EVERYONE IS TALKING ABOUT KATIE RUGGLE'S

SEARCH & RESCUE

FOUR-TIME AMAZON BEST BOOK

"I love Ruggle's characters. They're sharply drawn, and vividly alive. I'm happy when they find each other. These are wonderful escapist books."
— **Charlaine Harris**, #1 *New York Times* Bestselling Author of the Sookie Stackhouse series

"Gripping suspense, unique heroines, sexy heroes."
— **Christine Feehan**, #1 *New York Times* Bestselling Author

"Sexy and suspenseful. I couldn't turn the pages fast enough."
— **Julie Ann Walker**, *New York Times* and *USA Today* Bestselling Author, for *Hold Your Breath*

"Chills and thrills and a sexy, slow-burning romance from a terrific new voice."
— **D. D. Ayres**, author of the K-9 Rescue series, for *Hold Your Breath*

"Fast, funny read and a promising start to a new series."
— **Smart Bitches, Trashy Books** for *Hold Your Breath*

"The Rocky Mountain Search and Rescue series is off to a promising start."
— **RT Book Reviews**, 4 Stars for *Hold Your Breath*

"I cannot read these books fast enough. Waiting for the next book to see what happens is going to be pure torture. Is it October yet?"

—*Fresh Fiction* for *Gone Too Deep*

"As this series draws to a close, the most fascinating of the heroines is introduced. Her story is both heartbreaking and uplifting at the same time. She's a sympathetic sweetheart who carries the reader along on her journey to emotional healing."

—*RT Book Reviews*, 4 Stars for *In Safe Hands*

ALSO BY KATIE RUGGLE

ROCKY MOUNTAIN SEARCH & RESCUE

On His Watch (free novella)

Hold Your Breath

Fan the Flames

Gone Too Deep

In Safe Hands

After the End (free novella)

ROCKY MOUNTAIN K9 UNIT

Run to Ground

On the Chase

Survive the Night

Through the Fire

THROUGH THE FIRE

KATIE RUGGLE

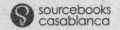

sourcebooks
casablanca

Published by Sourcebooks Casablanca, an imprint of Sourcebooks, Inc.
P.O. Box 4410, Naperville, Illinois 60567-4410
(630) 961-3900
Fax: (630) 961-2168
sourcebooks.com

Printed and bound in the United States of America.
OPM 10 9 8 7 6 5 4 3 2 1

For the rescue dogs who always, somehow,
end up rescuing us right back.

PROLOGUE

THE MATCH FLIPPED END OVER END, THE SPINNING FLAME creating a small pocket of light in the dim house. It landed in a pool of lighter fluid, and flames rippled outward with such speed that Alex took a startled step back, away from the quickly spreading fire. Arson was one of the few crimes she'd never had to commit, but the lure was understandable. The dancing flames were mesmerizing, and the potential damage significant. Lighting a fire was a powerful feeling—one she could get addicted to.

A little reluctant to leave and not see the end result of that one lit match, she slowly opened the back door, never looking away from the growing fire as it licked around the blanket-wrapped corpse.

"Sorry, sweetie." A flicker of guilt sparked and died just as quickly. "It was nothing personal. You just had what I needed." She patted the messenger bag looped over her shoulder, making the newly stolen car keys rattle lightly against the folder of documents. This moment had been a long time coming. She'd sacrificed so much to get here, and she was finally, *finally* close to getting her revenge. "I'll make a much better Elena Dahl than you ever would have, anyway."

With a final glance back, Alex stepped outside, blinking at the bright early-morning light reflecting off the snow. She walked with confidence, cutting through the secluded backyard. Long ago, she'd discovered that acting like she was supposed to be somewhere was the easiest way to get away with anything. The coming weeks would be the ultimate test of that.

This time it almost didn't matter. There was no one in this godforsaken semi–ghost town to see her slip away from the gradually growing light and into the waiting tree line. A deep satisfaction flowed through her, and she smiled. This was it. She was in the final stretch of her plan, and she could almost taste victory. *Finally*.

She quickly caught herself. It wasn't time for congratulations yet. First, she had to become Elena Dahl. The rest would come with time and patience.

Silently, she made her way through the snowy forest toward her new home.

CHAPTER 1

KIT HATED BEING LATE.

The thought of being late to her very first day of work was especially horrifying, and her muscles tensed as she shot another glance at her SUV's dashboard clock. She only had seventeen—*sixteen*, she mentally corrected as the digital numbers changed—minutes to find her new house, unhitch the rental trailer containing all her worldly possessions, and get to the police station on time. She swore under her breath as the pickup in front of her slowed to inch around a curve.

It wasn't looking promising.

Justice shifted in the back seat, giving a low groan as he settled into a new position. Flicking a look at the bloodhound in her rearview mirror, Kit couldn't keep from smiling. With his long ears and floppy jowls, Justice always looked adorably rumpled.

Quickly turning her attention back to the twisting road, she saw the achingly slow truck's signal light begin to flash.

"Hallelujah," she muttered, easing to a crawl as the pickup turned. For the past twenty miles, she'd been stuck behind the wheezing old vehicle, which had only sped up from its painfully slow pace whenever a passing lane appeared. She'd left the Denver hotel before five that morning, assuming that would give her plenty of time to get to work before seven, but she hadn't anticipated congested traffic on the snow-glazed roads.

At least the turtle-like speed allowed her to take in the views. This was only her second time in Colorado; the first was when she'd come to Monroe for her interview in late summer. The scenery was beautiful in a terrifying way, with shoulder-less roads edged by sheer drops and hairpin turns slicked with ice. A thick layer of snow covered everything except the road, piled off to the sides in dramatic, towering walls that narrowed the highway into claustrophobic corridors. The feeling surprised her. She'd figured being in such a small wilderness town would seem open and freeing, but the mountains and snow piles and even the twists and turns in the road pressed in on her, heavy and oddly menacing.

"It's just different from what we're used to," she told Justice, needing to hear a reassuring voice, even if it was her own. Her SUV topped a rise, and Monroe appeared before her, nestled in a valley and looking cozy enough to be the centerpiece of a snow globe. The sight of the adorable hamlet settled her nerves a little. How could anything bad ever happen in such a picture-perfect postcard of a place? Working here was going to be relaxing to the point of boredom. "This'll be good…much better than Wisconsin. We just have to get used to it. Right, Justice?"

Justice grunted, and Kit chose to take that as agreement.

Just as she passed a small sign reading WELCOME TO MONROE, ELEVATION 7,888 FEET, her GPS spoke up, telling her to turn right in half a mile. She obeyed, swinging her SUV wide so the trailer didn't cut the turn and catch on a curb. She shouldn't have worried. There was no curb. There was barely a street. Under the layer of packed snow, the road was painfully narrow and either gravel or so worn that most of the asphalt had given up, leaving only a potholed mess. She felt a pang for the townhome she'd left behind.

"Stop it," she ordered herself before she could jump into a full-fledged pity party. "This *will* be better. Justice will have a yard, and there won't be any shared walls, so you won't have to listen to the neighbors fighting over who put the empty milk carton back in the fridge. You're going to love it here."

As she rounded a bend in the road, the house came into view. She pulled up in front of the cedar-sided cabin and let out a long, relieved breath. It was perfect. She'd seen pictures, but photos could hide a lot of flaws. Tidy and well maintained, the small house looked exactly as she'd hoped it would. The drive and walkway to the front porch had even been cleared. There were a few other homes around, but they were definitely far enough away that she wouldn't hear any neighbors arguing unless they made a point of being heard.

"See, Justice? There's that big fenced yard I was telling you about."

Her relief didn't last long when she caught another glimpse of the clock. Even if she was extremely speedy, she was definitely going to be late on her first day. She muttered various creative swear words under her breath as she pulled her SUV and the trailer past the end of the narrow driveway.

As she started backing up, turning the trailer into the drive, she noticed another vehicle in the street behind her and quickly slammed on her brakes. Craning her head out of her open window, Kit spotted a dark-haired, bearded man behind the wheel of an elderly pickup. Her swearing was less muffled that time. It was hard enough backing such a small, wiggly trailer without an audience—an audience most likely impatient for her to get out of the way so he could squeeze past her SUV and get wherever he was going. If she rushed, she'd just end up sending the trailer cockeyed and getting it stuck in her new yard.

She looked at the snow mounded on either side of the skinny road. There was no way the pickup could go around, not without getting caught in the four-foot drifts. With a resigned sigh, she started backing up again. The pickup was far enough away that she wasn't in any danger of hitting him with the trailer. The only danger was humiliation if it took her a half hour to get the trailer into the driveway.

Turning the steering wheel, she watched as the back of the trailer lined up with the driveway entrance. Slowly, she started backing it in.

"It couldn't be this easy, could it?" she asked Justice, hope blooming in her chest, marveling at the way the trailer was obediently rolling up the lane. Even as she spoke, the trailer turned too far and headed for a snow-bank. Kit hit the brake before she got the trailer stuck in the drifts lining the yard. "Of course it can't. This is my life, after all. Everything has to be as painfully embarrassing as possible."

With a sigh, she shifted her SUV into Park and got out, heading for the driver's side of the waiting pickup. *Might as well get this over with*. The man rolled down his window as she neared, and Kit did a stutter step when she got her first up-close view.

He was the most beautiful person she'd ever seen.

Taking his features one by one, he wouldn't sound that attractive—short, dark-brown hair, matching beard, hazel eyes—but there was something about him that knocked her sideways. He was rugged yet refined, with sharp cheekbones, a full mouth, and a strong jaw and chin evident even underneath the beard. His lashes were long and lush enough to make pageant contestants weep. His model-like beauty was only emphasized by the contrasting mountain roughness of his untrimmed beard and utilitarian clothes, making him look like an actor playing the role of a backwoods lumberjack.

Taken altogether, he was startlingly attractive—and unexpectedly intimidating.

Kit blinked a few times to reorient herself and remember what she was going to say. Years of working with cops and other first responders had inured her to burly, masculine men...at least that's what she'd thought. This guy had taken her off guard, however. His unbelievably gorgeous face and silent regard were giving her a flashback to high school, and all the long-forgotten insecurities of a flat-chested, dorky teen tried to elbow their way back into her brain. She nipped those feelings in the bud. There was no way she was going to let anyone make her relive the misery of her teen years.

That thought and a sharp, cold gust of wind snapped her back to reality, and she realized she'd been standing there staring for much too long. She held back a groan. What a way to make an impression on one of her new neighbors.

Get it together, Jernigan.

"Hi," she said, trying to make her smile seem casually friendly despite her strange reaction. She had a trailer to park and a new job to start. There wasn't time to get distracted by a guy, no matter how distressingly pretty he was. "This is probably going to take me a few minutes. Can you back up and get where you're going a different way? Otherwise, I can drive around the block to let you get by."

His glance moved from her face to the trailer's torqued position and back to Kit. "I don't understand the problem."

She blinked. "Just what I said. It'll probably be a few minutes before the road will be clear. I'll need to pull forward to straighten the trailer before backing it into the driveway again." That was assuming she'd manage to keep it straight on the second attempt, which she highly doubted, especially with Mr. Gorgeous Lumberjack sitting there watching her.

He looked at the trailer again. "Why did you do that?"

"Do what?"

"Turn the trailer like that? Why didn't you just back it in straight?"

Great. Hot mountain man's an ass.

Kit bit back a rude answer and sent the man a steady look. She had to give it to him—he had a great poker face. Even though she knew he was being sarcastic, nothing in his posture or expression gave him away. He even rumpled his forehead as if honestly puzzled by her ineptitude. What was next—a crack about women drivers?

"I'm working on doing just that, but this small trailer's a bit tricky. Just give me a few minutes, and I'll be out of your way…unless you want to back up and use someone else's driveway to turn around in."

"What's tricky about it?"

She took a silent breath, trying to hold on to her impassive expression. Being a cop for eight years should've allowed her to perfect the look, but her emotions always showed too easily. Honestly, she didn't need some incredibly-hot-but-snarky jerk to mansplain as she prepared to humiliate herself in front of him…again. At least he didn't seem to be in any hurry. He could sit there and mock her, but she wouldn't have to waste time driving around the block to let him though. "Okay. I'm going to go give it another attempt. If you're going to stay, just know that my ability to back a bumper-pull trailer is inversely proportional to the number of judgy eyes staring at me."

His head cocked, and his full mouth turned up at the corners in a smile so unexpectedly sweet that Kit couldn't breathe for a solid four seconds. "Inversely proportional? You like math?"

The question threw her even more off-balance. "Sure, I guess? I mean, I like it more than backing in this trailer."

His smile widened, showing off white, mostly straight teeth. The front two overlapped a tiny bit, and she found that small flaw surprisingly endearing. "It's the same thing."

"What?" Still confused, she frowned at him. "No, it's not."

"Yes, it is. Everything is math."

"Uh…okay." Another gust of wind caught her, reminding her that she was still standing in the street, trying to figure out what this beautiful stranger was talking about, becoming later and later for work with every second that passed. She took a step away from the pickup and the odd, distractingly handsome lumberjack. "I guess I'm going to go do math, then." She hitched her thumb toward the trailer. "Hopefully, I'll remember enough high school algebra to get my trailer out of the way so you can get on with your day."

"Not algebra." The wrinkles in his forehead deepened as his smile changed, turning more quizzical than delighted.

"Right, of course. Geometry, then." She headed back to her SUV, shaking her head slightly as she got into the driver's seat, trying to brush off the strange encounter so they could get on with their lives. As she glanced in the side-view mirror, a movement caught her eye and she jumped.

The stranger had followed her, now standing right next to her back bumper—and he was *enormous*. Adrenaline nipped at her, and Kit mentally scolded herself for letting down her guard. She'd turned her back on a stranger even though she knew better than that. Just because a guy was hot didn't mean he wasn't a threat. As if sensing her tension, Justice sat up and peered out the window. When he caught sight of the stranger, his tail thumped against the seat. Ferocious, Justice was not.

Kit put a hand on the door latch, ready to get out of the car if the man came any closer, but he'd stopped. The tension in her muscles eased a tiny bit when he kept some distance between them, and she stuck her head out the window to give him a questioning look. Justice sniffed the air through the partially open window and then licked the glass with his broad tongue.

"I'll help," the mountain man said. "Otherwise, the trailer will end up stuck in the snow."

She frowned, pretty sure he'd just insulted her. "Help how?"

"I'll do the math, and you can drive. Together, problem solved." He swept his arm to the side in a dramatic wave that erased her lingering tension, making it impossible to be intimidated. With his enormous bulk and shaggy beard, she hadn't expected him to be so wonderfully *dorky*. He was like a nerdy, math-loving Sasquatch. Any remaining insecurities dredged up earlier were flushed away. She'd be willing to bet a lot of money that this guy hadn't been one of the popular kids in high school, either. No, this guy had been getting stuffed into lockers right alongside Kit.

She eyed his broad shoulders. At least, he'd been stuffed in lockers until he'd hit a growth spurt.

A smile tugged at her mouth as she lifted her hands in defeat and pulled forward, straightening the trailer before shifting into Reverse again. After turning in a circle on the seat, Justice lay down and closed his eyes.

"Turn the wheel eighteen degrees to the left," the man called, and she darted a glance at him in the mirror. He didn't look like he was joking. With a small shrug, she did as he suggested—or as close as she could manage. From his exasperated look, that wasn't precise enough for him. "I said eighteen degrees, not twenty-six."

Instead of annoying her, she found the mild scolding amusing, and she gave him an apologetic wave as she straightened the wheel slightly. It must've been acceptable to Mr. Tall, Hairy, and Exacting, because he gave a slight nod.

"Now continue backing up for four feet and eleven inches."

Four feet and eleven inches, Kit repeated in her head with a mental eye roll as she eased the trailer back. The extreme micromanagement struck her as funny, but she held back her laughter. The man seemed so earnest that she didn't want him to think she was making fun of him. He was being nice enough to help her out, after all.

"Stop!"

Startled by his shout, she slammed on the brake. Adrenaline rushed through her again as she leaned out the window, frantically trying to see behind the trailer. "What? Was I going to hit something?"

"No." He turned his puzzled gaze to hers. "You were about to go too far."

She stared at him, annoyed by the remaining anxiety threading through her body. "Did I actually go five feet instead?" Immediately, she felt bad for mocking him, especially when he gave her such a warm smile in return.

"No. You're perfect." Above the top edges of his beard, his cheeks darkened as he cleared his throat and looked away. "Perfectly positioned, I mean."

"Of course." A hundred teasing responses rose in her head, but she restrained herself and just stayed silent, waiting for the next instruction.

Staring at the snow-covered road, he rubbed at the back of his neck, and Kit had a feeling he was flustered. By *her*. That was a novel experience. Even as a kid, she'd always been considered one of the guys. It was rare that she induced speechlessness in a man—especially one as gorgeous as this one—and she was reluctantly flattered by his reaction.

Then her gaze moved to the dashboard clock, and the time made her stomach sink. She was going to be so horrendously late. "What's next?" Her voice was too loud, making him glance at her, startled.

"Right." He took a deep breath, the air expanding his broad chest even more, and he looked back and forth between the trailer and her SUV, his gaze calculating. "Straighten the wheel, and reverse another three feet, two inches."

Kit eased up on the brake and allowed the SUV to back up. Prepared this time, she didn't let his urgent "Stop!" startle her.

"Turn the wheel six degrees to the right."

Kit was quite impressed with her self-control, since she managed to keep a straight face throughout the process, even when his extremely specific directions included half inches. But she had to admit that his math-inspired technique worked. The trailer ended up in a perfect spot: right next to the walkway and leaving just enough room on the other side for her to park her SUV once she got home. Setting the parking brake, she hopped out and went back to unhitch the trailer, but the stranger was already on it.

Kit dug a good-sized rock out of the snow bordering the walkway and wedged it behind one of the tires as a wheel chock. As she straightened, she noticed the man eyeing her with approval. She flushed, thinking that he'd been focused on her bent-over backside, but he gestured at the rock instead.

"Good idea," he said, and she felt stupidly

disappointed that he *hadn't* been admiring her rear end—and then she felt silly for being so shallow.

"Thank you." She reached out to shake his hand. There was a pause where she wondered if he was going to accept the gesture, and then he took off his right glove and clasped her hand in his. It was warm and pleasantly rough, and his huge hand completely swallowed hers. That enveloping hold made her feel disconcertingly small, and she hurried to speak to distract herself. "This would've taken longer without your help."

"Yes." Now that he had her hand, he wasn't releasing it, and things started to feel awkward again. "A lot longer."

Once again, Kit wasn't sure whether to be offended or amused, but she settled on amusement. After all, the man wasn't wrong. Letting out a huff of laughter, she gently tugged her hand back. "I'm Kit Jernigan."

Finally releasing his grip, he gave a small nod but remained quiet rather than give his name.

With another small laugh, Kit headed back to the driver's seat of her SUV. The guy had just saved her a bunch of time and aggravation. The least she could do, she figured, was let him keep his anonymity. She'd return to cop mode soon enough.

Opening the car door, she looked over her shoulder at her new friendly neighborhood Bigfoot, who was still standing where she'd left him. "Well, I hate to math and run, but I'm already late for my first day at my new job. Thank you again, though."

With another short lift of his chin, he watched as she pulled out of the driveway and turned away from his pickup. Before she reached the next intersection, she couldn't resist another glance in the rearview mirror.

He'd moved next to his truck, but he was still watching her, and Kit jerked her gaze back to the road.

"What an interesting guy...whoever he is." She realized that she was smiling. "Just between us, Justice, I kind of like him...even if he is too pretty for his own good." The dog, who'd been snoozing for most of the trailer-parking process, opened his eyes and thumped his tail against the seat in what Kit took as agreement.

Blowing out a hard breath, she focused on getting back to the police station. It was still her first day at a new job in a strange town, but her encounter with the nameless Good Samaritan had given her a fizzy sense of hopeful anticipation.

If all her neighbors were as interesting and helpful as her mystery mountain man had been, life in Monroe was looking promising.

CHAPTER 2

SOMEONE HAD BLOWN UP THE POLICE DEPARTMENT.

It was bad enough starting a new job in a strange town, but it was even worse to find a charred shell where the building was supposed to be. Kit glanced at the printout of the most recent email from her new chief, but the address listed hadn't changed from the last time she'd been there: 101 Pickard Street, Monroe, Colorado. It was the same as what was printed on the Monroe Police Department sign—the sign directing her into the empty parking lot butted up against the blackened skeleton that, not too long ago, had been a functioning police station. Just a few months earlier, she'd been interviewed there. It was surreal to see the burned wreck it was now.

Justice whined from the back seat, and Kit reached back to pet his silky, floppy ears. "I know, buddy. As soon as I find out what's going on, we can finally get out of this car."

Pulling away from the curb, Kit drove back toward the town's main street. There had been a half-hearted effort to plow, but several inches of packed snow still covered the roads, making her grateful for her SUV's all-wheel drive. She slowly headed toward downtown, figuring Monroe was small enough that any random townsperson would know where the police department had moved. She just needed to find that person.

Like everyone else in the country, she'd heard the news about the attack on this tiny mountain town just a few weeks ago, but she was shocked by the extent of the damage. She'd interviewed with the Monroe police chief over three months ago, when the town was still intact and bustling with tourists. Monroe had seemed like a perfect escape then, with quaint shops lining downtown and quiet streets dotted with cedar-sided cabins. Set in a valley and surrounded by snow-peaked mountains with bright-yellow aspen trees scattered over the slopes, the town could've been used as a movie set.

Now, as she drove slowly through that same downtown, the difference was shocking.

The general store was gone, as was the diner, both just blackened holes in the line of shops. Most of the other places had CLOSED signs in the windows, and the streets and sidewalks were empty. It still looked like a movie set, just one with a postapocalyptic plotline—probably involving zombies.

Despite the cold, Kit rolled down her window several inches so she could hear what was going on outside her car. It was a habit she'd developed while patrolling, and now, even though she wasn't technically on duty, she felt uneasy with the windows up. The silence was eerie.

The town was too quiet for seven on a weekday morning. People should've been heading to work and getting their kids to school, but there was no one in sight. The only sound was her SUV's engine and the crunch of snow under her tires.

As she passed a shuttered restaurant, the VFW parking lot came into view, and she sat straighter. A dozen or so vehicles—including two squad cars—were scattered throughout the lot.

"Look, Justice," she said, glancing in the rearview mirror to see that the bloodhound was sitting up, ears perked as he looked out the window. "Actual people. I was beginning to think that we'd stumbled into a horror movie."

She pulled into the lot, backing into a space next to one of the squad cars. A Belgian Malinois in the back stood up and started barking, and Justice's tail thumped against the seat. He'd never met another dog he didn't like.

Kit smiled as she got out of her SUV. After driving through the creepy, bombed-out town, it was reassuring to see another dog. Being part of the K9 unit was her life—at least, it had been. She didn't feel so much like the last remaining survivor on earth anymore.

After checking to make sure Justice's heater was on, she carefully made her way across the snowy, icy lot to the VFW entrance. As she stepped inside, she removed her sunglasses and stayed in the entry for a minute, allowing her eyes to adjust from the bright sunlight reflecting off the snow outside to the dim interior. It smelled like every VFW she'd ever been in—a mixture of musty old building, years of cigarette smoke, and home-style food.

She followed the sounds of chatter and the scent of bacon into a dining area that looked as if it had been converted into some sort of restaurant. Remembering the destroyed diner down the street, she wondered if this was where they'd relocated. Scanning the patrons, she noted that most were older, and all were white. She braced herself for curious stares, since she was not only a newcomer to town, but half Korean as well. Her gaze immediately caught on a table with three uniformed cops, and she headed in their direction.

People quieted as she moved through the dining area, weaving between tables, and the cops spotted her quickly. All three were men, making Kit wonder if there were many women on this small-town force. She hoped so. Although she'd been in the minority at her last department, they'd had a great group of female cops. The thought of being one of only a few women in a sea of guys was daunting.

None of the cops watching her were smiling. Automatically, her shoulders drew back and she raised her chin a little, striding confidently to their table. If she was one of a few or—God forbid—the only woman in her new department, it was especially important to show them right off the bat that she could hold her own.

As she got closer, the guys got bigger, and she swallowed a groan. At a few inches over five feet, she was going to be dwarfed by them. She made a mental note to find whatever gym this town had as soon as possible. She might not be able to grow any taller, but she could always get stronger.

By the time she reached the cops' table, the diner was quiet except for the occasional clink of a coffee mug hitting a saucer and the sizzle of food cooking on the grill in the kitchen. With a mental grimace, she realized that she was going to become the crowd's morning entertainment. *Welcome to small-town life.*

"Hi." She held out her hand to the closest cop, who happened to be the biggest one. "I'm Kit Jernigan. I accepted a job with the Monroe PD. Today's my first day."

He studied her for a moment before accepting her outstretched hand. He looked reserved and wary, but not hostile. Kit took that as a good sign. "Otto Gunnersen."

Turning to the man sitting next to Otto, she offered her hand again.

This one had a shaved head and introduced himself as Hugh Murdoch as they shook hands. He studied her with a slight upward twist of his mouth, and she kept her expression bland, hoping he wouldn't turn out to be an asshole. Smirking was rarely a sign of a pleasant personality. Not really wanting to hear whatever smart-ass comment was going to come out of his mouth, she quickly turned to the last cop, the one with dark hair and eyes and a hard cast to his face.

He waited the longest before shaking her hand, but she refused to flinch, just holding his gaze while keeping her hand extended. Finally, he accepted it, giving a firm shake. "Theo Bosco. Have a seat."

She remained standing, knowing that these three would make her grueling hiring interview seem like friendly chitchat. "It's my first day, so I should check in with the chief. I just stopped in to get directions to the police station…the *new* location."

"Right across the street," Hugh said, typing something on his phone as he used his foot to slide out the chair across from him. "Sit. I've sent a text to the chief to let him know you're with us. Roll call's in a half hour, and Theo and I will be starting our shifts then. We'll show you where to go. Well, the two of us will. Otto's on nights, so he's done."

Resigned to her fate, Kit took the chair they offered, and a pretty server hurried over. The other diners had gradually started talking again, and the noise level returned to its earlier volume.

"Good morning. Coffee?" At Kit's nod, the waitress poured her a cup and then moved to the other side of the table to top off all the others' mugs. Kit watched as she worked, wondering why the waitress seemed so nervous. Even when she was in uniform, Kit knew her appearance wasn't intimidating—not like these three burly cops— but the waitress kept giving her anxious glances.

Once everyone's coffee mug was full, the waitress stopped next to Theo's chair. When he rested a hand on her lower back, she seemed to relax slightly, giving him a sweet smile before turning back to Kit. "Would you like a menu?"

"Coffee's fine, thanks." She gave the server a smile, figuring that would be the end of the conversation, but the woman lingered.

"Are you a reporter? I hate to ask, but everyone is going to harass me all day if I can't answer their questions about you." The server's words were rushed and thick with a Southern drawl. Her nerves would have been obvious even if her fingers hadn't been clamped so tightly around the coffeepot's handle that her knuckles had turned white. "Most of the news crews left last week, but we don't see many other strangers around here, especially now." Her laugh was quick and jittery. "Monroe isn't really a tourist destination at the moment."

Theo gave Kit a look she couldn't interpret before turning to the waitress. "Jules," he said soothingly, rubbing her back in small circles, "she's not a reporter."

"The newspeople were everywhere last week," Hugh explained to Kit. "Like a plague of camera-toting locusts.

I couldn't go anywhere without having a microphone jammed in my face and some well-coiffed journalist demanding to know how I felt about the town exploding. It was like twenty-four-hour mandatory counseling."

Otto grunted in what sounded like agreement, but Theo raised his eyebrows. "*Well-coiffed?*"

"What?" Leaning back in his chair, Hugh gave a slight pained wince. It was so quick that Kit wondered if she'd imagined it. "Are you mocking my excellent vocabulary?"

"Yes." Even though he was looking at Hugh, Theo continued rubbing Jules's back.

When Hugh started to respond, Otto cleared his throat gently.

"Right," Hugh said. "Back on track. Jules, meet Monroe's newest K9 officer, Kit Jernigan."

Jules jerked slightly, and Kit was pretty sure she would've taken a step back if Theo's hand hadn't been there. Kit studied the woman carefully, wondering why that information had scared the waitress. If appearances were correct, Jules was dating Theo and was friends with the other two, so the presence of one more cop shouldn't have been frightening. For some reason, though, it was. Although she tried to hide it, Jules was visibly nervous.

"Nice to meet you." Kit tried to keep her tone low-key and friendly, but Jules still looked like she thought Kit was about to leap out of her chair and grab her.

"Hi." Jules attempted a smile, but it trembled at the edges before collapsing completely. "Welcome to Monroe…what's left of it, at least." She turned her head, glancing behind her. "I'd better get back to work."

As she started to move away, Theo caught the hand not clutching the coffeepot. "Jules."

She smiled at him, but gently slipped free and headed for the kitchen. Theo watched her go before turning back to Kit. He didn't look happy. "Where are you from?" he demanded.

She had been expecting this. "Gold Mill, Wisconsin."

"PD or county?"

"Police."

"How long?"

"Eight years."

"All with the same department?"

"Yes."

"Why'd you leave?"

For the first time in their rapid-fire exchange, Kit hesitated. After numerous interviews, she should've been used to the question, but it still managed to throw her off guard, kicking up the same cloud of bitterness and grief it always did. It took a few seconds before she recovered enough to pull out her stock answer. "There was an incident that created some bad feelings. It was time for a fresh start."

From the look on Theo's face, he'd noticed her hesitation, and Kit knew the topic would come up again. Next time, he wouldn't let her get by on vague generalities. "Why here?"

"Gold Mill has about eighty thousand people and a huge opioid problem. After dealing with that for eight years, I was…tired." She almost laughed at the understatement. "When I interviewed with the chief in early September, Monroe seemed like a nice place, a peaceful place, somewhere I could be part of the community that I served. Plus, I like snowboarding, and it's much more fun here than the tiny hills we consider ski resorts in the Midwest." She attempted a smile at the last bit, but none of the other three returned it, so it quickly faded.

Her apprehension from driving around the bombed-out town had faded when she'd entered the VFW, but now it returned in a rush. These were her fellow officers, the people who were going to have her back when she was in a life-threatening situation—or they were supposed to be, at least. By the way they were staring at her, they'd just as soon toss her off the nearest cliff as work with her. She'd expected it to take a while before she integrated into the department, but she hadn't thought there'd be such instant resistance.

"Yeah, peaceful." Hugh huffed a laugh as he shifted in his chair and winced again. This time, Kit knew she hadn't imagined it.

"Are you okay?" she asked, and all humor immediately disappeared from his face. "Are you in pain?"

"I'm fine." The words came out with a sharp snap.

Otto turned his head toward Hugh. "What's wrong? Is it your arm?"

"No. My arm's fine."

"The cast just came off two days ago." By his concerned frown, it didn't look like Otto believed his partner's denial. "Shouldn't you have it in a sling?"

Hugh let his head fall back in an exaggerated motion. "It's fine. Want me to prove it?" He smirked at Otto. "I could punch you in the nuts, and then you could tell me if you think it's healed enough."

Although Otto didn't look too concerned about the threat, he stopped grousing and turned to Kit. She braced herself for more questions. Of the three, this one made

Kit the wariest, maybe because he'd been so quiet thus far. "You're K9?"

"Yes." She was much happier talking about dogs than about what had happened at her old department. "For the past six years. After working with a K9 partner, I could never go back."

Otto didn't smile, but he looked slightly less serious, so Kit decided it was close enough. "Bet it was hard to leave your dog."

"I didn't." She grinned, still thrilled that everything had worked out as it had—even despite the apocalyptic state of her new town. She'd found Justice at a rescue a year ago, and she'd done all of his training, so she would've been heartbroken to leave him behind. "My bloodhound came with me. Chief Bayard agreed he'd be an asset, so I bought him from my old department." They'd given her a really good deal, which hadn't surprised her. No one she'd worked with had been too impressed with Justice, but she'd known from the beginning that he was a diamond in the rough. Training him had been a long, slow slog, but it had paid off.

All three cops eyed her with renewed interest. "Patrol?" Theo asked.

"No." The memory of that complete fail made her grimace. "He doesn't have the drive. He's an amazing tracker, though."

"We don't have any trackers," Hugh said, rubbing his arm. Kit was pretty sure that he wasn't aware he was doing it. He seemed to be a show-no-weakness kind of guy.

"We do now," she said, trying to keep her voice light. It'd take time before they accepted her. She knew that, but sitting through this tense mini-interview with her new partners made her realize just how much it was going to suck until they did. Quickly shoving away the thought, she reminded herself that it couldn't be any worse than the past six months at her old department.

Hugh made a noncommittal sound just as Theo glanced at the entrance. "Incoming."

Resisting the urge to duck at his warning—which she felt she couldn't be blamed for, considering the current state of the town—Kit followed his gaze to the door. A tall, beautiful woman in a down coat, skinny jeans, and amazing boots that Kit instantly coveted walked in. After giving their table a quick, guilty glance, she made a beeline for the kitchen, tipping her head forward so that her hair—glossy and ink-black—fell forward to hide her face.

"Gra-cie," Hugh called out in a singsong voice, but she didn't turn or even look at him.

Theo snorted. "What'd you do to piss off Grace?"

"Nothing." Hugh stood up, his lips tightening slightly as he got to his feet. Although Kit recognized the pain that flashed across his face for a microsecond, she didn't mention it this time. He hadn't seemed to appreciate it when she'd asked about his arm earlier, and she didn't want to compound her mistake. "Everything was bubbles and puppies when I saw her last night. Something's up."

As Hugh started to weave his way through the tables toward Grace, Jules came out of the kitchen, and Grace nearly ran toward her.

Theo gave a long, drawn-out groan. "Jules is involved?" He got up and followed Hugh.

Glancing toward Otto, Kit saw he was tapping at his phone, frowning.

"What's going on?" she asked, feeling lost. It hit her how much she'd have to figure out—a new job, a new town, all these new people—and she was suddenly overwhelmed. Even though Gold Mill was a much bigger community than Monroe, she'd known the people there, known the players on both the shady and the bright sides, known who to go to for information, known where to find the suspects when they bolted, known which people to check on to make sure they had food and heat, known who to trust and who to listen to with a high degree of skepticism. The amount that she'd need to learn about Monroe and its citizens seemed momentous.

"Guess we'll see." Despite Otto's calm, even tone, the line between his eyebrows deepened as he glanced at his phone again.

Figuring she wasn't going to get any information out of him, she turned her attention to the other four. After a short, intense conversation with Grace, Jules peeled away and delivered the food she was carrying to a family sitting at a table in the corner. Although Theo stopped several feet away, he still seemed to be looming over her. As she passed him on her way back to the kitchen, she smiled, standing up on her tiptoes to kiss his cheek, not seeming at all intimidated by the looming. They exchanged a few quick words that Kit couldn't make out before Jules patted his arm and hurried away. After watching her for a few broody seconds, Theo started back toward their table.

Hugh, it appeared, was having a much more exciting time of it. He and the very stylish-looking woman—Grace, he'd called her—were having a low-voiced argument that involved a lot of dramatic gestures and facial expressions. Watching them, Kit was positive that they were together—or had been very recently. No one argued that passionately unless there was some chemistry involved.

Kit turned her attention back to their table as Theo sat in his recently vacated seat. He looked even crankier than he had before the mini-drama. When Otto raised his eyebrows in question, Theo gave an irritated shrug.

"She's going to fill me in later."

"About what?" Otto asked.

"News."

"What kind of news?"

Theo's frown deepened as he took a drink of coffee. He even drank angrily, Kit noticed, trying not to smile. "She didn't say." Glancing at Hugh and Grace, Theo scowled. "Doesn't look like Hugh knows, either."

"Sarah knows." Otto held up his cell phone for a moment, face out, and Kit saw a screen full of texts. "Says she'll tell me about it when she gets home from work this afternoon." He dropped the phone back into his pocket.

"Work?" Theo asked Otto, although his gaze found Jules and followed her around the dining area. "The general store is gone. Where's she working?"

"Grady's house. She's helping him with his insurance paperwork," Otto said absently as Hugh returned, dropping into his chair with an exaggerated scowl that Kit suspected hid a wince of pain. She glanced over to the door to see Grace leaving the dining area.

"That woman is incredibly stubborn."

Theo gave Hugh an incredulous look. "You're just learning this now?"

"She needs to be," Otto said mildly. "You'd steam-roll anyone who wasn't."

With a gasp, Hugh clutched his chest as if mortally wounded by Otto's words. When no one else reacted, Hugh dropped his hand and shrugged affirmatively. "That's probably true. Did either of you get any information?"

"No." Theo had mellowed slightly, but the reminder made him scowl again. "She said later."

Hugh grunted. "I didn't even get that promise. All I got was a 'mind your business.' Obviously, she's forgotten that *everything* is my business—everything interesting, at least. My curiosity is hungry and must be fed. Otto? Anything from the lovely Sarah?"

Otto shook his head silently.

"It has to be a new arri—" Hugh cut off so quickly that Kit was pretty sure someone had kicked him under the table. He turned to eye Kit with a thoughtful gleam in his gaze, one that made her want to scoot back a little to keep from being sucked into his shenanigans. Her younger sister, Casey, had a look very similar to that, and it had gotten Kit into a lot of trouble when she was little—a lot of fun, maybe, but mostly a lot of trouble. From Hugh's expression, Kit guessed he was even more of an imp than Casey had been.

He smiled, and her suspicions quadrupled. "Let's go, greenie."

Although she had to press her tongue against the back of her teeth to keep from telling him that she was *not* green, that she'd had eight years of experience in a much bigger and busier town than this bombed-out little hamlet, Kit managed to stay silent as she stood.

"Where are we going?" The suspicion in Theo's voice confirmed it. Hugh was planning something that would get them in trouble. So much for having a quiet first day consisting of filling out forms and getting measured for her uniform.

The way Hugh widened his eyes in a look of innocence made Kit brace herself and Theo groan. "We're giving our newest officer a tour of the town, of course. We could start at Jules's place. See if any...old friends happened to stop by for a visit."

"If you wait until this afternoon, Sarah will tell me what's going on," Otto said.

"I've always been bad at waiting. Want to tag along?"

"Can't." Otto didn't sound too disappointed. "I need to stop by Gordon Schwartz's to check on the animals."

"How's he doing?" Theo asked. "Is he staying out of trouble?"

"So he says." From Otto's shrug, he didn't fully believe this Gordon was telling the truth.

"I'd be surprised if he was," Hugh said as he headed for the door. "Once a paranoid, gun-collecting militia guy, always a paranoid, gun-collecting militia guy."

Making a mental note of Gordon Schwartz's name—since he sounded like someone she'd likely be dealing with in the future—Kit followed Hugh toward whatever trouble he was going to drag her into.

As they left the VFW, her stomach sank. Bending the rules was sometimes necessary when it was the right thing to do, but she had planned to stay out of trouble at her new job—at least on her first day. The problem was that she didn't know enough about the situation or Hugh to make a judgment. She glanced over her shoulder at Theo, hoping he'd be the voice of reason.

Instead of trying to rein in his partner, though, Theo was wearing a look of grim determination. With a silent sigh, Kit ignored her instincts and followed Hugh into the parking lot. It looked like she needed to start trusting her new partners. Hopefully, they wouldn't get her killed...

At least not on her first day.

CHAPTER 3

THE RED-TAILED HAWK WAS BACK, AND WES WAS PRETTY sure she was laughing at him.

She landed on the railing of the fire tower's observation deck, turning her head sideways and fixing one eye on Wes through the wall of glass that made up the south side of the tower room. He took a slow sideways step, his arm lifting ever so slowly as he reached for the camera sitting on the rolling workstation. If he hadn't been worried that the sound of his voice would startle the hawk, he would've used the voice command to move the wheeled table—and the camera—closer to him.

The red-tailed hawk was pathologically camera shy, but Wes was determined. The bird had been basically taunting him all summer and fall, posing like a *Vogue* model until Wes lifted his Canon. As soon as the perfect shot was a second away, the hawk took off—every single time.

Today looked like it was the day. He even had the right lens on. His fingers closed around the camera, and the hawk didn't startle or fly away. Instead, she stayed stock-still, watching him. Forcing himself to keep his movements slow and smooth, he raised the camera and peered at the blurry shape through the viewfinder. Far behind it, nestled in the valley, was the town of Monroe, its blackened buildings covered in a fresh layer of white snow. It would've looked like a Christmas card if not for the plume of smoke rising from the southwest side of town.

The camera's autofocus kicked in, but it was too late. Shot forgotten, Wes returned the camera to the table and grabbed his binoculars, barely noticing as the startled hawk flew away. Scanning the area, he searched for the smoke he'd spotted through his camera lens. Although Colorado's traditional wildland fire season was technically over, he still kept watch over Monroe and the forested acres that surrounded the tiny town.

Peering through the binoculars, he found the grayish-white plume again. Without looking away, he reached out again—for his radio this time. The town had already had a rough few weeks. The last thing it needed was another disaster.

Too bad that's exactly what it had.

"You can ride with me, greenie," Hugh said, heading for one of the squad cars.

"I'll follow. I have my dog with me." As if to prove her statement true, Justice popped up and stuck his jowly muzzle out of the partially opened window. All three of the other cops made beelines for her SUV, and she grinned, her spirits lightening for the first time since she'd met her new unit. Unlocking her car, she used her body to block Justice from leaping out until she could hook his leash to his harness. He was trained to wait for her command before exiting the car, but he was wiggling with excitement, and Kit knew he had a tendency to forget his manners when new people—and places and animals and smells—caught his attention.

The leash snap clicked into place. "Okay." As soon as she moved aside, he launched himself at the closest of the cops. His front paws hit Otto right in the belly as the dog tried to climb up the big man to lick his face.

"Justice, *off*." Kit was relieved when the dog listened, dropping to his haunches with his skinny tail whipping back and forth, making a one-winged snow angel. Otto didn't seem bothered by the enthusiastic greeting. Crouching in front of Justice, he ran his hands over the dog's long, floppy ears, and the tail-wagging accelerated into turbo mode.

"He listens well for a hound," Otto said approvingly, and Kit beamed.

"Thank you," she said as Hugh elbowed Otto aside to get to the dog. Theo shoved his way in as well. Justice gave a heavy, blissful sigh, in heaven from all the attention. "It took a lot of time and effort, but he does really well now. We're going to start working off lead once we settle in."

Hugh ran his hand over one of Justice's long ears and held it out to the side. "I can't get over these ears. They're so *floppy*."

Glancing at the sharply pricked ears of the Belgian Malinois in the back of the squad car next to them, Kit smiled. "Not quite what you're used to."

Three portable radios beeped in unison, and the men straightened, wincing at the crackle of feedback until Otto and Hugh turned their radios off, leaving only Theo's on.

"Fire Rescue One, there's been a report of a possible structure fire in the area of Hibberd Street and Canyon Road."

After a short pause, a male voice responded. *"Fire One copies. What's the address?"*

"Unknown at this time. The complainant is the forest service lookout at Sayer Tower."

"Copy. En route to the general area of Hibberd and Canyon Road." The firefighter didn't sound happy, and Kit couldn't blame him. Searching for the fire would take precious time.

"We respond to fire calls, so I guess you're getting a trial by literal fire," Hugh said as he headed for the driver's door of his squad car. Not wanting to lose his new friend and personal masseuse so soon, Justice tried to follow, but Kit's grip on his leash kept him close to her. "Follow me."

So much for getting a day to fill out paperwork, she thought, loading Justice into the back seat before climbing behind the wheel. As she cranked the engine, she smiled. If she was honest, taking a call was much more interesting than reading the SOP manual and completing a W-4. It wasn't what she'd expected from this sleepy-looking town, but nothing—from the time she'd arrived in Colorado until now—had gone how she'd thought it would. She just needed to roll with the changes and try to learn as she went.

As she followed Hugh out of the lot, Kit noted that his car and Theo's right behind them were marked with "Bedrock County Sheriff's Department." Only Otto's SUV, which turned in the other direction as he headed to Gordon Schwartz's place, had "Monroe Police

Department" painted on the sides. Kit wondered if they'd lost their vehicles when the station was bombed.

Lights and sirens activated, Hugh wove his way through the residential streets, and Kit followed, marveling again at the silent emptiness of the town. "Why do I feel like we're going to be fighting off zombies when we get to the fire?" she asked Justice, who made a quiet huff of what Kit took as agreement.

Despite the wail of the two squad-car sirens, it felt too quiet in her car. Ever since she'd left her old police department, the lack of a radio had left an aching hole inside her, as if it were a missing limb. She felt cut off and unhappily oblivious without that link, and she reached down to touch her cell phone where it sat in her pocket. Despite the layer of fabric separating her from it, the hard shape reassured her. She wasn't *completely* cut off from everything and everyone.

Theo slowed, and Kit assumed they were getting close. The air was getting hazier, and she could smell smoke—the acrid burn told her that it wasn't a cozy little campfire. Something was burning that wasn't supposed to be burning.

Kit turned, staying close to the squad car in front of her. It was a real-life version of Hot and Cold—with the potential for real-life property damage or even death. She scanned the area, looking for the source of the smoke. Their small convoy turned left and the haze thickened, irritating Kit's throat. She knew it would be hard to stop coughing once she started, so she fought the urge as they rounded a curve in the road. The houses thinned even more, making her suspect that they were getting close to the edge of town.

There it was. Kit felt a little silly for how she'd been peering around earlier, hunting for the source of the fire, when it was so obvious now that it was within sight. The lower-level windows of the two-story house glowed red, and smoke billowed from the eaves. She was no firefighter, but it looked to her like the interior was engulfed—at least the first floor.

There wasn't a garage that she could see, and no vehicles were parked in the driveway, so she hoped that this was one of the many homes that sat vacant over the winter. Without the right equipment or training, she couldn't run in to save anyone, but she didn't think she'd be able to stop herself if she knew someone was inside.

Hugh angled his car to block most of the road, and Theo whipped his squad car around and turned onto the next cross street. Kit assumed that he was going to block traffic on the other side of the burning house. She parked off to the side, as far out of the way as she could manage without driving into the snowbank. Without lights or a marked car, she didn't want to use her vehicle to try to control traffic—not that Monroe seemed to even *have* any traffic, except for their three cars.

"This is the Nailors' place," Hugh said, striding around his car to get closer to the burning house. "They're in California for the winter."

"No one should be in there, then." Kit's stomach unknotted slightly as she followed.

"Not unless they have a squatter," Hugh said, his face serious as he eyed the windows. Although they were still a safe distance from the house, the heat on her face went from gently warming to uncomfortable in just a few strides. Kit stopped, scanning around the structure for a propane tank or anything that might explode. It looked clear, except for the wooded area in the back-yard. She hoped the fire wouldn't spread. After just another step, Hugh halted as well. "Still, they're going to hate hearing about this."

The fire engine's siren wailed loudly as it turned the corner and came into view. Hugh jogged back to his squad car, backing it up a few feet so the truck could roll close to the burning house. A second fire depart-ment vehicle—a rescue truck—followed, and Hugh's car moved to block the road again.

Feeling useless, Kit did her best to stay out of the way. It grated on her to not be helping. After eight years with her old department in Wisconsin, she'd been at the point of almost always knowing what to do in any situation. Now, she felt like she'd been reduced to a rookie again.

Shaking off her moment of self-pity, she watched as a handful of firefighters got out of the trucks, pulling out equipment and unrolling hoses with quick efficiency. Hugh headed toward the firefighter who was giving orders next to the engine.

"Good thing it's unoccupied," the fireman said as he attached a hose to the side of the truck. "We're running on a skeleton crew here." He sent Kit a quick glance before refocusing on his task. "You must be new."

"Yes." Since his hands were occupied, she didn't hold hers out for him to shake. "Kit Jernigan."

"Steve Springfield." Although he didn't actually smile, still focused on his task, his raised eyebrows made him look amused. "Hugh's your PTO?"

Uncertain, she looked at Hugh, her stomach dropping at the idea. She knew she'd be assigned to an officer for her probationary training period, but she hadn't realized that it would be Hugh. He didn't seem all that impressed with her, so she hoped it wouldn't be two endless and miserable months until she was allowed to take calls on her own.

"That I am," Hugh answered her unspoken question.

Steve tightened the hose connection before sending Kit another fast but sympathetic glance. "Good luck with that."

"Hey!" Hugh protested, but they both ignored him.

"Thanks," Kit said dryly. Steve called out to someone manning the controls at the top of the truck before flipping down the face shield of his helmet and jogging toward the flaming house, hose nozzle in hand. He stopped to wave back a firefighter heading toward the house while carrying a wicked-looking ax.

"It's too far gone!" Steve shouted over the roar of the flames and the rumbling engines. "We need to keep it from spreading to the trees. Help Johnson!" The ax-wielding firefighter nodded and hurried toward the west side of the house.

Before Steve could move any closer to the fire, Kit called out, "Need help? I haven't had firefighter training, but I'd be happy to do any grunt work." Belatedly, she looked at Hugh. It hadn't crossed her mind to check with him before offering to help. She wasn't accustomed to asking permission from anyone except her sergeant or lieutenant. The whole starting-at-the-bottom thing was going to take some getting used to. "Unless Hugh had a different plan?"

He smirked at her. "Nice attempted save, but that's a good idea. Where do you need us, Steve?"

"Thanks." Steve whistled sharply, catching the attention of the firefighter on top of the engine. "Calvarone! Volunteers!" He pointed at Kit and Hugh before turning back to the fire.

"Both of you grab helmets from the cab, and I'll put you to work." Calvarone waved down at them from his perch on top of the truck before refocusing on the controls. As Kit and Hugh moved toward the passenger-side door of the engine, Steve's booming shout made Kit's head whip toward the fire.

"Back! Get back!" he yelled, and the firefighters retreated. One side of the roof sagged before the entire west side of the house started to droop. It felt like time slowed as the house caved in on itself with a deafening crash, sending flaming debris flying over the heads of the fleeing firefighters. Even Kit ducked, although she wasn't close enough to be in danger, and her gaze raked the area, looking to see who was injured. Her hand reached for a nonexistent portable radio, and she cursed her lack of equipment before remembering Hugh was there as well. She turned toward him, but he was already calling for an ambulance.

"Johnson! Lee! Chausky!" Steve, upright and appearing unhurt, immediately started calling for each firefighter's status. When the last one answered that he was okay, Kit felt her shoulders finally drop as the tension left her. She met Hugh's gaze, and they exchanged a look of utter relief.

"Firefighters are nuts," Hugh said as he fished out two helmets from the back seat of the cab. "Everyone knows you run away from fire, not toward it."

She laughed. "Just like everyone knows you run away from the sound of gunfire, not toward it?"

Handing one of the helmets to her, he shrugged. "I didn't say cops aren't nuts, too."

Kit spent the next few hours in a borrowed fire helmet, fetching tools and bottles of drinking water and everything else that the firefighters requested. Hugh and Theo helped as well, and Kit felt her first-day nerves ease slightly. It was good to see that her new partners were willing to lend a hand, even when it wasn't part of their job description. When the flames were out and the firefighters were digging through the ashes and blackened wreckage, searching for smoldering embers, Kit approached Steve. She was careful to stay out of everyone's way and far from anything that looked like it could fall on her head.

"Need anything else?" She handed Steve a water bottle, which he accepted with a weary smile of thanks.

"We're pretty much done here, except for the mopping up." Unscrewing the lid, he took a drink before slogging back into the blackened shell that had been a house just hours earlier. Looking over his shoulder, he called, "Thanks for your help."

"No problem." Now that she was standing still, Kit realized how tight her muscles had gotten. Putting her hands on her lower back, she stretched out her spine as she surveyed the scene. Water from the hoses and melting snow created a muddy moat around the burned skeleton of the ruined house, adding to the desolate picture.

"What a mess," Hugh muttered, echoing her thoughts as he walked up next to her.

Kit turned toward him. "Has someone contacted the owners?"

"I left a message, but they haven't called back

yet." He frowned, adjusting his borrowed fire helmet. "They've owned this place for decades. They're going to be crushed."

"At least no one was hurt," Kit said, watching Steve as he lifted a blackened board.

Hugh made a wordless sound of agreement.

"Steve seems less annoying than most firefighters," Kit said absently, and then darted a look at Hugh when she realized she was talking to her new PTO, whom she'd only known for an hour. But judging by his huge grin, he agreed with her.

"Yeah, Steve's a good egg. Too bad he's moving."

"Where's he going?"

"His brother has a ranch southeast of here. Steve's already sent his four kids there, but he's not leaving until his spot gets filled. As you can see, their numbers are already low." Hugh spread his arms, indicating the handful of firefighters scattered around the scene. Even though Kit knew they were in a much smaller town than what she was used to, it really was a ridiculously tiny number.

"Why are they so shorthanded?" she asked.

"Same reason Steve's leaving as soon as he can." Although Hugh sounded amused, there was a grimness underlying his voice. "The semi-apocalypse scared some people away. Well, that, and the fact that this town is always a handful short of a ghost town in the winter."

Kit could understand that. Just her short drive had almost been enough to send her out of town screaming, and, unlike Steve, she didn't have any kids to protect. "Can't really blame him for leaving."

Before Hugh could respond, Steve called them

over to where he stood in the middle of the wreckage. Exchanging a glance, Kit and Hugh jogged toward him.

"What is it?" Hugh asked, carefully picking his way through the still-smoldering debris.

"Remains." Steve's voice was grim as he bent over a blackened form.

"Human?"

Kit gave Hugh a sideways look at his question, but Steve seemed to take it in stride as he took out his cell phone. "Yeah. Pretty sure this is the point of origin, too."

"Shit." With a heavy exhale, Hugh reached for the portable radio on his belt. "Dispatch, we're going to need the county coroner and the chief."

"*Copy.*"

Tapping at his phone screen, Steve raised his cell to his ear. "Hey, Captain. You might want to call the fire marshal and then head this way. We're here at a structure fire with at least one casualty."

Kit pulled out her phone again and took multiple photos of the charred shape, staying several feet away so she didn't contaminate the scene. Although she'd worked on a few arson cases with the investigators at her old department, she wasn't an expert on burns and the effects of fire. What remained of the shrunken limbs was flexed in the pugilistic posture typical of burn victims, and the ash-colored skull had fractured into pieces.

Hugh gave a sharp whistle, making Kit look at him, but he was focused on catching Theo's attention. "Can you grab tape?"

Raising a hand in acknowledgment, Theo headed toward his squad car.

As soon as Steve ended the call with his captain,

Hugh asked quietly, "What do you think? Arson, or a lost hiker falling asleep with a lit cigarette?"

As he stared at the remains, the muscles tightened in Steve's jaw. "Only if they doused themselves with some sort of accelerant first."

Air left Hugh's lungs in an audible huff. "Seriously? Can't we catch a break? The worst crime around here used to be Mr. Wittlespoon stealing from the diner's take-a-penny dish, and now people are either blowing shit up or burning it down. For Pete's sake, are some petty misdemeanors too much to ask for?"

Steve didn't respond except for a small shake of his head. He looked tired.

Theo approached, carrying multiple rolls of police tape. "Casualty?"

"Yeah, and possible arson. We're going with Steve's first impression," Hugh said, keeping his voice low so it didn't carry past their small group.

Swearing under his breath, Theo rubbed his temple and then adjusted his borrowed fire helmet. Kit noted that he looked exhausted and grim, but not surprised. Her first-day nerves fired up again, but this time, she wasn't worried about whether she'd fit in or if her boss would be difficult. Her new town was a devastated wreck, and a possible murder-slash-arson had happened within the first hour of her first day.

She was beginning to wonder if she'd survive this new job.

CHAPTER 4

"LET'S SECURE THE SCENE," THEO SAID, HOLDING OUT A ROLL of tape to Kit. "We'll both start at that tree. You go clockwise, and I'll go counter. We'll meet at the back."

"Got it." Accepting the tape, she returned her borrowed helmet to the engine's cab before moving toward the tree he'd indicated. A small crowd had gathered on the other side of Hugh's squad car, so Kit pulled out her cell phone. The bystanders' attention seemed to be focused on Steve, Hugh, and the final efforts of the firefighters to soak any remaining hot spots, so she was able to take photos of the watchers.

"Good idea," Theo said quietly as she slid her phone back in her pocket, and she gave him a small smile.

As she unrolled the tape, she kept her eyes open, looking for anything—or anyone—that seemed out of place. Her effort felt futile, though, since debris from the burned house was scattered everywhere. The firefighters' efforts had created an even bigger mess, and she grimaced as she watched one soaking what was left of an exterior wall. Although she knew the work they were doing was necessary to put out the fire—and keep it out—it was still hard to watch as the crime scene was destroyed.

Rounding the corner of the yard, she wrapped the tape around a convenient small aspen tree and continued along the side of what had been the house. She noted which of the few neighboring homes had a clear line of sight, even as she hoped they weren't vacant for the winter. Finding a witness didn't seem too likely, though. The burned house was isolated and on the very edge of town.

Once she could see the backyard, Kit slowed, taking in the scene. If she were the arsonist, she would've entered and exited through the back. Except for the house a half block to the east, which looked empty, the backyard was hidden from view. A thick growth of trees bordered the south edge of the yard, providing a potential escape route.

Kit stepped into the trees a few feet before turning east. Most of the snow in the yard had been melted by fire and the firefighters' spray, but a slushy ridge remained just inside the tree line. As she made her way along the south side of the property, she kept her gaze on the ground, looking for any indication that a potential suspect had made their way into the woods.

Glancing up, she saw that Theo had stopped running tape along his side so that he could have a quiet conversation with Hugh. The sight of their small huddle made her chest twinge. She used to be part of something like that, but now she was the new cop, the interloper, the one not to be trusted. Impatiently yanking herself out of her moment of angst, she refocused on the ground around her as she continued unrolling the tape.

Right before she reached the edge of the property, she saw something in the half-melted snow bordering the tree line. Crouching down, she spotted a crescent-shaped indentation.

"Hey, guys," she called, pulling out her phone. As

Hugh and Theo made their way toward her, she took a picture of the mark in the snow, added a strip of police tape to the shot to give it scale, and then took another photo. "What do you think? Boot heel print?"

The two men squatted to examine it more closely. "Sure looks like it." Hugh straightened, looking at the ground around the print. "Any others?"

Kit stood and examined the area around the print. "Not that I can see. The yard's a mess, and there's not much snow cover in the wooded area. Want me to get Justice and see if he can pick up a trail?"

"Yeah." Now Theo was taking pictures, although he used an official scale instead of improvising with police tape like she had.

Hugh's face lit up. "Bring on the tracking dog! This is great. Now we just need an arson dog and a cadaver dog, and we'll have a dog for any occasion."

Rubbing the line between his eyebrows, Theo sighed. "Monroe doesn't need a cadaver dog *or* an arson dog."

His gaze moving pointedly from the burned shell of the house where Steve stood guard over the body and back to Theo, Hugh didn't say a word.

"These past few months have been an anomaly," Theo said, an annoyed growl underlining his words. "We *don't* need specialized K9s for cadavers and arsons. We *do* need people to quit killing and burning down buildings."

Hugh gave him a skeptical look. "Well, sure. Less death would be ideal, but it doesn't look like that's going to happen. We just got rid of a bomber, and an arsonist pops up. It doesn't seem like things are getting any less exciting."

Leaving the two men to their argument, Kit handed Hugh the remaining roll of police tape and headed back to where she'd parked. She pulled out the thirty-foot lead from the dog-supply bag she'd stowed on the floor in the back seat, grateful that she hadn't packed it in the trailer with the rest of her belongings. It was just luck that she'd tucked the long lead in Justice's travel bag. She never would've guessed that they'd be trailing an arson—and possibly murder—suspect on her first day.

Justice was quivering with excitement when she clipped the lead to his harness and gave him the command to leave the car.

"This way, goofy." She hauled on the leash, leading him toward the possible footprint in the backyard. His tail whipped back and forth as he trotted in front of her, his head swiveling as he sniffed the air, ready to head in whatever direction had the most interesting scents.

Hugh and Theo were still arguing when Kit and Justice reached them, but they broke off when they saw the dog. Both greeted Justice with thorough ear rubs and neck scratches. In thanks, Justice curled around them, his tail drumming a happy rhythm against their legs.

"I thought bloodhounds were usually reserved with strangers," Hugh said, massaging the loose skin at Justice's shoulders.

Kit gave a small shrug. "A lot of them are. Except for his excessive friendliness, Justice is a pretty typical bloodhound. He just doesn't have the shy gene." At the sound of his name, he looked at her, his tongue lolling out of his jowly mouth. "Ready, Justice?"

At the familiar words, he focused on her, his

brand-new friends forgotten. She indicated the footprint, and he snuffled at it.

"Will that be enough?" Theo asked, frowning.

Without taking her gaze off Justice, Kit lifted her free hand palm up. "We'll see. Justice, find."

The dog sniffed the ground, crisscrossing back and forth around the print. As he fanned out, Kit fed him more of the lead until he was fifteen feet away from her, heading deeper into the woods.

"*Aaah-rooo!*" His bay rang out, signaling that he'd picked up the scent, and Kit grinned.

"Find, Justice!"

The dog took off, and Kit followed, the lead stretching between them. Justice hauled her forward, wanting to run faster, but she kept him under control. In Wisconsin, she'd run almost every day, training herself along with Justice, but here the altitude was an issue. It was over eight thousand feet above sea level in Monroe, and the air felt too dry and thin as she pulled it into her lungs. After just five minutes of following Justice, Kit was already breathing hard. Annoyed by her weakness, she slowed Justice down and settled into an easy jog.

The sound of boots hitting the ground behind her let her know that Theo and Hugh were backing her up, and she felt her spirits lift with adrenaline and hope. This was what she'd trained for, what she loved to do—working with her K9 partner while her fellow cops had her back. The past six months in Wisconsin had been a pale imitation of this. She'd been disillusioned, and the other officers had become suspicious and hostile. She didn't regret blowing the whistle on her corrupt partner and would've done the same thing if she had a do-over, but she'd missed the camaraderie and sense of being in a close-knit team. This new start in Monroe might give her the opportunity to regain the love she had for the job.

If only the air wasn't quite so thin. The deer trail that Justice was following was narrow and winding, and dodging around trees and jumping over downed branches were good distractions from Kit's overworked lungs. The lead kept getting tangled in the brush, and she struggled to free it before Justice had to stop. The dog was easily distracted, and she wanted him to keep his mind focused on the trail.

Kit had half expected the scent to lead Justice a short way through the trees to another road, where the suspect would've parked a car and driven away after setting the fire. However, they'd been jogging through the woods for a good twenty minutes, and the dog didn't seem to be slowing down.

"Are you familiar with this area?" she asked over her shoulder, trying not to sound like she was gasping for air—even though she was. "Any idea where we are?"

"Yes." Theo's voice sounded annoyingly even, as if he were sitting in a chair with his feet up. There was no gasping on his part. "We're circling around the south side of town. Steve—the fireman—lives about a half mile to the right."

"Any guess where we're headed?" Kit gave up trying to make her words sound effortless and just sucked in air.

There was a pause that made Kit want to turn around and see the guys' expressions, but she was afraid that she'd fall on her face if she did.

"Possibly," Theo finally said. He'd loosened up

slightly since their first meeting, but it sounded as if all his guards had slammed back into place.

"Possibly?" Maybe it was the lack of oxygen to her brain, but Kit was extraordinarily annoyed by his vague answer. "Want to share what you think we're running into?"

From his grunt, she assumed Theo's answer was no.

She didn't bother asking any more questions. Obviously, he wasn't going to tell her, and she had a better use for the air she was dragging into her lungs. Her earlier hope slipped away. Maybe Monroe would end up being a better place than her last job, but it wasn't going to be all sunshine and happy times. She had a feeling she'd have to work for every step forward.

With a grimace, she pushed herself faster, and Justice happily surged ahead. She was so busy watching to make sure she didn't trip or run into any trees that it surprised her when the evergreens thinned and then disappeared as they ran into an open yard.

She slowed, blinking to get her bearings as Justice towed her straight for a dilapidated back porch. The entire house looked as if it would fall over in a stiff breeze, and Kit swiveled her head, trying to take in all the possible spots someone could ambush them from. There were too many. The evergreens that crowded around the property provided all sorts of hiding spots and darkened the yard to an eerie green. The windows facing them reflected the light, masking whatever—or whoever—was inside looking out.

"Whose home is this, do you know?" she asked, keeping her voice low. For all she knew, this place had been abandoned for years. It certainly looked like it should be vacant. When neither man answered, she risked a glance over her shoulder to see Theo and Hugh sharing a meaningful glance.

Trying to keep her face expressionless—and probably failing—Kit turned her head away from them, stewing. She didn't expect to be in on every inside joke in the department on her first day, of course, but she didn't expect them to withhold important information either. Her gaze locked on Justice. It appeared that the only ally she had at the moment was her K9 partner. Although he'd taken a while to catch on to things, he'd never intentionally let her down. Dogs didn't care about station politics. That was one reason they were so great.

As soon as it was obvious that Justice was headed toward the back porch, Theo skirted around them, pulling a key out of his pocket and quickly opening the door. He disappeared inside, leaving Kit to stare after him, confused.

"This is his house?" she asked Hugh.

"Not really." He quickly followed Theo into the house, the storm door automatically swinging shut behind him.

Running up the rickety-looking back steps, Justice reached the door and sat, his signal that he'd found the scent. As she joined him, still not sure what was going on, she absently pulled his favorite toy out of her pocket—a raggedy sock monkey. She found sock monkeys to be creepy as hell, with their empty eyes and evil red mouths, but the stuffed animal was Justice's favorite, no matter how hard Kit had tried to wean the hound off it. This particular sock monkey had been a joke gift from the other officers right after she'd adopted Justice, and she regretted ever offering the toy to her dog. It was the only stuffed thing he hadn't ripped to shreds…unfortunately.

"Good find," she crooned, offering the horrid thing to Justice, who accepted it eagerly. No matter what Theo and Hugh were hiding from her, her dog came first. "Good dog! Who's the best dog?" It was only after rewarding Justice for the successful—she assumed— trail that she followed the other two cops inside. Looking around the large kitchen, she noted that it was in a similar condition to the exterior, with missing and drooping cupboard doors and mismatched chairs. It was clean, though, and there were little personal touches, like an elementary school award letter proudly displayed on the ancient fridge and a row of boots of all different sizes lined up on a rag rug next to the door.

"Theo." Jules, the waitress from the diner, walked into the kitchen, looking surprised but pleased. "What are you doing here so early? And why do you smell like you've been rolling around in a tire fire?"

"A tire fire?" His face softened as he looked at her.

Stopping so that they were almost but not quite touching, Jules smiled up at him. "I was going to say a campfire, but that smells too nice. I hate to tell you, sweet pea, but you stink."

Jules echoed her earlier thoughts so closely that Kit snorted a laugh. The sound made Jules look over at her, Justice, and Hugh, who'd followed her into the kitchen and was standing behind her. Jules's welcoming smile faded as apprehension took over her expression.

"What's going on?" Jules asked, taking a step away from Theo.

He caught her hand. "How long have you been home?"

Her gaze flickered to the clock and then returned to meet Theo's as the worried grooves in her forehead deepened. "Just about an hour. Why? What's happening?" She gave Kit and Justice another anxious look.

"Are you the only one here?" Theo turned, putting his body between Jules and the hallway entrance.

"You need to tell me what's going on." Her Southern accent was thick. Kit had a feeling that Jules was about to lose it if Theo kept her in suspense any longer.

Theo, however, appeared to have missed the warning signs of his girlfriend's impending freak-out, because he kept his attention on the doorway. "I'll tell you as soon as we make sure the house is safe."

As Jules sucked in a breath, Kit winced. That had been the wrong thing to say.

"What?" Jules's voice rose several octaves, finally bringing Theo's attention back to her. "The house isn't safe?" When she started to make her way around Kit and Hugh toward the back door, Theo grabbed her hand, halting her progress.

"Where are you going?" he asked.

"To get the kids."

"The kids are fine," Theo assured her, but she gave him a flat look.

"Then what's going on? You're being all cryptic and weird, and it's freaking me out. Does this have something to do with…?" After a glance at Kit, she pressed her lips together in a frustrated line. "Just tell me."

"We're just going to check the house," Theo non-explained in a tone that Kit assumed was supposed to be soothing, but wasn't. She had to literally bite her tongue to keep herself from taking over the situation. All Theo was doing was panicking Jules, and he seemed oblivious to the fact that he was making things worse. There was nothing Kit could do, though. It was her first day. She didn't know the people involved or their backgrounds, and it wouldn't be good for her to act like a pushy know-it-all this early on, especially when Theo's girlfriend was involved. She snuck a glance at Hugh, and he bugged his eyes out in an *I know, right?* gesture before clearing his throat.

"Kit's dog tracked someone from a possible arson scene to your back porch," Hugh said, and Kit sighed inwardly as Jules sucked in a horrified breath.

"Here?" she almost shrieked before lowering her voice to a whisper. "Here? An arsonist was here?"

"Probably not." Theo scowled at Hugh before turning back to Jules, his expression gentling. "We're just going to take a look around, make sure the house is clear and you're safe. The dog is new."

Kit stiffened, shooting a glare at Theo. He didn't seem to notice as he continued.

"Besides, we don't know whose scent he was tracking. We don't even know if it was an arson. This was a long shot, and your house is just the dead end to a possible lead."

Kit held herself rigidly, swallowing back her words for another reason. Although she'd taken offense on Justice's behalf for the "new" comment, she couldn't argue with the last part of Theo's statement. The partial boot print had been a long shot, and it could easily have been from someone completely unrelated to the arson—if it actually had been an arson. Theo wasn't wrong, but it grated on her to hear him blame their failure on the dog.

Theo's reassuring words worked on Jules, though, and she visibly relaxed, no longer pulling against Theo's hold to get out the door.

"We're going to search the house, just to make sure it's clear," he said, and Jules tensed again.

Her face tightened with something other than fear, and Kit watched her expression with interest. Was that guilt? She wondered if Jules had someone in the house that she didn't want Theo to know about—another boyfriend, maybe? "Um…I'm not here alone."

Kit's eyebrows shot up. Even though she'd immediately suspected Jules of having an affair, she hadn't expected her to flat-out admit it in front of all of them.

"I knew it!" Hugh exclaimed, sounding more satisfied about being right than put out on his partner's behalf. "Gracie refused to tell me, but I knew what was going on the second I saw her chasing you down at the viner."

Kit blinked. Theo's girlfriend and Hugh's girlfriend were having an affair? This small-town policing had a lot more drama than she'd expected.

Theo's eyes narrowed as he looked at Jules. "Did another one of your…*childhood friends* show up unexpectedly?"

There was a third person? Kit was very confused at this point.

Straightening her shoulders, Jules met Theo's penetrating glare straight on. "Yes. Elena. She's very sweet and *extremely* shy, so you're not going to bully her."

Giving up on trying to figure out what was happening, Kit looked back and forth between them.

"Jules…"

"I know!" She threw up her hands. "You're just

worried, since all of my friends seem to bring an army of enemies with them. I can't turn them away, though." She sent Kit another of her wary glances, the kind that said she was verbally editing herself because of Kit's presence. "Elena just needs a safe place to stay for a while. Mr.— ah, I was promised that no one will be looking for her."

Hugh gave a forced cough. "No offense, Jules, but Mr. Ah's track record isn't the best, and I *just* got my cast off. I'd really like to stay off medical leave for a while."

Releasing Theo, Jules propped her hands on her hips, looking ready to face off with Hugh, but then her gaze slipped to Kit again. "Could we discuss this later? Maybe after you check to make sure there isn't an arsonist hiding in my house?"

After a moment of silent yet expressive shared glances between Jules, Theo, and Hugh, Jules's hands slipped off her hips. "Fine. She's in Sarah's old room. Be nice."

Hugh chuckled. "We're always nice."

Staring at Hugh skeptically, Jules said, "Theo?"

"We'll be nice." Theo moved toward the hallway, looking at Jules over his shoulder. "Stay in here. We'll check the house and then talk to Elena. This won't take long."

"Want Justice to lead?" Kit asked, and his tail started whipping back and forth at the sound of his name.

Eyeing them thoughtfully, Theo shook his head. "We'll do a standard search. Bring him along, though, and we'll double-check anything he lights up on."

Theo and Hugh worked together with the ease of two cops who'd done many, many searches together, and Kit stayed back, keeping an eye out behind them as she kept Justice from getting in their way. They searched a cluttered, ancient basement before working their way up. The house was charming, Kit had to admit, despite the fact that it looked like it was a lost nail away from collapsing on their heads. There were lots of small rooms and multiple entries that made the search tricky, but Theo and Hugh seemed to take it in stride. Kit could tell they were familiar with the place, and she wondered why Hugh knew the layout of Theo's girlfriend's house so well.

It wasn't until they climbed to the second floor that Justice's interest picked up, and he started pulling her forward down the hall. She made him wait until all the other rooms were searched and Theo waved her ahead of them before she allowed him to tow her to the last door on the left. Hugh and Theo took up positions to the side, their backs against the wall so they wouldn't be visible right away. Despite Jules's earlier assurances that Elena was sweet and shy, tension made Kit's fingers tighten around Justice's lead. As Justice snuffled at the bottom of the doorframe, Kit knocked.

Her heartbeat accelerated. Her dog's nose didn't lie. Whoever had been at that arson scene was behind this door, and she could be about to come face-to-face with a killer.

CHAPTER 5

"POLICE," KIT ANNOUNCED BEFORE TAKING A STEP BACK AND pulling Justice with her away from the door. In the tense seconds that followed, she listened, wanting a warning if the woman behind the closed door was trying to slip out the window or—much, much worse—racking a shotgun. The only sound was the creak of the floor and hurried, light footsteps.

The door swung open slightly, and a woman peeked out. She was tiny. There weren't many adults that Kit had to look down at, but Elena was one of them. Kit guessed that the woman was no taller than five feet and probably weighed ninety pounds. She looked to be in her mid-twenties, with straight, brown hair and big doe eyes framed by about a mile of dark lashes. Kit understood why Jules felt so protective. The woman sent a worried look toward Justice, who'd plopped down next to Kit in an unusual display of self-control.

"Hello. Elena?" Kit's voice was gentle, but the woman still flinched, even as she nodded slightly.

"I'm Officer Kit Jernigan. Is anyone else in your room with you?"

"No?" Her unsure response didn't inspire confidence in Kit that she was telling the truth.

"Mind if we come in?" She moved forward, and

Elena yielded, stepping back and opening the door all the way. As Kit walked into the small bedroom, she quickly checked for possible spots where someone could be hiding. The bifold closet door was open, and the quilt covering the bed barely came down to the bottom of the mattress, giving a clear view of the space under the bed. Shifting to the side, Kit glanced between the open door and the wall, but no one was there, and she relaxed slightly. "It's clear."

"What's this about?" Elena asked, wrapping her arms around her stomach.

Kit gave her a small, reassuring smile. "We just need to ask you a few questions." Without a digital recorder or even a notebook, Kit felt woefully unprepared for this interview. She glanced at Theo and Hugh, who'd moved into Elena's line of sight but stayed in the hall. Although Elena darted a look their way, her attention quickly returned to Kit. Widening her eyes at the other cops, Kit tried to send a silent message, but neither reached toward the recorders on their belts. She hid a grimace. It appeared that she was on her own. "What's your last name?"

Elena's gaze dropped to her feet before returning to Kit's. "Dahl."

"You're new to town?"

"Yes." Her mile-long eyelashes fluttered down and back up again before she continued. "I'm visiting my old friend Jules."

Hugh cleared his throat, making Kit glance over to see him exchange a partially amused but mostly exasperated look with Theo. Making a mental note to ask them what that was all about, she waited a few moments.

Instead of interjecting a question, he silently waved for her to continue.

"When did you arrive?" Kit asked, her tone losing some of its sympathy and becoming more matter-of-fact. Despite Elena's dropped glances and Bambi eyes, her voice was steady and her hands didn't tremble. Either the woman was excellent at hiding her nervousness or she wasn't as fazed by the sight of the police as she wanted Kit to think.

"This morning."

"What time?"

Elena dropped her gaze again, this time peering up at Kit through her lashes. If her little sister hadn't perfected the innocent-angel look, Kit might've softened. Instead, it had the opposite effect. "Um…" Elena hesitated. "I'm not sure exactly. Early?"

"Have you been here since then?" When Elena just blinked at her, either confused by the question or surprised that her damsel-in-distress act wasn't working, Kit forced some gentleness into her voice, rephrasing the question. "Have you left the house since you arrived?"

"No. I mean, I haven't gone anywhere. Why?"

Kit studied her, wondering why Elena's reactions seemed just a bit…off. "We're investigating a possible crime. Has anyone else been in the house?"

"Grace and the kids were here when I arrived," Elena said, biting the corner of her lip. "And Jules got home not too long ago."

"Anyone else stop by?"

"Nooo." The way she stretched out the word made her seem uncertain. "Not that I've seen. I've mostly been in my room, though."

Kit started to ask her next question, but Hugh interrupted. "Thank you for your help…Elena." When Kit gave him an *I'm not finished* look, he jerked his head toward the stairs in an unmistakable *yes you are* gesture. Turning back to Elena, Kit gave her a polite smile.

"Yes, thank you. If you think of anything else or see anything suspicious, please give us a call." Automatically, she reached for the pocket of her BDUs where she used to keep business cards only to realize that she hadn't even been able to fill out the card request form, much less have them printed. Hugh moved toward Elena, a card in his hand, and Kit gave him a nod of thanks.

"Okay." Elena accepted the card with a shy smile. She followed Hugh and Kit to the doorway. As soon as they stepped into the hall, Elena closed the door behind them.

Biting the inside of her bottom lip to keep from demanding to know why Hugh had stopped the interview, Kit forced herself to wait until Theo did a quick search of the third floor and the three of them returned to the kitchen.

"All clear," Theo told Jules with a slight, reassuring smile, and Jules let out an audible exhale, as if she'd been holding her breath the entire time. Theo wrapped an arm around her shoulders, and she leaned into his side.

"Every time I think we can relax just a little, some new scary thing pops up," Jules said, making Kit wonder what else — besides the police department getting blown up — had happened in this deceptively sleepy-looking town.

"Speaking of new scary things, should we expect the people your new roomie's running from to show up soon?" Hugh asked, leaning against the wall by the table.

At the mention of Elena, Jules straightened, although

she didn't pull away from Theo's hold. "No. Mr. Es—uh, the person who helped her get here said that he'd be surprised if anyone came chasing after Elena. She didn't tell me the whole story, but it's pretty clear that she's a minor player, and finding her is not a priority for anyone, especially since the main crime families are in chaos right now. Having her disappear was just a precaution."

"Uh-huh." Although he didn't say anything else, Theo didn't sound convinced, and his concerned frown deepened as he looked at Jules. Reaching up, she took his hand where it rested on her shoulder and gave him a reassuring smile.

"Mr. S?" Hugh said. "What does the S stand for? Smith?"

Giving him a flat look, Jules said, "It stands for *secret*. As in, you're never going to guess, and I'm never going to tell you, so you might as well give up and quit nagging me about it."

"But nagging is one of my things," Hugh said, not appearing to be fazed by her stern expression. "Most people find it to be one of my more endearing traits."

Kit couldn't hold back a laugh at that, even though she unsuccessfully tried to turn it into a cough at the last minute. The sound must've reminded the other three that Kit was listening—they exchanged warning glances and then dropped the subject.

Glancing at his watch, Theo said, "Do you have time before Dee gets home to give us a ride back to the scene?"

"Sure, if it's in town." Jules slipped out from under Theo's arm and snagged the purse sitting on the table. "What scene are we talking about here?"

"There was a fire."

The smile slipped from Jules's face. "Oh no. Another one?"

"Well, technically, all the other fires were really bombings, so this is the first." Although Hugh's words were joking, they had a tense-sounding edge. Kit couldn't blame him. From what she'd picked up, the town had been put through the wringer already.

"Was anyone hurt?" Jules asked.

"It was the Nailors' place, and they head to California for the winter," Theo non-answered. Kit was impressed by how neatly he sidestepped the question.

Jules looked relieved. "That's something, at least. Not much, but something." She waved at the back door as she headed for the hall. "Head on outside. I just need to talk to Theo for a moment. We'll meet you at the car."

As Kit headed back outside, Justice surging in front of her, she glanced back at Hugh, who was following her. "What was all that about?"

"All what?" His expression was pure innocent blankness, and Kit swallowed a sigh as she turned to face him head-on. She could already tell that she was going to have to work for every sliver of information she yanked out of him.

"Well, let's start with why there's a woman hiding from a crime family upstairs." Irritation surged through her as she remembered her truncated interview. "And why you wouldn't let me ask a possible suspect some basic questions."

His eyebrows shot up in what appeared to be honest surprise. "Suspect?"

"Yes." Justice slunk behind her, his belly low to the ground, and Kit tried to moderate her tone. She'd never managed to follow the "honey over vinegar" rule well. Her true feelings were always written on her face, or she simply announced them—loudly. Normally, she managed to stay relatively polite, but it had already been quite the day, and it wasn't over yet. Taking a deep breath, she forced her shoulders to lower and her hands to relax out of the fists she'd made. "A *possible* suspect. Justice led us right to her room. I'm just confused why you didn't want me to interview her."

"The women who live here"—Hugh jerked a thumb toward the house they'd just left—"Gracie, Jules, the kids, Sarah, and now Elena... They're just trying to escape bad situations. I know you're new, but you need to trust us on this. They're the victims, not the criminals."

Kit swallowed a scoffing reply, knowing it wouldn't help the situation. Still, it annoyed the heck out of her that Hugh was protecting a possible suspect. Kit's instincts were screaming that Elena was hiding something, and it went almost painfully against the grain to not at least *try* to get the truth out of her.

Small town, Kit reminded herself, mentally counting to ten before she said anything out loud. *Get used to it. This is your life now.*

She had a bad feeling that her new life was going to suck.

They waited next to the car in stiff silence until Jules and Theo emerged from the house, hand in hand. The sight reminded Kit of how her partners had protected Jules's new housemate from her, and her irritation flared again. She was a newcomer, true, but so was Elena. Hugh and Theo were treating Kit, a fellow officer, with more suspicion than a random stranger that Justice had trailed from a crime scene, merely because Elena had moved in with their girlfriends. It wasn't right. It was bad policing, and it was going to make Kit's life a lot more uncomfortable than it had to be.

Looking at the two men's closed expressions, though, she knew it wasn't a fight she was going to win. She resolved to let it go for now, and to keep an open mind as the investigation continued. If she dug in and decided that Elena was involved without actual evidence just because Hugh—and probably Theo—were determined to think the opposite, then no one would be doing any objective investigating. Taking in a deep, silent breath, she exhaled, trying to let go of her building resentment. It worked...sort of.

Jules waved at the passenger door in invitation, but Kit hesitated. "Do you mind having Justice in your car?" Kit asked. "He's a bloodhound, so he smells a little... well, houndy. I could walk him back."

Jules laughed. "Please. No dog smells worse than three teenage boys, including one who works at a kennel. Climb on in."

"Thanks." As she smiled back, Kit decided she liked Jules. Anyone who accepted her big, slightly smelly, occasionally drooly hound went onto Kit's good-person list. She opened the back hatch. "Load."

Justice jumped in, settling on the blanket that covered the floor, and Kit carefully closed the door. To her surprise, Theo and Hugh had gotten into the back, immediately starting a low-voiced conversation and leaving the front seat for her. Frowning a little in puzzlement at the unexpectedly polite gesture, she got in the car. She almost wished they'd decide to either be nice or be dicks, since this back-and-forth was messing with her head.

As the car bumped down the rutted driveway, evergreen branches slid along its sides. The trees blocked most of the light, making the narrow, curving lane seem claustrophobic. They couldn't be too far out of town, but it felt like the middle of nowhere to Kit, and the idea of being trapped in the wilderness with three almost-strangers made her tense. Her fear wasn't logical—she knew that—but her gut still twisted with unease.

"So…" Jules's voice made Kit start, and she gave an inward sigh at her jumpiness. If she was going to survive her new job, she would need to be better than this. "How do you like Monroe?"

"I haven't seen much of it yet," Kit said, figuring that was more tactful than saying it seemed like a postapocalyptic deathscape populated by unwelcoming cops and weird mountain people, at least one of whom was an arson-loving murderer. "The pass has been closed, so I just managed to get through this morning. I only had time to drop the trailer holding all my things at my rental house before heading to the station…or what *used* to be the station."

Jules winced as she turned onto the main road. "Poor thing. What a time to move here."

Anything Kit could've said in response didn't seem very tactful, so she settled on a noncommittal hum and a change of subject. "How many kids do you have?"

"Four. They're my siblings, actually." The nervous edge in Jules's voice disappeared as she smiled with obvious fondness.

"Wow. Four? That's a handful." Kit had a hard time

wrapping her head around the idea of having one dog dependent on her, much less four children. She loved kids and had volunteered at the Boys and Girls Club in her old town, but that wasn't the same as parenting. Plus, with Justice, she could crate him when she couldn't keep an eye on him. For Jules to take in her four siblings was impressive, and Kit found herself liking her even more.

"Sometimes it gets a little crazy, but Sam—he's the oldest—is a huge help. You'll probably meet him soon, since he works at Nan's." At Kit's baffled look, Jules clarified. "Nan owns the kennel the K9 unit contracts with."

That overwhelmed feeling hit Kit again at the reminder that the girlfriend of an officer knew more about her new department than Kit did. She did her best to shake it off. "I haven't been there yet. It's been a busy first day for me."

Turning onto the street with the burned house, Jules laughed again. "I bet." She sobered, peering at the blackened shell. "Oh no. That's awful. Our old barn burned down, and that was hard enough. I can't imagine losing our house like that." She did a U-turn in front of Hugh's squad car and stopped.

"Thank you for the ride," Kit said, unfastening her seat belt and climbing out. "It's a relief not to repeat that hike through the woods."

"No problem." Jules rolled down her window to accept a kiss from Theo, and Kit circled to the back of the car to retrieve Justice. After he hopped out and she closed the back hatch, she surveyed the scene. Although it felt as if their trek through the woods and the search of Jules's house had taken hours, the situation hadn't changed much. Another fire rescue, a couple of cops, and a man in street clothes had joined Steve by the remains.

Hugh headed toward the small group, and Kit hurried toward her car, intending to put Justice away. A sharp whistle made her stop and look over her shoulder at Hugh.

"Hang tight," he called. "The coroner has a flat. Can Theo use your SUV to pick him up? We need Theo's squad car to keep blocking traffic."

"Sure." Kit dug out her keys and tossed them to Theo, who gave her a nod of thanks.

"Give me one minute, and then I'll give you a ride to the station," Hugh said. "The chief should be able to hunt down a vehicle for you to use."

Kit waited as Hugh exchanged a few words with another cop she hadn't met yet. All the first responders on scene except for her were men, and she felt another rock join the stack already weighing down her belly. She knew it was a small department that shrank dramatically over the winter, but she was beginning to fear that she'd be the lone woman officer. Shoving the thought out of her head, she reminded herself not to borrow trouble. She didn't know for sure if that was true. If it was, she'd deal with it.

Right now, she needed to concentrate on making it through her first day.

Hugh jogged back to where she was waiting next to his car. "How's he with other dogs?" he asked, waving toward where Justice stood, his tail whipping back and forth in excitement at Hugh's approach.

"He loves everyone." Glancing down at the dog, Kit wondered what that was like, to be so happy and accepting. Even as a little girl, she'd never been as easygoing as Justice was.

"Good." Opening the back door, he leashed his dog before letting her jump out of the car. She approached the hound, her head and tail up with wary interest. "Justice, meet Lexi. She likes long walks, rawhide treats, and beheading stuffed animals."

Justice, being Justice, bounded over, his entire body wriggling with excitement as he play-bowed in front of Lexi, his back half swinging from side to side from the enthusiasm of his tail wags.

Grinning, Kit said, "Lexi, this is Justice. He's into sleeping, eating, and smelling things. Peanut-butter-flavored treats are his favorite."

After a thorough mutual sniffing, Justice was obviously deeply smitten, while Lexi was tolerant of his affection, albeit in a long-suffering way.

"This is the way it always goes." Kit sighed as Justice rolled onto his back, waving his ungainly paws in an attempt to get Lexi to play. "He loves so deeply, and then he gets clingy, starts texting too often, and drives them away."

"Justice. Buddy." Hugh crouched down next to the hound. "You need to stop trying so hard. Desperation is never attractive."

The dogs both cocked their heads at him as if they could understand, and Kit laughed.

Straightening, Hugh loaded Lexi and then waved for Kit to do the same with Justice. They watched for a few moments to make sure the dogs wouldn't have any issues with sharing the space, but they were fine. Lexi sat by the door, staring out the window, and Justice flopped down next to her, rolling his eyes up at her worshipfully.

"I don't think he took my advice," Hugh said as he headed for the driver's seat.

With another snort of laughter, Kit rounded the car and climbed in on the other side. "He just needs to learn these life lessons for himself, I think."

Even as her laughter faded, her smile remained. Their banter, as silly as it was, lit a spark of hope that she could find that same sense of camaraderie she'd had at her last department. Her move to a desolate, postapocalyptic deathscape might have been a good idea after all.

Glancing out the window, she took in the first responders clustered around the human remains inside the burned shell of what used to be a house, and she grimaced. *Or maybe not.*

CHAPTER 6

As Hugh pulled away, Kit's hands twitched, and she clasped them together in her lap. She was too much of a control freak to be a good passenger and would much rather be driving, but she was going to have to suck it up until her probationary training period was over and she could start making the decisions again. She couldn't wait.

"Get the chief to set you up with all of your equipment." Hugh turned east onto the main road running through town. "If you're going on calls, you'll need gear as well as a vehicle. It's not safe for you to be on your own without a radio, and you'll need an ID."

"I will." The thought of having a radio again made relief spread through her until the rest of Hugh's words registered. "I'm going to be on my own?" Since she'd only worked at one other department, she'd only gone through the probationary training process once, but she didn't remember being let loose by herself for at least a month. She wasn't sure if Hugh's plan to let her fly solo on her first day was a good sign or a bad one.

As if he could hear her reservations, Hugh gave her a sideways smirk. "Nothing dangerous. You'll be taking witness statements."

"What will you be doing while I'm knocking on the neighbors' doors?" she asked, a little wary of this plan.

He offered her a look of innocence that only made her suspicions deepen. "Other stuff related to the case. The state investigators are going to be helping, but we're still shorthanded for a major case like this. If we split up, we'll cover more ground."

Although Kit couldn't argue with that logic, she had a feeling that Hugh had an ulterior motive, one that involved keeping her at the periphery of this investigation. The amount of suspicion her new partners had for her seemed extreme, even for an insular, small-town force. She wondered why as Hugh pulled into the small lot by the station.

Instead of getting out, he looked at her expectantly. "I let the chief know I was dropping you off. He'll be here in just a bit to get you set up with equipment and a car."

"Why the chief?" Kit opened the door but didn't get out. "Isn't there a sergeant or lieutenant on duty?"

His mouth tightened like it did when his leg was bothering him, even though he hadn't moved it. "Not right now."

"Is that a winter thing or a small town thing?" At her old department, Kit had hardly ever even gotten glimpses of the chief. It seemed strange to have him so involved in such minor stuff.

"Neither." Hugh's frown deepened, and he stared through the windshield, looking more furious than she'd seen him so far. "It's what happens when your lieutenant turns out to be a back-stabbing criminal."

"Oh." She blinked, unsure how to respond. This job was not at all what she'd expected. "Sorry to hear that. Um…thanks for the ride." Feeling awkward, she hopped out of the car and got Justice out of the back seat. He was reluctant to leave Lexi, but obeyed when Kit ordered him out. "I'll let you know if I have any luck finding a witness."

As she closed the back door, Hugh rolled down the front passenger window and studied her for a moment, his unhappy expression fading with the change of subject. "You have your personal gun?"

"Yes." She felt the reassuring weight of her Glock where it rested in its holster in the small of her back, under her coat. Until she was in uniform, she preferred to have her weapon concealed, rather than on her hip, since people tended to get a bit antsy at what would appear to be a civilian open-carrying.

"Good," he said casually. "Be careful. Some people around here tend to be…nervous when strangers knock on their doors, and pretty much everyone owns at least one gun." With that unnerving advice, he rolled up the window.

Kit stared at the back of the squad car as it did a three-point turn and then took off the way they'd just come.

"Seriously?" she grumbled under her breath. Justice cocked his head at the sound of her voice. "All my witnesses are armed and paranoid? What kind of hellhole is this?"

When Justice didn't answer, Kit sighed and headed into the station, reminding herself that at least she'd be getting a radio.

"Have to look on the bright side of things," she said.

Justice thumped his tail against her legs, making her smile. She wished she had even half of her dog's optimism. For Justice, every side was sunny.

Climbing back into the pickup, Kit slammed the door a little too firmly, waking up Justice. He lifted his head from where it'd been resting on the center console and thumped his tail against the door. The dog was riding on the passenger seat next to her, since the area behind the front seats was filled with stacked cages. The truck was a loaner from the sheriff's department's animal control unit. Justice liked it, since he had a better view out the front windshield and had discovered a stash of dog treats in the passenger-door pocket. Kit was less enthusiastic, since the cab smelled like a musty mixture of wet dog, animal urine, and—oddly enough—skunk.

Blowing out a breath, she struggled to regain her sense of humor as she turned the radio to a nonemergency channel and rattled off Hugh's unit number into the mic.

"Go ahead, greenie."

She rolled her eyes, glad that her PT officer couldn't see her. "I've finished canvassing the area. What do you need me to work on next?"

"Any luck?"

It didn't really surprise her that Hugh took radio etiquette as casually as he seemed to treat everything else. "Negative. Only one house had someone in residence, a ninety-three-year-old Mrs. Velma Jones, and she didn't see or hear anything. She had, however, lost the keys to her Lincoln and wanted help locating them. I helped her look, but we didn't find them."

"Probably for the best," Hugh said. *"Mrs. Jones isn't supposed to be driving. If the car's still there, one of her*

kids probably took the keys for the safety of everyone in Monroe."

That had been Kit's guess, too. "The Lincoln is safely tucked in her garage." Rolling her shoulders to release some leftover stiffness, she heard her spine pop. It had been a rough few hours. With Hugh's warning niggling at the back of her mind every time Kit knocked on a door, she'd been tense since the chief had sent her out in the borrowed, smelly truck with an MPD ID on a lanyard hanging around her neck. She was antsy to join the other cops and see what leads they were following. "Anything on your end?"

There was a slight pause that Kit wasn't sure how to interpret before Hugh spoke again. *"Not really. Have you checked the houses all the way to Dry Creek Road?"*

Kit frowned as she examined the GPS map on the laptop screen attached to the dash. Dry Creek Road was about four blocks to the north. There was no way that any of the residents who lived in that area could've gotten a glimpse of what had happened at the burned house. Reminding herself that she'd just started working there, she kept it simple. "No, I haven't."

"Go ahead and do that. Maybe someone saw a strange car in the area."

Kit swallowed her protest that it would be a waste of time, since she had a feeling that arguing would be futile. "Has anyone interviewed the complainant yet?"

There was another pause. *"Wes? No, I don't think so. Why?"*

She gave the mic a bewildered look, happy again that he couldn't see her expression. "In case he saw something. Isn't it pretty standard to interview the complainant?" Although she'd known there were differing styles of policing, this seemed like an obvious requirement.

"*No need.*" *Apparently it isn't so obvious*, Kit thought as he continued, sounding a bit too blasé about the entire thing. "*If he'd seen anything more than the smoke, he would've shared it. Let me know if you find anything on your canvass.*"

It was Kit's turn to be silent for a moment as she worked things through in her head. Sure, this was a new department with different rules and ways of doing things, but good policing was good policing. She'd been a cop long enough to know how to investigate a serious crime, and there was no way she was going to skip over such a crucial step, even if it wasn't likely to lead to much. She didn't want to argue about it with her supervisor over the radio, however, so she kept her thoughts to herself, answering with a simple "copy" before she replaced the mic.

Justice shifted, and she looked over at him. "What should we do on our lunch break, Justice?" Cocking his head, he made a low *woof* sound. "What was that? Interview the complainant in a possible murder-and-arson case? Why, that's an excellent idea." A simple internet search of the closest forest service fire-lookout tower gave her an address, which she typed into the laptop's GPS program. When Justice shifted, drawing Kit's attention away from the computer screen, she smiled at him. "First day, and we're already rebels."

He thumped his tail against the seat in solidarity.

Following the directions, Kit took the main street west. As she left town and the road turned into a state highway, she divided her attention between driving, the directions, and the scenery. It still startled her how beautiful it was, with a layer of snow softening the vertical cliff's rough edges. It had a more severe and rugged look than when she'd visited in late summer, but it was wonderful just the same.

As she wove through the switchbacks, she made a mental note of each person's driveway or mailbox along the way. The sooner she knew her way around, the sooner everything would be easier. A couple of cars passed her on the highway, but once she turned at the GPS's urging, the traffic immediately thinned dramatically...to just Kit's smelly county truck.

The emptiness started to make her twitchy, and she glanced over at Justice's welcome shape next to her. The road she was on narrowed, the banks of snow on either side getting bigger and more intimidating with each second. Her trip into town that morning had been a piece of cake compared to the narrow, twisting lane she was driving on now. The GPS showed that she had a turn coming up, but she couldn't see any street signs. Slowing to a crawl, she spotted tire tracks in the snow turning to the right.

"Is this it?" she muttered, almost coming to a complete stop as she looked at the map on the screen, then the ruts in the unplowed snow. "Guess so." Justice, who'd sat up at the sound of her voice, looked out the window as Kit made a sharp turn onto what the map promised was a road.

The rear wheels of the pickup slid and spun as she turned, and her fingers clutched the steering wheel too tightly. Kit knew how to drive in snow, but that was in the Midwest, where everything was fairly flat and a too-tight turn wouldn't throw her off the mountainside.

She laughed at herself, but the sound came out stiff and harsh. "They actually plow roads in Wisconsin, too." Justice glanced at her and then returned to watching out the window. Kit focused on staying in the ruts another vehicle had made. If she had to call for help after getting stuck in a drift while using her lunch break to drive somewhere that Hugh had strongly suggested not to go, the other cops were never going to let her live it down.

The trail narrowed as it entered the trees, and Kit's fingers tightened around the steering wheel. The heavy evergreen branches filtered the sunlight, dimming it and turning it into an eerie green. Between the curvy road and the thick forestation, she couldn't see what was coming, so she slowed the truck to a crawl. At least one vehicle had gone this way earlier, which meant that there could be an oncoming car right around the next turn. With the trees lining the narrow trail, there'd be no room to get out of the way.

Except for the *scritch*ing sound of the pine branches brushing the sides of the truck and the soft hum of the engine, everything was quiet. She glanced at the radio display, making sure it was turned on and that she was scanning all the channels. Everything was as it should be. There just wasn't much radio traffic. The absence of the normal chatter made her feel very much alone.

Jumping to his feet, Justice gave a loud, baying bark, and the sudden sound made Kit jerk the wheel slightly. She quickly corrected, lining up the truck's tires with the existing tracks before bringing the vehicle to a stop.

"What's up, Justice?" she asked, leaning over to

peer out his window. She couldn't see any sign of what had caught his attention from that angle, so she shifted into Park and got out. The silence seemed even thicker outside the truck. Pressing away the uneasy feeling, she circled the front of the truck, scanning the area for the cause of Justice's alert.

As she reached the passenger side, she spotted a flash of red on the snow. She stepped closer to examine the spots. They were a vivid scarlet against the pristine white, and she tensed.

It was blood, and it was fresh.

CHAPTER 7

IF THE BLOOD HAD BEEN THERE FOR LONGER THAN A MINUTE or so, it would've frozen, leaving it a dull, orangey red. She wondered if it was from an animal, and checked around the area for any tracks. The few dots of blood led to larger blotches in the snow and then to an arc of what appeared to be arterial spray. Her stomach tightened with each new sighting, and she went still as she spotted a trail of prints—boot prints. Her head jerked up as she peered through the trees, mentally cursing the dim light and the shadows that made it too easy for something to hide.

Keeping her eyes on her surroundings, she opened the door and found Justice's lead by feel. The dog squirmed in excitement as she latched the leash onto the first hook of his harness. After grabbing her new portable radio, she gave him the command to hop out of the truck. Justice immediately snuffled at the blood.

"Justice, find." She kept her voice low and her gaze focused forward. There were a hundred noncriminal explanations for the blood and the boot prints, like a hunter or an injured hiker. Even so, the strange and eerie silence of her surroundings had her on high alert. It didn't help that she hadn't even been in town for a day, and there'd already been a probable arson and murder, but the current situation wasn't enough to call for backup, she decided. She slid her radio into her coat pocket.

The hound bayed, the sound echoing around them, and Kit flinched. *So much for staying quiet*, she thought, following Justice as he plunged into the forest. He barked again, the sound drawn out to a howl at the end, and Kit spotted movement through the trees. She ran faster, allowing Justice to tow her forward, and the motion came again. As Justice scrambled over a downed tree and circled a small grove of aspen, Kit was forced to keep her eyes on her footing. When she looked up again, a man stood just thirty feet away. She jerked to a halt, forcing Justice to stop as well.

The man looked to be in his early twenties, and Kit automatically cataloged his features in case she had to describe him later—or find a match in a photo lineup. He stared at her, menace radiating from every line of his body, and Kit felt a chill touch her spine. Her attention caught on the knife in his grip and the streaks of dark red that stained his coveralls and hands.

That's not a typical, harmless hunter, Kit thought, her muscles coiling with tension. There was something chilling about his dead-eyed expression—something threatening.

"Police! Drop the knife," she called, keeping her voice calm and commanding. "I just need to talk to you."

His face twisted into a sneer. "Pig," he snarled before turning to run.

"Stop!" she shouted, resuming her pursuit. "Police!"

The man ignored the command, speeding up instead. Justice bayed, caught up in the excitement of the chase, and Kit sprinted behind him. The adrenaline already had her heart pumping, and her lungs were hungering for oxygen, but she kept running. Branches whipped across her, scratching her face and catching on her clothes. The ground was rocky and covered in patchy snow, hiding bits of ice that made her slip every few strides. She managed to stay upright, but she worried with every slick patch that it might be the one to bring her down.

The person in front of her moved easily, as if he was accustomed to running through these woods. The trees grew thicker, blocking out most of the sun. It painted strange shapes on the ground, making it hard to tell what was an obstacle and what was merely a shadow. Despite the treacherous footing, Kit pushed her feet to move faster, and Justice happily picked up the pace when the lead slackened.

"Police! Stop!" she yelled again, hating how winded she sounded. She was used to pavement and manicured lawns, not this snowy wilderness. The only sounds she could hear were her own rasping breaths, the crunch of snow under her boots, and the swish of her coat as her arms pumped at her sides. Despite Justice's presence, the silent, towering pines made her feel small and alone, knowing that backup was miles away. It was up to her to keep herself—and her dog—alive. Shaking off her dark thoughts, she called out again. "Stop! Police!"

The runner didn't listen. As Kit dodged around a squat pine, the trees thinned, the forest opening up to a flat rock shelf. The man was nowhere in sight. Right in front of them, the ground abruptly ended, falling off into a deep gorge. On the opposite side of the crevasse, a steep cliff rose from the valley. Kit realized that she and her dog were running flat out…right to the edge of a cliff.

Justice was just a few strides away from certain death—and he wasn't slowing down.

Sucking in a scream, Kit immediately put on the brakes. Her boots slid on the rocky ground, bits of shale and grit rolling like ball bearings under her soles, not giving her any traction. Desperate to stop before hurling herself off the edge of the cliff, she grabbed for a nearby tree branch, but the spindly bough snapped off in her hands. Twisting her body, she reached for a sapling, even as her brain was yelling that it was too small to catch her weight, that its shallow roots were barely clinging to the rocky ground and would pull out at the slightest tug. She clutched it anyway. There was no other option, other than to go hurtling off the edge. It bowed in her grip, and she braced herself for the fall.

Somehow, miraculously, it held. Her body jerked to a stuttering halt right before the sheer drop.

Justice! She hauled on the lead, but she was too late. Justice's feet scrabbled against the ground, but the rocky surface didn't offer anything for him to grip, and his momentum carried him over the edge. Trying to think through the panic that was swamping her brain, she sucked in quick, terrified breaths and wrapped the lead around her arm. Holding tight to the sapling that had saved her, she braced for over a hundred pounds of falling dog to hit the end of the leash and drag her over the cliff with him. Even if his harness or lead didn't snap, there was no way she could keep him from falling when he weighed almost as much as she did. Clenching her molars together until her jaw ached, she prepared for the jolt and her dog's sharp yelp of pain.

It never came.

No. Oh no.

Releasing the sapling, she scrambled toward the edge, praying that he hadn't slipped from his harness and knowing deep inside that there couldn't be any other explanation. *He's fallen.* The horrible thought sent a spear of pain through her, and her lungs seized. He had to have fallen. Nothing else made sense. Her wonderful, loving, comical, irreplaceable partner was gone.

She couldn't take a breath. As she reached the brink, she leaned over the edge, dread and sorrow making her movements stiff and heavy. Forcing herself to look, she tipped forward—and froze.

Justice stood on a ledge only a few feet down from where Kit was standing. He eyed her curiously, as if wondering why they'd stopped. Kit blinked, afraid to believe her eyes, to hope that it was true—her dog hadn't fallen, hadn't plummeted hundreds of feet to his death. He didn't even have a scratch. The trail was tucked right against the cliff, hidden from her vantage point above, but as solid and real as her perfectly healthy and uninjured dog who was now impatiently waiting for Kit to resume the tracking session.

Her knees went watery with relief, and her breath starting coming in hard, ragged sobs. Even though she knew logically that Justice was fine, the rest of her mind was still mired in grief and panic.

Get it together, Kit, her brain reminded her sternly, and she fought to pull herself together. Jumping down next to Justice, she gave him a quick, hard hug, almost breaking down when he licked her ear in response. Releasing him, she stood, sucking in a hard breath and forcing herself to refocus on their current mission.

The armed and bloodstained man already had a lead on them, and she couldn't delay them any more than she already had. If he hurt anyone because she'd wasted time on what had turned out to be a stupid optical illusion, she wouldn't forgive herself. Even though there was no way she could've known about the ledge, she still felt silly for her panic, and she was glad none of her new partners were here to witness the embarrassing mistake.

"Sorry, Justice." Her voice shook a little, and she tightened her jaw. "Find!"

He eagerly leapt forward again, and she followed, trying to ignore the shaky weakness in her legs. She couldn't see movement ahead of them anymore, but she knew that Justice wouldn't lose the trail, so she concentrated on not getting smacked in the face by a tree branch or slipping on hidden ice.

Twisted trees grew in unlikely directions, forming around the scattered boulders. There was less snow, but the path was just as treacherous, since the rocky trail was as slick as the icy ground had been. Her footsteps echoed eerily off the rock faces, making it sound as if they were being pursued. Although she told herself that it was just an auditory trick, she couldn't shake the feeling that she and Justice were being hunted rather than being the hunters. She switched between watching her footing and craning her neck to search for a potential ambush.

Justice led her through a narrow space between two huge rocks and into an unexpected clearing. Bright sunlight, so different from the dimness of the claustrophobic, tree-lined path, blinded her for a moment, making her feel vulnerable. She blinked quickly, trying to adjust, before coming to a skidding halt.

Five people stood in a rough half circle, and they were all pointing shotguns at her chest.

She hauled back on the lead and towed Justice toward her. Her hand moved toward the small of her back, where her pistol sat in its holster beneath her coat, but one of the men racked his gun. Kit held her hands up at shoulder level instead, her right fingers still fisted around the leash. The radio in her pocket seemed impossibly far away. Even if she could reach it before being shot, it would be a long time before any backup arrived.

"Justice, heel." Somehow, her voice came out evenly, although her breath was ragged from exertion and fear. The hound sat at her side, close enough that he was leaning against her leg. "I'm a police officer."

In answer, another person racked her gun, and Kit fought the urge to take a step back. Her brain flipped through options, but none of them were good. She'd run far enough out of the trees that she couldn't sprint back to cover quickly enough. They'd have plenty of time to shoot her in the back. They were a good fifteen feet away, so she couldn't try to disarm one of them. If the person she ran toward didn't shoot her, the other four would.

Her eyes scanned the encircling crowd. They ranged in age from early twenties—the guy she'd been chasing—to a woman in her late sixties. There were three men and two women, and all of them appeared to be fully willing to shoot, judging by their determinedly unfriendly expressions. Hugh's warning about suspicious local gun owners popped into her head.

"I'm not here to harass anyone," she said, trying to keep her voice calm, even as she spoke loudly enough for all of them to hear.

"Why you chasing Bart, then?" one of the men demanded, his tone hostile enough to make Kit's heart rate kick up another notch. His light eyes narrowed in suspicion, and he spat tobacco juice to the side without taking the gun or his gaze off her. "With a dog, too."

"We were following a trail of blood through the woods. I was concerned that someone was hurt." *Or that someone had been hurting others.* Another quick glance around the half circle showed that no one was obviously bleeding. The guy who'd run from her, Bart, still had dark streaks of blood on his coveralls and hands, but he didn't appear to be injured.

The man—the group's spokesperson, apparently— barked a rusty laugh that didn't sound amused. His few remaining teeth were an unhealthy shade of brown. "Rabbit blood, one Bart trapped. Gonna arrest him for bunny murder?"

"No one's getting arrested." The thought that there were traps set in the woods she and Justice had just plowed through made her stomach lurch. Even though the more vicious varieties, like the leg-hold trap, were illegal, she had a feeling that the people currently aiming guns at a cop probably weren't the most law-abiding folk. "Now that I know everything's okay, I can be on my way. I'll just take my dog back to my truck and let dispatch know it was a false alarm." How she wished she'd called this in to dispatch. The guns didn't waver at her bluff. "I'm glad no one's hurt."

Bart snorted a humorless laugh. "Not yet."

Her stomach cramped as panic tried to hammer its way into her brain. Kit firmly blocked it out. If she lost the ability to think, she was going to do something instinctual and stupid—like pull her gun—that would get her and Justice killed. The dog whined, obviously sensing her distress, and leaned more heavily against her. Kit braced against his weight, barely keeping herself from stumbling to the side while her brain raced in circles, trying to figure out a plan.

"Let's keep it that way," she said, proud that none of her raging anxiety colored her voice. "Right now, we just have a misunderstanding. I thought someone was hurt and needed help, but you let me know that everyone here is fine. As it sits, there's no problem. I'll go back to my truck, tell dispatch all is well, and you'll return to your lives. If something happens to me, on the other hand, that will be a really bad thing for all of us. I'm a cop. That means that if I'm hurt, you'll have every law enforcement officer in the area descending on you, making your lives miserable."

Except no one knows where I am.

She paused, looking around at the group. None of their expressions showed any sign that she was getting through to them. Sweat trickled down the back of her neck, quickly turning cold. "All you have to do is lower your guns, and I'll walk away. It's an easy solution for all of us."

The first man laughed again. It sounded slightly more authentic this time. "Don't matter. We shoot you or don't shoot you. Either way, the cops'll be on us. Typical. The government'll take any excuse to stick their nose in."

"You have my word that no one will bother you if you let me go unharmed." Kit's voice shook slightly, and she dug her fingernails into her palm. The quick bite of pain steadied her. "You won't even be in my report. I won't mention you to anyone."

There was a pause that went on long enough to give Kit a spark of hope before he spoke again. "Liar."

He tilted his head, aiming the gun square at her chest. Her hand twitched, ready to go for her pistol, but there was no way she could draw and shoot five people before at least one of them managed to kill her. Justice whined, reminding her that she wasn't going to be the only one dying today. The idea of her dog getting hurt firmed her resolve, and she tensed, ready to grab her gun.

Time seemed to slow, and everything became very crisp and clear. She could see every detail of the man's shotgun and the way his knuckles whitened as he tucked the stock more firmly against his shoulder. His finger twitched on the trigger, and her hand whipped toward her gun, even as the echo of every lecture she'd gotten on tactical theory played through her head, telling her that action beat reaction every time. He was going to shoot her, and she wouldn't be able to stop him.

"What the hell are you doing, Rufus?"

The unexpected voice made her jerk, and she twisted her head around to look over her shoulder. A large, bearded man strode out of the trees toward her, and Kit recognized him as the person who'd helped her park her trailer that morning. She blinked, wondering for a fraction of a second if she was imagining him before slipping her hand under her coat to grab her gun. Real or not, he'd given her the time she needed to defend herself and her dog.

When he placed himself between her and her firing squad, however, she allowed herself to hope that he was really there and that there was a chance she could escape this situation without getting shot. She could smell him—woodsmoke and pine needles—and she was pretty certain that even the most welcome of hallucinations didn't carry such a sweet scent.

That and the sight of his broad back snapped her out of her shock, and she stepped to the side, pulling her gun but keeping it hidden behind her back. There was no way she was using a Good Samaritan as a human shield. Justice followed her, wrapping his gangly body around her and leaning against the back of her legs. Her dog didn't have any qualms about using her for protection, obviously.

"What's going on?" her rescuer asked, and the five people who'd been all too ready to shoot to kill exchanged looks.

"She's a cop, Wes," Rufus said, spitting on the ground next to him, although the tension in his hands had eased slightly. "Sent her dog after Bart for no reason."

Wes looked at Justice before returning his skeptical gaze to Rufus. "Bart was scared of that dog? He doesn't look too intimidating." As if in agreement, Justice thumped his tail against Kit's legs and ducked his head with a low whine.

"I wasn't scared," Bart protested.

"Shut it, Bart," Rufus snapped, although he was starting to look a little sheepish, and the barrel of his shotgun drooped a little toward the ground.

Wes looked at Bart. "Why'd you run if you weren't scared?"

"Well, I…uh…" He shot a frantic glance toward Rufus, as if asking for help, but the older man didn't offer any. "Dunno."

"Was it to lead her back here, where you knew there'd be people and guns?"

"Uh…" Bart just stared at Wes dumbly.

"What's the word for that? An ambush?" He made a *tsk* sound. "Intentionally ambushing a police officer and her dog? Luring her here just to shoot her? That's not protecting your property. That's premeditated murder."

His gun drooping at his side, Bart looked both bewildered and completely panicked. With an audible sigh, Rufus pointed his shotgun at the ground. The rest of the gun holders followed his lead and lowered their weapons. "Damn it, Bart. You're the dumbest of Chessie's kids, and that's saying something."

Relief started filtering through Kit, but she still kept her gun in her hand. "Tell you what," she said carefully, not wanting to ramp up the mountain people's tension again. "You let me and my dog walk out of here, and I won't pursue any charges. We'll call it what it is…a misunderstanding."

She stiffened her legs, which had gone soft with relief when the weapons had pointed toward the ground. She was so close to getting out of this situation. Now was not the time to collapse on the snowy ground, as much as her wavering limbs wanted to. "I saw some blood in the snow and thought someone was hurt, but it was just a rabbit. No one's injured, and we are all going to go our separate ways in peace."

Her nerdy Bigfoot gave her a quick look, arching one eyebrow in a way that showed he knew exactly what had been about to happen and what she was now trying to do. "Well, that sounds like a good solution. That's your truck on my road?"

She nodded, watching him but keeping the other five in her peripheral vision. Her fingers itched with the need to draw her weapon, but she knew that would just cause the tension to escalate again. Even with her newly arrived ally, it'd only take a second for one of the jumpy, suspicious mountain folk to raise their shotgun and blow off someone's head. No one was safe, not yet.

"Were you coming to see me?"

"You're the fire lookout?" she asked.

"Yes."

"Then yes."

He smiled at her, and she tried to return it, but her lips were numb from residual adrenaline. "I'll see you at the tower, then. I'm just going to talk to Rufus first."

"You'll be okay?" she asked quietly. He didn't seem to be worried, but she hated to leave the guy who'd just saved her life alone with that trigger-happy bunch.

He looked pleased. "Yes. I'll be fine."

When she didn't see any hesitation or concern on his part, she dipped her chin and started toward the trees. As she left, she kept her head turned and her gaze on the people watching her go, wanting to get out of the clearing before the backwoods five changed their minds. Her sweating fingers felt clammy inside her gloves as she tightened her fist around Justice's lead. She wanted to run, but she kept her steps even and at a careful walk. The dog kept close to her side, his tail tucked and his head low, still reading her fear. Her attention stayed focused on the group in the clearing, and she tried to hide the relief that flooded her as she reached the tree line.

Once there were several trees between Kit and the shotguns, she sucked in a rough breath and started to jog, following their previous tracks. Her bearded ally's voice filtered in after her.

"You can't go pointing shotguns at people willy-nilly, Rufus…"

His words quickly faded as she and Justice moved farther from the clearing. Justice soon perked up and took the lead, happy as could be with their second run. Kit carefully kept them in the tracks they'd made as they'd chased Bart, figuring that was the safest way to avoid getting caught in any of his traps. Ignoring the way her legs wanted to fold underneath her, Kit pushed herself faster, not slowing until they reached the truck.

Once she and Justice were both safely in the locked cab, she allowed herself to press her forehead against the steering wheel and take a deep breath. When it came out sounding more like a sob than an exhale, she squeezed her eyes shut and tried to steady her breathing. It didn't work. Her body shook as the scene in the clearing replayed itself in her mind. In her eight years of policing, she'd never been so close to death. The worst part of it had been that, except for Justice, she'd been completely alone. Even when things had been at their worst in her previous job, the other officers would've been there to back her up in a crisis. Here in Monroe, it felt as though she was on her own, and that was almost scarier than having shotguns aimed at her.

She wasn't sure how long she'd sat there before a wet tongue licked her cheek, jolting her out of her terrifying thoughts. Turning her head, she looked at Justice and caught another slobbery dog kiss across her nose. With a shaky laugh, she hugged her dog, burying her face into his silky shoulder.

He didn't give her long to wallow before he tried to

climb onto her lap, his huge feet pressing painfully into her thigh.

"Oof, Justice," she grunted with another watery laugh as she pushed him back to his own seat. "You're too heavy to be a lapdog."

Unoffended, he leaned over to give her face one last lick before giving himself a full-body shake. Following his example, Kit gave herself a mental one. She might not have a team watching her back, but she was still a cop, and she had a job to do. Having a breakdown was a waste of time. There was a witness waiting to talk to her.

Straightening in her seat, she shifted the truck into Drive and made her way up the mountain.

CHAPTER 8

KIT'S HANDS WERE STILL SHAKING A FEW MINUTES LATER AS she bumped over a rough stretch and the lookout tower came into view. It was actually quite pretty, with its stone base and windowed top with an observation deck circling the south side. The tower looked strangely out of place, like a lighthouse had been plucked from some ocean shore and deposited in the middle of the mountains. A small cabin sat next to it, making the tower look even taller in comparison.

As she pulled up next to the tower, Kit looked around the clearing. Despite the isolation, it was a beautiful spot that would've felt peaceful if she hadn't just been terrorized. She would've loved to see the area in the summer, with blooming wildflowers and all kinds of animals roaming around.

Getting out of the truck, she walked toward the heavy door set in the base of the tower. She stayed alert, still twitchy from her encounter with the armed mountain folk. The thick wall of trees surrounding the site should have seemed serene, but they held an air of menace. The silence was heavy—too heavy. By the time she reached the door, she was full-on jumpy, although she refused to turn back.

Instead, she knocked firmly on the thick door and

waited, doubting that the lookout had made it back before her. Only two seconds went by, however, before there was a soft *beep*, and the door swung in.

"Are you *kidding* me?" she muttered, peering into the dark entry. It didn't look like anyone was there, except for a pair of snow-covered boots that sat on the mat to the right of the door. She grimaced. Her nerves were already shot to hell, and the spooky, self-opening door wasn't helping. As bright as it was outside, with the sun reflecting off the snow, the thick stone walls blocked the light inside the tower, leaving it murky and dim. Chiding herself for acting like a nervous Nellie, she stepped into the tower.

Just after she cleared the entrance, the door closed behind her with a firm click. That sound, as soft as it was, made her jump.

"It's just an automatic door, dummy," she said quietly under her breath as she stood still, allowing her eyes to become accustomed to the dimness. Motion-sensing light fixtures had flickered to life as she'd entered, so it wasn't as dark as it had first appeared. Thanks to the eerie, self-opening door, she'd expected the interior of the tower to be creepy and strewn with cobwebs, but it was actually clean and even rather charming, with the curved stone wall and a spiral staircase in the center.

Cautiously, she started up the stairs, gripping the railing. Her footsteps sounded too loud on the metal, but she reminded herself that she wasn't trying to sneak up on the fire lookout. He was simply a complainant who'd first noticed the fire, so she was going to do a standard witness interview—the same type of thing she'd done hundreds, if not thousands, of times. Her frightening encounter, as well as the strangeness of her surroundings—not just the tower, but the whole isolated, bombed-out, deserted town—was making her twitchy, seeing danger where none existed.

Just as she talked herself into relaxing, a clicking sound made her freeze, her gaze locked on the top of the stairs. She waited as the sound got louder, a regular *tap-tap-tap* that made her tense up and reach toward her gun, although it wasn't enough yet to make her actually draw her weapon. There was a whir, and a small metal face—set in a robot-looking thing the size of a cat— peered over the top step at her. The single "eye" looked like a camera lens, and Kit raised an eyebrow at it. It was almost cute in a strange kind of way.

"I'm Kit Jernigan with the Monroe Police Department," she said to the metal cat creature, assuming that the fire-spotter was using it as a sort of mobile peephole to see who'd arrived at his door.

The mini-robot raised a...leg? arm? to give her a wave, and Kit had to smile. It was hard to stay on guard when a one-eyed pet/appliance hybrid was waving at her, especially when she already knew that its owner was an endearing dork who'd just saved her life. Spinning around, the fake cat clicked away from the top of the stairs, and Kit continued to climb. Although she was more relaxed than she had been before, it was still an odd situation. She wasn't sure what she would find in the lookout room, and she'd had enough unpleasant surprises for the day.

As she reached the top, she took in the circular room, half of which was wall-to-wall windows. There was a couch and several tables, one covered in a topographic map while the other two looked more like workstations, with a professional-looking camera and laptops and tools and bits and pieces that—now that she'd seen the metal cat thing—could only be robot guts. A woodstove sat in the middle of the space, and a compact kitchen was tucked against the wall on the opposite side of the windows. A partially open door appeared to lead to a bathroom.

Her mountain-man ally, now in BDUs and a long-sleeved T-shirt, stood in front of an open laptop, his gaze fixed on her.

"Hello." He gave her a tentative smile. "You made it back to your truck okay, then?"

"Yes. Thank you for your help." The words seemed so inadequate when he'd basically saved her life. She wasn't accustomed to being the one saved. With her job, she normally did the saving.

"You're welcome." He moved closer to her, stopping just a few feet away and leaning a shoulder against one of the vertical support beams. The way he crossed his arms made all the truly impressive muscles in his shoulders stand out, and she had to make a conscious effort to pull her attention back to what he was saying. "Sorry that happened to you. Most of my neighbors aren't very welcoming, especially to government employees."

The drastic understatement made her sputter out a laugh. "Yeah, I gathered that. Is this a common thing, then?" Her mind worked as she tallied up the pros and cons of making a report on the incident. It was one thing to threaten a cop who was chasing after them, but another if they were threatening people on a regular basis.

"No. Pretty much everyone leaves them alone. You startled them when you chased Bart, and then they felt trapped when they found out you were a cop. Despite what he said, I think he was scared when he ran from you." He watched her, as if knowing she needed a moment to process, before asking, "Are you going to report what happened?"

"No." Now that she and Justice were safe and unharmed, it was easier to see the advantages to not reporting Rufus and his family. "If they're not a threat to themselves or others, then the only thing I'd accomplish by reporting them is make an enemy…well, five enemies. Besides, I promised I wouldn't report them if they didn't shoot me."

He looked pleased by this. Both of them went quiet, and the moment started to stretch into awkwardness. He opened his mouth as if he was about to say something, but closed it before any words came out. She racked her brain for something to say to break the uncomfortable silence, but her mind was a blank.

"So…I assume you don't need more help backing any trailers," he finally said.

She laughed, charmed by his awkwardness. It seemed such a perfect match to her own. Her muscles had been tight since she'd spotted the blood in the snow, but now she felt them slowly release. "No."

"Did you need a different kind of help, then?" His shy smile was so adorably crooked that she couldn't help but grin back, more of her tension slipping away. "I also have some general knowledge of computers."

She realized that he was waiting for her to explain why she was in his tower, and here she was, just staring at him like he'd smacked her over the head. Shaking off her distraction, she focused on what she was there to do. "What's your name?"

"Wes. Wesley March."

Wesley March. The name burned itself into Kit's brain, but she tried to ignore the giddy, swooping thing her stomach was doing. "Do you go by Wes or Wesley?"

He stared at her for another long moment—so long that she ran her question back through her head, trying to figure out if it could've somehow offended him. It seemed innocuous enough to her.

"Is something wrong?" she finally asked when she couldn't take the silence any longer.

"No," he said slowly. "It's just that no one's ever asked me which one I preferred."

"So..." It was her turn to study him curiously. She didn't know what to make of him. "Should I call you Wes or Wesley? Or Mr. March?"

After another pause, he blew out an audible breath. "Not Mr. March. I like how the other two sound when you say them, though. Could I have some time to think about this and get back to you?"

She laughed, a delighted huff that she couldn't hold back. He was different, yes, but in a surprisingly lovely way, and talking with him was just what she needed after her terrifying experience. "Of course you can. Just let me know when you decide."

His smile stretched wider, showing off that slight overlap of one tooth. "Thank you. For as pretty as you are, I didn't expect you to be so nice."

Kit rarely became flustered, but the unexpected, sideways compliment made her face warm. "Thank you. I actually thought the same thing when we met...well, pretty much the same thing."

"You did?" His smile widened. "Why?"

Although she knew she should've just ended the conversation there and moved on to a more professional topic, her mouth ran ahead of her brain. "Well, look at you."

Glancing down, he studied his front for a moment before he gave Kit a puzzled look.

"You're...attractive." She almost snorted at the understatement. "And you seem very nice."

"Attractive?" His tone was doubtful as he looked down his front again. "I always thought I was just large and rather hairy."

Despite her still-warm cheeks, the exchange was making her stomach buzz with excited interest, a feeling she hadn't experienced for years. "Being large and hairy doesn't mean you can't also be handsome. And I think you're—" *What are you doing?* Desperate to change topics, she blurted out, "Um, I like your robot."

He smiled at her again, an ear-to-ear grin, and Kit found herself grinning back. Wes-slash-Wesley March's smile, it seemed, was dangerously infectious.

Desperate to distract herself, she glanced around the room again, this time noticing more of the gadgets and equipment. That reminded her of the self-opening door that had spooked her when she'd first arrived. "Do you have a camera at the door? Is that how you see who's there so you can open it remotely?"

"Yes, but after the first visit, I don't have to open the door. Once I approve you in the system," Wes explained, "the camera recognizes your facial features and automatically opens the door for you."

"Huh." Kit studied Wes, fascinated. "Did you design that?"

"Yes."

"That's impressive."

He gave her his wide, happy smile, and the buzzing in her belly started up again. "The robo-cat, too?"

His eyebrows drew together in confusion. "What?" When she gestured at the little metal creature, his forehead smoothed. "Oh, it's not a cat... At least, it wasn't supposed to be. If anything, I was thinking more along the lines of a dog."

"A dog?" Kit repeated, studying the mini-robot. "It's awfully small, but then I'm used to bigger dogs. My K9 partner is a hundred pounds."

Wes's face lit up. "You're in the K9 unit? What's your dog's specialty?"

"Tracking." Kit beamed back. He'd hit on the one topic of conversation she could gush about all day. "Justice is a bloodhound, so he's made for that."

"It's so fascinating how acute a dog's sense of smell is," Wes said, taking a step closer to her in his excitement. "Humans use sight almost to the detriment of our other senses. Dogs rely on scent over sight, which seems much more efficient. I can't imagine that smell lies very often—not nearly as much as we're fooled by what we think we see."

"Exactly." Kit shifted closer, nearly giddy to hear someone else—a very pretty someone else, too—bring up her pet topic. So often, people doubted Justice's reliability because they couldn't conceive of how an animal could detect something that they couldn't. "Scent doesn't lie. Even if someone figured out how to turn invisible, a dog would still know that they were there. We rely so much on our eyes that we miss seeing things that are right in front of us."

Kit's radio came to life as a sheriff's deputy let the dispatcher know he was on duty, bringing Kit back to reality. Here with Wes in his tower, it was easy to forget about the outside world.

Pulling out her phone, she tapped the screen, starting an audio recording before pulling up a blank page on her note-taking app. Turning back toward Wes, she said, "I'm actually here to ask you a few questions about the fire you spotted this morning." When he nodded, she started getting his personal information. "What's your middle name?"

"Alden."

"That's unusual." She typed out his full name.

"It used to be, but it's actually gaining popularity, especially in Hawaii."

"Really?" she asked, looking up from her phone. "That's interesting. I wonder if that has anything to do with—"

The dispatcher responded to the deputy on the radio. The interruption reminded her that she needed to finish the interview and get back to canvassing the empty neighborhood, no matter how fascinating Wes was. Clearing her throat, she started again. "Sorry. You're really easy to talk to." When he gave her that ridiculously endearing smile of his, she forced herself to focus on taking notes so she wouldn't be distracted.

"What'd you see this morning?"

"Smoke."

"Before that, were you watching the area?" When he shook his head, she glanced out the bank of windows, noticing how tiny Monroe was from their vantage point. "Were you using binoculars?"

"A telephoto lens on the camera, at first," he said. "After I saw the smoke, I switched to those." He pointed at a pair of binoculars on one of the rolling carts scattered around the space.

"After you started watching the smoke, did you see anyone around the house?"

"The angle's wrong." Picking up the binoculars, he offered them to Kit. She lifted them to her eyes and scanned the town. "It's the house on the far southwest corner of Monroe." She scanned over the snowy streets and buildings until she spotted the blackened shell of a house. "See how it's set back against the trees and the house to the north blocks the view of the yard?"

Although the lack of information was disappointing, she'd known interviewing Wes was a long shot. Still, it was good that she'd done this. If she hadn't talked to him, she would've felt like she'd skipped an important step in the investigation. She turned her head, still looking through the binoculars, and spotted a house surrounded by trees a mile or two east of the burned house. "Is that Jules's house?" She held the binoculars still so Wes could look through them.

"I'm not sure. Who is Jules?"

"One of the diner waitresses. She's dating Theo, another cop." She eyed Wes hopefully, but he looked blank.

"Sorry," he said, stepping back. "I don't know many people. If you want to take a picture and ask someone else about it, just push that button on the side. I'll send the photos to you."

She eagerly found the house she was pretty sure was Jules's again and pressed the button. It clicked, and she took a few more of the burned house and the surrounding area. "That's pretty awesome," she said, handing the binoculars back to Wes. "Did you make those?"

He gave a bashful half shrug as he turned the binoculars over in his hands. "Not really. I modified them a little, but that's it." She had a feeling his "modified a little" still meant some fairly impressive changes, but she didn't push it.

"Do you have pictures of the smoke from when you spotted it?" she asked. Although her instincts told her that Wes wasn't responsible for either the dead body or the fire, she needed to be sure. Facts trumped gut feeling, after all.

"Yes." He shifted to one of the monitors and brought a photo up on the screen. "Here." She moved next to him, once again noticing how good he smelled in a woodsy, clean sort of way. Shaking off the distraction of having him so close, she focused on the photo. The smoke was obvious, but the house looked intact, and she couldn't see any flames. She glanced at the time stamp, which was right before dispatch had sent them the fire call. She wasn't surprised at the proof that Wes couldn't have started the fire. He had such an honest and straightforward manner that it was hard to imagine him being capable of doing anything even slightly shady, much less arson and murder.

"Can you send me a copy of this, too?"

He nodded.

Reluctantly, Kit headed for the stairs. "Let me know if you think of anything else." Automatically, she reached in her pocket where she usually kept business cards and then remembered that they hadn't even been ordered yet, much less printed. "I can give you my cell number."

He waved toward the window at the mountain peaks

surrounding them. "No reception here, but I can email these pictures to you if you give me your address."

Happy that he'd have at least one way to contact her, she rattled the address off as he entered it on one of his laptops. "Thank you again for your help today." During the interview, she'd almost forgotten about her close call, but now fatigue was dragging at her muscles, reminding her how much adrenaline had been rushing through her body earlier. "I probably wouldn't be here if you hadn't intervened."

"I'm glad you're not dead," he said, making her snort.

"Yeah, me too." With a final wave, she headed down the stairs.

As the tower door swung shut behind her, she couldn't resist looking up at the observation deck, but the sun reflecting off the glass kept her from getting a final glimpse of Wes. She felt let down despite herself. Maybe it wasn't a good idea, but the excited flutter in her belly wasn't listening to reason. Wes was just so wonderfully interesting.

She was already thinking of an excuse for returning to the lookout tower sometime soon. It seemed that Wesley Alden March was addictive, and she couldn't wait for their next encounter.

═══════════════

After checking to see if anyone was watching, Alex quickly picked the lock on the back door to the garage. It was old and so simple that a five-year-old could've broken in, and it only took her a few seconds before the knob turned in her hand and the door swung open.

Picking up the gas can next to her, she slipped inside, carefully and silently closing the door behind her.

The Lincoln sedan was old but in beautiful shape, and Alex would have bet a good amount of money that Mrs. Jones only used it to drive to the grocery store and back once a week. Now that Alex had her keys, the poor old lady wouldn't be driving anywhere. As soon as she'd seen the car through the garage window early that morning, the keys dangling so temptingly on a hook by the door, she'd known it'd be the perfect getaway car. Alex sent a silent thanks to Mrs. Jones for unknowingly providing it.

She topped off the tank and retightened the gas cap. It had already been mostly full, but Alex knew better than to rely on chance. An empty tank, an unnoticed witness, an undeleted text message—those were the tiny details that could ruin a plan. Everything needed to be double- and triple-checked, because nothing was going to derail her plan. Not now. Not when she was so close.

The door to the house opened, and Alex whirled around, still holding the gas can, to see Mrs. Jones staring at her, her mouth open slightly in shock.

"Hello." Alex smiled her sunniest smile as her brain worked frantically. "I'm Susan. I work for your son? He sent me over to make sure you had enough gas in your car."

Mrs. Jones's mouth closed, but her eyes widened in obvious fear as she took a step back. "I don't have a son," she said, her voice high and shaky.

Well, shoot. Dropping the gas can, Alex rushed to grab the door before Mrs. Jones could close it. *Now I'm going to have to kill an old lady.*

With a choked cry, Mrs. Jones lurched back, tripping over a braided rag rug and falling to the floor. Alex grabbed a wooden nativity stable from the display on a table and brought it down hard on the woman's head. Mrs. Jones's skull bounced off the hardwood floor, blood spattering across the pristine floor, and she went still.

There. That had been simple enough.

Piece by piece, Alex carefully replaced all the nativity figures to their appropriate spots in and around the stable before grabbing Mrs. Jones's limp arms and dragging her down the hall.

"How unfortunate," she said conversationally. "This moves my timetable up. I'd better get the wheels in motion before anyone notices you're not answering your phone." Letting go of Mrs. Jones's wrists, she started opening the doors lining the hall. "Bathroom, closet... Oh, here we go—basement."

Bending to grab hold of Mrs. Jones's arms again, Alex felt a slight, almost clinical sadness at what she'd been forced to do, but she pushed it away. There was no time to dwell on things. She had a mess to clean up.

"I hope you have a nice, big chest freezer down here."

CHAPTER 9

KIT WOKE THE NEXT MORNING WITH RENEWED ENTHUSIASM, determined to win over her new partners and learn the ins and outs of her new town. Her optimism took a hit as she looked around the women's locker room at the temporary police station. It was basically a bathroom with a small bank of lockers—all of them empty—added as an afterthought. The place was echoing and abandoned, confirming her suspicion that any female officers had headed for warmer places to spend the winter.

"This is creepy," she muttered, and Justice, who was touring the perimeter of the room, sniffing along the tile baseboard, gave an absent wave of his tail at the sound of her voice. "How many horror movies have empty women's locker rooms in them? Answer: A lot. How many good, nonviolent things happen in these vacant locker rooms? Not many."

Her cell phone buzzed in her pocket, making her flinch in surprise. She laughed at her jumpiness. It was an old, empty bathroom. There wasn't anything to get spooked at. Reaching in her pocket, she pulled out her phone, not at all surprised to see Hugh's name on the screen. After one day working with him, she'd found that he called and texted a lot.

"Jernigan, where are you?"

Kit took advantage of her solitude to roll her eyes. It wasn't like she was running late. In fact, there was almost an hour before her shift started, but she'd wanted to get a draft of her report on the body found in the burned house done before roll call. She tried to keep the sarcasm out of her tone as she answered. "At the station."

"Cross the street. We're having roll call."

"Roll call? At the VFW?" She was confused.

"Breakfast, roll call, whatever. Get over here." He ended the call.

She studied her phone for a few moments, trying to decide whether to go. Part of her felt a warm glow that she was invited to their pre-shift ritual, but the other part balked at his bossiness, especially after he'd so obviously kept her out of the loop on the case the day before.

"He's your PTO," she reminded herself, pulling on her coat. "It's his job to boss you around for a few months. It won't be long before you're on your own, though."

Grabbing Justice's leash, she headed for the door. After making a detour to the animal control truck to put Justice inside, she crossed the road toward the VFW. As she looked around at the silent, snowy town, she wondered if she'd ever get used to the emptiness. The squeak of snow beneath her boots was too loud, the only sound in an otherwise quiet world. Kit had the same feeling she'd had the day before, like she was the only person left in the universe. A shiver ran through her at the thought.

It was a relief to push through the VFW door and hear the conversations and normal sounds of people breakfasting. She found Theo, Otto, and Hugh at their usual table, and Jules hurrying from one customer to the next, bearing coffee carafes and plates of steaming food.

Kit's stomach rumbled, reminding her that she'd been too tense to eat earlier that morning.

"'Morning,'" she said, taking the place across from Hugh, the same seat she'd sat in the previous morning. She had to smile. It was only her second day, and she already had a spot at their table. The men greeted her in unsurprising ways: Hugh with enthusiasm, Theo with a grunt, and Otto with a stoic nod.

"Decided to come back for another day?" Hugh asked, smirking a little behind his coffee mug.

"Sure." She made eye contact with Jules, who gave her a *be right there* wave. "Yesterday was so peaceful and relaxing, how could I stay away?"

Theo coughed, and Kit was pretty sure there was some amusement in the sound. "It used to be peaceful around here, especially in the winter. Not so much anymore."

"Yeah, ever since Jules and the kids arrived—" Hugh started, but Theo cut him off.

"The bombs didn't start going off until Grace arrived."

"The diner," Otto said quietly, gesturing with his mug as if to indicate that they weren't inside the now-exploded diner.

Theo frowned. "That was on us, though, not Jules."

Kit looked from one man to the other, listening intently. She'd pieced together some of the story, but there were still gaping holes in her knowledge about what had happened to her new town over the past few months.

"The explosions were fairly limited until Sarah arrived," Hugh said, giving Otto a look that Kit would've considered teasing if they hadn't been talking about the town getting bombed.

"Not her fault," Otto said calmly, not taking the bait.

"Never is," Hugh said, glancing around the dining area. "And now there's a new one. Wonder who'll come gunning for her." He grunted and glared at Theo. "Did you just kick me? What was that for?"

Theo just gave him a look, and Hugh sat back in his chair. By the way they were avoiding glancing in her direction, Kit was pretty sure they were silently arguing about her. She was starting to get a little aggravated by the secrets they were keeping for the women who lived—or used to live—in Jules's house.

The silence hung on until it felt too heavy, and Kit cleared her throat. Now that she knew she wasn't getting any more information by making herself semi-invisible, there was no reason to stay silent. "Did you find any new information about the fire yesterday? My canvass was a bust. Most of the neighboring houses were empty, and the three people who actually still live in town didn't see anything related to the incident."

"Any of those three greet you at the door with a shotgun?" Hugh asked.

She started and tried to hide the involuntary motion by reaching to flip her coffee mug right side up. "Nope. Guess I got lucky." Although she tried to keep her voice light, Hugh studied her with enough interest that she wondered if her nerves were showing. She looked back with as blankly curious an expression as she could manage, and he turned his gaze away. "So...anything on your end?" She suspected they'd purposefully not answered the first time she'd asked.

"Nothing too useful," Hugh said, turning slightly in his chair so he could stretch out his legs without bumping into Kit.

Silence fell over their table, and Kit wished that they'd forget she was there and start talking again. She tried to think of an innocuous conversation starter, but every question she wanted to ask was apparently a hot-button topic. She'd always been horrible at small talk. "So what's good to eat here?"

Again, Hugh was the one who answered. "Pretty much everything. For a psycho, Vicki's an excellent cook."

"Except for the oatmeal," Otto added.

"Right." Hugh gave him an approving nod. "Forgot about that. Definitely avoid the oatmeal."

Absently, she made a mental note to do just that, but most of her attention was back on Hugh's first comment. "What do you mean by psycho?"

"She's a practical joker," Theo said with restrained anger, his gaze locked on the kitchen door. His tense tone meant there was a story there—yet another incident that Kit didn't know about. The lack of knowledge was making her feel overwhelmed and antsy. She needed to learn quickly, or she was going to get herself into situations like the one yesterday, when she'd had five shotguns pointed at her. Her stomach twisted with remembered fear as for one brief moment she was back in that clearing, but she quickly shoved the memory away.

Digging her fingers into her thighs under the table, Kit forced her expression to smooth. Having mental freak-outs wasn't going to get her anywhere. She just needed to be smart and learn as much as she could—starting, apparently, with the diner staff. "Did Vicki prank Jules?"

Theo's attention turned toward Kit. "How did you guess?"

"You're too angry for her to have played the joke

on you, so Jules is the logical victim." Although Kit had only seen Theo and Jules together a few times, she could already tell that he was incredibly protective of his girlfriend.

He studied her for a few moments. "Yeah, Vicki locked Jules in the walk-in cooler."

"Whaaat?" Kit drew out the word in disbelief. "That's not a practical joke. That's dangerous and terrifying and just wrong. Poor Jules. How long was she stuck in there?"

"Just a few minutes." Theo gave her a slight nod, as if he approved of her horrified response. "Jules is claustrophobic, so she started screaming. I was at the diner—the original diner, not here—heard her, and let her out."

"No wonder you call Vicki a psychopath." Kit made a mental note to never, ever be alone in the kitchen with the cook. Although she could take care of herself, she didn't want to have to bring the woman down for some crazy stunt. Quiet settled over them again, but Kit refused to lose the momentum of their previous conversation and allow them to settle into awkwardness again. "Is that how you met Jules?"

"No." Jules was the one who answered as she poured Kit a cup of coffee. Kit hid her surprise. She'd been trying so hard to keep the other three talking that she'd missed Jules's arrival. "I met him a little before that, but I thought he was kind of rude." Kit turned her amused snort in a cough. Theo definitely wasn't the friendliest sort. Hugh didn't even try to hide his booming laugh, but Jules ignored it and continued. "When he swooped in to rescue me, I started to see him in a whole new light." She lightly bumped him with her hip, and he snaked an arm around her, giving her an adoring look that seemed so out of place on his harsh features.

"How long have you two been dating?" Kit asked, honestly curious now instead of just tossing out conversational topics randomly to see if one would stick.

Jules tilted her head, as if thinking, just as Theo said, "Three months next week."

"Really?" Jules asked. "It's been that long?"

Before Theo could answer, a new voice—a voice that was gruff and deep and put Kit's belly butterflies on high alert—spoke. "Excuse me."

Everyone at the table twisted around to stare at Wes. In fact, Kit realized, the entire diner had silenced, and all eyes were staring at their table... No, they were staring at *Wes*. It bothered her that everyone in town treated him like he was some wild, dangerous creature. It wasn't like the rest of the area residents—with their shotguns and paranoia and bombed-out buildings—were the picture of normalcy. Indignation on his behalf bubbled up inside her, and she smiled at him more fiercely because of it.

He was even bigger than she remembered—bigger and hairier. In his tower, he fit into his surroundings, among the rocks and trees and solitary cliffs. Here at the VFW, he seemed out of place, too wild and rugged for the cozy dining room.

"Hey there, March." Hugh greeted him calmly enough, although his eyebrows flew up high on his forehead. "What can we help you with?"

"Nothing."

Jules's amused and baffled gaze met Kit's, and Kit couldn't help but grin back. With all the effervescent bubbles rising in her chest, she felt like she was about to float off her chair with excitement. *Stop being silly*, she ordered herself. *You've only met the guy twice, both for very short periods of time. You need to calm down.*

"If we can't help you with anything, why are you here?" Theo asked.

"I'd like to talk to Officer Jernigan."

Kit pushed back her chair and stood up. "Of course. What did you need to talk to me about?"

He didn't answer. Kit took that to be him indicating that he didn't want to talk about whatever it was in front of an audience, which piqued her interest. What information could he have that he didn't want to share with anyone but her?

"How'd you two meet?" Hugh asked, looking back and forth between them.

Kit inwardly winced, resigned to admitting that she'd made a trip to the tower yesterday, but Wes spoke before she could.

"I helped her back up her trailer."

The guys exchanged looks.

"Is that a euphemism?" Hugh asked, and Kit hurried to round the table and usher Wes away.

"Should we head to the entry?" she suggested. "That's probably the closest private spot, unless we use one of the interview rooms at the station."

"The entry is acceptable."

Kit struggled to hide her smile. There was no reason why she should like the way he talked so much, but she really did. "The entry it is. After you." She waved him ahead of her.

The stares and whispers grew worse as they made their way through the diner, and Kit felt her irritation grow at how they were treating one of their own. It also made her wonder if she'd ever fit into this insular town. After all, Wes had been living here for years, and everyone was still treating him like a suspicious stranger. Glancing back at the silent table, she saw that even Jules and the other three cops were watching curiously.

What's that about? Hugh mouthed, and Kit responded with a shrug. She wasn't sure why Wes wanted to talk to her alone. Hugh's curiosity would just have to wait.

She followed Wes through the doorway and into the entry. He turned to face her but didn't say anything, his gaze fixed on her.

"Did you remember something about the fire?" she prompted after the silence stretched uncomfortably.

"No. Nothing that would assist in your investigation."

She smiled. A good part of his charm was that the way he looked didn't match the way he sometimes talked. His rugged lumberjack appearance made her expect him to communicate in grunts and short phrases, in a backwoods Tarzan sort of way, but there were times when his vocabulary rivaled hers when she got flustered. She liked that they shared that trait. Even though they'd just met, she felt a connection with him, a sort of awkward-nerd bond. Shaking off the wayward thought, she asked, "What did you need to talk to me about, then?"

"I've made a decision."

"About?" she prompted.

"What we discussed yesterday."

Confused, she mentally ran through the topics they'd covered during the short, strange interview the day before. "To which discussion are you referring?"

Inwardly, she rolled her eyes at herself for how quickly she'd fallen into his nervous speech patterns.

"The one where we talked about which name I prefer: Wes or Wesley."

"Oh." That was not what she'd expected. "Okay. Which would you prefer?"

"Wes."

"Wes."

He smiled slightly. "Yes. It sounds right coming from you. Wes sounds more…intimate." The skin right above his beard reddened. "I mean, Wes sounds more casual, not as formal."

The hint of panic in his voice made her want to smile. If he knew how increasingly interested she was in becoming more intimate, his face would probably catch fire from the heat of his blush. "I like it. So…Wes."

"Yes?" He tipped his upper body just slightly closer to hers, and she smelled his wonderful pine and woodsmoke scent. With him this close, he seemed even broader and stronger, and the butterflies swirled in her stomach. She took a step forward, drawn to his heat and marvelous weirdness.

"I—"

"Everything okay out here?" Hugh interrupted as he stepped into the entry. Kit took a quick step back, not wanting her PTO to see the way she was drawn to a witness on only the second day of her new job. Not only that, but the teasing would be unbearable. She spotted Otto and Theo hovering behind Hugh, a whole nosy army.

"Yes," she said. "Everything's fine." From Hugh's posture, she could tell he wasn't going to be leaving her and Wes alone again until his curiosity was satisfied, so she turned to Wes. "Thank you for letting me know."

"You're welcome." With a small lift of his chin at the men, which Kit took as a group goodbye, he left the VFW.

"What did he want?" Theo asked quietly a few seconds after the door shut behind Wes.

Kit wasn't sure how to answer, so she hedged. "He didn't see anything else related to the fire."

"What did he say?" Hugh asked, apparently not put off course so easily.

"Nothing, really." Lifting her hands palms up in a gesture of confusion, she shrugged. "He just said he hadn't remembered anything else about the fire."

All three men frowned at her. "Wesley March, the guy who leaves his tower less often than Rapunzel, came to town, walked into the VFW—a place he's never entered before—and sought you out just to say...he had no new information?"

"He never leaves?" Kit asked, confused. "He was in town yesterday morning."

The men exchanged a look. "Two days in a row?" Hugh said slowly, his expression turning gleeful. "How long's he been living up there? Six years?"

"Seven," Otto said.

Hugh nodded. "Seven years, and he's never come to town two days in a row. Something's up with the hairy tower princess."

All three cops eyed her with growing interest, even Otto. *Time for damage control.* "He didn't come to town just to see me. I'm sure he had something else to do."

"Uh-huh," Hugh said, dark eyes gleaming.

She gave a huff. "Can we talk about something else?

Like that arson and possible homicide we're trying to solve?"

Theo's expression immediately sobered. "No 'possible' about it anymore."

Her eyes widened. "It's been confirmed? The victim was murdered?"

"County coroner said it looks that way, but the remains are going to be sent to the state lab, too," Otto said in his slow, careful way. "The state is sending a couple of arson investigators here, as well. With all the incidents of organized crime we've been involved in lately, there's concern that this might be related. We think—"

Theo subtly nudged Otto's elbow, and the guys exchanged one of those silent-message glances that drove Kit nuts. Before she could ask any questions, though, the outside door swung open, drawing her—and the men's—attention.

Elena slipped inside the entry. Her body seemed to curl in on itself when she spotted them, her gaze darting from one person to the next. "Hello," she said in a wispy voice, and Kit struggled to stomp out the suspicion that flared when she caught sight of the other woman. Judging from the way the men's expressions had softened, none of them felt the same wariness when it came to Elena.

"Are you looking for Jules?" Theo asked in what was, for him, a gentle tone.

"Yes." A tentative smile touched her full mouth but then immediately faded. "Sort of? I'm supposed to meet Megan? Jules thought she might be able to get me a job?"

The uncertain way Elena spoke—with her sentences curling up at the end, turning them into questions—grated on Kit. As soon as the thought hit, Kit tried to shove it away. What kind of monster was she to be so irritated by this innocuous, frightened woman?

As she studied Elena, she wondered if that was the problem. Thanks to years of working with children rescued from abusive homes, Kit knew the look of fear—true fear—and Elena didn't have that. It was almost as if Elena was purposefully trying to play off the guys' protective instincts...and she was succeeding. Cocking her head slightly, Kit studied the woman, trying to see past her surface doe-eyed helplessness to what was underneath.

"I'm glad you're here, Elena," Kit said. "I wanted to ask y—"

"They're both inside." Theo cut her off midquestion, waving toward the doorway, and Elena scurried through into the dining room, her gaze fixed firmly on her feet. Kit pushed back her frustration at Theo's interruption. It seemed that the guys were constantly protecting Elena from her, and it rankled. After all, she was their partner—only for just over a day, but still—and Elena was as much a stranger to them as Kit was. Taking a deep breath, she decided she needed to ask, even if it didn't get her anywhere.

Once Elena was out of sight, Kit said quietly, "Are we going to talk about the coincidence that Elena arrived on the same day the homicide was discovered?"

The guys exchanged another set of looks.

"We've considered that," Theo said carefully, and Kit felt a surge of relief that she wasn't the only one suspicious of Elena. "Grace and Jules are going to check with her, see if she needs our help."

That relief instantly wilted as Kit realized that the

guys didn't share her suspicion after all. Instead, they just thought Elena was a fleeing victim. She figured she could work with that; at least it was a start. "Shouldn't we talk to her, then, and get her story? If she knows who's after her, we can follow up on that."

The men shifted uncomfortably, exchanging glances.

"That hasn't worked so well in the past," Theo finally said in a stilted way. "We ended up intimidating the victims rather than encouraging them to trust us. We don't want to do the same thing with Elena when she could be in danger. It's better this way."

"I'm not intimidating." It was something that Kit often wished wasn't true. "I could talk to her."

She hadn't even finished before Hugh was shaking his head. "Jules and Grace will see if she needs our help. Otherwise, we'll leave her alone." He gave Kit a pointed look.

All three of the guys' faces were closed off, and Kit swallowed any further arguments. She wasn't going to change their minds. That didn't mean, however, that she couldn't do some investigating. After all, her partners didn't have any say in what she did on her own time.

The silence thickened until Kit waved in the direction of the dining room. "No sense in standing out here. Our food's probably ready."

Although they all made agreeable noises, it took a moment for them to move, since they were all waiting for the others to precede them. With a snort, Kit led the way into the dining room. *This is what happens when a bunch of cops are together*. She liked that they had similar habits, though. It reminded her of their commonalities and gave her hope that she'd fit in their team…someday.

They took their seats in stilted silence, but Kit didn't care about the awkwardness. Her mind was working. Whatever her new partners thought about her, she was first and foremost a cop—and an effective one. If they weren't going to share information about the case, or Elena, with her, then she was going to have to do her own investigating. Their distrust of her wasn't going to stop her from doing her job.

"Here you go," Jules said cheerily as she lowered a packed plate to the spot in front of Kit. "I didn't know what you like, so I had Vicki make you a sampler. There's a little bit of everything on there."

"Thank you," Kit said, staring at the mounds of food. It was enough to feed her for a week. "No oatmeal though. That's good."

Jules laughed as she slid plates in front of the other three. "I'd never do that to you."

It was Kit's turn to laugh. She liked Jules more every time they talked. If Theo's distrust didn't spoil it, she could see the two of them becoming friends.

"Did Elena find you?" Theo asked.

"Yes." Jules tipped her head toward the kitchen door. "Megan's giving her an interview right now. I hope it works out. Elena, bless her heart, could use a confidence boost."

At Jules's fond tone, Kit felt a flash of guilt. So far, she was the only one who wasn't sold on Elena. If no one else—including some street-wise fellow cops— found anything suspicious about the new arrival, then the problem was probably Kit's. She resolved to try to be as fair and open-minded as possible when she talked with Elena.

She pictured Elena's wide, dark eyes and heard her wispy voice, and her gut tightened in warning. Despite everyone else's reaction to Elena, Kit's instincts were loud and clear: Elena was not to be trusted.

Don't worry, she told the part of her that was yelling at her to be wary. *I'll do my best to be fair, but that doesn't mean I'm going to be stupid about it.*

Everyone's food disappeared quickly. Kit managed to make a sizable dent in the mountain on her plate before passing the leftovers to Otto, who said that he'd take it home to feed to his chickens.

Just then, Elena slipped through the kitchen door, and Kit knew it was her cue to set her new plan into motion. "Excuse me for a minute," she said, pushing back her chair. She could feel their suspicious gazes following her as she headed for the entry, but she reminded herself that she could talk to whomever she wanted. Elena was moving fast, and Kit had to almost run to catch up.

"Elena," Kit called as she stepped into the entry, just as Elena was pushing open the door. Elena stopped in surprise, taking a step back so that the door swung closed again. Her tentative smile came a second too late, jarring Kit and making her stop abruptly. She tried to hide her discomfort. There was something a little off about Elena, and it wasn't a good oddness, like Wes's was. Kit pushed away the thought, reminding herself to wait until she had the facts to make any judgments about the woman.

"Kit, right? Did you have more questions for me?"

"No. Well, not official questions." She put on her best friendly smile and hoped it didn't make her look clownlike. Too many of her social graces had been warped by her years as a cop. In Wisconsin, all her friends—both male and female—had been coworkers, which was one of the reasons it had hit her so hard when most of them had turned their backs on her. "I was just thinking that, since we're both brand new in town, we should hang out." When Elena just blinked her huge eyes rapidly, Kit pressed on. "Would you be interested in getting coffee sometime? I don't know about you, but I'm getting the feeling that it's going to be a while before this small town accepts me."

The silence stretched until it was uncomfortable, but Kit wasn't about to give Elena an easy way out of the offer. Her patience paid off when Elena's smile returned, brighter this time.

"Uh…sure!" Again, Elena's enthusiasm came just a hair too late to seem sincere. "Jules and Grace have been very sweet, but it would be nice to have a friend outside the house."

"Someone to listen when you need to complain about the roommates?" Kit asked, not having to fake her smile that time. She was one step closer to finding out why this woman was in her new town.

Elena laughed a little. "Exactly. I'm supposed to start working tomorrow, since Megan—the owner—said that their dishwasher suddenly quit to go work at a ski resort. Want to get together after my shift ends at two?"

"Perfect." It really was promising. Maybe her crazy first day and a half was improving. "I'll wait and take my lunch break then. Want to meet here? I think the only other place that serves coffee and isn't boarded up is the gas station."

"Here's good. See you then." With a shy wave, Elena slipped out the door.

"What are you doing?"

Kit turned around to face Hugh. When she raised a speaking eyebrow at his lurking, he just held his hands up in an innocent-looking shrug.

"Nothing," she said.

"Do I need to tell you again to leave her alone?"

"Nope." Moving over so that she could see out a narrow window into the parking lot, her gaze scanned the cars. Elena reversed a sedan out of her parking spot and sped down the main street. Kit frowned. Her driving didn't match her fearful, timid personality—at all. "I'm not going to question her." At least not in an official capacity. "I just want to get to know her…to understand her." Hugh seemed to be actually listening thoughtfully, so she let a bit of her suspicion show. "There's something a little weird about her."

With a snort, Hugh moved over next to her so he could also see out the window. "If a little weirdness meant someone committed murder and arson, then half the people in town would be guilty. The whole town would be burned down."

Kit gave him a speaking look. "Half the town *is* burned down."

"Touché, young'un. Touché."

"Aren't you younger than me?"

Hugh gave a small shrug before pushing open the door. "Maybe, but my soul is older than the mountains."

She couldn't hold in a small choke of laughter, and

Hugh gave her a triumphant look before pausing in front of the door. His expression turned serious, and Kit braced for a lecture.

"It's fine if you want to make friends with Elena," Hugh said, and Kit sent him a sharp look, expecting him to follow that up with a warning.

"But…?" she prompted when he stayed silent.

"But nothing." He shrugged. "You both are new in town and could use a friend. I know we're a prickly bunch, especially after what happened with the lieutenant. His betrayal was a blow."

Kit studied his face, looking for any sign that he was teasing, but he seemed sincere. "Thank you."

One corner of his mouth quirked up. "If you're going to be hanging around Elena, just be aware that Jules's friends tend to attract explosions and snipers and kidnappers and things."

Kit blinked. "Uh…okay. Good to know."

Giving her a wink, Hugh started across the parking lot. As she followed him, that tiny bubble of hope rose in her chest again. As nosy and distrustful as the other Monroe cops could be, they were growing on her. Now she just had to prove to her new partners that she could be trusted.

CHAPTER 10

ALEX STOOD IN FRONT OF WHAT USED TO BE GRADY'S General Store and swallowed a string of creative swear words. It was as if fate was making this part of her plan as difficult as possible.

Think, Alex, she told herself firmly. *The only thing you'll accomplish by having a hissy fit in downtown Monroe is drawing attention, and that won't help the situation.*

It was horribly frustrating, though, that the only place to buy a gun in Monroe was now a bombed-out wreck.

The only legal *place to buy a gun*, the logical voice in her head corrected her. Too bad she didn't have any connections in this backward place. From her research, it had seemed like every resident was armed, from toddlers on up, but that didn't do her any good unless she had a way to get hold of a gun. Any trip out of town would need to be explained to her extraordinarily nosy roommates and their cop love interests, and the required background check would be noticed by a certain Mateo Espina, and she didn't want to make him curious enough to visit "Elena Dahl"…not until her plan had been set in motion. She'd been hoping that the Monroe general store owner could be convinced—either by flirting or cash—to forego the background check, but she hadn't taken into consideration that the store wouldn't still be standing.

"What happened?" The querulous voice made Alex whip her head around to see an elderly man standing next to her. She silently reprimanded herself for letting him sneak up on her while she'd been staring at the burned-out remains of the store.

"I don't know," she said, putting on her innocent Elena persona even as she eyed him carefully. Despite his frail, stooped body and the hazy cast to his eyes, she knew better than to underestimate anyone. "I'm new to town. Are you visiting?"

"'Course not. I've lived in Monroe since 1962." He straightened as if offended by the idea that he wasn't a local.

"You don't know what happened to the store?" she asked.

His indignation faded, replaced by what appeared to be confusion as he studied the building's blackened skeleton. "I don't…" His voice trailed off, and then he turned toward her. "Have we met?"

"Not yet." An idea began to sprout as she put on her sweetest smile and held out her hand. "I'm Elena Dahl. I'm staying with Jules… She works at the viner?"

His eyes lit in a moment of clarity. "Jules! Yes, she's my favorite waitress. She always remembers that I don't like onions. Nasty things. Even if you pick them out, the whole meal still tastes disgusting." He shook her hand. "It's a pleasure, Elena. I'm Bernard Wernicutt, but everyone calls me Bendsie."

"Very nice to meet you." Alex wasn't lying. This was perfect. Even if Bendsie remembered giving her information on how to get a gun, he could be easily discredited. "Since you've lived in town so long, I'm sure you'll be able to answer my question."

"Bet you're right." His thin shoulders pulled back. "I know pretty much everything there is to know about Monroe."

Her smile wasn't fake anymore. "Jules's place is so isolated. I would feel so much safer with some home protection. Now that this happened"—she gestured toward the bombed store—"where can I buy a gun in this town?"

"Well," he said. "Word is that Gordon Schwartz has a whole armory. Bet he'd be willing to part with a pistol for the right price."

Bingo. "Where can I find him?"

"Find who?" His gaze had gone hazy again, and Alex held back a groan.

"Gordon Schwartz."

"Why do you need to find Gordon?" His tone grew scolding. "Nice girl like you should stay far away from that wild boy. He's going to get himself into serious trouble one day. After he blew up the Johnsons' beehive, he didn't seem sorry at all…just sorry he'd been caught." He peered at Alex's face. "Who are you?"

She sighed silently and mentally revised her plan. "Elena Dahl. I'm friends with Jules, who always remembers you hate onions. You were just telling me about your favorite gun."

"My favorite gun?" He seemed confused but not unwilling to follow her lead. "The Peacemaker?"

Ugh. "No, the semiautomatic." She was fishing, but she really didn't want to be stuck with a single-action revolver.

"The Springfield pistol?" His eyebrows drew together. "That's not my favorite. I just kept it because my nephew gave it to me. Can't think of any way to sell it without hurting his feelings."

"I'd be willing to take it off your hands. Let's go get it now."

"Uncle Bendsie!" a man shouted from down the block. He started hurrying toward them, and Alex saw her opportunity slipping away.

Turning so her back was to the approaching nephew, she grabbed a Sharpie out of her messenger bag. Tugging up Bendsie's sleeve, she scribbled *32 Blank Hill Lane* on the inside of his wrist. "Bring the gun to this address. Can you remember that?" He nodded, but she was still doubtful, so she added *Springfield* before tugging down his sleeve again.

"Thirty-two Blank Hill Lane," he said slowly, smiling slightly. "Delilah Garmitt's place. She's a beauty."

Alex didn't know who this Delilah was—probably some woman from Bendsie's past—but she happily took his memory and ran with it. "That's right, and beautiful Delilah needs a gun for protection." Slipping the pen back into her bag, she saw that Bendsie's nephew was just twenty feet away, and she gave him a friendly wave before turning back to Bendsie, lowering her voice. "You need to bring the gun to Delilah."

His wiry white brows drew together. "Is her no-good dad drinking again?"

The nephew was close enough to hear, so she just nodded deliberately, hoping that Bendsie'd remember with the help of the address on his arm.

"Uncle Bendsie, there you are." Turning toward

Alex; Bendsie's nephew gave her a tight smile that warmed as he gave her a quick up-and-down glance. She quickly hid her annoyance at the interruption beneath a shy smile. "My uncle tends to wander off as soon as I'm distracted. At least he remembered to put on his coat this time. Half the time he comes outside in his bathrobe."

"You live close by, then?" she asked, mentally working out yet another plan in case Bendsie didn't come through for her.

"Yeah, just a block or so away." Bendsie's nephew turned and pointed down the street. "See the house with the inflatable snowman in the yard? Ours is the one right past that—two-eleven—in case you find my uncle wandering around again."

"Who are you?" Bendsie asked.

With an apologetic grimace, his nephew took his arm and started escorting him down the snowy street. Alex watched as they walked away, the wheels turning in her brain. If this worked out, if Bendsie managed to remember long enough, he'd bring the gun right to her.

Not only that, but he'd most likely forget he'd ever met her. Alex felt a slow smile stretch across her face. Maybe fate wasn't laughing at her. Bendsie Wernicutt was better than Grady's General Store ever could've been.

━━━━━━━━

Just seconds after Kit sat down in the chief's office with her pile of paperwork, Justice sprawled out on the floor next to her chair, Hugh opened the door and stuck his head inside.

"Hey, young'un. Grab your dog and let's go."

Standing, Kit snatched her jacket from the back of the desk chair and pulled it on. Justice bounced to his feet, as happy as she was to escape the tedium of the office, and she clipped on his lead. Despite her excitement about being interrupted, she had to ask, "Am I going to get into trouble with the chief for blowing this off for the second day in a row? I know he let me skip the paperwork yesterday because of the fire, but eventually I'm going to have to sign up for health insurance."

"That can wait. This is a matter of life and death." Without elaborating, Hugh charged down the hallway, leaving Kit to scramble after him. Even though her responsible side was pushing her to stay and finish what she needed to get done, her adrenaline-junkie side easily won. If she missed an important call just because she insisted on doing paperwork, she'd never forgive herself.

"Whose life and whose death?" she asked, catching up with him.

"Bendsie Wernicutt is the answer to both." He surged forward, making her have to trot to keep up. For someone who'd recently injured his leg, Hugh was really fast.

"Whosie Whatsie?" she asked, trying to hide the fact that she had to skip every second step to not get left behind.

"Bendsie. He's elderly, has dementia, and wandered away from his caretaker. Bendsie's Springfield nine-millimeter pistol is also missing, although his nephew isn't sure when the gun disappeared. Bendsie's been randomly giving away his possessions lately."

Despite her concern for the man, Kit felt a tiny hop of excitement at the thought of getting to do a search with Justice. "What are we waiting for?" She sped up so that Hugh fell behind her that time. "Let's go find Bendsie."

They basically raced to the squad car, where Lexi was already waiting. She looked like she was just as excited about the call, bouncing in the back of the car, her legs straight like pogo sticks. After loading Justice in the back, Kit automatically reached for the driver's door, but Hugh cleared his throat. Hiding her grimace, she circled the car and got in the front passenger seat, twisting around to look in the back and make sure the dogs were settling in.

Justice was obviously ecstatic to be with Lexi again, basically curling his wriggling body around her, his tail whapping against the back of the seat. Although Lexi tried to feign long-suffering endurance of his affection, Kit saw the Malinois's tail wag a few times before she got it under control again.

They pulled up to Bendsie's address just four minutes after they left the makeshift station. Theo was already there, trying to question a middle-aged man who was pacing the walkway in front of the house. Kit got out and opened the back door. When she hooked the lead to Justice's harness, his whole body quivered with excitement. He knew exactly what it meant when she used that loop—he was going to work, and there was nothing he enjoyed more.

"Finally!" The man plowed through the snow-covered yard toward them once Justice surged out of the squad car. "I hope the dog means you're actually going to look for my uncle, rather than stand around flapping your lips."

"Do you have something that smells like him?" Kit asked, falling into the familiar routine. "An item of clothing he's worn recently that hasn't been washed yet, for example?"

"Yeah, hang on." The man reversed course and hurried into the house.

Once he disappeared inside, Kit shot a bland-faced Theo a sideways look. "You're flapping your lips again?"

Behind her, Hugh coughed. Kit was beginning to recognize that as his way of smothering a laugh. "Yeah," Hugh said in a low voice that didn't carry to the house. "Theo's a nasty lip-flapper."

When Theo just gave them a flat, unimpressed stare, Kit met Hugh's gaze and had to quickly look away again before she started laughing. *A man is missing*, she reminded herself, sobering quickly as the nephew reemerged, holding what looked like a flannel shirt.

"Here," he said, holding out the balled-up fabric.

"Thank you." Kit accepted the shirt. "Do you know if your uncle left out the front door?"

"He had to," Bendsie's nephew said. "The back door's blocked. This is the only way out of the house."

Kit offered the shirt to Justice, who snuffled at it furiously. She had to hold back a smile at how he never simply *sniffed* something. Instead, he threw his whole self into it, nearly burying his head in the fabric in his enthusiasm. After giving him a few seconds, she withdrew the shirt and told him, "Justice, find."

The dog dropped his head toward the ground, his long ears flopping over his face, and started to search for Bendsie's trail.

"Here." Hugh held open a paper bag he'd just retrieved from the squad car and Kit dropped the shirt into it with a nod of thanks. Justice made ever-widening loops around her as she fed him more of the twenty-foot lead, focusing on staying out of the dog's way.

When Justice lifted his head and let out his characteristic baying bark, Kit grinned. He charged down the driveway and into the street, quickly taking up all the slack in the lead. Kit chased after him, slipping a little on the packed snow in the road. Justice turned east, running back toward town.

Behind her, Kit heard the squad car's engine start up. Since Hugh was jogging to her right, she assumed that Theo and the nephew were driving behind them. Justice turned again, to the north this time, trailed the scent a block, and then turned so they were once again heading east. Kit settled in, finding a pace that she could hold for miles and not letting Justice yank her out of it. Right away, she felt the same squeeze of her lungs that she'd felt the previous day running through the woods, and she slowed her pace a little more, even though she hated to do it.

"You don't have to do that." Hugh sounded irritated, and she glanced at him, confused.

"Do what?"

Now he *looked* annoyed, as well. "Slow down."

"If I don't, I'm going to be sucking air in about five minutes." Her tone was a little snappy, but she couldn't help it. She prided herself on her fitness, but this was a whole new environment. "The air's a lot thinner here than I'm used to. I'll adjust eventually, but you need to give me a few days."

His aggravated expression dropped, replaced by surprise. "Oh. Sorry. Thought you were slowing down for me. I'm used to Theo and Otto trying to baby me."

"Why would I slow down for you?" she said. "If you can't keep up, just get in the car."

"Oh, I can keep up." He sounded like he was back to his usual self. "We could run all the way to Denver, and I'd still keep up. In fact, I could run even faster than you, much faster, but I don't want to get ahead of the handler."

"Hugh." She gave him a sharp look, knowing why Theo always seemed to be at the end of his patience. Her competitive nature had flared at his words, but she'd be a miserable, air-sucking mess if she allowed him to goad her into running too fast. "If you keep this up, I'm going to have to race you, and we'll both lose, because I'll be puking and you'll be limping and Theo will yell at us."

Although he snickered, Hugh didn't say anything else, and he gave a salute that Kit took as agreement. A tug on the lead brought her attention back to Justice, who was following his nose to the other side of the road.

They were running down Main Street, the highway that passed through town, and Kit was thankful for the following squad car keeping any incoming traffic from running them over. It'd only been six months, but she'd forgotten what it was like to have competent partners who had her back. Despite Hugh's regular teasing and the occasional feeling that he and the other cops were holding back information, things were so much easier when she had a team helping her. For the first time in months, all she had to worry about was letting her dog lead her to the missing person.

As they passed through the center of the tiny downtown, people poked their heads out of the few businesses that were open to watch them jog down the road—dog, pedestrians, and squad car with the lights flashing. Kit got a glimpse of a few people in front of the VFW, but her attention was focused on Justice. As soon as they passed the vacant lot where the old diner had been, Justice took a sharp turn into the post office parking lot. Kit had a moment of hope that Bendsie was safe inside the heated building, but Justice didn't pause. Instead, he headed straight for the trees bordering the back of the lot.

Hugh groaned.

"Last chance to catch a ride in the car," Kit puffed as they plowed through the snowdrifts toward the tree line. He just shook his head stubbornly.

Once in the forest, the snow was only a few inches deep, and it got a little easier to keep from sinking. It wasn't all easy going, however. The trees were closer together and the undergrowth was thicker here than in the woods they'd run through the day before. Justice wove his way through the evergreens, finding dog-size openings between the trees and brush, forcing Kit to stop occasionally so she could untangle the lead and find a human-accessible path. There were branches hidden under the snow, and she kept tripping over them. From the amount of swearing coming from Hugh, he was having the same problem.

Finally, the trees opened up, leaving plenty of room for two people and a dog to maneuver.

"Stop," Hugh ordered, coming to a halt at the bottom of an old metal windmill.

Although she obeyed, she frowned at him. At the pace they'd been moving, they had to catch up with the elderly man soon, even if he had almost an hour's head start. "What's the problem?"

"I know this place." He waved at the windmill as if that explained everything.

"So?"

"So I'm wondering what exactly is up with your dog." He crossed his arms and stared at her, his frown belligerent.

"What? Nothing is up with him. He's trailing Bendsie, who we need to find before he freezes to death!" Her voice had risen with each word, and she took a breath, trying to regain her sense of calm. "I think the question is what is up with *you*."

"Fine." From his tone, though, nothing was fine. "Let's go. See where he's taking us. Ask yourself if it seems familiar."

"Nothing in this town is familiar," she grumbled, but she turned to Justice, who looked as confused as she was feeling. "Justice, find."

He picked up the trail in an instant, moving through the trees as quickly as Kit would let him. She ran a little faster than she should've, but she wanted to find Bendsie and get this call over with. Hugh was silent, but she could almost feel his judgmental gaze burning into her back. Shaking off the sensation, she followed her dog. It didn't matter. Hugh's strange, illogical temper tantrum didn't matter. All that mattered was finding an old man with dementia and getting him home where he'd be safe.

It only took a few more minutes for Hugh's accusation to make sense.

Justice burst out of the trees into a clearing, Kit behind him. *No, not a clearing*, she realized with a clenching stomach, *a backyard*. It was Jules's backyard, to be precise, exactly where Justice had led them yesterday. She stared at her dog, confused. What was wrong with Justice? Even when he couldn't figure out obedience commands to save his life, he was a natural tracker.

Was he broken? Had the move to Monroe wrecked him somehow?

He didn't look broken or wrecked or in any way uncertain as he towed her around the side of the huge, dilapidated house.

"I'll have to ask the twins if they left a bag full of hot dogs somewhere around the house," Hugh said. Although his tone was light, Kit felt her face heat with embarrassment, and she kept her gaze fixed on Justice to hide her expression.

"Let's see where he takes us before assuming he's wrong," she said.

"This is the second time in two days he's led us here," Hugh said, not sounding as amused anymore. "Unless Bendsie started that fire yesterday and then moved in with Grace, Jules, and the others, the dog is confused."

Quick words in Justice's defense rose to Kit's lips, but she clenched her teeth, holding them back. "We'll see."

"Hopefully soon," Hugh grumbled as they jogged along the side of the house where the snowdrifts were higher.

Justice bounded around the corner to the front yard, pulling harder now. In front of the porch steps, he stopped abruptly and sat, facing the house. Her stomach sinking, Kit followed, looping the excess lead as she did so. It reminded her so much of the day before, when Justice had signaled at the back door, rather than the front. If Hugh was right, she'd never live it down at the station, and no one would ever trust her or her dog again.

Passing the overgrown, snow-heaped shrubs next to the porch steps, Kit came to an abrupt halt right next to her dog. A grin spread across her face, wider and wider until it ached with a wonderful, righteous burn.

"Good dog." Pulling out Justice's sock monkey, she played a quick game of tug with him—rewarding him for a successful track—before turning to the elderly man sitting on one of the porch steps. She heard Hugh talking on his radio, giving their location. "Hello. You must be Bendsie."

He turned to look at her. "Who's asking?"

"I'm Kit, and this is Justice." The hound wagged his tail at the sound of his name. "That's Hugh. We're officers with the K9 unit, and we've been looking for you. Did you bring your gun with you?"

"My gun?" He glanced down at the empty hands resting in his lap and then back at her.

"Your Springfield nine-millimeter pistol."

"Oh, I gave that to someone who needed it more than me." His voice trailed off at the end, making the last few words a mumble. Turning his head, he looked into the trees bordering the yard.

"When was that?" she asked, and he looked at her blankly. "When did you give your gun away?"

"What gun?" His eyes narrowed. "Who are you?"

"I'm Kit." She gestured toward the step. "Mind if I join you?"

When he didn't object, she sat next to him, and Justice settled by their feet. Bendsie was wearing a coat and boots, she was happy to see. His hands and cheeks, although red from the cold, didn't have the waxy appearance of frostbite. For an elderly man who'd just wandered a few miles, he looked better than she'd expected.

"Hugh," she said, once he'd finished talking on the radio. "Mind lending Bendsie your gloves?"

"'Course." He immediately removed them and helped Bendsie put them on. "How's that? Warmer?"

"Murdoch, is that you?" Bendsie asked, rather than answering the question.

"That's me," Hugh said, straightening from his crouch.

"How's that wild kid of yours? Still think he's going to follow in the footsteps of your jailbird brother?"

Hugh's smiled turned into a grimace as Kit raised an eyebrow at him. "Nah," he said. "Hugh grew up to be a cop. He still likes picking locks, though."

"A cop." Bendsie shook his head. "Imagine that. Thought that kid would be locked up by his eighteenth birthday for sure, after that prank he pulled."

Hugh's forehead wrinkled. "The thing with the green paint?"

"No, the cow stunt."

"Right." Hugh looked amused and a bit nostalgic. "I'd forgotten about the cow."

Kit looked back and forth between the men after they both fell silent. "You can't just leave it there. What happened with the cow?"

Hugh made a zipping motion over his lips, and Theo's squad car pulled up in front of the house, distracting Bendsie before he could answer. As she helped the elderly man stand, Kit decided she'd have to stop in and have a chat sometime. Not only could she check on him, but she also might be able to get the details of Hugh's wild childhood. She needed to hear the cow story—and hopefully get some ammunition to torture Hugh with when he teased her about Wes.

Payback would be sweet.

CHAPTER 11

Alex slid into her seat at the kitchen table, feeling the thrift-store chair wobble underneath her. "Hello," she said shyly in her best Elena voice. Jules and the younger kids answered, but Sam stayed silent, simply eyeing her for a long moment before returning his attention to his plate.

Sam always looked at her as though he could see right through her. *I just need to work harder to win him over,* she thought grimly. *He's a guy, after all. He's bound to crack sooner or later—they all do eventually.* She caught his gaze and shot him a sweet smile, but he frowned and focused his attention on the cat that had draped itself across his shoulders. The cat was eyeing her with almost as much disdain as Sam was.

"Here you go," Jules said, setting a glass of water and a plate in front of her. "How are you feeling this morning?"

Alex faked a flinch. "Okay, but I'm still a little shaken up about that poor woman who was killed, especially since they haven't caught the guy."

"I know. It's terrible." As she settled in a chair between Dee and Tio, who was absently tracing shapes in the condensation on his glass, Jules gave a visible shiver. "I still can't believe that happened. I thought all of that was over." She gave Alex a sharp but sympathetic look. "Do you know anything about who might have done that? I know it's scary, but you have to remember that none of what happened to you is your fault. Theo can help you if he knows what's going on."

Alex had been surprised when she first realized how earnest her housemates were, how they honestly cared about keeping her safe. It made things much easier. Dropping her gaze to her lap for a moment, she said hesitantly, "Nothing happened to me. I mean, I don't know anything."

Reaching across the table, Jules patted her shoulder. "Just remember that help is here when you need it."

A slight twinge of guilt pinged in Alex's stomach, but she ignored it the way she always did. "Thank you."

"Guess what Theo told me?" Jules asked the table at large, obviously changing the subject, and Alex's ears perked up, even as she kept her head down. It was an unexpected bonus that Jules and Grace were dating two local cops. A little eavesdropping and a hidden app on their phones, and Alex knew pretty much everything that was going on. The only problem was the suspicious new cop—Kit—but Alex knew she could be handled. No one in town trusted Kit yet. Alex just had to play on that, to encourage the other cops' distrust of their new partner, and no one would believe anything that Kit had to say. People were easy to manipulate. Everyone was always so willing to believe the worst.

"What'd he say?" Dee asked eagerly.

"Mr. Wernicutt wandered away from his nephew again." Jules scooped some pasta onto Elena's plate. "Guess where he went?"

"Where?" Ty asked. Even Tio was listening.

"He walked through town and into the woods and finally sat down on our front porch."

"Our porch?" Dee echoed. "Did you find him?"

"No. It was the new officer, Kit. She has a tracking dog that followed Mr. Wernicutt's scent and led them all the way here."

"Oh." Dee looked sad for a moment. "I wish I'd seen that."

That had been close. Alex hadn't expected Bendsie to show up so soon. She'd barely gotten the gun and darted back inside before the dog had rounded the corner of the house. It could've been a disaster. The new cop was much too suspicious and didn't seem to be as easily influenced by a sad story and a pair of big, dark eyes as her partners were.

"Wh-wh-what k-kind of d-d-dog?" Sam asked, breaking his habitual silence.

"A hound of some kind." Jules's eyebrows pulled together as if she was trying to remember the name. After a few seconds, her expression cleared and she smiled. "A bloodhound. That's what he is. He's adorable. I gave them all a ride back to town yesterday, including the dog."

"They were here twice, and I missed it both times?" Dee's mouth pulled down in disappointment. "School wrecks everything."

There was a chorus of laughing responses from everyone except Sam, who stared off into space silently. Alex surreptitiously studied him, trying to figure out what he was thinking. She didn't like how much influence Sam had over his older sister, especially since it was so obvious that he didn't like Alex. Jules might be sympathetic to Alex now, but that could change if Sam shared his suspicions—and Alex's plan depended on keeping Jules's trust. It was infuriating, really. She'd played her best game, used techniques that should've lured in the most suspicious minds, but Sam stayed aloof. Alex hadn't given up yet, though. She wasn't about to let a *teenager*, of all people, best her.

She'd convince him that she was innocent, fragile, and harmless. All her marks fell eventually. It was just a matter of time before Sam fell, too.

And if he didn't, well, there were ways to take care of even the most stubborn stumbling blocks.

"That's it!" Tio said suddenly, and everyone's attention turned to him as he pulled what looked like a Swiss Army knife out of his pocket and set it on the table.

"What's it, T?" Ty asked, eyeing the knife with interest.

"I'm trying to convert this to use touch commands for each implement," Tio explained, pushing the knife into the center of the table so that everyone could see. "I've been having trouble setting it off unintentionally, however, which causes issues when I'm carrying it in my pocket. I just thought of how to prevent it from accidentally opening." He tapped the side of the knife and the blade extended, quickly enough to make Ty, Sam, and Jules jerk back in their chairs.

"Tio," Jules said sternly. "Did you just make a switchblade?"

He cocked his head to the side, blinking at the tool for a few moments before saying, "Not…technically?"

"Retract it," she ordered, and he tapped the side twice, making the blade disappear with a click. Jules picked it up tentatively, handling it like she would a bomb, and set it on top of the refrigerator. "No one touches this until Theo can dispose of it." She gave Tio a flat, no-nonsense stare. "No more switchblades."

"But what about my touch-command experiment?"

"Dull implements only for all future projects," Jules said firmly, waiting until he nodded in reluctant agreement before retaking her seat.

A switchblade—how handy. As she gave Tio a sympathetic look, Alex made a mental note to retrieve it before Theo's next visit. She'd need all the weapons she could get once her plan was set in motion. She never liked to kill, but sometimes it was the only way forward.

She smiled across the table at Dee, who immediately beamed back. *Such a sweet, trusting family,* Alex thought. *It was so good of Mr. Espina to lead me right to them.*

Wes couldn't sleep. It wasn't uncommon for him to have insomnia, but it usually happened when he was working on a project or was trying to sort out an especially tricky problem. This time, it felt different. Excitement was running through him, making him feel like he'd downed a half dozen espressos in the fifteen minutes before he'd gone to bed.

He couldn't blame caffeine for his sleepless state, though. No, it was all the fault of a beautiful woman who'd almost gotten shot by Rufus. The memory made him frown, hating the idea that she'd been in danger. After seven years working in his tower and living year-round in the small adjacent cabin, Wes had earned the wary respect of his neighbors. He wouldn't call them friends, but he'd be able to knock on their doors without getting his head shot off.

Probably.

Giving up on attempting sleep, Wes climbed out of bed and tossed his winter coat over his drawstring pants and T-shirt. Stuffing his feet into his boots, he clumped outside. He glanced at his watch. It was close to four, but the world was as dark as if it were the middle of the night. The stars were bright, though, giving the snow an eerie blue-white glow. One of his favorite things about his home was how quiet it was, especially at night in the winter. In the small city where he'd grown up, there'd always been noise, sounds overlapping other sounds until it was impossible for him to concentrate on anything. Here, it was just the slight thud and brush of his boots connecting with the snowy ground, then the quiet beep and click of the tower door unlocking and opening.

Once upstairs, there were more distractions—the crackling of the fire in the woodstove and the whir and beep of various electronics he'd hooked to the motion sensor—but everything was familiar and expected. Usually, the sameness of his tower was comforting, but tonight he was restless. He'd gotten a taste of the heady excitement he'd felt in Kit's company, and he wanted more. For the first time, the tower felt empty.

"Radio on," he commanded, needing to hear human voices other than his own. After he heard the beep indicating that the digital radio had powered up, there was still silence, and he almost laughed. Why had he thought anyone would be communicating at this hour? It was tiny Monroe after all. "Radio scan." Although he still didn't have high hopes of hearing any communications, even with all the channels open, that at least increased the odds. Walking over to the bank of windows, Wes peered into the darkness, not seeing anything except his reflection.

"Dispatch, Unit 2242. I'm about to make a traffic stop on the 200 block of Main Street. Plates when you're ready."

The voice belonged to one of Wes's more sane neighbors, Otto Gunnersen. The cop and his new wife, Sarah, lived a few miles away.

"2242, go ahead." The dispatcher sounded sleepy. As Otto rattled off the license plate number, Wes wondered if Otto's transmission had woken her up.

It wasn't long before the dispatcher spoke again, sounding wide awake this time. *"That plate comes back to a blue Honda Accord, registered to a William Kyle Yarden. He has a warrant."*

"Copy." Otto didn't sound fazed by the information, which wasn't surprising. Although Wes didn't know Otto well, he got the impression that it took a lot to rattle the big cop.

"2268." Wes's stomach jumped with excitement when he recognized Kit's voice. *"Need some help, Otto?"*

"I've got this, thanks," Otto answered. *"Bill never gives us any trouble."*

"Copy. Let me know if you can use a hand. I'm just around the corner, so I could be there in five minutes." Kit sounded a little disappointed, and Wes wondered if she was having just as much trouble sleeping as he was. He liked that idea. It made the early-morning hours seem less lonely when he knew she was awake as well.

On impulse, he switched the radio to a seldom-used channel and picked up the wireless mic. "3537 to 2268 on eighteen."

There was a pause long enough to make Wes wonder if she was scanning channel eighteen or if his attempt to reach out had been lost to empty air. *"2268 to 3537. Wes, is that you?"*

He smiled. "Yes, it's me."

"What are you doing up so late?" she asked. Her voice was warm, and it made his blood feel carbonated again, all those fizzy bubbles swirling through him. He couldn't stay still, so he paced over to the windows, peering through the glass even though he knew he couldn't see her house without the binoculars.

"I couldn't sleep. How about you? Are you working nights now?" He hoped not. There would be fewer chances to see her if their sleep schedules were reversed.

"Nope to both. Can't sleep, but I'm not on nights. Too bad. At least then I'd be paid for staying up."

He moved from Window 1 to Window 12 and then back again, needing to move so his brain didn't freeze with the pressure of talking to Kit. "Why can't you sleep?"

Although he'd only met her a few times, the sound she made was already familiar, and he could picture her doing a half shrug as she made it. *"I'm not sure. New place or too much excitement yesterday or something. Who knows. My brain does what it does, giving no explanations."*

"Yes." Her words resonated inside him. "Mine, too. Our brains match in that way."

"Please." Amusement filled her voice, and it made his throat tighten with anxiety at the thought of her laughing

at him. "*As if my brain could even hope to match yours. I've seen your tower. You're a stinking genius.*"

The words ran through his mind a few times before he was reassured that she was complimenting him, and he ducked his chin, his face heating from pleasure and relief. As he lifted his head, his reflection in the window caught his attention, and he was glad Kit couldn't see his flushed cheeks. Realizing that his pause had probably stretched too long, he scrambled to come up with an answer. "You're just as smart. I think your brain could hold its own."

"*Now I'm picturing our brains battling it out.*" Her words were filled with laughter, and he was pleased that he was actually managing to banter with her.

At least, he was pretty sure that they were bantering. He made a mental note to call his sister, Leila, later and ask.

"Are they using swords or light sabers?"

"*Neither. They're bouncing off each other like lumpy, armless sumo wrestlers.*"

His own laughter took him by surprise, and he felt a rush of affection for Kit. It had been a long time since he'd been able to talk to anyone so easily. "Of course. That's the only battle that makes sense."

"*Could you two take your weird flirting somewhere else? Somewhere I don't have to listen to it?*" The dispatcher cut in, making Wes grimace. He hadn't thought anyone would bother scanning channel eighteen, but he'd forgotten about the dispatcher.

"*Sorry,*" Kit said. "*I'll talk to you later, Wes. Try to get some sleep.*"

"You, too." He already knew that sleep would be an impossibility. If he'd been antsy before he'd talked to

Kit, now he'd be bouncing off the walls. He didn't want to give up his connection with her, but it was different now that he knew the dispatcher could hear everything they said. "Good night, Kit."

"*'Night, Wes.*"

He set the mic down and switched the radio back to channel one. Instead of returning to his cabin, he moved over to the tower windows again and watched over the town—and Kit—until the sun rose, replaying their latest conversation in his mind.

Kit was still smiling as she entered the VFW the next day. She was pretty sure she hadn't stopped since finding Bendsie. If it had just been her pride on the line, it wouldn't have mattered so much, but it was her dog's competence that Hugh had questioned. Justice had proven himself to her over and over, and she'd defend him ferociously if she had to. Even her mostly sleepless night hadn't dampened her mood, especially when she thought about the radio conversation with Wes.

She took her usual seat at the table where she and the other cops had their daily morning roll call, and Jules gave her a wave from across the room. Kit waved back, scanning the room automatically. Several people were having a late lunch, but she didn't recognize anyone besides Jules. They were all looking at her, still obviously fascinated by the stranger in their midst—and the new cop, at that.

The townspeople's distrust had an upside, at least. That morning, when Hugh had sent her off on an errand, very transparently wanting her out of earshot while they discussed the arson and possible murder case, Kit had taken the opportunity to spend some time at a computer in the records room. Without a previous location, she wasn't able to track down anything using Elena's name, but she did run the woman's license plate number. Oddly enough, Elena had already changed the address it was registered under to Jules's house in Monroe. Kit found that to be suspiciously fast, telling her that Elena was hiding something. The vehicle registration did give her Elena's full name and birth date, however. Once she found out where Elena used to live, her research should really bear fruit.

Kit's thoughts were interrupted when a tall, blond teenager with the sturdy frame of an athlete cautiously approached her table. She watched him in her peripheral vision, pretending not to notice him. His wary expression and careful way of walking made her think that any sudden moves on her part would send him darting back to his table like a startled rabbit. When he was a few feet away, he stopped, and she slowly turned her head to look at him.

"Hi," she said, glancing away again. She saw Jules by the kitchen door, staring at them with an odd look that Kit couldn't identify—Worry? Anxiety? Possibly a little hope thrown in there?

"H-h-hey." The teenager's husky greeting brought her attention away from Jules and back to him.

"I'm Kit, but you probably know that already." She kept her gaze moving, not wanting to lock on him with her usual penetrating cop stare and drive him away. She couldn't say why, but something was telling her this was important.

"Y-yes."

"Want to sit?" She borrowed a move from Hugh and pushed out the chair across from her with her foot.

"No."

She bit the inside of her cheek to stop herself from laughing at the bald rejection. "Okay."

"Y-you're the n-new c-c-cop."

"Yes."

"Jules t-told me y-you have a t-t-track-king dog."

That was interesting. Kit wondered why Jules had been telling this kid about her. As she glanced again at Jules, who was still watching them closely, it suddenly clicked. This had to be one of Jules's siblings. She turned her attention back to him. "I do. He's a bloodhound."

Interest lit his expression, almost overtaking the wariness, and he shifted a half step closer. "D-did he really f-f-find Mr. W-Wernicutt?"

It took her a second to recognize the name. "Oh, Bendsie! Yes, Justice tracked him."

"D-did you t-train him?" He slid another step closer, placing one hand on the back of the chair she'd pushed out for him. "W-was it hard?"

Kit laughed a little, thinking back to Justice's snail-like progress. "Yes. So hard. Not the tracking, really, but everything else."

His other hand clutched the back of the chair as he leaned closer. "I w-work at the k-k-kennel, and there's a resc-cue d-dog there n-now—a b-bloodhound. N-Nan said that I c-c-can t-train her, b-but n-none of the g-guys have t-trained a t-tracker b-before."

The words *rescue bloodhound* would have won her over if she hadn't already been completely suckered in by the wary dog-loving kid who was awkwardly trying to ask her for help. "I'm planning on training Justice to be able to work off lead, and I'll need someone to help. If you're willing, I'll help you train your rescue in exchange. Sound good?" She would've helped him no matter what, but she knew the importance of keeping things from being lopsided. For her, accepting help was tough, especially when she didn't have a chance to pay the person back.

The kid's entire face lit up, and Kit couldn't hold back her own smile. "I have school and w-work at the k-kennel, b-but I b-bet N-Nan w-will let m-m-me have t-time off for t-training w-with you."

"Great." Still smiling, Kit fished out her phone and held it out to him. The kid was almost ridiculously endearing. "Put in your number. Oh, and Nan's and your parents'. I'll call everyone and make sure we're on the same page."

His mouth went tight as he focused on the screen of her phone. "No p-p-p... It's j-just m-m-my sister." He flicked a glance at Jules, who was still sending frequent looks their way even as she bustled back and forth between the tables. "J-Jules."

"Ah," Kit said. That confirmed her guess. "Put in Jules's number, and I'll talk to her before we start training."

His face relaxed slightly, although his cautious expression had returned. After tapping at the screen for a bit, he handed Kit her phone back. She glanced at the screen and saw he'd entered his number simply as "Sam."

"So what's the story, Sam?" When panic flashed in his eyes, Kit's curiosity grew, but she simply clarified, "Where'd the bloodhound at Nan's come from?"

Again, the tightness in his muscles visibly eased. "N-Nan runs a rescue, and the bloodh-hound w-was b-brought in from another shelter. She w-w-was returned fr-from three homes that d-didn't w-work out."

"I'm guessing she ate the couch in at least one of them," Kit said wryly, remembering the furniture and shoes and even the cell phone she'd lost to Justice's need to chew.

He laughed, just a tiny huff of an exhale, and Kit felt like she'd won something. "How'd you g-g-guess?"

Before she could answer, Elena slid into the chair that Kit had pushed away from the table for Sam. "Hey, Sammie," Elena said, turning around to speak to him. "What are you guys talking about?"

As quick as a security door slamming into place, Sam's expression blanked, all amusement or interest gone in a fraction of a second. Without answering Elena, he turned away, heading back toward the table with the three other kids. Now that she knew about the connection between Sam and Jules, Kit assumed that all four were Jules's siblings. When Sam sat down next to the little girl, Kit turned away, pushing back her curiosity while promising herself she'd find out more in the future. She mentally added Sam's past to the long list of things she needed to learn about the residents of her new town.

"He was talking to you for a long time." Even though Elena was giving Kit her usual sweet smile and wide, innocent eyes, Kit sensed the slightest hint of irritation. "He never says a word to me. What's the secret to getting him to open up?"

"Mutual interests." Kit gave a one-sided shrug and

decided to change the subject. Even though she'd only just met Sam, she felt oddly protective of him. The kid acted like he'd already drawn the short stick too many times in his young life. It felt wrong to be discussing him with someone he obviously didn't trust. She wished Elena had waited another few minutes before joining them, since Sam had been starting to relax and open up. Pushing down her resentment at the interruption, Kit forced a friendly tone as she asked, "How was your first day of work?"

"It was hard." Elena dropped her gaze to the table. "Sorry. That was ungrateful of me. I'm sure I'll get used to doing dishes and cleaning the kitchen. It's just not what I'm used to, and Vicki can be kind of…mean."

Glancing at the kitchen door as Jules pushed it open, Kit caught a glimpse of the cranky-looking cook. "I bet she can be. Hugh mentioned something about her liking practical jokes."

Elena's gaze snapped up, her eyes widening. "She does? I didn't know that. She hasn't tried any on me. Not yet, at least."

"At least you have Jules," Kit said. "She seems like she could never be mean."

Elena dropped her gaze to the table. "Yes. Jules is very sweet."

"So I take it your last job didn't involve dishes?" She probed gently, trying very hard not to slip into interrogation mode.

"No." There was a pause that went on just a hair too long. "No dishes. It was an office job."

"Oh? Where was that?" As hard as she was trying to sound casual, Kit knew she was failing. Apparently, talking shop with cops and interrogation were all she was good at anymore—except with Wes. She swallowed a smile at the memory of their radio chat. Conversation was always easy with Wes.

"Um…Chicago." The frightened bunny expression accompanied the obvious lie. To her relief, Jules arrived at their table at that moment, and her honest smile eased the tension.

"Hey, Elena. Hi, Kit. Did y'all want lunch menus or just coffee?"

As if on cue, Kit's stomach grumbled. "Lunch for me. I'm only halfway through a long day, and Hugh ate most of my breakfast."

Jules laughed. "That's Hugh for you. I swear, eating with him around is like being in a prison cafeteria. You have to protect your food with your life." She filled their coffee mugs. "How about you, Elena? Are you hungry after washing all those dishes?"

"Yes." Elena smiled back, but Kit noted a slight stiffness to her expression. Glancing at Jules, Kit couldn't see any tension on her side, just kindness and a friendly openness. She took a sip of her coffee, savoring the rich heat absently as she studied Jules and Elena. For two people who were supposed to be old friends, they acted more like new acquaintances. The mystery of Elena deepened with each new encounter.

"I'll bring you both menus, then." With a final smile, Jules turned away and crossed the room to fill coffee mugs at other tables on her way back to the front.

"It must be tough living with so many people," Kit said, trying to think of the best way to get the answers she needed in the most casual, roundabout way possible.

"I've just had one roommate. I can't imagine having, how many? Six?"

"It's fine," Elena said. "Do you have any roommates now?"

"No...not unless you count Justice, my K9 partner."

"You're lucky." Elena dumped four sugar packets into her coffee and then tore the top off a fifth as Kit watched with disgusted fascination as she turned her coffee into syrup. "Did you have a roommate when you lived in Wisconsin?"

The mention of her previous home jarred Kit, and she took a sip of coffee to hide her reaction. "At first I did," she said, keeping her voice neutral. "Not for the past six years or so, though. It's just been me, and then me and the doggo."

Elena played with her mug and then glanced up through her mile-long eyelashes. At the shy look, filled with sympathy, Kit stiffened, bracing herself for whatever Elena was about to say. "I'm sorry about what happened to you. That must've been so hard."

It took a great deal of effort to keep her voice even. "What must've been hard?"

Elena's eyes widened. "Having all your friends turn on you like that, especially since you were just doing what you thought was right."

Her skin went cold enough to make goose bumps pop up on her arms and the back of her neck. "What are you talking about?" She tried to keep her tone casual and even, but she was pretty sure she failed by the way Elena flinched as if Kit had threatened to slap her.

"Nothing." Releasing her grip on the mug, Elena tucked her hands onto her lap. "Never mind."

Kit stayed silent, barely containing the urge to shake the information out of Elena. Instead, she waited, knowing that Elena would eventually share whatever she knew.

"Sorry." Elena shot her a quick, mortified glance. "I just thought that if *Grace* knew about it, then it was common knowledge. I didn't mean to offend you or hurt your feelings or anything."

Despite having her painful past dragged out by an almost stranger, Kit forced herself to sit back in her chair and even smile a little. "Oh, I'm not offended; I'm confused. What are you talking about?"

Elena's brows drew together slightly at Kit's casual response. "Grace said you turned in your partner for something, and everyone in your old department started calling you a rat. Isn't that why you moved here?" She offered an earnest look. "If that didn't happen, I'll let Grace know to stop spreading false rumors."

"That's okay." Kit took a sip of her coffee, proud that her hands were steady. "I'll talk to Hugh and Grace myself."

As Elena's eyes widened in alarm, Kit pressed her lips together to hold back a satisfied smile. *Got you.* "Oh, I wish you wouldn't. They're going to think I'm not trustworthy. It's my fault for passing along the story."

Kit offered Elena a sugary smile. "It's not your fault. Don't worry about it. I'm just going to set the record straight and see where she got her information. Go right to the source, and all that."

As Elena's mouth set in an unhappy line, Kit saw Hugh in the doorway. He waved at her in a *come on* gesture.

"Work calls." Secretly grateful for Hugh's appearance, Kit set down her coffee and stood, digging in her pocket for a five-dollar bill. "Sorry to interrupt our lunch, but that's the life of a cop. We'll have to do this again sometime." She gave Jules, who was approaching with menus, an apologetic shrug before heading toward where Hugh was waiting in the entry.

"Bye," Elena said faintly, and Kit gave her a wave over her shoulder without slowing.

"Thank you," she said as she reached Hugh. "What's up?"

His eyebrows shot up at her overly enthusiastic greeting. "Got a call from the county deputies. A small avalanche just west of town caused a multicar accident, and they asked for our help. Sorry to interrupt your lunch."

"No apologies necessary. That was painful." The words were out before she could stop them, and she instantly regretted her blunt honesty when Hugh's amused expression disappeared in an instant.

"From what Grace has told me, Elena's having a really tough time right now," he said, pushing open the VFW door, and Kit used the moment when he wasn't looking at her to make a face at his back. Of course he was sympathetic to Elena. She'd forgotten for a second that she was the odd woman out in this. "It's easy to be judgmental when you haven't been in a situation where you're scared and helpless."

She stopped abruptly next to her car, her hand outstretched toward the back door handle. "You think I haven't felt scared and helpless?" Anger surged inside her. "I've been a cop for eight years. I can promise you that I've been in a lot more dangerous situations than Elena has."

He waved off her protest, and her annoyance

intensified at his casual dismissal. "You've been trained for it, though. Elena's a victim. Maybe if you let go of all the competitive crap, you'll be able to see that."

Heart pounding, Kit bit her tongue hard enough to hurt as she turned to get Justice out of her car. The waves of anger must've been rolling off her, judging by the way he shrank down, eyeing her warily. She took a deep breath and blew it out, closing her eyes for a moment, annoyed at herself for scaring her dog, even unintentionally.

"Sorry, Justice," she muttered, and he popped right back up, surging toward her eagerly. He was nothing if not resilient.

"Listen," Hugh said, his voice softening a little. "I get it. When Grace first arrived, I investigated her like nobody's business. Then she was almost killed. Elena is the fourth person to move into that house, so we know the drill now. They're not the problem; the criminals who come after them are. Like I said, these women are the victims."

Kit used the few seconds it took to get Justice leashed and out of the car to get a firm hold on her temper. Elena wasn't the reason for this anger. It was that her new partner—someone she was supposed to be able to trust—had been spreading rumors about her painful past. When Kit finally managed to put a lid on her anger and turn toward him, she was pretty sure her expression was controlled—or at least she wasn't trying to kill him with eye lasers.

"We're cops. We investigate things," she said, choosing her words carefully as they headed for Hugh's squad car. "I knew that you, Theo, and Otto wouldn't hesitate to look into my background. Honestly, I'd do the same thing if I were in your shoes. I just wish you'd asked me for my side of the story before sharing what you found out about my history with your girlfriend."

Hugh blinked at her, his face blank with confusion. "Wait. What are we talking about now?"

A movement inside the diner caught Kit's attention. As soon as she glanced at the window, Elena turned away, but it was obvious that she'd been watching them. An uneasy feeling prickled up Kit's spine, and she suddenly felt exposed in the open parking lot.

"Let's talk about this in the car," she said as she opened the back door for Justice. He leapt in, enthusiastically greeting Lexi, whose expression once again feigned indifference even as her tail whapped against the seat. As Kit closed the door and got into the front passenger seat, she wished that she and Hugh could consistently get along as well as their dogs did. He got in the driver's seat and pulled out of the parking space as soon as her seat belt clicked into place. His hand circled in a *go on* gesture.

"Elena heard about my professional history from Grace. Since I haven't shared the details with Grace—or anyone in town—I assume you did some digging. I understand why. Like I said, if our positions were reversed, I probably would've checked into your past." Even as she said it, she doubted that she would have. She'd like to think that she would've at least given Hugh more than a few days to trust her enough to share something like that.

"I'm still not following. What did Grace tell Elena?" Frowning, Kit examined Hugh's profile, looking for signs that he was trying to wiggle out of an uncomfortable conversation by feigning ignorance. His confusion appeared to be legitimate, though. "Elena knew that I reported my former partner, and that the majority of the people in my old department..." She tried to think of the best way to put it. "They let me know that they didn't agree with my decision."

Hugh gave her a quick, thoughtful glance before returning his attention to the road as he turned out of the parking lot. "What'd your partner do?"

"He profited by misusing the power of his position." Her stomach twisted as it always did when she had to think about Chad.

With a snort, Hugh asked, "Has anyone ever told you that your vocabulary expands when you're angry?"

"Yes." It was a habit that had started when she was a teenager and realized that staying calm and using big words in an argument really annoyed her sister.

"Okay." He grew serious again. "Back to the point. Grace didn't tell Elena anything."

Kit huffed, opening her mouth to challenge his statement, but he held up a hand.

"I didn't even know about your ex-partner, so there's no way Grace knows. I'll ask Theo if he said anything to Jules, but I doubt it."

Her eyebrows shooting up in disbelief, Kit had a hard time keeping her calm tone. "Are you telling me that you didn't do a background check on me five minutes after meeting me?"

His look of innocence wasn't very believable. "Five minutes after meeting you, we were still eating breakfast at the diner, followed by an arson-and-murder crime scene, followed by a run through the woods. There are limits to googling things on my phone, you know."

A short laugh escaped, annoying her. She didn't want to find Hugh amusing right now. "How'd Elena hear about it, then? My department handled the situation internally, so there wasn't even any media coverage."

He gave her another one of his penetrating looks. "He was fired?"

"Forced to resign." Anger added an extra twist to her already sore gut. "He's working for another town not too far away from my old department."

The sound Hugh made was hard to translate. Kit hoped it was disgust that a dirty cop had been found out, but the discovery of his crimes had barely made a blip in his life. It could've meant anything, though. After what had happened to her and the way she'd basically been forced out of her last department, she knew better than to assume that everyone had a moral code.

"I'll talk to Theo," he repeated. "And I'll have a word with Grace. Maybe she does have another source at the department." His voice lightened at the end, however, telling Kit that he really didn't believe that Grace told Elena about her. As they sped along the highway toward the multicar accident, Kit felt the all-too-familiar sting of having a partner who didn't trust her. She firmly pushed it away, vowing not to let it affect either her mood or her work.

She'd already been driven out of one job. She'd be damned if she'd allow it to happen again.

CHAPTER 12

THE SNOW CRUNCHED UNDER WES'S BOOTS AS HE CLIMBED. It was a beautiful day, with the late-afternoon sun shading to orange as it approached the mountain peaks it was about to hide behind, but Wes didn't pay much attention to the scenery. He was intent on reaching the bat cave.

Despite its name, the bat cave was more of a rock overhang than a cave, but the bat part was true enough — it housed a good-sized colony of silver-haired bats. Researchers and animal-loving hikers frequently visited the location. Although Wes had gotten some striking photos at the bat cave, he hadn't even brought his camera with him this time. He was more interested in the cell reception.

When the trail evened out, leading to a large, flat rock overhang, he pulled out his cell phone. Sure enough, he had reception. Finding his sister's name in his short list of contacts, he called her. As he waited for her to answer, pacing back and forth across the granite ledge, he made a mental note to set up a cell-signal booster at the tower. He should've done it before, but he hadn't missed phone service. Having to mindfully go somewhere with cell reception allowed him to control when and whom he called. It wasn't enough now, though, not when there was someone he was hoping to call — as soon as he got her number.

"Wes!" Leila sounded winded. "What's wrong?"

"Nothing's wrong." Well, nothing except his social skills when women—not including his sister—were around.

"Oh." There was a pause. "I thought there was an emergency. You never call except for every other Sunday afternoon."

"No emergency." He tried to mentally plan out his question. "I need some advice."

"Advice?" Another silence fell, and Wes could almost hear the gears in her brain turning. He smiled. Leila was even smarter than he was, and she was a whole lot more intuitive and perceptive. That's why he was calling her. "Does this have something to do with a woman?"

"Yes."

She squealed, the sound so excited that he smiled wider even as he winced and pulled the phone slightly away from his ear. "Are you dating someone? What's her name? When do I get to meet her? What does she do? Is she funny? Pretty? Smart? A badass? Tell me details, Wes!"

"Answering most of your questions might be premature." As much as he wanted to talk about Kit, Wes knew it could be dangerous. The more he said, the more real the possibility of something happening with her felt, and he didn't want to build up hopes too high. After all, the more excited he got, the harder the disappointment would hit if she never wanted to talk to him again.

"Fine." Although Leila was obviously trying to sound calm, Wes could tell that she was thrilled, and it made him wonder if he'd done the right thing by calling his sister. Now there might be two extremely disappointed people if nothing happened between him and Kit. "Just answer the basic ones, then. Are you dating?"

"No. We've only met three times." He didn't think their radio conversation counted.

"But you like her?"

"Yes. I like her." It seemed like a barely adequate phrase to encompass the fizzing excitement he'd felt around her—and even later, when he was alone and thinking about her. "I'm…interested in her." That didn't seem much more accurate.

Leila let out another small squeal, and Wes looked up at the sky, even as he felt his face heat. "Sorry," she said as if she could see his long-suffering expression. "That's out of my system now. Back to basic questions. Is she interested in you?"

"I don't know." Crouching down, he absently picked up a few small pebbles, his brain fully occupied with the mystery that was K9 Officer Kit Jernigan. "That's what I wanted to discuss with you."

"Hang on. I think I need to get comfortable for this conversation." There were a few rustling noises, and then Leila spoke again. "Okay. I'm ready. Let's start with the first time you met. Tell me what happened."

"I needed propane, so I refilled my tank at the station on the southeast side of town. I wanted to be back home before things got busy—"

"Wesley," she interrupted. "I've been to your Podunk town, remember? It never gets busy. There are, like, ten buildings and eight people total."

"The population of Monroe—"

"Nope. Don't care. Tell me the story."

It never hurt his feelings when Leila cut him off like

that. In fact, he appreciated her directness. It was easier than trying to guess what a person was thinking by their body language or tactful words. "Four days ago, I was driving west on Mule Drive at six fifty-four, but I was forced to stop due to an SUV backing a small utility trailer into a driveway." He frowned at the memory. "*Attempting* to back a small utility trailer into a driveway."

"Go on. No, wait! Let me guess. Did you save this woman from getting run over?"

"No."

"Oh." She sounded disappointed. "Go on, then. What did happen?"

Wes smiled slightly. His sister was terrible at listening to stories. She didn't have any patience, wanting to rush right to the conclusion instead. "After talking with the driver, I didn't think she'd move the trailer into the driveway efficiently—which meant I'd be late—so I got out of my truck in order to help."

"She was the driver?" Her voice was hushed, amusing Wes.

"Yes."

"That's so romantic!"

His eyebrows scrunched together. "It is?"

"Well, not really, I guess. I think I'm just anticipating that it's going to be romantic soon. Go on! Get to the good part!"

He hesitated. "I'm not sure what you'd consider the good part."

Her gusty sigh was audible. "Just tell me the rest. I'm dying of curiosity here!"

"I helped her get the trailer into her driveway and unhitched it."

"And then?"

"She drove away."

There was a long beat of silence. "That's disappointing."

"It was."

"Did she tell you her name, at least?"

Wes found himself smiling. "Yes. Kit Jernigan."

"Kit," Leila repeated, trying out the name. "I like it. It sounds unpretentious and a bit sporty, but clever, too."

"She is all of those things."

"What does she look like? I bet she's pretty."

"She's beautiful." His face was flushing again. He could feel the heat as he pictured Kit in his mind—her taut, subtle curves and the warmth in her almond-shaped eyes and the eight freckles dotting the bridge of her nose.

Leila cleared her throat loudly.

"What?"

"Details!"

He struggled to put what made Kit so incredible into words. "When she's just being polite, she smiles with her lips together. When she means it—when she thinks something is funny or I say something that she honestly likes—her teeth show."

With an exaggerated sigh, Leila said, "Give me the basics first. You can't start with her toothy grin like she's the reappearing Cheshire cat."

"You know I hate *Alice in Wonderland* references."

"I know, and rightfully so. It's a creepy book and even creepier movie. Back on track, though. Is Kit short? Tall? Round? Skinny? Black? White? Hair color? Length? Give me something I can mentally slap that smile onto."

"I'd estimate she's five feet and two inches. She's not round or skinny, but athletic, like she exercises rigorously and consistently. I haven't asked her what her ethnic background is, but I'd guess that at least one of her parents is of Asian descent. Her hair is black. It was all up in a bun, but I believe it would be long when loose." Now he was picturing how it would feel to release her hair from the knot it was twisted into, to watch it fall heavily over her shoulders and down her back in a dark sheet of silk. Uncomfortably warm, he coughed to ease the constriction in his throat.

"That's perfect, Wes. She sounds gorgeous."

"Yes." In his mind, Kit was both perfect *and* gorgeous.

"What happened the other times you met her?" Leila asked eagerly. A corner of Wes's mouth twitched up at her excitement. He hadn't expected her to be so thrilled that he'd met someone he liked. "Did you ask her out?"

"No." His small smile died. "I was planning to during our last meeting, but her partner interrupted before I had a chance."

There was a shocked pause on the other end of the call. Wes didn't know what had caused his sister's silence, so he kept his mouth shut, waiting for her to tell him.

"Her...*partner*?" she finally repeated, and Wes understood her surprise.

"Kit is a police officer. A member of the K9 unit," he explained.

Leila's relieved sigh was loud enough to make Wes pull the phone away from his ear. "Oh! *Partner*. I thought you were talking about a *partner*-partner."

"What?"

"Never mind. The important part is that this Kit is single. She's single, right?"

"As far as I know. She wasn't wearing a wedding ring." Even as he tried to assure his sister, doubt filled him. A lot of people didn't wear rings, after all. Maybe he'd imagined the interest on her part. The thought brought him back to his reason for calling. "I need you to tell me if she's flirting or just being nice."

"O…kay." She sounded doubtful. "What did you say to her, and what did she say back?"

Wes recounted their conversations to the best of his ability, which he knew was pretty accurate. Everything Kit said was burned into his memory. It was embarrassing, sharing his awkward first encounters with his sister, but it was worth it to get her take. He needed more data, and Leila was excellent at interpersonal interactions, something he had never mastered. He felt like he could understand Kit better than he could most people, since she seemed so straightforward, but he didn't trust himself. Reading people wasn't one of his strengths, and he needed a second opinion.

"Huh."

He didn't like the sound of that. "What? Do you think she's not interested?"

"No." His heart gave a hopeful little hop, only to sag at her next words. "Maybe. I'd need to watch her while she's talking to you to give a more definitive answer."

"Do you want to come visit me?"

She laughed. "I do, but I can't. It's this damn dissertation. I'm in the homestretch and determined that I'm going to finish it before Christmas."

Disappointment struck, but only for a moment before

an idea occurred to him. "Next time we talk, I could take a video of her."

"Nope." Leila's response was firm. "That is guaranteed to backfire horrifically. She's going to think you're either a weirdo who takes excessively long selfies or a perv. Do you know how many movies I've seen where this exact thing happened and the guy always, *always* regrets doing such a stupid thing?"

"You shouldn't base your decisions on what works in the movies," Wes said, although he mentally nixed the idea of capturing video of Kit. Even as the thought of recording her had popped into his head, he'd dismissed it. Leila had just confirmed his original instinct—she was always right when it came to things like this.

"Promise me no hidden video," she said.

"Promise. You sure you can't come and visit?"

She blew out a long breath. "If I could spare the time, I'd be on the next plane. I'm dying to meet Kit already. Since I can't, though, you know what you're going to have to do, right?"

His stomach tightened with nerves, part of him knowing what she was about to say, even as he asked, "What?"

"You're going to have to be brave and ask her out."

That's what he had been worried she was going to say.

"I know it's scary," she said when he remained quiet, "but you have to ask yourself: Is she worth the possible rejection?"

"Yes." His answer came immediately. There was no question in his mind. The chance to be with Kit was worth possibly humiliating himself a thousand times.

"Then you have to ask."

"Okay." He took a deep breath and let it out slowly, but it didn't calm any of his raging nerves. "I'll ask her."

Leila let out a loud *whoop*. "I love this! Call me right after. If I don't get regular updates on this continuing saga, I might actually die of unsatisfied curiosity."

"You won't die."

"I might. You don't understand how invested I am already."

Although he snorted at her exaggeration, he also smiled a little. "I love you, too."

CHAPTER 13

It was stupid. There was little to no chance that Wes would be awake at this insane hour, much less wanting to talk to her, and the radio wasn't the place for their chats anyway. They'd just annoy the dispatcher again. Kit knew all of those things, yet she still couldn't sleep, her attention focused on the silent radio on her nightstand, even as she told herself she wasn't waiting for Wes to call out her unit number. She'd been like that for hours, jumping at every occasional transmission and random beep, but Wes hadn't said a word.

"Time to sleep," she told herself for the fiftieth time. The sound of her voice must've woken up Justice, because his snores stopped briefly before starting up again. It was a good thing she had the next day off work, since she was going to get about fifteen minutes of sleep if the rest of the night continued as the first half had.

"Wes to Kit on eighteen."

Despite the fact that she'd been secretly hoping for it, the sound of Wes's voice still surprised her. Her arm flailed out as she tried to grab the radio and sit up at the same time, and she knocked it off the nightstand. Cursing, she grabbed it off the floor and hoped that the fall hadn't damaged it. Everything looked intact, so she turned the channel to eighteen and tentatively pushed the mic button.

"Hey, Wes." She tried to make her voice sound casual, but her words came out annoyingly breathy. "Can't sleep again?"

"*I haven't tried yet.*"

With a frown, Kit checked the time, noting that it was close to two in the morning. He was definitely a night owl, then. "Working on an interesting project?" Although she didn't know for sure, he seemed like someone who'd always have something fascinating in the works. After all, she'd seen his tower room and all the gadgets inside.

He paused. "*That's one way to put it.*"

Okay. That's vague. Kit's ever-present curiosity flared to life. Before she could ask more about his mysterious project, though, she remembered what had happened the night before. "We should probably go before the dispatcher yells at us again."

"*It's fine.*" Wes didn't sound concerned. Then again, he wouldn't be the one who'd have to work with a dispatcher he'd pissed off. An angry dispatcher could make a cop's life miserable. "*Geoff's working tonight. He consistently naps between one and four thirty.*"

That seemed dangerous. "What if there's a call?"

"*The phone wakes him up, and everyone on night shift knows to speak loudly if they need to call in.*"

Kit filed away that new piece of town information. It stung a bit that even Wes, with his hermit-like tendencies, was more in the know than she was. "No wonder you're talking so softly."

"Not softly enough, bitches," said a crabby male voice. *"It's two in the morning. Hush up and go to bed."*

"Sorry!" Kit hoped that she wouldn't be put on nights for a while, at least until Geoff forgot that she'd been partially responsible for waking him up. "I'll see you later, Wes." Realizing that she had no idea when she would see him again, she wished that he had cell reception at the tower. He'd sent her the binocular photos of the town, so she had his email. It made her feel a little better to know that she had some way of communicating with him.

"Want to meet for breakfast tomorrow?" The words came out rushed, all jammed together like a verbal six-car pileup. It was strange to hear Wes sound flustered, when his usual way of speaking was so precise. When she finally figured out what he was trying to say, excitement shot through her. She hadn't felt so thrilled by a crush asking her out since…ever. *Get it together*, she told herself. *You're an adult who just got asked out by another adult. You're not in high school, and you weren't just invited to the prom.*

Her stern internal lecture didn't help. She was still giddy.

She realized that Wes—and probably Geoff now, too—was waiting for an answer. "Oh! Um…sure. That'd be nice." She made a face at the understatement. "What time? At the viner, I assume?" There didn't seem to be any other place to go out to eat in town.

"Yes, if by viner, you mean the VFW that is now being used as a diner?"

"I do. Viner is a little less wordy. It saves time that we could use for…other things." She closed her eyes at the unintended sexual innuendo. She knew that Geoff would be sharing every detail of the conversation with her new colleagues. *Wonderful*.

Wes must've pressed his mic too early, because his strangled cough came through clearly. *"Um...yes. Is six okay? That's when the diner opens."*

She cringed at the thought of getting up so early on her day off, especially since that was less than four hours of sleep away, but she figured she would be too excited to sleep in, anyway. "Six it is. See you tomorrow."

Geoff cleared his throat. *"Today."*

"See you later this morning," Wes said, back to his normal, calm manner. He didn't seem bothered that Geoff was eavesdropping openly as they planned their first date—if it was a date?

Placing the radio back on the nightstand, Kit flopped spread-eagle on the bed, grinning. It didn't matter if it was a date or not. For the next—she glanced at the clock—three hours and fifty-three minutes, she was going to assume it was a date and enjoy every moment of anticipation leading up to it.

Her hair was just as beautiful down as he'd imagined it would be. Wes shifted his weight and fought the urge to fidget with the salt and pepper shakers. He didn't know what to do with the excess energy that was coursing through him. He'd asked her on a date, and she'd agreed. Even though hours had passed and the date had begun, he still marveled at it. If it hadn't been horribly early, he would've called Leila to let her know it had worked. His bravery had been rewarded.

Seeing her was worth enduring the heavy weight of the other diners' stares and the buzz of their whispers. He normally did his best to avoid all the townspeople, but he'd ignore their avid interest for Kit's sake. It was difficult, though. Even the sleepy waitress gave him a curious, wide-eyed look when she stopped at their table to fill their coffee cups and chat lightly with Kit. After she walked away, Kit said quietly, "That's Jules. She and Theo are together."

He nodded. "You're good with people." She reminded him of Leila that way. Both women always seemed to say the right thing, even when they didn't know someone. "That must be useful when you're working."

She studied him with a slight smile that was kind, rather than mocking. "Thank you. I'm not always the most tactful, so I sometimes get myself into trouble that way. I do best with kids."

"I can see why. You're both very honest." His interactions with children had been minimal as an adult, but he remembered the sometimes brutal honesty of his peers from when he was a kid.

She laughed a little, and the sound warmed his insides. "'Honest' is the nice way of saying that we don't think before we speak sometimes."

"That can be good, though." He couldn't look away from her. From the sheen of her black satin hair to the way her green sweater followed her slight curves, she was riveting. He felt like he could stare at her for days and not get bored. "My sister, Leila, always tells me the truth, even when it's uncomfortable. That's so much easier than trying to figure out how people really feel when their words don't match their thoughts."

"If everyone were that honest, my job would be a lot easier."

"That's true." He watched as she picked up her coffee mug with both hands and took a sip. Her fingers were small and slender, with unpolished, short nails, and he marveled that she could use them to take down people twice her size. The mention of her job reminded him of something. "One of my neighbors stopped by the tower."

"Rufus?" she asked, setting down her coffee. He saw a muscle twitch in her cheek and felt a remembered jolt of fear at the thought of how close she'd been to losing her life.

"No. Murphy." She seemed to relax a little as she watched him, waiting patiently for him to continue talking. He loved how she wasn't in a rush. Her manner calmed him and made conversation, which was usually a minefield of missed cues and uncertainty, so much easier. "He spends a lot of time in the woods south of town. Trapping, mostly."

Wes paused, wondering if she would question him about Murphy's activities. He'd never actually caught his neighbor in the act, but Wes had found a few illegal leg-hold traps that he was pretty sure belonged to Murphy. He was still trying to figure out the best plan to convince Murphy to stop, since the traps were dangerous, as well as cruel. Kit didn't say anything, just kept her gaze on him, giving him her full attention.

"My neighbors don't trust law enforcement…or any government agency, really. In the last year, they've started to come to me with a few things. They know I work for the forest service, so I believe they consider me an intermediary, someone halfway between them and the government, if that makes sense?"

"It does." Her coffee forgotten, she stayed completely locked on him, and he felt the rush of that focused interest. "You're their backwoods ambassador."

His laugh was a surprise, even to him, more pleased than amused. It was such a pleasure to be understood. "Yes. Exactly. I pass on the information they give me to the right agency, and they can hold on to their anonymity."

"Win-win." Pushing her coffee mug aside, she laid her forearms on the table so she could lean even closer to him. "What did Murphy tell you?"

"Are you still working on the case of the house that burned down last Monday?" Even if she wasn't, he still planned to tell her the information he'd gotten from Murphy. If he was the backwoods ambassador, then she was the Wes ambassador. He was acquainted with the other cops, and he didn't have any problem with them since the crooked lieutenant had been arrested a few weeks ago, but he already trusted Kit. She might have been new to the area, but he had a gut-deep feeling that she wouldn't betray him.

"Yes."

Wes lowered his voice, even though the closest other diners were several tables away. "Murphy was checking his traps and saw someone leave that house minutes before it went up in flames."

"How close was he?" Kit had softened her voice to match his.

"Approximately fifteen feet from the edge of the house's backyard."

"Could he describe the person? Does he know them?"

Although the words were quiet, there was an urgency to them that made his blood run faster. It wasn't a bad feeling. Ever since he'd met Kit, he'd felt so much more alive.

"He said it was a stranger."

The sound of a harsh inhale a few feet from their table made Wes start. Turning his head, he saw a small, dark-haired woman in a diner uniform, two menus in her white-knuckled grip.

"Elena." Kit greeted the woman. Although her voice was cordial, there was the slightest of tensions there, telling Wes that she didn't trust this newcomer. "Are those menus for us?"

"Oh, yes." The woman seemed to snap out of her paralysis, and she offered them the laminated sheets. "Sorry. Jules is busy, so she asked if I'd run these out to you."

"Thank you," Kit said. There was a pause as Elena continued to hover, and Kit glanced at Wes, their eyes meeting ever so quickly. That brief look connected them and made him feel like they were a team. He wished Elena would leave so they could go back to their intense discussion where it felt like there were only two of them in the whole viner.

When she didn't move away, Kit said, "We'll probably need a minute before we order." She gave Elena a closed-lip smile, the one Wes recognized as her polite expression. "We're both new to the viner's offerings."

"Oh! Okay." A frustrated look passed over Elena's face—so quickly that Wes almost wasn't positive he'd really seen it—before the doe-eyed, terrified expression returned. He was fascinated by how she could switch masks so quickly. "Just let Jules know when you're ready to order."

"Will do," Kit said cheerily, her attention turning to the menu. Her body stayed alert, though, and Wes knew her focus was on Elena. After hovering for another few seconds, Elena darted back toward the kitchen, almost running into a sharp-faced woman in the doorway. The other woman barked out a "Hey!" as she recovered her balance. Wes couldn't hear Elena's response before she ducked into the kitchen. The other woman headed for the restroom.

Kit met Wes's eyes. There was that look again, the one that said they were a team. It was a thrilling feeling to be a part of something with Kit.

She waited several moments after Elena had disappeared into the kitchen before saying very quietly, "I don't trust her."

Wes thought that was wise. "She hides what she's really feeling."

"Yes!" Kit raised her hands as if in triumph. "Exactly. I'm also beginning to suspect that she's an instigator."

"In what way?"

"She knew some information about my past and lied about it." Her features hardened, a dramatic change from her usual soft expression when she looked at Wes. "She said that Hugh's girlfriend gossiped about me, but both Hugh and Grace—that's the girlfriend—denied knowing anything about it."

Wes considered her words carefully. Hearing about these types of interpersonal exchanges made him glad he spent most of his time at his tower alone. "Couldn't Hugh and Grace be the ones who lied?" After he asked it, he hoped Kit didn't think he was doubting her. It was just in his nature to question things.

"It's possible." She sounded thoughtful, rather than offended, and Wes's tension eased with relief. "My internal lie detector is usually pretty good, though, and it's telling me that Elena was the one not telling the truth." She made a wry grimace. "I might be biased, though, since something about her rubs me the wrong way."

"You shouldn't question your instincts," Wes said. Leila had repeated that over and over when he was a kid and had a hard time figuring out people's motivations. She'd always told him to trust his gut, that it would tell him whether someone was meaning to be kind or cruel. "With your job, I can see why you'd get good at knowing when someone wasn't being honest. You shouldn't disregard that."

Smiling slightly, she studied him. "Thank you, Wes. You give excellent advice."

He blinked, never expecting to be complimented on *that* particular skill. "You're welcome."

"Enough of my mini-dramas." She took another sip of coffee. "Tell me more about what your neighbor saw. Can he describe the person he saw leaving the house?"

"I don't see why he couldn't, since he was close enough to get a clear look."

Kit raised an eyebrow at him, looking slightly amused when he stared back, not sure what she was waiting for. "So, he didn't describe the person he saw?"

"No." Murphy had heard something and disappeared into the trees before Wes could get anything more out of him.

"What's his name and address?" She pulled a small notebook from her coat pocket. "I'll go interview him this afternoon."

At the thought of Murphy's reaction to a strange cop showing up at his house, Wes winced. "That probably won't work, especially since I don't know his address."

After eyeing him for a long moment, she dropped the notebook back in her pocket. "Is this neighbor one of the gun-toting, paranoid set?"

"No. Not of the group you met. He does like guns, and from what I've seen, he's probably suffering from paranoia."

"Great." Kit closed her eyes and let out a hard breath before reopening them. "So, he hasn't pointed a gun at me yet, but he probably will in the future?"

"If you continue to visit the area around the tower," he said, hoping she would indeed keep visiting him, "then yes. That's not an unlikely scenario."

Despite his words, she was smiling at him again. "I like how you talk."

The simple, straightforward compliment completely knocked the wind out of him. Before he could even start to think of how to respond, Wes raised his head, inhaling deeply. There was a smoke smell that didn't fit with the others in the viner—acrid and unfamiliar. "Something's burning."

Kit looked toward the kitchen. "Did someone neglect the toast?"

"No. It's not food." He inhaled again, but he still couldn't identify it. "It's—"

A low beeping from a fire alarm interrupted him, and thick, black smoke immediately started pouring out of the kitchen. The sharp-featured woman ran out of the restroom toward the kitchen door, and Wes stood, peripherally noticing that Kit got up at the same time.

"Don't go in there," Kit called across the diner, but the woman ignored her. As she pushed through the door, a billow of black smoke escaped into the dining area, and the cries of alarm turned into coughs. The waitress started hurrying toward the kitchen as well, but Kit stopped her. "Jules, get everyone outside and call Fire."

Jules, her face pale and anxious, switched directions and started herding customers toward the front entry. Wes stayed next to Kit, who moved quickly through the dining area to the kitchen door, pausing only to grab the fire extinguisher from its spot hanging on the wall. He entered the kitchen, his eyes instantly tearing from the smoke. It wasn't the pleasant burn of woodsmoke, but the chemical harshness of melting plastic. He paused, taking in the scene, but it was hard to see more than a few feet in the haze.

From the little he could see, the kitchen appeared to be empty, but that couldn't be true. They'd watched Elena and the other woman enter, so they had to be here somewhere. "Elena!" he called, and the smoke immediately scratched at his lungs, forcing him to cough. That just made it feel worse, though, so he stopped coughing and called again. "Anyone else in here! You need to get out now!"

Kit passed him, moving quickly. "Flames this way."

He followed, continuing to scan the space for the two women. The dark shapes of equipment and counters looked alien in the thick smoke, and his eyes watered, creating a distorting lens that made it even harder to see. The haze thickened as they got closer to the flames leaping against the back wall, growing even worse as Kit sprayed the fire with the fire-extinguisher foam.

A dark, human-sized form darted across the room. *There!* Wes moved toward it. "This way! Come this way, and we'll get you out!" Yelling tore at his lungs, and he started to cough again, feeling like every heave just pulled in more smoke. Wiping at his watering eyes, he peered through the gloom. The figure wasn't moving toward them, and Wes wondered if they were disoriented by the smoke or panicked. Pressing his arm against his nose and mouth to try to filter some of the smoke, he moved toward where he'd seen the movement. The haze was thicker, and his urge to cough was almost too strong to resist.

Squinting, he peered across through the smoky room, hoping that Kit was okay. He tried to reassure himself that she was trained to deal with emergencies like this, but he still wanted to get her to safety.

There! He saw someone in the gloom, just as the back door was yanked open.

Light flooded the room as the flames behind him leapt higher. He heard Kit curse, and he turned to check on her, his heart accelerating with concern. Seemingly unhurt, she was still working on putting out the flames, and she'd been joined by someone else with a second fire extinguisher.

"Help! Let me go! Someone, help!" A woman's screams made him whip around, just before the outside door slammed shut, cutting off the sunlight and her cries. Wes's brain tried to make sense of the situation. What'd just happened? Had someone just been dragged outside against their will?

"Kit!" he yelled, trying to be heard over the noise of the flames and the fire extinguishers and the shouts from

Vicki and Kit. He managed somehow, and Kit turned toward him. "It sounded like someone was dragged out through that door!" His voice was rough, but Kit seemed to have understood, immediately rushing toward him. "Through there," he said, the words rough from smoke inhalation as he pointed toward the back exit. She ran past him toward the door.

Wes followed Kit, catching up to her as she yanked open the door. The cold daylight flooded in, making his lungs and eyes sting even more, and he coughed and blinked, trying to clear his vision.

A loud *crack* split the air. Kit shoved Wes back into the viner, even before his brain identified the sound as a gunshot. Shocked by the familiar yet unexpected noise, he allowed her to push him back into the smoky haze, resisting the urge to protect her by putting his body between her and the shooter. The logical part of his brain reminded him that she was a cop and knew what she was doing, but the rest of him simply wanted to do whatever he needed to in order to keep her safe.

Bam! Bam! Bam! Another three loud shots were fired in quick succession. He crouched automatically, reaching out to tug Kit with him, but she was already down and was drawing her gun.

"Are you okay?" he rasped. "Are you hit?"

"Code four," she clipped, her attention locked on the alley behind the viner.

He tried to translate that, but his brain spun uselessly, not finding the answer he needed. "What?"

"Sorry." She gave him a quick glance over her shoulder before returning her focus to what was happening outside. "Cop speak. I'm fine. You?"

"I'm okay."

"Good." He couldn't miss the wealth of relief in her voice. Despite the bullets and the flood of adrenaline and the smoky confusion, her concern warmed him. She shifted forward, cautiously peering around the doorframe. Wes tensed, but the alley outside was silent. The shooter had stopped…for now. "I'm moving to the side of that Dumpster," she said, her words hushed but authoritative. "Wait here until I give you the all clear."

The urge to go with her, to protect her, filled him, but he shoved it down. He needed to help her by following her orders. If he let his instinct to keep her safe at all costs take over, he'd just get in her way—and that might get both of them killed. "Got it."

Tensed for another round of gunshots, he held his breath as she darted into the alley, her gun at the ready. All of the sounds around him—the still-crackling flames, the swearing of the woman trying to put out the fire, the hiss of the fire extinguisher—were drowned out by his heart beating in his ears. Every one of his muscles was clenched with fear as he watched Kit speed across the alley. She was only exposed for seconds, but it felt like an eternity. One shot could've taken her out, and he could do nothing to stop it.

Kit dove behind the green metal bin, and Wes let out a hard breath. Now that she was somewhat protected from the shooter, he relaxed slightly and shifted into the doorway to get a better view.

She checked the area and then darted down the alley, staying to one side, close to the buildings. Wes chased after her, his gaze moving from side to side, trying to check all the possible sniper locations at once. He hated that Kit was so exposed, that the shooter could be anywhere—right around the corner, hiding in the doorway, ready to take aim at her as soon as she ran by.

Turning her head, Kit shouted, "Grab Justice out of my SUV!"

He hated to leave her, but he knew she needed her K9 partner. Turning, he ran around the side of the VFW, his boots sinking into the snow with every step and slowing him down. There weren't any tracks, but he was still tense, waiting for another round of gunfire to cut him down. In a way, it would've been a relief, since that would mean the gunman wasn't about to ambush Kit in the alley.

As he reached the lot, he scanned the vehicles, finding three SUVs. Even if he hadn't recognized her SUV from the first time they'd met, the bloodhound in the back seat would've told him which one was hers.

He rushed to it, opening the door and expecting Justice to surge out, but the bloodhound stayed in the SUV, his entire body wiggling with excitement. Relieved to see that the dog was already wearing a protective vest, Wes looked for a leash but didn't see one. He stepped back to give Justice an opening. When the hound just danced in place, Wes figured he was waiting for a command.

"Out!" he tried. "Down!" Justice lay down, his big paws stretched in front of him. That wasn't the one. Wes tried to think of other possible commands. "Off! Here!" He racked his brain for other words that made sense, but nothing was coming to him. "Okay…"

Justice leapt off the seat, almost knocking Wes over on his way out of the SUV. Once down, he jumped and played, his directionless excitement leading him to run a few feet away and then spin to rush back to Wes.

Slamming the door closed, Wes ran toward the side of the VFW again, Justice following. The fire engine pulled into the lot, and he turned to see some cops rushing out of the station and across the street. "Fire's by the back wall in the kitchen," he called out to Theo, the closest cop. "One person's still putting it out. Someone dragged a woman out of the kitchen and shot at us. Kit's chasing them west down the alley."

As Wes ran toward the back of the viner, he heard Theo shouting, repeating the information that Wes had just shared with him. The dog sped up, running in front of him, giving him occasional backward looks as if he wasn't sure where he was supposed to go. His ears were pinned back, and his tail was tucked, telling Wes that his playfulness was switching to anxiety. Wes felt guilty and scared for Kit, but he didn't know how to get Justice to track her and the shooter. For Pete's sake, he didn't even know the command to get Justice out of the car.

Frustration filled him, battling with his fear for Kit's safety, and he fisted his hands at his sides. He needed to do this, to calm down and communicate with Justice. *Think of it as a puzzle*, he told himself. *It's dog training, after all. If Justice understands, then surely I can figure it out.*

"We can do this," he said, and the dog crouched a little at his harsh tone. Wes cringed and made an effort to soften his voice. "Sorry, Justice. Help me out here. I need you to follow Kit."

Justice perked up, his head cocking to the side and his tail waving tentatively.

"Kit? Is that a word you know?"

His tail whipped back and forth in what Wes was pretty sure was an affirmative answer.

"Look for Kit!" Justice just stared at him, so Wes tried another possibility. "Search for Kit! No? Track Kit!" There was still no response except for enthusiastic tail wagging every time he said Kit's name, and Wes felt frustration building up again. He shoved it back, knowing that he couldn't let it creep into his voice and scare Justice again. "Follow Kit! Find Kit!"

That got a reaction.

The bloodhound immediately lowered his head and made ever-widening circles, so focused that Wes felt hope rise in him. Letting out a loud bark, Justice started running down the alley in the direction Kit had gone.

"Good dog! Good boy, Justice! Let's find Kit!" Letting out excited bays, the dog quickly outpaced Wes, turning south between two buildings. When Wes reached the spot where Justice had changed direction, the bloodhound was long gone, and Wes had to switch to following the boot and paw prints in the snow.

His heart was pounding heavily in his chest, but it was more with adrenaline and anxiety for Kit's safety than from exertion. Breathing was hard, thanks to the smoke, and he struggled not to cough, knowing that it would just slow him down. He heard pounding footsteps behind him and looked over his shoulder to see that Theo was following him. As Wes faced front again, two gunshots rang out, followed quickly by a third. *Kit!* Heart in his throat, Wes ran faster, barely preventing himself from calling to her. He didn't want to distract her if she was fighting for her life.

The tracks turned again, disappearing behind a

detached garage, and Wes tore toward the structure, dreading what he might find behind it. After the gunshots, he braced himself for the worst. What if he was too late to save Kit? His heart thumping painfully against his ribs, his imagination painted horrible scenarios in his head as he rounded the corner.

Taking in the scene, Wes dragged in a deep breath and immediately started coughing. When he came into sight, Kit spun to face him, putting her body between him and a crying Elena. Recognition and relief passed over her face, and she turned back toward the other woman. Justice was bouncing in excited circles, returning to attempt to lick everyone's face. Elena cried harder as she pushed the dog away with black-smudged fingers. Wes approached with Theo close behind, and Kit took a step back, hauling the dog with her by his harness.

"Sit, Justice," she said before turning to Theo. "Can you call in a BOLO for a white sedan? Elena said the plates were covered with snow and unreadable. She thinks it turned east on Main, but she's not certain. There're at least two people in the vehicle, the driver and the man who tried to abduct Elena. She couldn't give a good description, except that he was male, tall, and strong, and he was wearing dark-colored pants, coat, and a ski mask."

Theo repeated the information into his radio as she turned back to Elena. "Are you hurt?" Kit asked gently. "Theo can call for an ambulance if you need one."

"No," Elena said between shuddery breaths, "no ambulance."

"Okay. Can you stand?" Kit asked as Wes moved to take Justice's harness. She gave him a smile of thanks before returning her attention to helping Elena up.

"Do you have any idea why he tried to kidnap you?" Theo asked, stepping closer. With renewed sobs, Elena threw herself against Theo's chest, burying her face in the front of his coat. Wearing a startled expression, Theo held out his hands as if he had a gun pointed at him. Wes took an automatic step back, tugging Justice with him. He was very glad that Elena hadn't chosen to throw herself at him.

As Elena clutched Theo's coat, Wes noticed the black smudges on Elena's right fingers again. "What's that on your hand?" he asked. Kit moved closer to look, but Elena yanked her hand back, tucking it between her chest and Theo's.

"Probably soot from the fire," Theo said, trying to step back to get a better look. Elena's hands fisted in his coat, making it impossible for him to budge. Wes made a skeptical sound. The black marks had looked more like gunpowder than soot. He eyed a still-sobbing Elena, wondering if she'd been the one who'd shot at them. Anger gripped him at the thought of Kit getting hurt, and he clenched his teeth to keep himself from accusing her. He'd mention it to Kit, but he knew she'd already seen it. She wasn't stupid. She'd know what it was and quickly reach the same conclusion that Wes had. He looked at her, at the way her narrowed gaze took in Elena and the scene around them, and he knew Kit was already there—and probably a few steps ahead of him.

But if it was true, why would Elena go through such trouble to stage her own fake kidnapping?

"We should get a couple people to tape this area off, as well as the alley right behind the viner," Kit said, her gaze cool and thoughtful as it rested on Elena. "Did you see if the man who grabbed you tossed the gun or kept it on him?"

Wes saw the tiniest jerk of Elena's shoulders at the question. "Nooo," she said between hiccupping breaths, drawing out the word uncertainly. "I don't think so." She sniffed and released Theo to blot at her face with her sleeve. "It's cold out here. Can we go back to the viner?"

"Okay," Kit said, raking the area with her gaze a final time. "Let's head to the station. We can talk in the warmth there."

CHAPTER 14

AFTER LISTENING TO HER STORY FOR THE SECOND TIME, KIT left Theo with a still-sniffling Elena and headed for the viner. She'd vainly attempted to convince Theo that they should do a gunshot residue test on Elena's fingers, but he'd shot her down, saying that the tests were too expensive to waste when the marks were most likely just soot. She'd been in a fire, after all, and had similar smudges on her face. Kit had pushed it until he'd firmly suggested she check in with Hugh at the viner.

Wes was still sitting in the back seat of her SUV, sweetly petting an ecstatic Justice, and she gave him a wave as she passed. The sight of the two of them together eased some of her lingering angry tension. She was impressed by how calm Wes had been, how he'd been just as willing as she was to run toward danger. Almost as remarkable was how well Justice responded to him. Normally, her dog obeyed only her commands, and that was after a long, intense year of training. Today, however, Justice had listened to Wes, and Kit loved that. Secretly, she liked to think that it meant that her dog approved of Wes.

She ducked under the police tape and entered through the front door of the VFW, skirting around the enormous fans the fire department had used to clear the smoke from the building.

The dining area looked normal, with only a hint of smoke. The walls of the kitchen were darkened from soot, and the burned back wall was a mess, but the room was surprisingly undamaged. A tall woman with a sharp-edged face was scrubbing off one of the workstations, ignoring the milling cops, firefighters, and EMTs. Kit headed her way.

"Hello," Kit said in her most calming tone as the woman's dark gaze threatened to pull out all of her internal organs and tie them into a slippery knot. "I'm Officer Kit Jernigan."

The woman laughed, a dry bark of a sound that was as far from amused as you could get. "Great. Another one."

With some effort, Kit ignored the sarcastic comment and held her smile. "What's your name?"

"Vicki Burt."

The name was familiar, and Kit remembered hearing stories about Vicki and how her love of practical jokes bordered on the sadistic. "Can you tell me what happened?" Kit always liked to leave her questions open-ended. She found that witnesses—and suspects—shared more information that way.

Vicki shot a glare at the crowd of first responders milling around the kitchen. "I can't, but I'd bet you a gazillion bucks that Elena could tell you *exactly* what happened." After scrubbing the counter viciously for almost a full minute, Vicki finally spoke again. "I suppose you think she's all pixie dust and angel sneezes, too," she muttered.

"Not really," Kit said quietly. Normally, she wouldn't have said anything about her suspicions, but she really wanted to find out what Vicki knew. She had a feeling that the cook wouldn't respond well to heavy-handed orders, so Kit decided to try to bond with her instead. "I actually find her to be a bit of an instigator."

The scrub brush paused. "Instigator?"

Lowering her voice even more, Kit said, "Shit stirrer."

This time, Vicki's bark of laughter seemed more genuine. Kit noticed Hugh glance over at the sound, but she ignored the other cop. If she started second-guessing her technique mid-interview, it wouldn't do Kit or the investigation any good. Vicki started scrubbing again, more gently this time. "That is exactly what she is." She pointed the brush at Kit. "You nailed her perfectly."

"What do you think happened?" Kit asked again.

Vicki glanced over at the other first responders again, but this time the look was more furtive than furious. "That little bitch caused this. I know it."

Holding back the torrent of questions that wanted to pour out, Kit waited for Vicki to elaborate.

"Megan thinks she's great," Vicki continued in a low voice. "Jules is all protective of her. But neither of them see that it's just an act. I know what scared looks like. Hell, Jules was scared when she first started here, but that Elena isn't scared. She's tricky, but she's not scared." After rinsing off the scrub brush, she shook it at Kit as if to emphasize her point. "Normally, I don't mind tricky. I can even respect bitchy. That whimpering victim crap, though… I don't have any patience for that. If you're going to be a vicious bitch, then you own it. Not her, though. She's owning nothing." Vicky raised the brush and brought it down hard on the counter before starting to scrub again.

"What makes you think she caused the fire?"

"From what I heard, she's trying to say that some stranger in a ski mask came through the back door while I was in the bathroom—trying to clean off the honey *she'd* 'accidentally' dumped on me. This random pyro started the fire, dragged her out, threatened her with a gun, and tried to stuff her in a car. Supposedly, she was barely able to escape." Vicki smirked.

"You don't believe that?" Kit asked, attempting to keep her voice neutral. She definitely thought something felt off, but she was a cop. Extreme suspicion was her thing.

As if she could read minds, Vicki gave her a flat look. "Do *you* think she's telling the truth?"

"I don't have enough information to make a decision yet."

Vicki made a *humph* sound. "I don't need more information. My gut tells me there's something off about that woman."

"How is Elena involved, do you think?" Kit asked. She had her own theory, but Vicki was proving to be a font of information so far.

"I think she set that fire and faked the kidnapping for attention." Vicki answered quickly enough that Kit was pretty sure she'd already been considering the question. "Or maybe she wanted to get rid of something in that fire."

"Get rid of something? Like you?" The question popped out before Kit could think about it, and she hid her wince. What a thing to ask. It was as if Vicki's bald frankness drew the same quality out of Kit.

After a startled beat of silence, Vicki tipped her head back and roared with laughter, drawing the other cops' attention again. When she'd finally recovered enough to speak, Vicki reached out with her non-brush-wielding hand and slapped Kit on the shoulder. "You're okay, new cop. In fact, you're the best one out of all those other donkeys." She tilted her head toward the other officers.

"Vicki! How could you say something so mean?" Hugh asked as he joined them. "I thought I was your favorite!"

Kit swallowed a curse. She'd just established a rapport with Vicki, and Hugh had interrupted before Kit could get any valuable information from the cook. Although Kit tried to catch his eye and send him a silent *go away* message, Hugh was focused on Vicki and missed all of Kit's nonverbal hints.

"So, Vicki," he said as Kit resisted the urge to elbow him for hijacking her interview—an interview that had just been getting interesting. "Tell me what happened."

Vicki's expression returned to its previous sour lines. "Why bother? Hasn't the princess given you guys the story already?"

His eyebrows shot up, and he finally glanced at Kit. It was too late to resuscitate the connection she'd formed with Vicki now that Hugh had stuck his big head in it, so she just gave him a flat look as she leaned against the counter. "You sound like you don't care much for Elena," he said, turning back toward Vicki.

Her laugh was that humorless crack again. "How'd you guess?"

After studying her for a few moments, he waved his hand. "I still want to know your version of what happened."

As Vicki started scrubbing again, Kit shifted a little farther away. Judging by the speed and ferocity of Vicki's movements, Hugh was already managing to seriously piss her off. "Well, my *version* of what happened is that it was an inside job, no matter what little Princess Firebug says."

Hugh straightened, interest clear in every line of his body. It reminded Kit of Justice when he caught a fascinating scent. "Princess Firebug? Are you saying that you saw Elena start the fire?"

"I was in the bathroom, so I didn't *see* it, but I know it was her."

Some of the sharp interest in Hugh's gaze faded. "What makes you suspect her?"

"Seriously, Hugh?" The scrub brush clattered to the counter as Vicki dropped it so she could turn to face him, her hands fisting on her hips. "A *masked* man broke in during the three minutes I was in the bathroom, started a fire, and dragged Elena out? Three minutes, Hugh. I left the princess in the kitchen, and when I came back, there was a fire that she didn't even try to put out. Kit and *I* grabbed the fire extinguishers. Kit and *I* put out the fire. *She* just cried big, fat crocodile tears as she supposedly got dragged down the alley."

Although he regarded her thoughtfully, Hugh didn't look convinced. "That's a little harsh, Vicki. Not everyone is good in a crisis."

"You think that's harsh?" Vicki growled. "That's nothing compared to what I would've done if this place burned down and I had to set up *another* kitchen. I just did that a few months ago after that first crazy bitch blew up the diner, and I'm not doing it again."

"Vicki," Kit said quietly, knowing she needed to intervene before there was an assault. "Let's go up front to talk."

"No." Despite her answer, Vicki sounded a little calmer. "I'm done talking to you guys. You're not listening to a thing I'm saying, anyway." Pivoting around, she headed for the next counter.

Kit gave Hugh a speaking look.

"C'mon," he said, either ignoring her silent reprimand or completely missing it. "Let's see if County or State has spotted the car."

In her gut, Kit knew that Vicki was right—something strange was going on, and it revolved around Elena. Still, she followed Hugh. If she tried to fit the evidence to her theory, rather than letting the facts lead her to the answers, she wouldn't be a very good cop. Folding up her irritation, she tucked it into a drawer in her mind so she could pull it out later, once there weren't so many possible eavesdroppers.

Strange things were happening in her new town, and she was determined to find out the truth.

Alex scrubbed her hands fiercely, angry with herself. If Theo had listened to Kit and done that gunshot residue test, Alex would've been caught. She knew better than to shoot a gun without gloves on. She blamed it on her impromptu pseudo-kidnapping and not having time to plan out all the details. When she'd overheard the weird tower lookout telling Kit that someone had witnessed her leaving the house she'd burned, she'd panicked.

Stupid, she mentally berated herself. Impulsive decisions were never a good idea. It was done, though. The only thing she could do was move forward. Taking a deep breath, she let it out slowly as she dried her hands. Her thoughts calmed, falling back into their usual logical order.

One thing was very clear. Kit was a problem. Killing her would be difficult, since she was trained to defend herself and already distrusted Alex. She'd need to up her efforts to discredit Kit. Since she was closer to Jules and Grace than with the other cops, she'd start there.

The bathroom door opened, jerking her out of her thoughts, and she had to quickly mask her flash of annoyance at the sight of Sam.

"S-sorry," he muttered, turning to leave when he saw her.

"Wait!" Her mind was working, processing what she knew about Sam, about everything his stepmother, Courtney, had done to him, and about how protective Jules was of her brother. Alex wondered if there was a way to use that information to fix her Kit problem. Courtney, that idiot, had told her every terrible thing she'd done to those kids after Alex had lied and said that private investigator/client privilege was a thing, and that everything shared with Alex would be confidential. She'd learned a lot of useful information from Courtney. It'd been worth killing off the previous PI to get that job.

She gave Sam her sweetest smile, even as he eyed her with his usual suspicion. "I'm done in here. It's all yours."

Slipping past him, she made her way down the hall toward her room, feeling much more cheerful than she had a few minutes earlier. A solid plan always made her feel better.

CHAPTER 15

I<small>T</small>'D BEEN ANOTHER ROUGH WORKWEEK, BUT K<small>IT</small> HAD survived, and she was determined to enjoy her day off. If she had her way, it would be free of other cops—especially secretive, suspicious ones—and full of her favorite things: dogs, kids, and sleep. *And Wes*, her mind added, and the butterflies in her stomach fluttered around in agreement.

"Here it is," she said to Justice, turning at the cockeyed mailbox. Both times she'd been here—after her dog had led them to Jules's house twice—they'd been leaving, rather than arriving, but she recognized the driveway instantly. It was little more than a two-track path that led her through the woods, the trees close enough to run scratchy branches over the sides of her SUV. The thick evergreens blocked out the early-afternoon sun, turning the twisting, narrow driveway into a gloomy tunnel.

"There can't be two driveways this claustrophobic," she muttered as she came around yet another turn and saw the path continued even farther into the trees. "This must be the one they use in every single horror movie." It seemed to take forever, but she finally rounded the last curve. The trees thinned and the yard opened up, revealing the huge, dilapidated wreck of a house.

Pulling up in front of the house, she parked and got

out as Sam and the three kids she recognized from the
diner as his siblings piled onto the porch. Jules was the
last out of the door, but she quickly took the lead down
the steps toward Kit. Although she gave a welcoming
smile, Jules's expression was unusually guarded.

"Hey, Jules," Kit said, smiling wider to try to break
the strange awkwardness. "Thank you for letting me
borrow Sam. I've been hoping to start Justice's off-leash
training for a while, but it requires a competent helper,
and not that many people have the patience to work with
bloodhounds."

Jules looked a little startled before her expression
eased and her smile became more genuine. Kit opened
the back door of the SUV, letting Justice hop out,
although she kept him next to her.

"Is it okay if Justice says hi to the kids?" she asked,
feeling him quiver with anticipation under her restraining hand. "He's very friendly."

"Of course," Jules said. "Everyone here loves dogs."
She gave the youngest a glance. "Some more than
others, right, Dee?"

The little girl didn't seem to have heard the question.
She was too busy staring at Justice with longing eyes.
"Oh, he's beautiful. Can I pet him? Please?"

"If you do, he'll be your lifelong friend," Kit said,
smiling as she released Justice. Immediately, he
bounded straight for the kids, nearly bowling Dee over
in his enthusiasm. The little girl didn't seem to mind.
As the kids, including Sam, swarmed around the dog,
who basked in the attention, Kit made her way closer to
Jules. "I really do appreciate you letting Sam help me
with training."

Jules eyed her searchingly before her smile returned—as did her caution. "He's very excited about learning to train Fifi, the rescue bloodhound. Theo's been trying to help, but…" She spread her hands out in an exaggerated shrug, making Kit laugh.

"It's like I told Sam," Kit said. "Training a bloodhound is a…unique experience, requiring a lot of patience." They both watched the kids fawn over Justice for a few seconds. "It also requires a high tolerance for drool."

That made Jules laugh, and her shoulders dropped slightly, making Kit realize how tightly the woman had been holding herself. "Will you be at Nan's?"

"We'll pick up the dog Sam's working with there, but I was thinking we'd go a few more miles north, get a little farther into the mountains where there are fewer dogs and people to act as distractions."

Jules's tension returned. "A few miles north? Where will y'all be exactly?"

Hiding a small flash of embarrassment, Kit concentrated on keeping her voice even. "I was thinking the fire lookout tower, if Wes doesn't mind."

"Wes?"

"Wesley March, the forest service fire lookout," Kit explained, feeling a warm glow in her belly as she thought about him, even as she mentally laughed at her silliness. She was a grown woman, a cop, and she still found herself wanting to grin dopily when she said his name. "He was the big, bearded guy sitting with me at the diner."

"Excuse me a second," Jules said, taking a few steps away as she pulled out her phone. She tapped a message on the screen, and Sam took a step closer to Kit. His face looked a little flushed.

"Sorry," he said quietly. "She's p-prot-t-tective."

"Understandable." She gave him a smile. "That's what big sisters do. I have a little sister, so I know all about it."

Despite her words, he glanced away, looking uncomfortable.

"Question for you," she said, drawing his gaze back to her.

Instantly, a shield dropped down, hiding Sam's expression. "Wh-what?"

"The dog you're working with… Is her name really Fifi?"

A quick flash of relief crossed his face before he answered. What horrible question had he expected her to ask? "Y-yes. Unf-fortunately."

She groaned dramatically, covering her face with her hands.

"I like the name Fifi," Dee protested, and one of the twins made a fake gagging sound.

Kit scrunched up her face in an exaggerated way to make Dee laugh. "For a tiny toy poodle, maybe, but a bloodhound?" Crouching down next to Justice, she cupped his head in her hands and squished the loose skin forward, so he was all wrinkles and floppy ears and jowls. He groaned with pleasure. Having the attention of multiple kids was heaven for Justice. Kit tipped the dog's head toward Dee. "Does a face like this say Fifi to you?"

Dee and the twins started laughing. With a final rumple of his ears, Kit released Justice, who immediately rolled over onto his back, angling for belly scratches. The three younger kids complied, and Kit sent Sam an amused grimace.

"I don't know how we're going to get him to leave."

Dee looked up eagerly. "He can stay here with us."

"Nope." Jules must have finished texting, because she pocketed her phone. "Theo said Wes is a stand-up guy—despite his...uniqueness—so we're going to go take care of the cat you're pet-sitting, and Justice needs to go with Kit and Sam so he can learn new things. Ty and Tio, you'll be coming with us."

"Can't we go with Sam?" Ty asked. "Dog training sounds more interesting than watching Dee clean a litter box."

Jules looked worried. "With everything that's happening, I'd rather have you where I can keep an eye on you."

"We'll be with a police officer, Sam, and two large dogs, so we should be just as safe as we would be with you," Tio reasoned. "Plus, you just said that Theo approved of Wes."

"Please?" Ty gave his sister a pleading look.

After a few moments, Jules gave a reluctant nod. "Okay. You can go with Kit and Sam...if that's okay with you?" She turned toward Kit.

"Of course. The more helpers we have, the easier training goes." The twins looked to be in their early teens, so they were old enough to assist, rather than have to be babysat.

"Okay, y'all. Be aware of your surroundings, and let me or Theo know if anything—anything at all—seems wrong." Jules gave each of her brothers a telling look, and Kit wondered what wasn't being said. Although she fully understood why Jules had been nervous after the body was found in the burned house, plus the strange fire and kidnapping attempt at the viner, Jules's reaction seemed slightly off. Kit studied Jules, trying to work out what she wasn't saying. This odd little family was a mystery.

"I wish I could help train the dogs," Dee said a little sadly, breaking the strange tension.

Jules gave a small laugh, gently bumping her sister with her hip. "You have an embarrassment of riches." When Dee just looked at her, puzzled, Jules explained. "Too many animals to pet, not enough time."

Dee's face lit up. "That's the way I like it."

Kit chuckled. The little girl reminded her of herself. When she was growing up, she couldn't get enough of animals, either. "Do you have any pets?"

"A cat, Turtle."

"Turtle?" Kit repeated, amused.

Jules gave an exaggerated *what-could-I-do* shrug. "It was the only name everyone agreed on."

"I like it." Kit grinned at Dee. "It's unique. I bet there aren't too many other cats in the world named Turtle."

Dee's return smile was huge. "I—"

"Kit!" Elena interrupted, stepping out onto the front porch. "What are you doing here?"

"Elena. Hi." Although Kit tried to infuse her voice with enthusiasm, it came out flat as all her questions about what had happened a week ago flared to life again. Kit sharply reined in her suspicions, reminding herself that, as far as she knew at this point, Elena had been the victim. "How are you feeling? Are your lungs still bothering you?"

"Better, thank you."

"I can't believe something like that would happen at the viner," Jules said, sympathy thick in her voice. "I'm so glad no one was seriously hurt."

I can't believe something like that would happen, either, Kit thought wryly before she caught herself. *Remember,* she scolded herself, *she's a victim until proven otherwise.*

"We're going to train dogs," Ty told Elena eagerly. "Do you want to come?" Sam stiffened, sending his brother a sharp glare.

Before she could answer, Kit interjected, "I'm so sorry, Elena, but there's no more room. Justice would have to sit on your lap, and he weighs almost as much as you do."

Elena ducked her head, and Kit felt a flash of guilt, despite knowing Sam would not feel comfortable if Elena came along. Ty's disappointed expression didn't help. Kit hated mean-girl behavior, and it bothered her that she was acting that way, but her need to protect Sam outweighed Elena's hurt feelings…or her desire to keep a close eye on the other woman.

"Ready?" she asked with a glance at Sam, pushing away her uncomfortable feelings. He looked relieved, which made her feel better about not allowing Elena to tag along. Sam tipped his chin down slightly in a nod. "Let's go."

As the boys and Justice headed for her SUV, Kit turned back to Jules, who still looked nervous as she watched her brothers. "We shouldn't be more than a couple of hours," Kit said, wanting to reassure her. "Bloodhounds tend to have short attention spans."

Jules smiled, but it still looked strained. "Thank you. Theo agreed that it'll be fine, but everything that's happened makes me worry."

"Understandable. I promise to watch out for them."

With a wave to Dee and Elena, Kit headed toward her driver's side door. The twins were in the back, with Justice between them, and Sam was up front in the passenger seat. Jules watched as Kit started the car and began the slow, bumpy trip down the driveway. A glance in the rearview mirror showed that Elena was heading back into the house, but Jules was still standing where they'd left her, Dee leaning against her side.

"Sorry," Sam muttered, his eyes fixed on the side-view mirror, even after they went around the curve and his house disappeared from sight.

"I get it. Like I said, it's a big-sister thing." Although she kept her voice light, her brain was trying to work out the puzzle of what had just happened. Seeing Jules act so worried bothered her. Despite not knowing Kit very well, Jules was aware that she was a cop and worked with Jules's very protective boyfriend. Why was she so concerned about Sam training with her? And why didn't she want to send the twins along? Kit gave the two boys in the back seat a quick glance in the mirror, checking to make sure that their seat belts were buckled. The twins were both strapped in and petting a blissful Justice.

Tucking the questions away until later, she glanced at Sam. "I've only been to the kennel once, and Hugh was driving. Would you mind letting me know when a turn is coming up?" She had a good sense of direction and was sure she'd be able to make it to Nan's on her own, but she wanted to get Sam talking.

"Y-yes."

They reached the end of the driveway, and the trees opened up, allowing the sunshine to hit the SUV. It wasn't until Kit found her shoulders lowering that she realized her muscles had been clenched. The dark, claustrophobic feel of the driveway made her uncomfortable.

"Left," Sam said. Once she'd turned onto the quiet road, she gave the twins another glance in the mirror.

"You two will probably need to correct me on your names a few times." She made an apologetic face. "Ty, you're on the right, and Tio's on the left, right? I mean, correct?" The twins looked almost exactly alike, although Tio was a little slighter and his expressions tended to be less animated and more guarded.

A wicked smile started to stretch across Ty's face, but Sam jumped in, giving his younger brother a stern look. "C-c-correct."

Kit lifted an eyebrow at Ty. "You were just going to mess with me, weren't you?"

"Maybe." Ty shrugged, not looking at all put out that his plan had been foiled. "Everyone in town and at school knows us now, so we can't play that trick much anymore."

"That's too bad," Kit said in a dry voice, exchanging a look with Sam. The moment of shared amusement only lasted a second before his face tightened and he turned toward the window again.

For the rest of the ride to Nan's, Sam stayed quiet, except to give occasional directions. The twins made up for their brother's silence, however. By the time she pulled into the kennel's small, snow-packed parking area, Kit had learned that they ran a shady-sounding "security" business at their school. Tio had also been perfecting a touch-activated Swiss Army knife, but Jules had vetoed that project, thanks to the knife's switchblade-like qualities. Kit felt that probably had been a wise move on

Jules's part. The twins weren't too crushed, since they'd returned to building a miniature drone.

"Impressive. Why miniature?" she asked, reaching for the door handle.

"So that we don't have to register it with the government," Ty said blithely, and the boys and Justice hopped out of the car.

Kit huffed a laugh as she climbed out. It sounded like the twins were too smart for their—and everyone else's—own good. Still smiling, she glanced around the kennel. It consisted of several buildings and multiple fenced areas where a variety of dog breeds eyed them with interest, barking to announce their arrival. Before Justice could go investigate, Kit called him over so she could leash him.

"You must be Officer Jernigan." A tall woman with a graying ponytail poking out from under her stocking cap was striding toward them. "The brave soul who's going to help Sam teach Fifi to track. I'm Nan."

"Call me Kit," she said, smiling as she shook Nan's hand. "I've trained one bloodhound and managed to survive, so I figured another wouldn't kill me."

Nan looked doubtful. "You're braver than I am. Hi, Sam, Ty, and Tio. Sam, Fifi's in the southeast yard. Are you going to work with her here?"

"N-no," Sam said. "W-we're g-g-going t-to the f-fire look-k-out t-t-tower. K-Kit said it'll b-be q-q-quieter there."

"Sayer Tower?" Nan's eyebrows disappeared under her hat. "Is the lookout okay with that?"

Kit hid the now-familiar mix of embarrassment and exhilaration at the mention of Wes. "I'm going to check with him first. If he has a problem with it, we'll find somewhere else."

"Huh." Nan looked doubtful.

"Do you think he'll not want us there?" Kit asked, starting to wonder if visiting the tower unannounced was a good idea. Wes seemed to value his privacy, and they'd only been on half of an official date. It was a little early to be popping in without an invitation or any prior warning.

"No idea," Nan said bluntly. "The lookout is a strange one, though, just to warn you. He only comes to town when he has to, and even then it's only in the very early morning when not many people are around. Fire season's over, but he stays in that cabin through the winter, all by himself."

"That d-doesn't sound so b-b-bad," Sam said, and Kit grinned at him.

"Not when you're living with six other people, huh?" she asked, and he made a wry face before catching himself and looking away. Kit turned back to Nan. "Any reason I should avoid him, or is he just antisocial?" She felt like she was betraying Wes just by asking, but she was curious why the whole town was so fascinated by him, even as they kept their distance. He'd never been anything but sweet to her, so the locals' attitude was baffling. No matter what the townspeople's reasoning was, it wouldn't affect how she viewed Wes. She liked him, and no one else's opinion would change that.

Nan gave a small shrug. "I don't know enough about him to answer that. There aren't any dead wives in his back shed…none that I know about, at least."

Kit blinked. "That's…uh, good, I suppose." Glancing at the twins, she saw their rapt interest and cleared her throat. "Anyway, we won't be too long, no matter where we end up doing the training."

"Thank you for doing this," Nan said, going along with the change of subject without hesitation. "It'll be hard to find a new home for her as she is right now. If she learns how to track, though, there are a number of search-and-rescue teams and law enforcement agencies that would be interested in adopting her. You're doing a good thing, Sam."

He flushed, ducking his head. "W-we sh-sh-should g-go." He hurried away, flustered, and Kit followed after giving Nan a final smile and wave. She caught up with Sam and walked next to him on the packed-down snow, giving Justice enough slack so he could happily plunge through the deeper snow at the side of the path. The twins stayed by the parking area, tossing snowballs at each other.

Kit glanced back to see Ty throw a snowball that immediately dissolved into powder. "The snow here is useless for snowball making."

"Th-that's a g-good thing wh-when the twins are around," Sam said, making her laugh. As they passed the exercise yards, small groups of dogs jumped onto the fence, excited to see them. Sam quietly greeted each one by name as Kit observed, liking the way he was calm around them. With people, he seemed to be tense and stressed, but he appeared to relax around the dogs. He barely stuttered when talking to them. She was relieved to see it. If Fifi was even half as sensitive to tension as Justice was, then having a tightly strung handler would've been a challenge.

They reached the last gate, and a bloodhound came

galumphing toward Sam until she spotted Kit. Coming to a screeching halt, she dropped her tail and head.

"A little shy with strangers?" Kit asked, keeping her voice low and soothing.

"Yeah." Sam slipped into the yard, and Fifi hurried over to him, still slightly crouched. She wrapped herself around him, her tail thumping against his leg. "She g-gets over it p-pretty f-fast, though."

As if she understood him and wanted to prove him right, Fifi cautiously approached the gate, eyeing Kit and her dog. Fifi snuffled at him through the chain link, and Justice practically turned inside out with excitement at meeting a new dog, enthusiastically licking whatever part of her he could reach. Forgetting about Kit's newness, Fifi started wagging her entire hind end as she play-bowed.

"Think she's ready for us to join her?" Kit asked Sam.

He looked surprised—and pleased—that she'd asked. "Y-yes."

Kit unlatched Justice's lead and let him into the yard. The two dogs immediately began romping. When Justice tripped over his own big feet and went face-first into the powdery snow, even Sam let out a rusty laugh. Kit hid her surprise at the sound, carefully keeping her gaze on Justice as he shook off the snow and took off after Fifi again. She wondered what horrible things had happened to this sweet kid to make him so cautious and serious. Thanks to what she'd seen in her job, she could imagine too many terrible possibilities.

After a few more minutes of playing, both dogs ran up to Kit and Sam, and Fifi acted as if she'd known Kit all her life, thrusting her floppy muzzle under her hand for pets.

"Let's head back to the car and see if the twins

managed to burn the mountain down while we were gone," Kit said, hooking Justice's lead to his harness.

Sam gave her a look.

"What?" she asked.

"You j-just m-m-met them." He grabbed the leash hanging on the gate and attached it to Fifi's collar. "B-but it's like you kn-now them already."

"They remind me of my sister. That girl can find trouble. Thankfully, she's smart enough that she usually can get herself out of it."

"The t-twins are like that, t-too." He grimaced slightly. "Somet-times."

Smiling, Kit opened the gate, and the two of them walked the dogs back to the car, collecting the twins on the way. She couldn't stop the flutters of excitement at the thought of seeing Wes again. Breakfast had been too short, and she also needed to talk to him about what his neighbor had witnessed. If Murphy could identify the person he saw leaving the house, that could be the break they needed in the arson-and-murder case.

And it might finally vindicate the growing unease she felt around Elena.

It wasn't just the cop in her that needed to visit Wes again, though. Kit simply wanted to see him. She couldn't seem to stay away from her wonderfully dorky lumberjack.

CHAPTER 16

HE HAD AN UNEXPECTED VISITOR. WES DIVIDED HIS attention between the SUV that had just pulled up in front of the tower, giving him a view of the top of the vehicle, and the camera monitors. The sun reflected off the SUV windows, so he couldn't see inside, and not knowing who was there bothered him. He knew the vehicles of his neighbors, and the only other people who came to the tower were a handful of the Monroe cops.

The back passenger doors swung open, and two people got out. Even from this angle, Wes could tell the boys looked enough alike to be twins, and they were barely in their teens.

Kids? He frowned, not sure if the fact that two of the visiting strangers were children made it better or worse. Wes didn't have much experience being around kids—at least, once he'd stopped being one—but he suspected that they would find him strange and off-putting, just as adults did. Children, however, would more likely be outspoken about what they thought of him. Again, Wes didn't know if that would be better or worse, and his indecision made him uncomfortable. The whole situation was uncomfortable.

The front passenger door opened, but Wes barely had a chance to take in the older teenage boy before the driver got out. His heart gave an odd little jolt that made him press his hand to his chest. It was Kit.

As soon as he saw her, he was up and moving. He hurried to the stairs and started rushing down when he heard the beep and click of the door unlocking. As it swung open, flooding the ground level of the tower with natural light, Wes reversed, charging back up the stairs. At the top, he paced to the windows and back, just out of sight of the people coming up the steps.

The robot dog—or cat—whirred to life, scooting across the floor toward the top of the stairs. Wes had a moment when he was tempted to give the video record command, but he stopped himself. If Leila believed that Kit would find it creepy, then it was almost certainly true. It wasn't worth the risk, even if he would've loved to get Leila's impression of Kit. He decided to ask her if he could at least take a picture to send to his sister.

Only seconds later, Kit poked her head out of the stairwell. "Wes, hi. I hope it's okay to just show up. You don't have cell reception, so I couldn't call, and I didn't want to anger any more dispatchers. They can hold a grudge like no one's business."

He stared for a moment, struck as always by her beauty. It didn't seem to matter how often he saw her; each time she was even more attractive than he remembered.

Her smile slowly faded, and a small crease formed between her eyebrows, reminding him that he needed to respond. "I'm glad you're here," he blurted.

Her expression brightened again, so it must have been the right thing to say. Wes felt rather triumphant. Climbing up the last few stairs, she moved out of the way of the other three. The robot moved with her, and

Kit reached down to pat its smooth, shiny head. "Hello, Robo-Cat."

A cat it is, then.

While he'd been focused on Kit, all three boys had spilled into the room, and one of the twins stared out the glass wall. "Whoa! You can see everything. The town looks tiny from up here." Following the curved wall of windows, he looked out at what Wes tended to forget was a truly awe-inspiring sight. "Can I go out on the deck?"

Wes started to give him permission, but Kit interrupted. "Better not. If I don't return you three to Jules alive and in the condition in which I borrowed you, I don't think she's going to let you help with training anymore."

"Okay." He seemed to accept that easily. "How do you get out there, anyway?"

"Window four, open," Wes said clearly, figuring it was easier to show him than to explain. The glass pane rotated out, creating a floor-to-ceiling opening onto the deck. A cold wind immediately blasted into the room, making Kit cross her arms over her chest to protect herself from the chill.

"That's pretty amazing," she said.

Despite the chill, Wes felt warm from the compliment. "Thanks. Window four, close."

As the pane rotated back into place, making a solid glass wall again, Wes glanced at Kit, who was shivering.

"Fire, light," he said, and the woodstove ignited. The twins both made an *ohh* sound, and even the oldest kid looked impressed.

"That's a wood fire," the twin who hadn't spoken yet said as he crouched next to the stove and peered inside.

"If it was gas, I'd understand how you did that, but how do you have voice control over a wood fire?"

"It's a—"

"Wait!" the boy interrupted, opening the cast-iron and glass door and peering into the firebox. "Don't tell me. Let me try to figure it out first."

"Okay." He liked the kid already. Wes always enjoyed trying to figure out how things worked. Only when he was absolutely stumped did he ask for an explanation.

Turning back to Kit, he was pleased to see that she was watching him with a soft, warmly amused expression. "Since you said you borrowed these three, I take it they're not yours?"

"They're Jules's brothers. Ty"—she pointed at the twin still looking out the windows—"Tio"—she indicated the other twin who was closely examining the fire—"and Sam."

Wes nodded at the oldest boy, who eyed him warily. He seemed to be the most reserved, judging by the fact that he hadn't spoken since they'd arrived. There was a short pause, and Wes realized that he was a host... with guests. His visitors rarely stayed long. Normally, anyone who stopped by just said what they needed to and left. Now, Wes needed to remember what the rules for hosting were.

He doubted that he ever knew what the rules were.

"You live here?" Ty asked, interrupting his growing panic, and Wes turned toward him in relief.

"No." Wes pointed at where the roof of his cabin was barely visible through the trees. "That's my home. I just spend the days up here." He didn't mention that he'd spent many nights in the tower when he couldn't get his brain quiet enough to sleep. There was something about looking at the vividly bright stars and the dimmer lights from the tiny town that soothed his mind.

"Your job is to watch for forest fires?" Tio asked, looking up from his examination of the stove. When Wes gave a nod, Ty and Tio's gazes met for a few seconds of silent communication before they looked back at Wes.

"This is going on the list," Ty said.

Wes glanced at Kit, but she looked as confused as he felt. "What's going on what list?"

"Fire lookout." Ty looked out the windows again. "We have a list of future careers that sound like they'd be fun."

"We don't believe that we'd do well in a typical office environment," Tio said as he moved to crouch by the robo-cat, having apparently figured out the stove's firing mechanism. Smart kid. "Jules agrees."

"What about being a K9 cop?" Kit asked. "That's a fun job. Well, not exactly *fun*, most of the time, but rewarding. Interesting, too."

"We considered it," Tio said absently as he examined the robot closely without touching it. "We have concerns about passing the background check, however. Is this a camera?"

"Do any of you want something to eat?" Wes hurried to ask. He didn't want Kit to think he was recording her.

The twins' heads popped up as their gazes locked on Wes. Sam looked suddenly interested as well. Wes's distraction attempt had been successful.

"What do you have?" Ty asked, moving away from the windows.

Wes mentally ran over his inventory. Although there were all sorts of things, like ground beef and soup and rice and frozen vegetables, he didn't think that offering to whip up a meatloaf would go over well. He decided on his favorite food. "Pop Tarts?"

Although all three of the boys' faces immediately lit up, Kit laughed, and Wes eyed her, trying to figure out what he'd done that she'd found funny.

"I didn't expect you to offer Pop Tarts," she explained, as if reading his expression. "Beef jerky or a protein bar or trail mix or something, but not Pop Tarts."

"I do have all of those other things if you'd prefer. Pop Tarts are just my favorite."

"Oh, no." Kit waved a hand, as if brushing away the other options. "I love Pop Tarts. Do you have the chocolate kind?"

Opening one of the cupboards above the two-burner stove, he pulled out two boxes and held them up. "S'mores or chocolate fudge?"

"You have s'mores Pop Tarts?" Ty asked, sounding impressed. "Maybe we could have a sleepover here sometime."

Kit laughed again, but Wes was pretty sure she wasn't laughing at him. "I'll take a rain check on one of the s'mores, since we should probably get the dogs' training done first," Kit said. "I promised Jules we wouldn't be too long."

Disappointed, Wes returned the boxes to the cupboard. "Okay. Whenever you want a Pop Tart, let me know. I have a good supply, since I stock up in case there's a blizzard."

Her smile was small, but her eyes were dancing. "Understandable. You can't be trapped here without toaster pastries. How would you survive?"

Was she teasing him? He was pretty sure she was teasing him. Were they flirting? His heartbeat quickened. "I wouldn't. Pop Tarts are critical."

She laughed, and he felt another strong surge of triumph. *He'd* done that, made her laugh, by saying the right thing.

He caught Sam looking back and forth between the two of them, his eyebrows raised, but Wes couldn't read his expression. As soon as they made eye contact, Sam quickly looked away, and Wes refocused on Kit. He might not be able to translate most people's body language—or even verbal cues—but he felt like he understood Kit already. By her affectionate expression, he was pretty sure that she got him as well. Their gazes met and held. The chatter of the twins as they explored and Sam's quiet presence faded to the background as the moment stretched, the connection between him and Kit so solid that it felt almost like a physical thing.

A cold gust of wind hit him, breaking his focus, and he looked to see that one of the twins had opened one of the windows.

"T-Tio," Sam said sternly. "C-c-close th-that."

Kit cleared her throat, and Tio looked over guiltily, pulling Ty away from the opening. "Sorry. I wanted to see if the voice control was personalized. Window eight, close."

Unconcerned, Wes just gave him an *it's fine* wave. If he'd been in Tio's shoes, he would've wondered the same thing. He understood curiosity. For him, it wasn't something to punish.

Kit looked a little sheepish, and he wanted to tell her that he wasn't bothered by the boys' explorations. He loved showing off his tower. She spoke before he could get his thoughts in order, though. "Sorry. We'll get out of your hair. Is it okay if we train the dogs outside?"

The question confused him. "Why wouldn't it be?"

"Since it's your front yard, I thought I should ask."

"I don't really think of it as my property. It's all national forest land. I'm just lucky enough to live on it."

She gave him a questioning look, but he wasn't sure what she was asking, so he just returned her gaze silently. Finally, she asked, "So…we're good to train in your national forest?"

"Yes. It'll give me something to watch." He immediately wanted to retract the words, but she smiled, seemingly not bothered by the idea of him watching her from his tower.

"Aren't you supposed to be watching for fires?" Ty asked, sounding more curious than critical.

"The official wildland fire season's over," Wes explained. "Most fire spotters leave for the winter, but I always request to stay. I'm not paid during the off season, but I don't have to pay rent, since the cabin would sit empty otherwise."

"How do you make money then?" Tio asked, and Sam cleared his throat.

"Th-hat's k-k-kind of a pr-private q-question, Tio."

His gentle correction reminded Wes of something that Leila would say to him when he overstepped, and he smiled at Sam as he said, "I don't mind answering. I don't really need the money. I have patents on a few gadgets I designed, and I do some wildlife photography. It's good that I can stay out here, since, like Ty and Tio, I don't think I'd do very well working in a typical office job." Inwardly, he shuddered at the thought of being trapped in a cubicle all day, surrounded by coworkers who thought he was strange. He'd never experienced it, but he assumed it would be similar to the hell that was high school, only with adults.

"Agreed." Kit looked amused, but Wes wasn't sure why, so he asked.

"Why?"

"Why do I think you'd hate an office job?" When he nodded, she continued. "Because you seem to fit here, out in the wilderness. An office job seems like it would be too confining for you. Wouldn't being around a lot of people all the time wear on you?"

"Yes." He didn't even have to pause and consider that. As he studied her, he felt a now-familiar warmth bloom in his chest. Although they hadn't spent much time together yet—certainly not as much time as he wanted—Kit always seemed to get him. In the past, so many people had misinterpreted what he'd said or meant or felt, but Kit usually understood right off the bat. He was suddenly and intensely glad that she'd moved to Monroe.

Tio looked around the space again and gave Ty a nod. "This job will definitely go on the list."

Kit appeared a little flushed as she clapped her hands together. "Okay, let's get to training before Jules sends a search-and-rescue team after us." With a final smile at Wes, she headed for the stairs, herding the kids in front of her. Now that Wes knew they weren't her children, he was even more impressed by her ease with them. "We'll come back for snacks once we're done working with the dogs, if that's okay?" she said, and Wes nodded, just glad that he'd get to see her up close again.

As soon as the door banged closed behind them, Wes hurried to the windows to watch. Each time he saw Kit, he worried that this time would be the last. After all, he rarely saw anyone in town more than a few times a year. The idea of never seeing her again made his tower in the woods, which was normally his safe haven, seem lonely.

As she and Sam leashed up one of the bloodhounds that had been waiting in the back of her SUV, Wes pushed away his depressing thoughts and concentrated on Kit. He'd enjoy every second he could have with her—even if that meant watching her from his tower like he was a big, hairy-faced Rapunzel.

CHAPTER 17

Kit couldn't stop smiling. Every time she saw Wes, he seemed smarter and more interesting and even more attractive than the last. She knew she was developing a mega-crush on him, but she was also aware that there was nothing she could do to stop it.

Justice gave an excited whine, drawing Kit's attention back to the three kids and two dogs waiting for her instructions.

"Let's work with Fifi before and after we train Justice," she said to Sam, who was listening so intently it was both flattering and rather nerve-racking. "With bloodhounds—especially at the beginning—it's important to do frequent, short sessions and always end on a positive note."

"Ok-kay," Sam said, moving to leash the dog, who was excitedly trying to jump out of the SUV. After retrieving a huge bag of training treats from the floor of the front seat, Kit joined him.

"Here. Let me take her for a second, and you stuff your pockets with these. Lots of them."

Although he quickly traded leash and blocking duties for the bag of treats, he gave her a questioning glance. "Theo and the others use t-toys, rather than f-f-food," Sam said as he filled his pockets.

"I use a toy for Justice now, too, but it took a lot—and I mean *truckloads*—of treats to get to that point." Using her body, Kit blocked Fifi from jumping out of the back. Even though Justice was shaking with excitement, he stayed sitting like the well-behaved dog he was, and Kit felt her usual warm glow of pride. "All stocked up?" Sam nodded, patting his bulging pockets. "Great. Let's start with waiting to get out of the car."

After fifteen minutes of working with Fifi on sitting and not jumping out of the SUV until Sam gave her the release word, they gave her loads of praise and pats. Returning her to the SUV, they got Justice out. A little mournfully, Sam eyed the dog as Justice sat fairly calmly next to Kit.

"He's so m-m-much easier," he said, and Kit snorted.

"Yeah, after a year of training. Do you know how many swear words I yelled in my head during that year? A lot." When Sam still looked unconvinced, Kit continued. "Fifi picks things up much faster than Justice did. She's less confident and more sensitive than him, so it's important you don't get impatient or harsh. If you can keep training fun and interesting for her, though, she's going to progress really quickly."

"Y-you think so?" Sam looked through the window at Fifi, who'd curled up to take a nap.

"Absolutely." Kit looked around and spotted the twins examining something on the side of the tower. Putting two fingers in her mouth, she gave a sharp whistle, and they both whirled around in a way that just shouted guilt. Nothing seemed to be on fire or broken, though, so she put it aside to ask them about later and just called over to them, "Come help us with Justice."

Ty and Tio trotted over willingly.

"What will we be doing?" Ty asked curiously.

"Well, I'll be the handler, Sam's observing, and Justice is tracking, so you two"—she pointed back and forth between Ty and Tio—"get to play the victim. Who wants to be lost in the woods first?"

After Justice found Ty and Tio several times each, they worked on his off-lead obedience skills for a short time before switching dogs again. This time, Kit had Sam start Fifi on tracking. Ty and Tio only moved a short distance away, and she caught on quickly, hauling Sam toward whatever twin was "lost" as soon as he gave her the command to find.

"You're right," Sam said, lavishing treats and praise and ear scratches on Fifi after the last successful "search." "She's so m-much b-better at this than ob-bedience."

"Welcome to my hell," Kit said. "Seriously, though, it makes sense that tracking is easy for her. This is what she's been bred to do." She met Sam's gaze steadily. "You're doing a really good thing, you know. There aren't a lot of homes for a bored, untrained bloodhound, and there aren't a lot of people patient enough to turn her into a well-behaved tracking dog. This will save her life."

He flushed a dark red, focusing on the top of Fifi's head. Kit gave his shoulder a pat, and he stiffened under the quick touch. Dropping her hand, she turned toward the twins—only to find they'd climbed halfway up a pine tree.

"Let's go get Pop Tarts," she called. "Be careful coming down. If either of you get broken, Jules will probably make me buy you, and, no offense, but I'd rather not take you home with me. I have a hard enough time keeping just me and Justice alive." Despite her joking tone, she watched them carefully as they quickly shimmied down the tree, jumping the last few feet. Her stomach didn't unknot until all four of their boots were back on the snowy ground. "How Jules doesn't have ulcers, I don't know," she muttered, following behind them as they ran toward the tower.

"She p-probably d-does," Sam said quietly, falling in next to her while holding Fifi's lead.

"She's a braver woman than I am, taking on four kids." She kept her gaze on the twins, making sure they didn't climb any more trees or hurl themselves off a cliff or something equally disastrous. Although she was curious as to what had happened to their parents and why Jules had ended up with custody, she didn't feel like it was her place to ask. If Sam wanted to tell her, he would. "You guys are lucky to have her."

"We kn-now."

As they stepped out of the trees, the base of the tower came into view, and disappointment swept over Kit. There was a squad car parked next to her SUV, and Theo was talking with Wes. She made an irritated sound in her throat.

Sam gave her a sideways glance. "D-did you j-j-just *growl*?"

"Yes. Sorry." She kept her voice low as they approached the men. "It'd just be nice to have one day— an afternoon even—away from work."

Sam was eyeing her strangely, and the corner of his mouth twitched up ever so slightly.

"What?" she demanded a little more harshly than she meant to, but she was annoyed. It seemed as if Theo didn't even trust her to keep three kids alive for an afternoon.

Surprisingly, Sam's tiny smile grew. "N-nothing. J-just that you're usually so c-c-calm. It's f-funny to see you all ruffled."

Although she tried to shoot him an annoyed stare, she couldn't hold it. He was normally so serious, and his small grin transformed his whole face. It made her want to squeeze his cheeks like a doting grandma. "Ha ha," she said flatly, having trouble keeping herself from truly laughing. "At least I don't basically live with him."

Sam shrugged. "I d-don't m-m-mind." His voice lowered to a mutter, so low that Kit barely caught the words. "B-b-better than liv-v-ving w-with Elena."

"Amen," she grumbled, making him give a short, surprised crack of laughter that caught Theo's attention. He stared at Sam in surprise while Wes gave Kit a sweet smile that she returned. Sam led Fifi over to the rear hatch of Kit's SUV, and Theo shifted his focus to Kit. She figured she might as well find out what the situation was. "What's on fire now?"

Theo gave an amused huff. "At this moment, nothing that we know of, but considering the way things have been going around here, I doubt that'll last long."

She looked at him with raised eyebrows. "So, if there's no emergency, why are you here?"

Before he could answer, the sound of a vehicle engine caught her attention. As they watched silently, an SUV came around the final curve of the narrow road leading to the tower. Kit recognized it as Jules's even before she saw her in the driver's seat with Elena sitting next to her.

Still confused as to why everyone was descending on Wes's tower, Kit stayed silent as Jules pulled up behind Kit's SUV. Dee rushed out of the back seat and bounced over to them.

"Hi, Theo! What are you doing here?"

Kit coughed to cover her laugh. "I asked, but he won't tell me. Maybe you'll have better luck getting an answer." She noticed that Wes had retreated and was leaning his back against the tower, and she wished she could join him. All she'd wanted was to spend her day— afternoon—off training dogs and eating Pop Tarts with Wes, but that didn't look like it was going to happen.

"Where's Sam?" Jules asked, sounding harried and even more Southern than usual. Theo started toward her.

"Right here, J-Ju," Sam said, straightening from where he'd been bent over under the hatch door fussing with Fifi. "Wh-what's the m-m-m-m…wrong?" As Kit watched, his gaze snapped to the twins and then Dee, as if checking on each sibling.

"Nothing." Jules leaned back against her car as Theo reached her side. "Sorry, Sam. Sorry, everyone. I didn't mean to scare y'all. Elena and I were talking, and then I started worrying, and no one was answering my texts, and I just needed to see with my own eyes that y'all were okay so I could stop imagining all sorts of terrible scenarios."

"The cell phone reception up here is almost nonexistent," Wes offered, drawing everyone's attention. "The closest place to call or text is the bat cave." He gestured to the rocky slopes on their right.

"Bat cave?" Kit repeated. "As in full of bats or full of Batman?"

"Full of bats." His face lit up. "I'll show you sometime. We can hike there."

"Okay." Her insides warmed at the thought of another date with Wes.

"Elena was worried about Sam being alone with Kit," Dee said in her clear, childish voice.

Kit looked at Elena, keeping her face carefully blank, and saw the other woman's eyes widen as she made anxious patting motions with her hands. "Just because of everything happening... I mean, Jules and I were really shaken up by what happened at the viner..." Elena trailed off for a second time as her eyes grew shiny with tears. "Then there was the house fire and that poor woman who was burned, so Theo was going to check on you and the kids, but he wasn't texting back either." She blinked rapidly, managing to hold the tears back, although her lashes grew wet and spiky. "We were worried."

"I'm sorry, Kit," Jules said, a slight flush on her cheeks. Theo wrapped an arm around her and tucked her against his side. "I'm overprotective, but usually I'm more rational than this. With everything that's happened lately, I'm having a hard time letting the kids out of my sight. They've gone through so much..."

Sam gave his sister a horrified, betrayed glance before dropping his gaze to the ground.

"It's okay." Kit smiled at Jules. "To be fair, the twins climbed a really tall tree when I was distracted, so your worries are somewhat valid."

Waving a hand, Jules said, "Oh, climbing trees isn't

a problem. As long as they're not crashing helicopters, it's a good day."

"Dee was the one who crashed the helicopter," Tio said as the twins joined them. Apparently, playing in the snow was less interesting than the drama happening by the tower. "She was also commended for it."

"Fine." Jules kissed Theo on the cheek before slipping out from under his arm. "As long as y'all don't crash *non-enemy* helicopters, then it's a good day." She walked over to Sam and started talking to him too quietly for Kit to hear. Kit blinked at the thought of little Dee crashing a helicopter. What was *wrong* with this town?

"Wes has a robot cat," Tio told Dee, and her eyes rounded. "He also has a remote ignition system for his woodstove, but I expect that you're more interested in the robot cat."

"A robot cat?" Dee breathed, proving Tio's assumption correct. "Is it fuzzy or metal on the outside? Does it do cat things, like meow and purr?"

"Neither." Wes was the one who answered from right behind Kit. "Its exterior is a polymer, and it doesn't make any sounds. If it did, I would've made it bark, since I assumed it was canine until everyone corrected me."

Dee immediately switched her rapt attention from Tio to Wes. "What's a polymer?"

"A compound of high molecular weight made up of multiple smaller molecules." Both Dee and Tio stared at him. While Dee appeared confused, Tio had a look of complete hero worship.

Trying to hide her amusement, Kit suggested, "Why don't we just show her?"

At that, Ty's face lit up. "Can we have Pop Tarts now?"

"I'll ask Jules," Kit said, heading toward where Jules was still talking with Sam. As Kit approached, she tried to make it obvious so she didn't unintentionally sneak up on them. Despite her best efforts, Jules and Sam were too focused on their hushed conversation to notice her. As Kit was about to call out to them, Sam's voice got louder until his agonized words were clear.

"...you c-c-can't *say* th-things l-l-like that, J-J-Jules. Sh-she's g-g-going to f-figure out wh-what I d-d-did! I d-don't want her to kn-n-now."

"Sam..." Jules sounded like her heart was breaking. "You didn't *do* anything. None of that was your fault."

Even as the cop part of Kit's brain clicked into gear, running through the possibilities of whatever crime Sam had committed, the rest of her knew that whatever it was, it most likely had been self-defense or an accident, especially after Jules's reassurance. From what she'd seen, Sam was a sensitive, conscientious kid who felt responsible for his siblings. Also, his demeanor just screamed abuse victim. Her jaw tightened, her back teeth pressing together as anger rushed through her. She wished she could get her hands on whoever had hurt this kid.

"Hey, Jules," she said quietly, making both Jules and Sam jump and snap their gazes to her. "Dee would like to see Wes's robo-cat, and the twins are hoping for a couple of his Pop Tarts. Is it okay if we go up into the tower?"

Jules brushed at her cheeks, scrubbing away evidence of her tears as Theo approached and rested a hand between her shoulder blades. He eyed the three of them carefully, as if trying to figure out who was to blame for making Jules cry. "Robo-cat?" Jules repeated a little shakily, and Theo frowned.

"Wes made a robot cat," Kit explained, keeping her tone gentle. Both Jules and Sam looked brittle enough to crack. "Want to see? He's interested in electronics and that sort of thing. His tower looks like a robotics lab and a mad scientist's lair collided. Plus, his favorite food is Pop Tarts. The twins are fully won over."

Jules hesitated, studying Sam's expression. "It sounds fascinating." Her gaze darted over to Elena, who still looked upset. "I've already butted in enough today. I'll take Elena back home now that we know our worries were unfounded." She gave a small, shaky laugh. "I feel bad for feeding her fears. Poor thing's already had a rough couple of weeks."

"Next time we come up here, you'll need to come along," Kit said, giving Sam a glance. His face was stiff and expressionless as he studied the ground, not giving her any indication if she was helping or just making things worse. "You can see the tower then, and you can watch Sam train Fifi. He's pretty impressive."

Jules gave her a brilliant smile, and even Theo let out a grunt of approval. "That sounds wonderful. Oh, and please come to dinner tonight at our house. It'll be casual—just us, Hugh, Grace, Otto, and Sarah. Wes, you're welcome, too." Kit felt her stomach warm at the invitation—and from the automatic assumption that Wes would be her date. She sent him a sideways questioning look. Despite a slightly panicked expression, he gave a nod.

"Thank you," Kit said. "We'll be there."

"Good. It's about time we got to know each other, especially since you and Sam will be training the dogs together." Jules reached toward Sam, as if to squeeze his arm affectionately, but he stiffened before she could touch him. Jules froze for a moment, her hand hovering in the air next to Sam's elbow, before it dropped to her side. "Did you want a ride home, Sam-I-Am?"

He gave Kit a quick look that she took a rough guess at interpreting. For as young as he was, the kid sure could hide his emotions. "If you're interested in getting a Pop Tart first, we'll all fit in my car. Now that we know Fifi and Justice get along, they're fine in the back together, so we can squeeze Dee in the back seat with the twins."

As Sam studied her, Kit met his gaze evenly. She didn't know what he'd done or what had happened, but she knew in her gut that Sam was a good kid, and she wanted to protect him...from any threat. She resisted the urge to glance at Elena.

"I'll r-ride w-w-with K-Kit."

His stutter sounded worse than it had been when she'd picked them up—and much worse than when they'd been training the dogs. Kit had to force herself not to frown, wishing that unfounded fears hadn't ruined the enjoyable day they'd been having.

"I'll stay," Theo said, earning a smile from Jules. "I'd like to see the robot cat."

Kit glanced away so he couldn't see her roll her eyes. She knew why Theo was staying, and it wasn't robot-related. It was so he could babysit them. Obviously, it was going to take time and a herculean effort to win their trust.

"Elena, ready to go?" Jules asked.

"I'd like to see the tower, too," Elena said in her shy, tentative way.

After a quick glance at Sam, Jules gave Elena a com-miserating smile. "We'll have to come back another time. I need to get home, and they're already going to be stuffed into Kit's car."

After a short pause, Elena said, "Another time, then."

"Dee," Jules called as she and a reluctant Elena headed for her car. Dee turned around. "Kit's going to bring you home. Be on your best behavior." Giving her sister a wave of agreement, Dee hurried to the tower entrance.

"I'm hoping 'best behavior' means no crashing helicopters," Kit muttered to Theo.

Instead of laughing, Theo winced. "With these kids, you never know."

After giving Theo a sideways glance, Kit moved to Wes's side. He smiled at her in that pleased way that made her feel like the most beautiful, interesting person on the planet. "You don't have anything potentially explosive in your lab, do you?" she asked.

"Yes."

Of course he does, she thought with a sigh. "Help me keep an eye on the kids. Apparently, they have a habit of leaving destruction in their wake."

Instead of looking concerned, his face lit with interest. "What did they destroy?"

"A helicopter."

"The biggest thing I blew up as a kid was a car."

Startled, she blinked at him, and his nostalgic smile faded. "Don't worry. No one was in it."

"That's...good, I suppose." Mountain people were nuts. "Will you help me keep them from destroying your tower? I'm getting kind of fond of it."

His grin was huge. "You like my tower?"

"Yeah." She couldn't help it. She had to smile back at him.

"I'm glad." He paused, focusing a little too hard on the tower wall. "Want to train here again tomorrow?"

Her heart gave an odd little flutter and skip. "Sure."

"I have t-to w-w-work tom-morrow," Sam said, sounding disappointed. His words reminded Kit that she and Wes weren't alone, and she looked over at Sam. He seemed to be a little more relaxed now that Elena and Jules had left, but he was still holding himself more stiffly than he had while they'd been training.

"Let's talk to Jules and Nan. Between the four of us, we should be able to figure out a time when we're both free to train." Kit gave him a stern look. "In the mean-time, you and Fifi can work on your homework."

Instead of looking chagrined at the mention of home-work, Sam's face lit up at the thought of working with Fifi, and Kit had to resist the urge to hug him. Under his protective outer shell, Sam was such a sweet, dog-loving kid. "W-we w-w-will."

"Good." She tried to keep her tone firm. "Remember that frequent, short sessions are best. Too bad she's stay-ing out at Nan's. Is there any way Jules would let you keep Fifi at your place while you're training her?"

Dee must've had a sixth sense when it came to the possibility of having a dog at her house, because she immediately ran from where she'd been waiting by the tower entrance, her face bright with hope. "Fifi might come home with us?"

"Maybe." Sam sounded more cautious than Dee. "She m-might say n-n-no. F-Fifi is k-kind of w-w-wild. B-besides, w-we're n-not in a g-good p-place to g-get a d-d-dog r-right n-n-now. Rem-m-member?" He gave Dee a telling look that caused her smile to droop, which made Kit intensely curious. What did he mean that they weren't in a good place for a dog? Their isolated house on the edge of town seemed like the perfect home for a big dog, so Sam must've meant something else. Kit again wondered what their background was, what had happened to their parents so that Jules'd had to take custody of her four siblings.

"I bet she wouldn't say no if *you* asked," Dee said, her excitement returning even as Theo, who'd obviously overheard, groaned. "You never ask for anything."

Sam was quiet for a moment. "I'll ask."

Dee gave an excited whoop. "We're going to get a dog!" Sam's grin broke free, lighting up his face again.

Kit had to laugh at their excitement. She could sympathize, since she couldn't think of a better thing than bringing home a new dog. Then Wes took her hand, and she felt her stomach give a small, excited leap. She kept her gaze forward as the corners of her mouth turned up at the feel of his palm pressing against hers.

Maybe she could think of *one* thing that was better.

When everyone was occupied with checking out all of Wes's gadgets, Kit noticed Theo was standing alone by the wall of windows and made her way over to him. He gave her a sideways look.

"I never really got an answer," she said quietly, looking out at the snow-covered forest spread out around them, with the miniature town in the distance.

"To what question?"

"I know why Jules showed up, but why did you decide to crash our dog-training party?"

His grimace was so slight she almost missed it. "Jules couldn't reach you or the boys, so she texted me, asking if I could swing by. After what happened to Elena last week, Jules has been on edge."

"Okay," Kit conceded. "Why did Jules and Elena drive out here, if she'd sicced you on me?" Although she kept her tone light, learning that Jules didn't trust her with her siblings did sting. Kit wasn't used to not being trusted. She'd been the responsible one for so long, even before wearing a police uniform, and the amount of suspicion almost everyone in town was aiming her way was wearing at her confidence.

One of Theo's shoulders lifted in a partial shrug. "She worries."

"More than most sisters, even sister guardians, it seems." Kit couldn't help but probe a little.

Theo didn't even shrug that time. His expression closed down so tightly that Kit knew she wasn't getting anything out of him about Jules and her family—not that she'd expected to. Theo seemed tight-lipped about everything, so it made sense he wouldn't blab about his girlfriend's situation. That didn't stop Kit's curiosity, though.

She was about to ask about his feelings regarding Elena when Wes approached, grabbing her attention.

"Would you like to see my vacuum?" he asked, and she eyed him as Theo gave an amused snort.

"Is your vacuum interesting?" Since this was Wes, Kit had a feeling he could make even boring household appliances fascinating.

"Yes. It's automated, but it doesn't just bump around

blindly like the commercial versions. This one can actually make decisions regarding suction and direction."

"Then yes." She moved to stand next to Wes, and he
gave her a pleased smile. "I'd love to see your vacuum."

When Theo gave a choked laugh as they started to
walk away, Kit raised an eyebrow at him over her shoulder. Although she kept her expression innocent, she
knew perfectly well why he was smirking like a twelve-
year-old. For some reason, Wes offering to show her his
vacuum sounded like a proposition—although it could
just be that her mind focused on sex when she was with
Wes. She couldn't help it; he was irresistibly attractive.

He caught her hand and tangled their fingers together
again, and her stomach warmed. *Irresistibly attractive
and just so very nice.*

CHAPTER 18

WALKING INTO JULES'S HOUSE FELT COMPLETELY DIFFERENT from the last time she'd been inside—when they'd been pursuing a possible arsonist. It helped that she had a noisy gaggle of kids and dogs entering with her, as well as a very tense Wes. Once they'd gotten back in cell range, Sam had called Jules to ask if Fifi could stay overnight, rather than having to return to the kennel. Kit had a feeling that Fifi wouldn't just be staying one night.

In the front entry, Kit waited until the kids had shed their boots and coats and were loudly stampeding toward the kitchen before stepping close to Wes's side. "Would you rather skip out of this dinner and head to my house? There's not much food there right now, but I could probably scrounge up something."

"Yes," he said quickly, his obvious nervousness easing. "I don't think that would be polite, though."

"Probably not." She pulled a face, hoping to make him laugh. All he managed was a poor attempt at a smile, but she appreciated the effort. "It's tempting, though, isn't it?"

His expression grew intent as he studied her, his gaze warm on her face. "Yes. Very tempting."

Feeling herself flush with heat, she slipped her hand in his and tugged him toward the kitchen, knowing that she'd be tempted to kiss him if they stayed alone in the hallway much longer. "If you need to leave at any time, feel free," she said seriously, catching his gaze and holding it. "No one will be offended."

"Thank you." He was giving her that look again, the one that made her want to tackle him and have her way with him. Resisting temptation, she walked into the kitchen, keeping a tight hold on his hand. She loved that they were together like this, on an official date, especially since this was the first social event with her new partners. There was still a long way to go before they learned to trust her, and vice versa—she knew that—but getting invited to this dinner felt like a giant step in the right direction.

The kitchen was noisy and packed, and Kit felt Wes's hand tighten around hers as they walked into the chaos.

"Kit and Wes! You came! Welcome!" Jules called from her spot by the stove. Theo was leaning against the counter right next to her, and he gave Kit and Wes a lift of his chin in greeting. Elena, standing on the other side of Kit, gave them a tentative smile before ducking her head.

"Hey, greenie. Glad you could make it." Hugh sounded sincere, and Grace gave her a friendly wave from her spot next to him at the kitchen table. Justice and Theo's dog, Viggy, were underneath the table, trading off two well-worn chew toys. Dee hadn't wasted any time and was busy setting up a board game on the table. Hugh and Grace immediately began tussling for possession of the red game piece.

"Food'll be ready in twenty," Jules hollered at the kids gathered around the table. "The game better be put away and the table set by then."

"It will!" Dee and Ty chorused as they hurried even faster to finish setting it up.

"Hi, I'm Otto's wife, Sarah." The relatively quiet voice brought Kit's attention away from the group playing the game to a small, almost fragile-looking woman standing next to her. By the way Otto was hovering right behind her, Kit would've known who Sarah was even without the introduction.

"Nice to meet you," Kit said, hiding her surprise at the other woman's delicately pretty appearance. For some reason, she'd expected Otto's wife to be tall and strapping and Nordic, just like he was. "This is Wes March."

"The fire lookout." After shaking Kit's hand, Sarah offered hers to Wes. "We're sort of neighbors, give or take a few miles."

As he shook her hand, Wes gave a jerky nod of his head, and Kit knew he was still feeling overwhelmed by the packed room. She shifted so that she could lean her shoulder against his arm in support. He gave her hand an appreciative squeeze.

Sarah didn't press Wes to talk, simply turning back to Kit when he stayed silent, which made Kit pretty sure that she was going to like Otto's wife.

"I'm glad they finally hired a new K9 officer," Sarah said, glancing up at her tall husband with clear affection. "Winters are so short-staffed anyway, and with the lieutenant…" She trailed off, her lips pressing together. "I worry when these guys don't have backup available."

Although she wanted to know the full story of what happened with the lieutenant's betrayal, Kit knew now wasn't the time to get it. "It's surprisingly busy here, too."

Sarah winced even as she laughed. "This town…"

Instead of finishing her thought, she looked over her shoulder at Otto. "Would you mind grabbing me some water?" He gave her a sweet kiss on the top of her head and crossed the kitchen to a cupboard missing a door that held a motley collection of glasses. "How are you liking the job?" Sarah asked, turning back toward Kit.

"It's not boring," Kit said honestly. "I haven't had a chance to work with Otto much, since we're on opposite shifts, but so far," she leaned closer, lowering her voice, "he's my favorite."

"I heard that!" Hugh yelled from his spot at the table. From his green game piece, it looked like Grace had won the wrestling match.

Kit rolled her eyes at Sarah, making her laugh. "As I was saying, Otto's so wonderfully quiet. He's *definitely* my favorite."

"He's mine, too," Sara said mock-seriously, giving a blushing Otto a huge smile as he handed her a glass of water.

"Mine, too," Grace called, shrieking with laughter as Hugh immediately started to tickle her.

Leaning more heavily against Wes, Kit felt his free hand rest lightly on her waist, and her skin lit up under his touch, despite the multiple layers of fabric blocking his skin from contacting hers. Standing in the warm, crowded kitchen, Wes pressed against her, listening as her new partners and their families talked and laughed, Kit felt more content than she'd been in a long time.

Turning her head, she looked at Wes, marveling at how familiar his beautiful, bearded face was already, at how this man was quickly making Monroe feel like home.

A gust of cold air swept through the kitchen as the back door swung open.

"K-Kit?" Sam stuck his head inside. "D-do y-you have a m-m-minute?"

"Of course. Let me just grab my coat." As she turned toward the hall, Wes reluctantly released her, but she kept hold of his hand, pulling him along with her. "You're not getting away from me that easily," she said quietly enough that only he could hear.

He gave her a sideways glance, looking both pleased and relieved.

After getting their coats and boots on, they went out the front door and circled around the house, rather than tromping back through the kitchen. The night was clear and cold and surprisingly still, the ever-present wind missing for once. The snow crunched under their boots as the air cooled Kit's overheated cheeks, and she had a moment of thankfulness for the chance to be here in this beautiful place with this beautiful man on this beautiful night. Tipping her head up, she met Wes's gaze. It might've been wishful thinking, but she was pretty sure the same gratitude was mirrored in his eyes.

They rounded the corner of the house into the backyard, and Fifi galloped over, breaking the mood but replacing it with an even happier one. After rumpling the dog's ears, Kit crossed the yard to join Sam.

"What are you working on?" she asked.

He looked glum. "Recalls."

Although she tried to hold back her laugh, she couldn't completely, and Sam shot her an offended glance. "Sorry," she said, restraining her amusement. "I'm not laughing at you. I'm laughing at memories of trying to teach Justice to come when I called. The crazy things I tried out of sheer desperation… Anyway, the trick is lots of repetition, and a huge reward."

"I have treats." He patted his pocket.

"You need to have the best treats, and"—she held up a dramatic hand, and he watched her, his mouth twitching with the barest smile—"you have to make it into a party."

"A…party?"

"Every time she comes to you when you call, it has to be the most fun time she's ever had."

"Okay." He blew out a breath, as if she'd asked him to do something painful. "A party. Fifi, here!" The dog cocked her head and then trotted toward him.

"Party time," Kit reminded him under her breath.

"Good girl!" Sam fed her treats as she reached him.

"More fun. Ultimate party time," she urged.

"Yay!" Sam's voice got higher-pitched and more enthusiastic than she'd ever heard, and Fifi started dancing in excitement. "Good Fifi! You're so smart! Such a good dog!"

Trying to hold back her laughter at both Sam's and Fifi's antics, she said, "Yes! Better! More treats, and then we'll have Wes hold her on the other side of the yard until you call her."

By the fifth recall, Fifi was galloping over immediately, and Sam was doling out happy praise and treats unrestrainedly. Kit had lost her fight to hold back her laughter, and she was doubled over at the sight of the hound and the teenager jumping up and down in excitement. Even Wes was chuckling.

Crouching down, Sam rubbed Fifi's wriggling body as she enthusiastically licked his face. He turned his

head and gave Kit a huge smile, so open and happy that
it stunned her into silence.

"Thanks, Kit."

He turned back to the dog as Kit watched them,
wanting to rub her chest where it ached in a good way.
Clearing her throat, she said, "Don't thank me. This is
all you and Fifi."

Wes walked over to her side, and she leaned against
him, the same gratitude from earlier hitting her again,
even harder this time. She tipped her head back to look
at the stars, since she knew she'd tear up if she kept
watching Sam beaming so proudly at Fifi. "What a nice
night," she said.

Wes wrapped an arm around her shoulders, as if he
knew that she needed that warm, comforting weight to
ground her right now. "Yes. It is."

―――――――――

Wes was proud of himself, and grateful for Kit. He'd
survived dinner, and she'd been a huge help with that,
staying close by his side and filling in any awkward
silences. There'd been several pauses when he was
pretty sure he was supposed to do something but didn't
know what, and Kit had been there every time, smooth-
ing over the moment and saying exactly what needed
to be said. Instead of being torturous, as the few social
events he'd attended always seemed to be, the evening
had actually been...quite tolerable.

Of course, being able to touch Kit—to hold her
hand or brush arms at the table or put an arm around
her shoulders—was a big part of what made the event

enjoyable. That, and how she kept glancing at him, smiling in a way that meant she wasn't bothered that being in a crowded space with a bunch of strangers and almost-strangers had reduced him to a silent lump.

"Wes?" Tio asked, hovering a few feet away from the arm of the couch. "Would you mind helping me with our drone?"

Only after Wes was on his feet and headed for the hallway did he remember that he'd left Kit behind. Glancing back sheepishly, he saw she was smiling at him.

"Go ahead." She waved him off. "Just keep them from blowing up the house."

"Please," Jules added.

Giving them both a salute, Wes followed Tio up the stairs to a rabbit warren of a second floor. The doorway into the twins' bedroom was low enough that he had to duck to get in. Eyeing the small chair next to the crowded desk holding the drone, Wes suggested, "Should we bring that to the kitchen table?"

To his relief, Tio agreed and led the way back downstairs. They'd just settled in at the kitchen table when Wes's cell phone rang. He jumped, unaccustomed to the sound, before checking the screen.

"Excuse me, please," he said to Tio. "It's my sister."

Tio nodded, his attention mostly focused on the drone. "You should take it, then."

"Hang on a minute, Leila," Wes said as he headed for the front door, pausing to put on his coat and boots. Once he was outside in the crisp chill of the night, he put the phone back to his ear. "Hello?"

"What's going on?" she asked. "I expected to leave my usual 'call me back' message, but instead you answered, which you normally never do, and I hear talking and laughing and what sounds like a...party? Are you at a party?"

He smiled, satisfaction rolling through his chest at the thought of actually impressing his social sister. "Yes."

Her excited shriek made his smile broaden, even as he held the phone away from his ear to protect his hearing. He started wandering around the perimeter of the house, retracing his and Kit's steps from earlier that evening. "Is this a date?" He could almost hear Leila holding her breath as she waited for him to answer. He didn't think it was possible for his grin to stretch any farther.

"Yes. With Kit."

There was another scream, but Wes was prepared for it this time, and a part of him was screaming in excitement right along with his sister. "So you're dating? You two are dating? You and Kit?"

He walked into the backyard and stopped abruptly before he ran into Elena, who was also speaking on the phone. Her back was to him, and her hushed, serious tone, so different from her normal, tentative way of speaking, made him go silent and listen to what she was saying. "...sure, Courtney. One of my police contacts ran Sebastian's prints and confirmed that it's him. The rest are here, too, including Juliet. You should come as soon as you can."

Juliet? Who's that? Jules? He frowned, trying to think of why Elena would be running anyone's fingerprints, and how that could be connected to Jules.

"Wes? Weeessss! Did we lose our connection? If we did, I might die of curiosity. Why do you have to live in the middle of nowhere with the crappiest cell service in the history of the world? *Why?*"

Elena either sensed him or heard Leila, because she whipped around, fear flickering across her face before her usual shy expression locked into place. "I'll need to call you back," she said quickly, some of her uncharacteristic confidence still lingering in her voice as she let the hand holding the phone drop to her side.

"Hang on a minute, Leila," Wes said, not looking away from Elena. She'd just become a very interesting puzzle, and he wanted to know whether Jules was in any kind of trouble.

"Wes? Yes! Go someplace with better reception. I don't want to miss a word of this," Leila said, but his attention was focused on Elena, and he barely heard his sister. He lowered his own phone as well.

"Is something going on with Jules?" he asked baldly.

Elena blinked rapidly, either because she was confused by his question or because she was trying to think of a lie. "Jules? No, why?"

"Who's Juliet?"

"Oh!" Elena gave a small laugh. "Juliet works at the public library. After what happened last week, I don't want to work at the viner anymore. Don't mention it to Jules, though, please? She gave me such a good reference, and I don't want to let her down, but it's really hard being in that kitchen. You understand that, right?" Even in the low light of the moon, he could see the tears starting to pool in her eyes, but his discomfort was outweighed by his need to find out what the call had been about. Apparently, his curiosity was as strong as his sister's.

"If that was about working at the library, why were you talking about running someone's fingerprints?"

"What?" She shook her head slightly. "We weren't. You must've misheard."

He knew he hadn't, but he also knew that was a pointless argument, so he said nothing. She gave him a tight smile and hurried back inside. He stared at the back door, lost in thought, until he heard Leila calling him and remembered that she was still on the phone.

"Sorry," he said, refocusing. He'd worry over the puzzle that was Elena Dahl later.

"It's fine." He could almost picture her dramatically waving away his apology. "I can hear you really clearly now. So, tell me everything."

He opened his mouth and then closed it again, not sure of where to start or what Leila's version of "everything" entailed. "Why don't you ask questions, and I'll answer them."

"Okay. How many dates have you been on?"

"One and a quarter official dates."

"A quarter?"

"There was a fire and a possible but unlikely kidnapping."

Silence filled the line for several moments, and Wes waited patiently for the next question.

"Were you involved in either the fire or the kidnapping?" she finally asked.

"No. I—" He broke off when the back door opened and Kit poked her head out.

When she saw him, she smiled and stepped onto the porch. "You okay? I was worried that you might've turned into a human-shaped ice sculpture."

"I'm fine, but you don't have a coat or boots on. Go

back inside before you freeze." Despite his scolding words, he found himself smiling back at her.

"Is that her?" Leila demanded. "Is she right there? Let me talk to her! No, take a picture, and send it to me, and *then* let me talk to her. Oh, we can just Facetime!"

"She can't stay outside to talk to you. She'd freeze. Inside it's too loud. We'll hike up to the bat cave soon and maybe you can talk to her then."

"Fine. At least take a picture!"

Lowering the phone, Wes said, "Leila would like a picture of you."

"Leila?" Kit repeated.

"My sister."

"Oh." Kit gave him a wicked grin. "Fine, but you need to be in it, too. Let's take a selfie together."

Grumbling slightly, since he hated having his picture taken, he joined her on the porch, pulling up the camera mode on his phone. "If it's two of us, is it still a selfie?"

"An us-ie, then." She grabbed his wrist to move the phone where she wanted, and he crouched down so that both of their faces were in the shot. "Smile! Okay, one more." He centered the picture again before tapping the photo button. At the last second, Kit turned and pressed a kiss on his cheek. The phone made the clicking sound of the picture being taken, but Wes was frozen, unable to process the fact that Kit had just kissed him.

Kit had just kissed him.

"Brrr!" She gave an exaggerated shiver. "Tell your sister hi from me, but I'm going back inside. It's freezing out here." She rushed back inside, leaving him alone on the porch, his arm holding the phone still outstretched.

"Wes!" Leila's voice jerked him out of his reverie

for the second time that night. He shook off his daze and hurried to send her the first picture of the two of them, Kit smiling and him looking grumpy as he did in all photos. The second photo wasn't for Leila. That was for him to look at later that night, when he had time to replay the moment in his head.

"Oh, Wes!" His name was just a gasp, and then there were muffled sounds. Wes frowned.

"Leila? You okay?" It sounded like she was crying.

"I'm perfect!" It came out as a wail. "You and her, and she's so beautiful, and you took a selfie with her, and it's so amazing and wonderful and I love her already and I'm going to hang up now so I can send this to Mom so she can cry, too!"

"Wait, Leila…what?" It was too late. She'd already ended the call. Wes wondered if his mother would be calling him later and crying. The thought made him uncomfortable.

"Wes!" Dee, bundled up in coat and hat and mittens, came flying out the door, the start of a wave of kids and dogs and adults. "We're going to play footer in the snow!"

"Footer?" Still a little rattled by the kiss and the call and his sister's tears, Wes zipped his phone into his coat pocket.

"It's football mixed with soccer, plus some made-up rules," Tio explained, bumping a soccer ball on his knee before Ty stole it. "I thought we could work on the drone after, if that's okay?" Wes nodded, and Tio's face lit up. "Thanks." He chased his brother, tackling him and reclaiming the ball.

Kit, now wearing appropriate outerwear for the weather, grabbed his hand and pulled him toward the kids. "Come on." She smiled over her shoulder at him. "Let's play footer."

"I'm not sure about the made-up-rules part."

She shrugged. "It'll be fun. You'll see."

He believed her. After all, she made everything more interesting. Why not footer?

CHAPTER 19

THE NEXT DAY, KIT LOADED JUSTICE INTO THE BACK SEAT of her SUV to make the short drive to the grocery store. It wasn't even a mile away, and Kit felt silly driving such a short distance, but she knew she'd appreciate the vehicle when she had multiple heavy bags of groceries that she didn't have to lug through the snow. Also, despite all the patrolling they did on the job, Justice still loved car rides. Smiling, she glanced at her dog as he rested his jowly muzzle on the back of the seat so he could gaze out the rear window.

She wished she could borrow some of his simple peace. Her mind hadn't stopped working since Wes had told her the night before that he'd overheard Elena talking on the phone about taking someone's fingerprints. That seemed so...odd, and Kit couldn't make sense of it. Wes had heard her mention the names Juliet and Sebastian, and Kit had spent half the night going over the reports from the homicide and arson, as well as the viner fire and kidnapping, trying to find a mention of those names. The closest she could find was Jules. She decided to arrange another meet-up with Elena. Kit had a lot more questions for her.

As they approached the bombed-out building where the police department had been, Kit slowed and

frowned. There was a sleek, low-slung car parked in the
lot that she didn't recognize. Even though she had only
been working in Monroe for a couple of weeks, she was
beginning to get to know the residents and their vehicles, and she would've noticed this one if she'd spotted
it before. The car looked almost ridiculously impractical
sitting in the snowy lot, its yellow paint blinding in the
bright mountain light.

Curious, Kit pulled into the lot, parking behind the
car. After she jotted down the license plate number, she
got out and approached the front left door, automatically looking through the back windows as she went.
Except for a woman sitting in the driver's seat, the car
was empty, its seats bare and clean. There was a rental
sticker, which surprised her.

The window rolled down a crack as Kit reached the
driver's door. The woman looked to be in her thirties
at first glance, but Kit revised that by at least a decade
when she looked closer and recognized the signs of plastic surgery. Around the edges of the huge sunglasses, the
driver's skin was smooth to the point of looking frozen.

"Everything okay?" Kit asked. This woman, like her
car, didn't fit in Monroe.

"I need to speak with a police officer." Her voice
was low and husky, but calm, almost cold. She gestured
toward the blackened shell of the building in front of
them. "This is obviously not the right place."

"I'm a police officer," Kit said, smiling through the
woman's skepticism, which was easy to read despite the
Botox and oversized sunglasses. "I'm off-duty at the
moment, but I can show you where the station is now."

"I would appreciate that."

"Follow me. It's not far." She headed back to her SUV and reversed out of the lot. As Kit waited for the woman to get her car turned around, Justice stood up and rested his muzzle on her shoulder. Eyeing the adorable mass of wrinkles smooshing his jowls and cheeks, Kit lifted a hand to rub behind his ears. "Maybe we should get you some Botox injections," she told him, and he rolled an eye to look up at her face, making her laugh. "You're right. You're perfect just as you are."

With a drawn-out sound, Justice let his head rest more heavily on her shoulder as she massaged his neck. Glancing at the bright-yellow car still in the lot, Kit echoed her dog's groan, but for a different reason.

"Of course she's stuck," she muttered, easing out from under Justice's heavy head and getting out of the SUV. The woman had reversed into a drift, and her wheels spun as she managed to bury the car even deeper into the snow. Kit tapped on the driver's side window, and it slid down, revealing the woman's glare. Kit knew she would've looked furious if her face had been capable of forming expressions.

"You need to push," the woman said, and Kit held back a laugh.

"There's no way you're getting out of this snowdrift without the help of a tow truck," Kit said, taking a step back so she wasn't blocking the door. "Leave it here. I'll give you a ride to the station, and you can call for a tow from there. It'll be warmer than waiting here." Kit hoped there was a local service. Knowing Monroe, all tow-truck drivers might have moved south for the winter.

The woman pressed her artificially full lips together before giving an audible huff. "Fine." Climbing out of the car, she yelped as her feet sank shin-deep into the snow. Kit knew the feeling of snow dropping into too-short boots, and she grimaced in sympathy.

"Do you have a coat?" she asked when the woman shivered.

"Yes." Popping the trunk, the woman waved toward the rear of the car, but didn't make any move to walk toward it.

Although Kit knew immediately what the woman wanted her to do, she feigned ignorance, staying still and waiting quietly for the indignant squawking she knew was coming.

"Well?" the woman asked after just a few seconds had passed. "Are you going to get my coat? It's right on the top. You can't miss it."

Kit couldn't help herself—she laughed. "No, I'm not getting your coat. This isn't what 'public servant' means." With another amused snort, she headed back to her SUV. "Besides, it's my day off."

When she reached her car, she saw that the woman was still staring at her, mouth slightly agape.

"Grab your coat and let's go before you freeze," Kit called before climbing into her blessedly warm SUV. Justice had spotted the woman, and his tail was whipping back and forth as he pressed his nose against the window. "Don't get too excited, buddy." She kept her voice low, aware that the woman had finally grabbed her coat and was stomping through the snow toward them. "I doubt you're going to get many ear scratches from this one."

Her words didn't seem to affect Justice's enthusiasm, however, and he wiggled with excitement as the woman yanked open the passenger door, her affront clear in every line of her body. As she settled into her seat, Justice poked his head between the seats, looking at the new arrival with the confidence of a dog who believed that everyone loved him.

The woman drew away from Justice with a disgusted hiss, and Kit restrained an eye roll. Did the woman have to bring every cliché to life? Then again, maybe she was allergic or fearful of dogs. Kit chided herself for being judgmental. "Justice, down."

Throwing a mournful look at the woman, he obeyed, lying on the back seat. Once his slight whine faded, silence settled over them.

"I'm Officer Kit Jernigan," she offered, feeling like she should make an attempt to be polite. Also, her curiosity was still raging.

There was a pause before the woman introduced herself. "Courtney Young."

"What brings you to Monroe?" Kit asked.

The woman let out a quiet huff. "I'd rather wait and discuss that with a detective."

"A...detective?" Trying to hold back a laugh, Kit focused on the road in front of her a little too intently. "I think you're overestimating the size of the Monroe Police Department, especially in the winter."

The woman waved an impatient hand. "Whatever. I need to talk to someone who actually has some influence, not a jumped-up meter maid."

Instead of being insulted, Kit just wanted to laugh again. Courtney Young was coming off as such a caricature of an evil rich person that Kit couldn't take anything the woman said seriously. She looked forward to telling the other K9 cops about the encounter. Hugh, especially, would get a kick out of it. Kit smiled a little at the thought. Despite what had happened at the tower the day before, she was still hopeful that she could become part of the K9 team. Once they got to know her better, they'd figure out that they could trust her to have their backs—and watch out for their kids.

"Why are you going so slowly?"

Courtney's complaint interrupted Kit's thoughts, bringing her attention back to her passenger. "With this snow, driving can be treacherous…as you discovered. I'm surprised the car rental agency didn't recommend a more snow-worthy vehicle."

"They tried to switch and give me something like this." Her hand flicked toward the SUV's dashboard, contempt thick in her voice. "I refused. How was I supposed to know that this backwards hole wouldn't plow its streets?"

Kit was about to tell Courtney that the streets *were* plowed and she'd gotten stuck because she'd driven her very impractical car into an unused parking lot, but she just sighed instead, knowing it would be a waste of breath. Besides, they were right in front of the station. Kit pulled up to the curb and parked. "I'll walk you in."

Courtney's attention was fixed on the squat building across the street. "What's that?" Her tone was surprisingly interested, considering she was looking at a dingy, small-town VFW.

"That's the VFW and the temporary home to the town diner." She wasn't even finished speaking when Courtney opened her door and jumped out. As Kit watched, the woman hurried around the front of her SUV and across the street toward the viner entrance. She moved surprisingly fast on the slick pavement for someone wearing boots with four-inch heels.

Kit jumped out of the SUV and followed, her curiosity reignited. "You're heading the wrong way. The station's over here."

Without pausing in her dash toward the viner, Courtney tossed over her shoulder, "I'm going to get some coffee."

Although that was actually a good idea, since the quality of the station coffee varied greatly from barely drinkable to almost tolerable, depending on who made it and how long it had been sitting, Courtney's manner was a little too urgent. The fire had caused more of a mess than true damage, so the viner was already open again for business. Kit hurried to catch up with her, following her closely into the entry. From the intent look on the woman's face, Kit figured that Courtney had an ulterior motive for coming into the viner—unless she *really* loved her coffee.

Just as she entered the dining area, Courtney stopped, forcing Kit to shift to the side so as not to crash into her back. There was an almost immediate hush, one that Kit recognized from her first trip to the viner. The sight of a stranger in town was apparently a big deal.

Jules turned from where she was clearing an empty table and caught sight of Kit by the door. She started to smile, lighting up with genuine welcome, when her gaze moved to Courtney.

Her face instantly blanched of all color. The tray of dishes in her hands wobbled and fell, hitting the floor with a crash and breaking the frozen silence.

"No!" Jules darted across the room, and Kit tensed, trying to figure out what was happening. It felt like an accident scene, filled with action and chaos and requiring split-second decisions on her part—but she had no idea whose lives were in danger or why.

Jules skidded to a halt in front of a booth where Sam, the twins, and Dee were sitting. All the kids wore horrified expressions that made Kit tense even more. Something was wrong—very wrong—but Kit didn't know what. All she knew was that Courtney was somehow the cause.

"You!" A tiny, triumphant smile slipped across Courtney's face before disappearing just as quickly. Raising her arm, Courtney pointed at Jules dramatically. "Officer! Arrest that woman!"

Movement in her peripheral vision caught her attention, and Kit turned her head to see Elena retreating into the kitchen. Kit let her go, her focus switching between Courtney and Jules's protective stance in front of her family. She wished she'd brought her radio with her, but she had to settle for pulling out her cell phone and calling Theo. As it rang, Courtney charged forward toward Jules.

"Hold up!" Kit grabbed Courtney by the arm and hauled her back a few steps. When the woman started fighting her grip, Kit held her phone to her ear with her shoulder and used both hands to restrain Courtney. "Settle down and just stay here until we get this— whatever it is—worked out. Ms. Young, if you don't stop fighting me, I'm going to have to use restraints— Theo," she interrupted herself as Theo answered. "I need backup at the viner. Appears to be just a verbal dispute at the moment, but Jules is involved." Her voice lowered. "She's terrified."

"Five minutes," Theo clipped out before ending the call.

Courtney's struggles had stopped, so Kit kept one hand

on her arm while using the other to turn on the recording app before dropping her phone into her coat pocket. "Okay, let's go across the street and figure this out."

"No!" Courtney twisted out of her hold, and Kit grabbed her again, this time putting the other woman into an arm bar. "You have to arrest her immediately. If we leave her alone, she'll just steal my children away from me again!"

Startled, Kit blinked before giving Jules a questioning look. A white-faced Jules just stared back, not denying the accusation, and Kit tensed. For now, she was the only cop on scene, so it was up to her to keep things under control.

"Jules, could you take a seat next to Dee?" she asked.

Acting as if she hadn't heard, Jules continued staring at Courtney as if the older woman had stepped right out of Jules's nightmares. If Jules tried to run before Theo arrived, Kit was going to have to chase her, which meant either letting Courtney go or dragging her along. Her gut told her that Jules was more trustworthy than Courtney, but she really didn't want to have to leave either unguarded.

"Jules." Kit put more force into the command. "Sit down."

Tearing her gaze from Courtney, Jules met Kit's eyes before flicking from the entrance behind Kit and Courtney to the kitchen door. Kit's muscles tightened, preparing to move. She knew what Jules's look meant. It meant that desperation and panic were warring about which absolutely wrong decision she was about to make.

Kit softened her tone. "Jules, Theo's going to be here in just a minute. Nothing is going to happen until then.

Once he's here, all of us are going to talk and figure out what's going on. You trust Theo, right?"

Although she didn't answer, Jules focused on Kit again. Her panic was still obvious, but she looked as if she was actually listening now. It seemed that Theo's name was the magic word.

"Why don't you have a seat," Kit continued, using the same calm, hopefully soothing tone. "It looks like Dee could use your company. We'll stay over here, and you sit with your family, and when Theo gets here, we'll work everything out." Tensing in Kit's grip, Courtney took a breath, but Kit squeezed her arm before the woman could say anything. Kit knew for certain that nothing Courtney added to the conversation would help. Even worse, it would likely be the trigger that sent Jules and the kids bolting for the door.

Jules stayed frozen for several moments—long enough that Kit thought that her persuasive monologue hadn't helped—but then she glanced quickly at a terrified-looking Dee, who was staring at Courtney with huge eyes. "Oh, sweetie," Jules said softly, sounding heartbreakingly sad as she stiffly eased down on the bench next to her sister. Her voice was so quiet that the only reason Kit could hear her words was because everyone else in the viner remained completely silent.

On the other side of the booth from Jules and Dee, Sam started to slide out of the seat, but Kit caught his eye and shook her head. His expression looked just as frantic as Jules's. Normally, he was so good at hiding his emotions, and Kit knew that he must be completely panicked if his guard was down like that. Ignoring her silent signal, Sam stood.

"Please sit down, Sam," Kit ordered. Sam's gaze flickered over to her for only a brief second before returning to glare at Courtney. Kit braced herself, anticipating that Sam would rush at them. If she was occupied with Sam, she wouldn't be able to restrain Courtney or watch Jules and the other kids. It would be chaos.

His gaze flicked to Jules, and they exchanged a quick, telling look before Sam faced Kit and Courtney again. Dread filled Kit's belly as she read his expression, a mixture of determination and resignation that told Kit he was going to throw himself to the lions in order to save his family. He knew that she wouldn't be able to stop Jules and the other kids from running if he charged them—and as much as Kit was on their side, as a cop, she *had* to be a neutral party. She couldn't just let them run. Kit glanced briefly around the diners for someone who could help, but the average age was approximately eighty. She was on her own.

Hurry up and get here, Theo!

"Wh-wh-why are y-you h-here?" Sam demanded. His fists clenched at his sides, but he stayed by the table... for now.

"How can you ask that, Sebastian?" Courtney sounded choked up, but a quick glance showed that her face was as smooth and expressionless as ever. It was a discomforting juxtaposition. "I've been heartbroken since you were stolen away from me by that...that...*bitch*." She paused to glare at Jules, who stood up to stand next to Sam. "Your poor father..." Her voice broke, but it was eerily empty of emotion. This woman didn't love these children. Kit knew it deep in her gut, but she couldn't let her feelings affect how she handled the scene. It was one of the hardest things she'd ever done, to see Jules, the twins, Dee, and—worst of all—Sam, her sweet training buddy, stare at her as if Kit was a betrayer, a monster. She couldn't let the family just run out of the diner, though. It went against all of her instincts as a cop. "It took away his will to live." Her tone changed from sorrow to fury. "You killed him, you ungrateful bitch!" Jules flinched at that, turning chalk white, and Sam's face went blank with what Kit guessed was shock.

"Dad's dead?" Dee asked, sounding bewildered, and Jules reached behind her to grab the little girl's hand. The twins both stared at Courtney from their positions in the booth, silent and still for the first time since Kit had met them.

Courtney pressed her fingers to her lips as she let out a sob, but her smooth cheeks remained dry. Kit eyed the woman, her brain working through the information that had just been revealed. Courtney was either Jules's mother or stepmother—stepmother would be Kit's guess—and she was accusing Jules of kidnapping her siblings. Pieces clicked into place—Jules's mistrust and paranoia during the training session, the clear signs that Sam had been abused, even Theo's overprotectiveness. He'd known that Jules had committed a crime, and the entire K9 unit had been trying to hide it from Kit. It felt like a repeat of what had happened at her last department, only worse, since it seemed Jules had a very good reason to commit her crime.

Kit's gaze turned to Courtney, and a bone-deep loathing filled her. This woman had hurt those kids, hurt them badly enough that Jules had felt the need to commit a serious crime to get them away from her. Her thoughts filled with every domestic violence case that Kit had tried to intervene in. So many times, she'd been forced to stand by, watching as the system failed the victims, as abusers walked free, as children were returned to homes where Kit knew they weren't safe. The maddening frustration of each of those situations hit her in a wave, the memory of every time justice had failed because there hadn't been enough evidence or someone had screwed up.

This couldn't be one of those times. She couldn't be the person who sent these kids—these sweet, wonderful kids—back to their abuser.

Catching Jules's agonized gaze, Kit jerked her head toward the kitchen. Jules straightened, her shoulders jerking back in shock, looking confused for only a fraction of a second before she flew into action, motioning the terrified kids out of the booth.

"Where are they going?" Courtney's voice grew shrill as the kids piled out and Kit didn't say a word to stop them. "You're letting them go? What kind of police officer are you? This woman *kidnapped* my children, and you're just allowing them to leave? Stop them! Stop them right now, or you'll never work as a cop again!"

Kit faced forward, trying not to flinch at Courtney's threat as the kids ran for the kitchen door, followed by Jules. For nearly ten years, Kit had tried her best to follow the rules, to make a difference in the strict confines of the law, but she couldn't do this. She'd seen how happy the kids were with Jules, and she couldn't rip that away from them.

A swirl of cold air and the thump of boots in the front entry made Kit glance over her shoulder to see Theo, Hugh, and Otto rushing into the viner.

"Wait!" Theo made a beeline for Jules, who froze at the kitchen entrance, her expression a mix of love and grief. "Don't run, Jules. We'll fix this. We'll figure it out together."

After taking in the scene at a glance, Otto and Hugh moved over to Kit, and she felt her shoulders fall slightly in relief. Her partners were here to back her up. That might not be something she experienced for much longer, if Courtney had her way, and it made her even more grateful for their presence.

"They can't go back," Jules said, a sob in her voice as she clutched the edge of the door, her gaze jumping between Theo and the kitchen, where the kids must be waiting. "I won't let them go back."

"*We* won't let them." Theo stepped closer, his face both tender and fierce, all at once. "They won't go back to her. I promise. Whatever we have to do to keep that from happening, we'll do it."

Jules crumbled, her legs sagging underneath her, and Theo rushed to hold her up. She collapsed against him, and he supported her as she cried against his shoulder. Kit swallowed as her throat tightened in reaction to the other woman's relieved sobs.

"Sam, Ty, Tio, Dee." Theo said each child's name seriously, as if they were also a vow. "Come back in here, please. No one's going back with Courtney." His gaze flashed to her, ferociously cold anger in his eyes. "Ever."

The kids filed back in and clustered around Theo and Jules.

"You're all crooked cops," Courtney spat out, glaring at Theo and then at Kit. "Every single one of you."

"Okay!" Hugh clapped his hands loudly, making

half the people in the diner jump in their chairs. "Unless you're a cop, being restrained by a cop, or you're related to Jules, breakfast is now over. Everyone out!"

There were a few grumbles, but all the customers quickly gathered their coats and hurried out the door. Silence descended on the viner except for the soft murmur of Theo's voice as he spoke too quietly to Jules for Kit to hear. When the door thudded shut behind the last customer, Otto locked it and returned to the dining area as Hugh turned to Courtney.

"Who is this?" Hugh asked, his mouth a grim line. It was a sharp contrast to his usual good-natured expression.

"Courtney Young." Kit was the one who answered. "Jules's stepmother, apparently."

Hugh and Otto exchanged a look.

"You brought her here, to Jules?" Hugh demanded.

You're glaring at the wrong person, Kit thought, but kept her voice even as she answered. "No, I brought her to the police department. She came here and spotted Jules. That's when I called for backup."

"I saw that kidnapping bitch on the news, standing in front of this building," Courtney spat. "She was wearing a waitressing uniform. Last night, my PI confirmed that she was here with the kids, and I caught the first flight this morning."

Otto cursed under his breath, and Kit's eyebrows shot up. She'd never heard him swear since she'd met him.

"Pretty much, big guy," Hugh said with a sigh, looking back and forth between Courtney and the frightened family huddled around Theo.

"Let me go." Courtney tried to twist out of Kit's hold.

"I don't understand why I'm being treated like a criminal. I'm the victim! My children were stolen from me."

Kit hung on. "If we were treating you like a criminal, you'd be in handcuffs in an interview room across the street. Let's go to the station and get this straightened out."

"It's not a *disagreement* that needs to be 'straightened out.' This was a heinous crime, and Juliet needs to go to prison!" As Courtney's voice carried across the viner, Jules's face whitened even more and Theo looked like he wanted to murder someone. Sam's fists had clenched again, the twins' expressions were grim, and Dee started to cry.

Kit turned back to Courtney, determined to get her across the street, even if she had to drag her, but before she could make a move, a stranger's deep voice came from the doorway.

"That's enough, Ms. Young."

Jules gasped audibly, but Kit didn't look at her, too focused on the man who'd just entered the viner. He was tall, broad, and looked to be in his thirties, darkly attractive despite his scars and scowl. He strode into the dining area with such confidence that Kit immediately wondered if he was a state or federal investigator. Courtney stiffened in Kit's hold.

"Who are you?" Theo asked sharply.

"And how did you get in here?" Hugh didn't wait for the stranger to answer before adding, "That door was locked."

"My name is Mateo Espina." He ignored Hugh's question. "I'm here because I received a text from Jules last night, telling me that there was an emergency, and that I was needed." His gaze flicked to Courtney. "I see she was telling the truth."

Everyone's eyes moved to Jules, who looked confused. "I didn't text you," she said.

Mr. Espina frowned slightly before appearing to dismiss that, at least for now. "I have some information about the current situation that you might find useful."

"Don't listen to him!" Courtney's voice had a shrill note that revealed her fear and made Kit even more interested in what Mr. Espina had to say. "He's a criminal, just like Juliet. They're in on it together. He blackmailed me, made me promise not to go to the police. If it wasn't for him, I would've found where Jules was hiding the kids months ago."

Mr. Espina didn't looked fazed by her words. Instead, he simply cocked his head slightly, as if he found what she was saying only mildly interesting. "And what evidence, Ms. Young, did I use to blackmail you?"

Courtney tried to take a step away from him, but Kit blocked her path. "It's not evidence. It's lies and doctored video." Seeming to regain some of her confidence, Courtney straightened. "Also, it was illegally obtained. My lawyer isn't worried about it, so neither am I." After shooting Jules a triumphant, poisonous glance, she looked back at Mr. Espina. "There's no way I'll be convicted, but *she* will be."

Dee started to cry harder, and Kit frowned. "We need to move this to the station. The kids shouldn't be hearing this."

Otto moved toward Mr. Espina, and to Kit's surprise, he didn't object as the cop approached. Instead, Mr. Espina just said mildly, "Left jacket pocket."

Otto cautiously reached in and pulled out a flash drive as Mr. Espina lifted the large envelope he was carrying and dumped it out on the table in front of him. Glossy pictures scattered over the surface of the table, and Kit peered at them, unable to see the photos at that angle. By the way the muscles in Otto's jaw tightened and twitched, however, they were upsetting.

"What are those?" The shrill note was back in Courtney's voice as she pulled against Kit's hold. "If those are what I think they are, then I will sue you. How dare you invade my privacy like tha—"

"Quiet," Otto ordered, the harsh word as effective as a slap. Courtney snapped her mouth closed, her face paling under the layers of contoured makeup.

"I gave you a choice, Ms. Young." Mr. Espina idly straightened the corner of one photo, lining it up squarely with the one next to it. "You chose poorly. Jules might be going to prison, but you *will* be joining her."

"No!" The word burst from Courtney, but then she calmed, even smiling slightly. "Like I said, I discussed this with my lawyer. Those pictures, whatever you have on that flash drive, aren't admissible evidence. So what if my relationship with Sebastian was a little...inappropriate? What boy wouldn't want to be in his place?"

Kit glanced at Sam, fury and heartbreak at what had happened to him sweeping over her. He stared at the floor, refusing to look at anyone. "What else did you do to them?" Kit asked, trying to keep her voice neutral even as she raged inside. She knew that there'd be more. With people like Courtney, there always was.

Courtney gave an impatient huff. "Nothing."

"Nothing?" Jules's voice shook. "You hit me, locked me in a closet for hours, *tortured* me. You call that nothing? And what about what you did to Dee at the pageants? Burning her with the curling iron if she didn't sit still? Not letting her use the bathroom all day?"

"It was for her own good." Courtney waved a hand at Dee. "Look at her. A couple of months away from me, and she looks like a homely boy. As for you, you were a difficult child. I didn't do anything you didn't deserve. You don't know how hard it was. I was basically a single mother."

"You're going to jail," Theo gritted out, flat hatred in his gaze. "I'm going to enjoy helping to send you there."

"Please," Courtney scoffed, sounding as if she was regaining her confidence. "I'm not going anywhere except back to Florida with my children. All of that so-called evidence was obtained illegally by someone who doesn't even have his mob buddies backing him up anymore." She smirked at Mr. Espina. "Yes, my PI told me how pathetically powerless you are now that all your criminal business associates are either dead, in prison, or in hiding.

"All that's left is my word against a kidnapper's— and a few crooked cops that are in on it with her. You all knew about it for months and didn't turn her in. I'll need to check with my lawyer about the proper terminology, but I believe that's called 'aiding and abetting.'" The triumph in her voice was almost as sickening as the casual way she'd admitted to abusing her stepchildren. "No court is going to convict me—but they will convict all of you and give me custody of my children."

The diner went almost silent for a frozen moment. The only sound was Dee's muffled crying.

"Y-y-you f-forg-g-got ab-bout m-m-me." Sam took a step toward his stepmother, his skin so pale it was almost green.

"What?" Courtney gasped on a sharp inhale.

"I'll testif-f-fy ag-gainst y-you."

Jules pressed a hand to her mouth, silent tears streaking her cheeks as she stared at her brother.

"Sebastian! How could you threaten to do such a thing? You know you enjoyed every second of it." As Courtney tried to move away, Kit tightened her grip, giving the woman's arm a harder tug than technically necessary. She didn't have to see the photos to know what was in them, and her heart broke for sweet, brave Sam, even as disgust for the woman she was restraining filled her. Courtney tensed, and her expression went cold as she gave a sharp, short laugh. "You think anyone will believe you? They'll all think you're lying."

"He's not lying." Ty's face was tight and his voice had a slight quaver, but he didn't drop his gaze from where it was fixed on his stepmother. "I'll testify, too."

"Of course you'd defend your brother," Courtney scoffed. "That doesn't mean anything."

There was a short, intense silence, and Kit could see the effect of Courtney's words on Sam. His rigid posture started to collapse as his resolute expression flattened to blankness. Kit couldn't stay quiet and watch him take all the blame for something that was not his fault.

"I believe them," Kit said, meeting Sam's surprised gaze when it darted to hers. "And the jury will believe both of us, since I've recorded this entire conversation—including when you confessed to child abuse. Courtney Young, you're under arrest." Glancing around the room, she saw that only Theo was in uniform. "Theo, can I borrow your cuffs?"

He grinned at her—the happiest, friendliest smile

she'd ever seen on him—as he pulled a pair of hand-cuffs from the case on his belt. "Definitely." He tossed the cuffs to her, and she grabbed them out of the air one-handed. It wasn't until one of Courtney's hands was restrained that she realized what was happening and started to struggle.

"I'm not the criminal here!" she yelled, trying to twist free. Hugh helped restrain her as Kit secured Courtney's other wrist before double-locking the cuffs with the key Hugh offered. "How *dare* you arrest me? By the time I'm through with you, you're going to be jobless and destitute, do you hear me?"

Hugh took a firm hold of a still-shrieking Courtney and met Kit's gaze. His small smile was grim. "I commend you on not getting rough with her. If I'd been in your place, I don't know if I would've had the willpower to resist."

Kit returned his smile with a humorless one of her own. "I was tempted." As Hugh led Courtney toward the door, Kit glanced around, her mind clicking through what she needed to do. When her gaze landed on Sam, who was having the stuffing hugged out of him by his siblings and Theo, sharp anger pierced her. Taking a deep breath, she pushed the knowledge of Courtney's abuse and the accompanying rage aside to dwell on later. Right now, she had a viner full of witnesses and victims and who knew what else.

Otto was returning the photos to their envelope, his expression hard, when Kit caught his attention. "Can you escort Mr. Espina across the street to one of the interview rooms?" Otto dipped his chin in acknowledg-ment before ushering the other man toward the door.

"Wait!" Jules called. "I want to talk to you before you leave town again, and I know that Elena, Sarah, and Grace will want to see you."

Mr. Espina turned toward Jules. "Tomorrow. We'll meet at your house at eight."

After he and Otto left, Kit turned to Theo and Jules's family, letting her expression soften to a smile when the kids looked at her anxiously. "Let's move this next door so the viner can reopen for business."

Jules gave a watery laugh, her arms around Dee and Tio, gripping them to her sides, as Sam and Ty stayed close and Theo loomed protectively over them all. "The poor customers keep getting chased out of here. They're going to start getting their food to go."

"Nah," Kit said. "They like being in on the excitement. This way, they're first on the gossip chain."

"True."

Kit switched her attention back to Theo. "Is there an interview room they all can fit into?"

From his grimace, she took that as a no, so she thought about other possibilities.

"The women's locker room will work in a pinch." When Ty looked like he was going to complain, Kit spoke again before he could. "Right now, I'm the only woman who might be wandering in there, so you'll be safe."

They gathered up their coats, seemingly unwilling to break out of their tight family huddle, and Kit thought that was sweet. She felt a slight pang that she didn't have anyone close by, but she was glad that Jules wouldn't be ripped away from her siblings, and she was very happy that Sam and the others wouldn't have to live with the awful, vicious Courtney Young.

"Wh-wh-why d-d-did y-you br-br-br...l-lead h-her in h-h-here?" Sam's accusing question broke the comfortable silence, and Kit looked at him in surprise.

"I didn't—not intentionally. I just brought her to the police station because she got her car stuck in the snow. When she darted across the street toward this place, I wasn't sure what to think." She met Sam's eyes and was unable to tell whether he accepted her explanation or not. "I'm sorry for my part in springing her on you. That must've been terrifying."

Sam gave her a tiny nod before looking away, but Jules managed a tight smile. The rest of the kids looked overwhelmed and stressed, reminding Kit to focus. There was a lot to do before everyone could head home.

She gave Theo a rueful look. "Every time I try to take a day off, I end up in the middle of some incident."

He tipped his chin. Although the gesture was slight, his gaze was warm, and she finally felt like she was part of the team. "Welcome to Monroe."

CHAPTER 20

BY THE TIME KIT ESCAPED THE POLICE STATION, THERE WAS only an hour or so of daylight left, but she still wanted to go to the tower. She was tired and needed to see a friendly face—especially if that face was Wes's. It had been a long day. Mr. Espina had contacted a lawyer, who'd arrived with custody documents and other contracts for Courtney to sign. In return, she had been released.

It bothered Kit that Courtney wasn't getting any jail time for what she'd done to Sam—and the others— but Sam had assured her that he didn't care if she was punished. All he wanted was to stay with Jules and his other siblings, without the threats of having to return to Courtney or Jules going to prison hanging over their heads. Since Courtney had signed legal custody over to Jules, all the kids were ecstatic. They didn't even want the inheritance left by their father, but they agreed to accept it when the lawyer mentioned how it would drive Courtney crazy to only get a tiny sliver of the fortune their father had possessed.

"Honestly," she told Justice, who'd spent most of his day happily hanging out with Jules and her siblings, "I'm glad they're sticking around town. I'd hate to lose my training buddies." She hoped they wouldn't hold it against her that she'd unintentionally led Courtney right to them, especially since everything had turned out for the best.

As she neared the turnoff for her street, Kit hesitated, tapping her fingers against the steering wheel and peering at the darkening sky. It would get dark even more quickly, thanks to the gloomy clouds that'd gathered. She hadn't realized how accustomed she'd become to the sunny weather until it changed.

She passed the turnoff, continuing toward the western pass. Sticking his head between the seats, Justice rested his chin on the center console, his droopy jowls spreading out to either side.

"I know," she said as if he were judging her. "We'll get a half hour of work in before it gets dark, and we don't have a helper, so we probably won't get much accomplished, but I don't care. Wes is probably waiting for us. I did tell him we'd come to the tower to train today. The only way to tell him I couldn't make it would be to call on the radio, and then everyone and their brother would be in our business, and we'd probably piss off another dispatcher." She knew she could also email him, but she honestly didn't want to chance that Wes would tell her not to come.

Justice heaved a long sigh.

"Fine." The only reason she was making the trip to the tower was because she wanted to see Wes again, and it was a little silly to try to convince herself—or Justice, who couldn't understand a word of what she was saying—otherwise. "Today was tough, and the only thing that got me through was knowing that I'd get to see Wes. We'll do some basic obedience training, have a Pop Tart, and get home in time for dinner. Sound like a plan?"

Half asleep, Justice didn't respond.

"Good. That's what we'll do, then." It probably wasn't normal to discuss her plans with her dog, but that was the nice thing about her new town: the weirder she was, the more she fit in with everyone else.

They'd just gotten over the pass when the snowflakes started to fall. They were big and beautiful, like something out of a Christmas movie, but the closer Kit got to the tower, the thicker the flakes got. As she turned onto the two-track path leading to the tower, the previous tire marks were blurred, filled halfway with new snow.

The wind picked up, and she was grateful that the surrounding trees blocked the worst of it. She wouldn't want to be on the highway in this, since the visibility had to be just a few feet. In the midst of the trees, the snow swirled around her SUV, the fresh, white covering giving the forest a magical appearance. Despite the sparkling fairyland around her, Kit's shoulders tightened as she slowly rolled through the falling snow. Considering Wes's inhospitable neighbors, this was not a good place for her to get her vehicle stuck.

It wasn't until she pulled into the clearing surrounding the tower that Kit allowed herself to relax, exhaling a long breath. She felt like she'd been holding it since the snow started falling. Now that she was out of the shelter of the trees, the wind hit the side of the SUV hard, making it shudder from the strength of the gusts.

Parking next to the tower, she braced herself and opened her door. Although she thought she'd been mentally prepared, the cold wind still shocked her, blasting through her layers like they were tissue paper. Hurrying to get Justice out of the SUV, she revised her plan. There was no way they were going to do any training in this snow-storm, not without her losing a few toes from the cold.

By the way he huddled at her side, rather than jumping around like a wild thing in the snow like he normally did, Justice agreed with her. He stuck close to her as she hurried for the tower door, silently thanking Wes for his genius when the door swung open as soon as she looked toward the camera.

Stepping inside, Kit almost ran into a broad, flannel-covered chest. "Oh!" she said, looking up at Wes. "I thought you'd be upstairs."

"I saw you pull up and wanted to open the door before you froze." He closed the door behind them, and the howling wind was instantly muffled. Justice slipped his head under Wes's hand and was rewarded with ear strokes. "Heavy rain or snow messes with the facial-recognition. I'm working on fixing that."

"Thank you." There was a coatrack next to the door, so she removed her boots and coat, hanging it next to his before following Wes up the stairs. Justice bounded ahead, back to his bouncy self now that they were out of the wind and snow. "I should've checked the weather before heading out, but I was in a hurry, worried about running out of daylight to train in." She gave a huff of laughter. "Guess it doesn't matter whether it's light out or not now. There's no training in this."

"Did you want to use the tower?" he offered as they reached the top. The large, round room was warm and bright and welcoming, smelling of split pine and woodsmoke, just like Wes.

"I think I'll give Justice the day off. I'd prefer to stay here until the snow and wind let up, if you don't mind?" She dreaded making the drive back to town in the middle of the nasty storm. Despite their predicament, though, she wasn't sorry she'd come. Just seeing this big, bearded, flannel-draped man made the tension of the day ease out of her. She hadn't realized how tense she was until she'd set eyes on him and everything inside her had suddenly relaxed.

"No."

She blinked. That was unexpected. "We can't stay?"

"No." He let out a huff and stared at the lofted ceiling for a moment. "That isn't coming out right. No, I don't mind if you stay. Yes, you can stay. I want you to stay. So please stay."

Once again, she was reminded how much she loved his mannerisms and the way he always said exactly what he was thinking, and she smiled for what felt like the first time in a long, stressful day. "Thank you."

"You're welcome." There was another long pause as they stared at each other. Justice, finished exploring the space, returned to lean on Wes and did his head-under-the-hand trick again. Wes blinked, as if pulled from his thoughts, and asked, "Would you like something to eat?"

Kit smiled more broadly than the offer probably deserved. "Yes. That would be wonderful."

Wes's thoughts ran in high-speed circles. He'd never felt so nervous—and yet so excited—before in his life. Kit was here, in his tower, and they were alone—except for the dog—and he needed to get her some food before she started wondering what was wrong with him. As he moved toward the cupboard, the dispatcher's voice came from the radio, announcing that both the east and west passes were about to be closed due to the winter storm. He wasn't surprised. With this wind, the visibility had to be terrible.

Wes grabbed the s'mores box and held it up in question. When he saw Kit's frown, he started to return it to the shelf.

"No, that would be perfect. I'm just thinking about the pass being closed. Is this storm supposed to continue all night?"

He froze, the consequences of the closed pass suddenly hitting him. Normally, he left his home so rarely, especially during the winter, that the road conditions didn't affect him too much, but this time, it was different. Kit couldn't leave, which meant she would need to stay. With him. Possibly all night. He swallowed hard, his brain temporarily experiencing a whiteout that rivaled the conditions outside. "Uh…"

Looking concerned, Kit walked over to the wall of windows and peered out into the snow-filled dusk. "Last time I was snowed out of Monroe, when I first got to Colorado, it was for almost a week." Turning, she gave him a tentative smile. "If you're stuck with me and Justice that long, you'll probably end up tossing us out in the snow after a few days."

"No!" he said, and realized that came out too vehemently when she looked startled. The idea of being trapped with Kit for hours—if not days—was sending blood racing through his veins. This would be the true test of how they got along, and he worried that she'd be the one wanting to toss him into the snow, rather than the other way around. He tried to speak again, more calmly this time. "I can't imagine ever getting tired of you." When her eyes widened again, he mentally swore. Had that sounded too intense? He felt like he was trying to navigate a minefield while blindfolded. Conversation—especially a conversation with a woman he liked—was not his strong suit.

"Good." Her surprise seemed to have faded, and she was smiling again, so Wes let out the breath he was holding. "Could I check the weather forecast?" She gestured toward one of his computers.

"Of course." As he moved toward the closest laptop, he realized that he was still holding the box of Pop Tarts, and he handed it to Kit as he passed.

When she laughed, he hesitated, trying to figure out why, but she waved him on. "I've got this. I'm not the best cook in the world, but I can manage to toast a Pop Tart. Did you want one?"

"Yes." He pulled up the weather site. It loaded slowly, but Wes had expected that. He was glad the satellite internet was working at all, since it tended to go down during storms. When the site finally displayed, his stomach gave a hop of excitement. "The snow will continue until approximately midnight, but there will be high winds through the night."

She made a face but didn't appear to be overly upset, which made Wes hopeful that she didn't mind having to stay the night. "The plows won't even try to clear the passes until the wind dies down, since the snow would just blow right back over the highway. Guess you're stuck with us. In hindsight, I should've checked the weather forecast before coming out here. Sorry about this."

"I'm not... Sorry, I mean," he blurted out.

"You're sure?" Kit was eyeing him closely, and he felt that warm feeling in his chest again at the way she seemed to really care what he thought and felt. "I know you have to really cherish your privacy to spend the winters out here. I hate to intrude on you like this." Justice settled on the rug by the woodstove with a loud groan, making Kit laugh. "Obviously, my dog doesn't care that he's intruding."

Wes smiled—he loved the sound of her laughter. "Neither of you is intruding." He wanted to change the subject, since he was worried that the more she apologized, the greater the risk was of him admitting how extremely glad he was that she was here. "Did you figure out the toaster?"

His topic change worked. "I think so." She glanced at it, tilting her head as she examined the appliance. "It's not like any toaster I've ever seen before."

"I modified it." He joined her in the small kitchen area and checked to see that she'd gotten it working. "Heat-producing appliances typically use the most energy, so I…" He glanced at her, not sure if she would want to hear the technical details. If Leila were here, she'd definitely be telling him she didn't care. He decided to play it safe and not delve into the process. "I made it more energy-efficient."

"Huh." She examined the toaster and then returned her gaze to him. "You're really smart, aren't you?"

"In some areas, yes." At the moment, he would've traded a good portion of his technical knowledge for a few more social skills. "Other things are harder for me."

Kit made a *hmm* sound. "I think we're all that way. I like police work and training dogs and mentoring kids, but if I try to do anything more technical on a computer than writing a case report, it tends to go badly."

"Go badly?" he repeated, carefully extracting one of the pastries from the toaster and juggling it from hand to hand until it was cool enough to pass to Kit. It wasn't until she accepted it with a wry look that he realized she might not want to eat something he'd just handled extensively. "Sorry. Did you want that one instead? I won't touch it."

Waving off the offer, she took a bite. "At my last job, the joke around the station was that I had hands of death when it came to computers. I'll be innocently trying to set up a spreadsheet or answer an email, and *bam*"—she held the Pop Tart in her mouth so she could clap her hands together once before rescuing the pastry—"blue screen of death. I seriously should come with a warning label."

After glancing around at the array of computers and electronics, Wes picked up the second Pop Tart. "Good to know."

She laughed. "I'm also horrible at art or decorating or anything creative."

He loved hearing about things she was bad at. If she'd been as perfect as she'd first appeared, there'd be no way she'd ever be interested in him. If she had foibles and flaws, though, then there was a chance she could see past all his idiosyncrasies to what was inside. Except for his parents and his sister, no one had ever bothered to look that deeply, but the way Kit listened to him so closely and watched him for his reactions made him hope that she would try.

"Sooo…" she said, drawing his attention away from his thoughts.

He waited, not sure what that drawn-out word meant.

"Since I've revealed a few of mine, what are your weaknesses?" she asked.

Surprised, he stared at her for a long moment before speaking. "You can't tell?"

When she rolled her eyes at him in response, he smiled. The gesture seemed like she was teasing, rather than mocking him. "Of course I can't. You are a mad-scientist-level genius—minus the 'mad' part—and sweet and modest and brave enough to get between me and five loaded shotguns. I'm not seeing any negatives, and it's making me a little self-conscious here."

That made him blink as his brain tried to wrap itself around her words. She'd dumped out so much in front of him that it made his head spin with delighted disbelief. "*I* make *you* self-conscious?"

She picked crumbs off her hoodie, peeking up at him through her lashes in a way that he found almost unbearably appealing. "A little, yeah. You're just so smart. It's a little intimidating."

"I'm intimidating?" He huffed a laugh, having a hard time believing the picture she was painting.

"Not obnoxiously so." She hurried to amend her words. "You're too nice to rub your brains in my face." After a short pause, they both laughed. "Sorry, that was kind of a graphic way of putting it, wasn't it? I just meant that you're not pretentious or snobby, even though you're smart enough that you could get away with that. It makes you really easy to like."

His insides were so warm that he felt like he was positively glowing. Not only had she just admitted that she found him smart, and nice, and brave, but she'd also said flat-out that she liked him. Even if she left the tower and never returned, the memory of her words would be enough to keep him company for years on the long, lonely winter nights. It was such a huge deal to him, what she'd just said, that he couldn't think of any worthy response. Instead, he took the chicken's way out and changed the subject...again.

"Are you thirsty?"

She took the switch in topics with easy grace, and it made him like her even more. "Oh God, yes. Ever since I moved here, I feel like I can't drink enough water."

"Are you having any trouble adjusting to the altitude?" Grabbing a spill-proof travel mug, he filled it with water from the tap. After screwing on the lid, he handed it to her.

"Not really. I've found I can't run as fast as I could at sea level, but that just motivates me to work out more." She examined the mug with a wry expression. "Leave it to you to have a glass that astronauts probably use in space." Pushing the button on the side to open the lid, she took a long drink.

He ignored her space-cup comment, figuring that she didn't want to hear facts about space travel. It was getting easier to know when to share and when to be quiet, he realized, and he gave Leila a silent thank-you for always being so blunt with him. "Once your body adjusts to it, you'll be able to visit your former home state and run even faster there without getting breathless."

"That's something to look forward to." The radio chirped, and the dispatcher assigned a traffic-accident call east of town to a county deputy. When their voices went silent, Kit asked, "Mind if I use your radio to let the dispatcher know I'm not reachable by cell phone?"

He gave her a go-ahead gesture, and she moved over to the radio, careful not to step on a snoring Justice's tail. She quickly gave the dispatcher the information. Before she could even take a step away, an amused voice came through the radio.

"Whatcha doing at the tower with Wes?"

He recognized the voice as Hugh Murdoch's and eyed Kit to see how she was taking the teasing. She just grimaced in a good-natured way as she picked up the mic again.

"None of your business."

A long, exaggerated sigh came over the radio, and Kit met Wes's gaze. Her long-suffering but amused expression made him smile, and he loved how it felt as if they were a team, the two of them against the rest of the town. If he had Kit on his side, the gossip and the stares of the rest of the area residents didn't matter. With just that small gesture, Kit had turned things around so that it felt like they were the normal ones. For the first time in his life, Wes felt like he was on the inside of something, and he felt a huge surge of affection for Kit for making that happen.

"Greenie," Hugh continued on the radio. *"Spill. It's been a rough day…and week. And year. I need a distraction, and my soap is in hiatus right now. Help a partner out."*

The dispatcher spoke before Kit could. *"Mind taking this gossip session off channel one in case there's a real emergency?"*

Kit snorted before raising the mic. "Excellent idea. Good night, Hugh. Stay safe." She replaced the mic and walked away from the radio. "I don't know how Grace—Hugh's girlfriend—doesn't strangle him on a regular basis. I consider myself pretty even-keeled, but he tests my patience sometimes."

Wes tried to imagine riding around in a vehicle with someone for eight or more hours a day and shuddered. For him, that would be hell—unless he was able to partner up with Kit. She'd be the only one he'd be able to tolerate being in such close quarters with for an extended length of time. Most people made him feel tense, but Kit had the opposite effect. She actually relaxed him, making him feel calm and almost unbearably excited at the same time. As she sat on the couch, curling her socked feet underneath her, he couldn't look away. There was a sinuous grace to her movements that fascinated him, making him feel as if he could happily watch her do simple daily tasks for hours on end.

Her gaze turned curious, making him realize that he'd been staring. As much as he wanted to keep watching her, he knew it would make him come off as strange.

As he sat on the opposite end of the couch, he hunted for a socially acceptable question and finally came up with "Do you like working there?"

Tilting her head, she glanced down as if considering the question. "Right now, it's challenging," she finally answered, sounding as if she was picking each word carefully. "I think it'll get better once I get to know the people and the area, and my partners learn that I can be trusted." She gave him a quick glance, and he wondered if she'd realized too late how much that last bit revealed. "It's been a hard few months for Monroe and its police force, so it's natural for everyone to be…cautious."

Even though he was isolated geographically, he couldn't have missed the news about the lieutenant who'd been arrested for working with the people who'd attacked Monroe. Kit was right about it being a hard few months for everyone in the area, especially law enforcement, but he still felt a strong need to defend her. Why couldn't everyone see how trustworthy and *good* Kit was? Wes had known immediately, and everything she'd said or done after that had just confirmed her integrity. "Are they making it hard to do your job?" he asked.

She smiled at him, a surprised yet open grin that made him blink from the brilliance of it.

"What?" he asked, still a little stunned.

"You live up here by yourself, rarely interacting with other people," she said.

"Yes." He spoke slowly. Although her words were accurate, he wasn't sure what she was getting at.

"I didn't expect you to be one of the most intuitive people I've ever met."

"Intuitive?" He said the word slowly, feeling it out. No one had called him that—ever. "I don't feel like I'm intuitive."

"You are." The way she sounded so certain made him start to believe it was true. "How else could you have managed to get your crazy-ass neighbors to trust you? And whenever we talk, you always know exactly how to sort out my scattered thoughts."

He considered that for a long moment, feeling that unfamiliar warmth in his chest spread even more. *Intuitive*. It wasn't a word he'd ever attributed to himself, but he really liked that she saw that in him. "I'm not sure if you're right," he said finally, "but I hope you are."

The silence that fell after that wasn't awkward, although it wasn't exactly *comfortable* either. The sparking tension between them reminded Wes of the air right before a thunderstorm rolled in, when everything was still and charged and thick with anticipation of what was about to come.

Breaking their eye contact, Kit placed her water

bottle on the rough-hewn wood of the coffee table. Wes sat back, surprised to find that he'd been leaning toward her. With the tense moment interrupted, he felt like he should say something, and he glanced around for inspiration. He was still hunting for words when she spoke.

"Do you have any cards?" she asked, making him frown.

"Playing cards?" When she nodded, he glanced around again, as if he could pull them out of thin air. "No."

"Board games?"

"No." He was the worst host in the world. It had never occurred to him to have any cards or games, since he simply played on his tablet or his computer when he had the urge. That reminded him that the tower wasn't completely out of entertainment options. "Want to play *Call of Duty*?"

"Oh yeah." She beamed at him. "Although I need to warn you that I'm really, really good at it."

"Yeah? Controllers." The robot cat retrieved them and zipped across the room to offer them to Wes. "Then I need to warn you that I'm probably better. Screen down." A large monitor lowered from the ceiling to hang six feet in front of the couch.

"Enjoy those delusions of superiority while you can," Kit warned, teasingly elbowing him in the side. His skin lit up at the touch. "I'm going to enjoy destroying you."

He stared at her until she glanced over and made a face.

"Too far?" she asked.

"No." His voice sounded rough, and he cleared his throat and focused on handing her a controller. "No, that was just right."

CHAPTER 21

THEY PLAYED FOR HOURS, UNTIL JUSTICE INDICATED IN NO uncertain terms that it was time for dinner and a trip outside. With a groan, Kit dropped her controller and stood, stretching on her tiptoes with her fingers reaching for the ceiling. Turning her head toward Wes, she noticed he was watching her with a heated stare. When he caught her looking at him, he dropped his gaze and fumbled his controller.

"I can only say that I warned you," she said, trying to keep her tone light and not reveal the answering flame his hot eyes had lit inside her. It was hard to remember that they hadn't known each other for that long when she felt as comfortable with him as if they'd been friends for years. Her strongest feelings, however, weren't that friendly, especially since they'd gradually eased closer to each other as they'd played until they'd been sitting side by side, close enough to brush arms.

"You did warn me. And you were right. You're very, very good at *Call of Duty.*" A tiny smile twitched up the corner of his mouth. "Almost as good as I am."

"Whaaat?" Her protest had as much laughter as indignation in it. "I was very clearly the victor. Do I need to beat you *again* to prove I'm better at this than you?" Plopping down on the couch, she grabbed the controller she'd just abandoned. "Sorry, Justice, but your dinner will need to wait. That kind of whopper can't go unchallenged."

Holding up his hands as if warding her off, Wes let out a deep laugh. "No more! No more! I admit your superiority!"

Although she managed to hold her smug expression, Kit felt a bit dazed by the beautiful sight of a belly-laughing Wes. Even when he was serious, he was intimidatingly attractive, with his model-meets-lumberjack appearance, but happiness made him positively radiant. "Well, then." She stood again, trying to look away as he continued to chuckle. "My work here is done. Justice, want to go outside with the reigning champion?"

Wes's laughter finally faded, and she was able to breathe normally again. "Don't go far. It's easy to get lost in a storm like this."

"We won't." She headed for the stairs, watching over her shoulder as Wes told the screen to retract and the robo-cat to pick up the controllers. At her chuckle, he gave her a questioning look.

"I love all your gadgets," she admitted. "It's like living in an old *Jetsons* episode."

He looked pleased and a bit bashful at that. "I'm just lazy."

"Sure." She didn't believe that for a second. "So lazy you design and build all sorts of things *and* you watch for fires *and* you take professional wildlife photos *and* you rescue stray cops from your gun-happy neighbors." She started down the stairs with Justice right behind her. "Lazy, my ass."

His low chuckle followed her down, and she was very

careful not to look back at him. Just the sound made her shiver, and she knew the sight of him laughing would stop her in her tracks. Poor Justice needed to get outside.

After pulling on her coat and boots, she stepped out of the tower door. The wind shoved at her and threw sharp pellets of snow against any uncovered skin. Huddling against the door once it closed, she gasped at the shock of cold and buried her chin in her collar. Squinting eyes that wanted to water from the cold and force of the gusts, she peered around the area. Her shiver wasn't just cold-related.

Compared to the warm, friendly brightness of the tower room, the woods outside seemed almost menacing. The puddle of artificial light didn't touch the trees, and they rose, black on black against the starless sky. The forest seemed to press in on her from all sides, reminding her that anything could be hiding in that darkness…hiding and watching her. She tried to dismiss the unsettled feeling in the pit of her stomach, but she couldn't escape the creeping sensation of having hostile eyes focused on her.

Even typically oblivious Justice didn't look any more thrilled than she was as he went just far enough to do what he needed to do. His caution made her even more aware of the surrounding woods and the possible dangers lurking in it. She watched him carefully, alert to any sign that he might catch a scent and head into the dark, treacherous wilderness surrounding them. To her relief, he took care of business quickly, not even glancing at the encircling trees before trotting over to her. If she hadn't been tense, anticipating some nebulous threat, and if her eyelids hadn't been threatening to freeze shut, she would've laughed at the way her dog's ears blew to one side, flying horizontally in the wicked wind.

Remembering that the facial-recognition part of the automatic lock didn't work well in a snowstorm, Kit pounded on the door a few times as she turned her face toward the camera. One of those two methods worked, because it swung open immediately, letting them back inside. It wasn't until she and Justice were both inside and the door had shut and locked behind them that she relaxed. Even though she doubted that there was really something dangerous waiting in the gloom outside, it was still reassuring to be safe behind a locked door and thick stone walls.

After shedding her outerwear, she hurried up the stairs, drawn by her desire to be close to Wes again, as well as a wonderful smell.

"Is that beef stew?" she asked, marveling that he'd cooked something that smelled so delicious in the short time she and Justice had been outside.

"Yes. I'm just warming it up." Standing at the two-burner stove, he glanced over his shoulder at her. The sight of such a big, burly man cooking for her made the heat in her belly—which had quieted to a simmer during her cold trip outside—flare to life again, hotter than before.

She abruptly looked away, moving to the coffee table to grab her travel mug of water. "It smells great."

As he dished the stew into three bowls, she smiled that he'd thought of Justice. Normally, she kept dog food in her SUV for emergencies, but the move had messed with her usual routines. There was even a large mixing bowl filled with water on the floor that Justice was currently lapping at. Kit held back a snort. Leave it to her to be more impressed when a man did nice things for her dog than she was when he did nice things for her.

Wes put one bowl on the counter—to cool so Justice wouldn't burn himself, she assumed, which made her heart turn into an even bigger mushy mess than it already was—and brought the other two over to the couch where she waited.

"Thanks," she said, trying not to smile too widely as she accepted the bowl. It smelled even better close up. Sitting on the couch in her spot from earlier, she took a bite and gave a happy groan that sounded a lot like the noise Justice made when she scratched his ear just right. "This is wonderful."

He beamed. "Thank you. It's surprisingly rewarding to feed someone else."

They grew quiet as they ate, finishing their food quickly. Kit hadn't realized how hungry she'd been. It had been a long day. Except for the Pop Tart Wes had given her earlier, she hadn't eaten since breakfast.

"Did you want more?" he asked, taking both of their empty bowls.

"No, thank you." She rubbed her now warm and fed belly. "It was great, but I'm full."

With a nod, he placed the bowls and spoons in the sink before setting Justice's bowl on the floor. The dog sat in front of the bowl, staring at Wes with hopeful eyes and a string of drool hanging from his jowls.

"What's he waiting for?" Wes asked.

"I make him wait to eat until I give him the release word," she explained, joining him in the kitchen. "That way, he doesn't just gulp down whatever rotting hot dog smells good to him before I can tell him no. Justice, okay."

The dog dove into the bowl, eating even more quickly than Kit had. She grinned down at him. "You make me feel so delicate and dainty in comparison, Justice." Without taking his face out of the bowl, he wagged his tail at the sound of his name. Still smiling, she met Wes's gaze again. "Since you cooked, I'll do the dishes."

"No need." He got that half-bashful, half-excited look that she was beginning to recognize.

"You have some high-tech, super-efficient gadget for washing dishes, don't you?" she asked, not at all surprised when he nodded and opened one of the lower cupboards to reveal what appeared to be a normal— albeit small—dishwasher. After placing their dirty dishes into the appliance, including Justice's well-licked bowl, he pushed a few buttons on the front.

She waited for it to start, but it was silent. When she glanced at Wes, he gave her a small smile. "It's working," he said, as if guessing her unasked question. "It's just quiet."

"Huh." Skeptically, she examined the appliance again, looking for a light or some indication that his invention was more than a silver box filled with dirty dishes. "How long does it take?"

"Three minutes."

Now she really doubted him. "That's it?"

"Yes." Instead of looking annoyed by her inability to believe in a silent, three-minute dishwasher, he appeared to be holding back his amusement. A low beep brought her attention back to the appliance, and she watched as Wes opened it.

Wordlessly, he pulled out a bowl and handed it to her. It felt warm and looked completely clean. "That's amazing." She held it up to eye the bowl more closely. "My last dishwasher took an hour. Is this one of the gadgets you have a patent on?"

"No." He shrugged the compliment off, as if it were no big deal that he was a miracle-producing genius. "It's still a work in progress. This small version works fine, but the standard-size units have a few bugs."

Justice, obviously bored with the discussion, wandered back over to his place by the woodstove and stretched out on his side. That reminded Kit that they were going to be spending the night at Wes's. The idea of sleeping in the same small space as him made her jittery and, at the same time, filled with anticipation.

"So…" She hesitated, glancing out the windows, even though all she could see were blackness and a few white flakes hitting the glass. "You don't usually sleep up here, do you? I mean, the cabin is your actual residence, right?"

"Yes, but it's not exactly… It's not set up for…" Wes made a frustrated sound, and Kit could relate. He seemed as flustered as she was by the topic. For some reason, that calmed her nerves, and she almost laughed. They were two adults. They could talk about sleeping arrangements without getting tongue-tied—or at least they should be able to.

"Let's make this easier," she said. She was hugely relieved that no one she worked with was here. The teasing would've been infinite and unbearable. "Justice has picked his bed. Where would you like me to sleep? I'm fine with whatever—bed, couch, floor, chair. As long as we're not sleeping outside, I'm grateful."

Even though she'd tried to lay it out in a straightforward way, Wes still looked a little stiff and uncomfortable. "My cabin is very small, and there's only one bed. There's no couch over there, and it's cold. I don't want to leave you alone up here by yourself, so I thought I'd take the couch, and you could—if you like—take the bed." He nodded toward the wall next to the kitchen, and Kit peered at the spot with interest. It didn't look like anything but a section of wall but, knowing Wes, he'd most likely press a button and make a castle-like master bedroom appear, complete with housekeeper.

When he eyed her uncertainly, as if checking on her reaction, she gave a firm nod. "Sounds like a good plan, but you get the bed, and I'll take the couch." When he started to argue, she waved off his objections. "It's silly to put you on the sofa. Your feet would hang off the end."

He grudgingly agreed, and Kit relaxed. Not knowing where she was going to sleep, especially in relation to Wes, had made her tense. Now, with everything figured out, she didn't have to worry about any surprises. She was also glad that they wouldn't be staying in the tiny, dark, probably chilly cabin next door. The tower room was warm, and she was comfortable here.

"Want to watch a movie?" he asked, breaking into her thoughts.

"Sure." She briefly considered asking him for a T-shirt to wear to bed, but that seemed too girlfriendy a thing to do. Instead, she started to strip off layers.

"Uhh…"

When she saw Wes's startled expression, she flushed. "Don't worry," she assured him. "I'm stopping before I get to skin."

True to her word, she left her long underwear on before returning to her spot on the couch. Wes had to clear his throat before the screen would obey his command to lower. Pulling a fuzzy fleece blanket off the back of the couch, Kit opened it and laid it over her legs.

Once she was settled, Wes handed her a tablet. "These are the movies I have."

As she scrolled through the list, Kit blinked. "You have quite the extensive movie collection," she said.

"Winter can get long."

"True." She fell silent as she skimmed the titles, growing more and more impressed with his choices. Looking at the kinds of movies he enjoyed made her feel as though she knew him a little better, and she liked what she was learning. "Oh, here we go. I haven't seen this one yet." She tapped on her selection and handed the tablet back to Wes.

He gave her a sideways smile. "I'm not surprised you like superhero movies."

"Yeah." She snuggled into her corner of the couch, tucking her blanket around her. "I'm not subtle."

After starting the movie, he dimmed the lights, and the music drowned out the sound of Justice's soft snores and the howling wind outside. Glancing over at Wes, Kit smiled and focused on the screen again. Being full and warm and entertained and this close to an interesting guy was much better than fighting her way through a snowstorm. The day had started rough, but it was turning out to be pretty doggone perfect.

Wes woke with a start, his body jerking in place as he tried to figure out where he was. Just as he realized he was on his couch in the tower, overhead lights dimmed and the screen down but off, something else caught his attention. There was a warm weight draped over his chest and along his side.

Kit. Even before he remembered the events of the evening, he recognized her smell—cinnamon and well-maintained leather, with a hint of something minty from her shampoo. He blinked at the dim ceiling, not wanting to shift even a little, worried that the moment she woke, she'd realize that she could be wrapped around another man who wasn't frozen in awed indecision by the press of her clothed body.

She sighed, making a sleepy grumbling sound that brought an instant smile to his face. He couldn't stay still anymore. If this was accidental cuddling, and she'd wake up to pull away and never come close to him again, he didn't want to waste this opportunity. Moving slowly, he wrapped his arms around her, hugging her more firmly against his chest.

It was bliss, but uncertainty nagged at him, making him wonder if he was doing something wrong. If she'd been awake, would she have pushed him away? Was he taking advantage of her sleeping state to steal a hug she'd never have offered him if she'd had a choice?

"Kit?" he whispered, needing her to make the decision, for her to move away or not. It felt too good to hold her for it to be tarnished by worry. "Kit, wake up."

She squirmed against him, fighting the return to consciousness, wiggling and squirming and turning her head back and forth under his chin. He could feel the second that clarity returned, because she jerked her head up, nearly clipping him in the jaw as she did so.

"Wes?" Her sleep-roughened voice had a sexy burr to it that he immediately wanted to hear again. "Sorry. Was I climbing you as I slept? I have a bad habit of aggressively sleep-cuddling."

"Yes, but I didn't mind." Wes struggled to find the best way to ask and decided that he'd just be honest. It seemed the easiest, although also the scariest. "Sorry to wake you up, but I wanted to make sure that you knew it was me."

She studied his face intently, and he wondered if she realized that they were still pressed together from the chest down. A slow smile stretched across her face. "I knew it was you."

"It wasn't just auto-cuddling with the nearest warm body, then?"

Blinking at him, she slowly lost her smile, although the look in her eyes was hard to read. Affectionate? Warm? Warmly affectionate? "You're so much more than a warm body."

He didn't know how to respond. It felt so fragile, this heated peace between them, so intense, yet gentle, and he worried about destroying that feeling by saying the wrong thing. In his experience, the chance of him blurting out something ridiculous was about ninety percent. It would be best, he decided, not to risk it. Instead, he just looked at her, enjoying their closeness and the press of their bodies.

Her expression changed, and the air between them suddenly became fully charged. It was hard to breathe, and then he forgot about oxygen entirely as Kit leaned closer, her lips opening ever so slightly. Everything slowed down, and a dim corner of his brain thought he should be taking notes, since they'd obviously figured out the trick to manipulating time.

It seemed like forever and no time at all before Kit's mouth was inches above his, looking full and soft and lush, even in the half light of the overhead fixtures. She paused, but he couldn't stand it anymore. He had to know what her mouth felt like on his.

Lunging up, he kissed her.

They both froze at the contact. Even though he'd been expecting it for what had felt like an eternity, the kiss still startled him into stillness. Her lips really were as soft and yielding as they looked, and they seemed to have an electrical short, judging by the charge jolting through him. This was a first for him— not the kissing, but his fiery, intense reaction to such a delicate touch.

He needed more. Reaching up, he cupped her cheeks and urged her down farther. When she went willingly, deepening the kiss enthusiastically, a thrill cut through him. As they kissed, exploring each other's mouths, Wes's arousal grew until he felt like he was burning from the inside out. Each touch, each nip, each kiss made him more frantic with need.

He slid his fingers into her hair, feeling the silky slide of the strands as they fell around them in a heavy curtain. Running his hands over her head and down her neck and then to her shoulders and upper back, he marveled at the contrast between her soft skin and the strength of the muscles underneath. She was small but so powerful, and he was both amazed and honored that he was here with her, kissing her, feeling her in a way he'd never thought he'd have a chance to do.

When she nipped his lower lip, he forgot everything in the world except this moment. Every part of his brain—even the one that kept him up at night by constantly spewing ideas and solutions and doubts—focused on the feel of the woman above him, of her lips and tongue, of her hands in his hair and her hip pressing into his side.

It wasn't enough. The more they kissed and touched and explored, the more he needed her. With a groan, he rolled them over, barely remembering in time that they were on the narrow couch. He managed to turn so that they ended up still on the couch, but with her beneath him this time. Wes held himself on his elbows and knees, not wanting to crush her into the cushions.

The movement distracted him enough that he managed to break the kiss, although the sight of her swollen lips and the way her chest moved up and down as she panted for breath lured him back. He leaned closer, about to kiss her again, but somehow he managed to resist the urge to press his lips against hers.

"I can put the bed down," he said, his voice so thick and deep with desire that he hardly recognized it. There was a light thump behind them, and he turned to see that the bed had unfolded, dropping out of the wall obediently. He turned back to see that Kit was smiling. Somehow, seeing those lips curve made them even more tempting than they'd been before. With a huge effort, he managed to keep from kissing her again. "Guess I said that a little too loudly."

Her laugh was just a puff of air, but her eyes were smiling at him. "The bed is a good idea."

He swallowed, his body dropping to press down on hers instinctually. "Both of us?"

Her laughter faded as heat replaced it, and she pushed her hips up to meet his, making him groan. "Yes."

His eyes nearly rolled back in his head at the thick need she'd put into that single word. "I'm not rushing you?" He had to be sure. The further they went, the harder it would be to stop, and he wanted to make sure she didn't have any reservations. It could be hard for him to read people, to know what they were really thinking, so he wanted to ask, to put it out there in words that couldn't be misread or misinterpreted. It was so intense for him, and he wanted her so badly, but he needed her to be just as sure. He couldn't ruin this. It was too important, too critical for his happiness to have this with Kit. Even though what they had was new, he already knew that to be true. Life without her would be empty.

Reaching up, she cupped his face, her gaze meeting his directly. Her touch lit a fire under his skin, but it was also comforting, both burning heat and soothing warmth at the same time. "You aren't rushing me at all. I want this. I want it so badly that I might spontaneously combust if we stop now."

He met her gaze and held it, caught up in a whirl of anticipation and excitement and affection and exhilaration. This was actually happening. He'd been wishing for it since she'd first appeared at his truck window, all understanding charm and understated power, and that wish was actually coming true.

"I know it's been fast," she continued when he was too caught up in his swirling emotions to say anything. "But I feel like I already know you." He nodded, his stubble rasping against her palms. "And I want to know more. Show me."

He would show her, and he knew that she'd keep everything he offered her safe. He could trust her.

She watched him, as if waiting for a response, but he didn't have any words to express how he felt. Instead, he pressed his lips to hers again, pouring all of his emotions, everything that he felt the two of them could be, into the kiss. Wrapping her arms and legs around him, she reciprocated just as eagerly, clinging tightly as he stood, holding her against him.

He moved over to the bed, tumbling both of them onto the mattress. Kit gave a laughing shriek as they fell, never letting her grip on him loosen. Wes caught his weight on his hands before he could crush her, hovering over her as he kissed and nipped a line down her throat. She arched her neck, making small sounds that showed exactly how much she was enjoying the feel of his mouth on her skin. The evidence of her pleasure heightened his, tightening his muscles with hungry need.

When he reached her collarbone, licking and nibbling at the exposed skin above the neck of her top, she gently pushed him back until she could sit up and yank her shirt over her head. Without hesitating, she unhooked her bra and slid the straps down her arms, revealing her breasts.

He stared, entranced, feeling like a teenager who was seeing a woman naked for the first time. It wasn't until she visibly shivered that he ripped his gaze away. She was smiling a little, but she seemed uncertain.

"You're beautiful," he said, reaching out to touch her, still amazed that he could, that this wasn't a dream, that he wasn't going to wake up alone and aching in his cabin loft. Her skin was so, so soft. "I can't believe I get to touch you like this."

Tugging at the bottom of his T-shirt, she smiled, her hesitancy gone. He must've said the right thing. "Take this off. It's only fair that I get to touch you, too."

Before she even finished asking, he grabbed the back of his shirt and hauled it off, tossing it away. As soon as his upper half was bare, her hands were exploring his chest. Overwhelmed by the sensation of her fingers on his skin, he had to close his eyes for a moment, but that just intensified the pleasure. He was startled by how amazingly good it felt.

His skin grew hot and tight, shivering under each brush of her hand, each light scratch and pinch. With a groan of intense pleasure, he reached for her, pressing her back onto the bed so he could kiss her deeply as their bare chests touched.

It was almost too intense. His desire flamed higher, and he wanted more. Catching her long underwear and her panties, he pulled them down her legs and off. Her toes, small and dainty, distracted him. He kissed the arches of her feet as he smiled.

"What?" she asked, returning the smile even though she didn't know the cause of his.

"Your feet are so cute." He brushed his lips over her ankles and then slowly worked his way up her calves. "They're always hidden in your steel-toed police boots, though, so no one else knows how adorable you are." It was as if they had a secret, as silly as it was. He liked that feeling.

She snorted a laugh that turned into a gasp as he nuzzled her thigh, working higher and higher until he found her center. He kissed her there, touching and sucking and licking as he watched for every tensed muscle, listened for every gasp or pleased sigh, learning what made her climb higher and higher until she came, gripping his hair tightly.

Her climax nearly set him off, and he hurried to strip off the rest of his clothes as she lay back on the rumpled covers, so beautiful with her face relaxed and eyes half-lidded in the aftermath of orgasm. He moved toward her before he remembered condoms, and he swore.

"What's wrong?" she asked, propping herself up on her elbows, her hair mussed in the sexiest, most alluring way. It distracted him for a moment, until she shifted again, starting to look alarmed. Turning away reluctantly, he started hunting in drawers and cupboards. "What are you doing?" She sounded a little amused this time.

"I know I put them somewhere…" He pulled out the top drawer of his workstation and then the next. In the third, he hit pay dirt. "Found them!" Grabbing the box, he rushed back to the bed, and Kit started giggling. He straddled her on his knees, looking down at her laughing face, loving that something he'd done—although he wasn't sure what—had made her this happy. "What's so funny?"

Taking a deep, shivering breath, she managed to stop laughing, although her huge smile was still in place. "You're just normally so serious. It was fun to see you act so…goofy."

"That was an important mission I just went on," he said, perfectly fine with being called goofy if it made her laugh. He showed her the box of condoms. "I need to program the robot to bring these on voice command."

She was laughing again. "Robo-Cat is going to fetch your condoms? In the middle of…*everything*?"

It made sense to him, since it would save him from scrambling around when he was naked and desperate to be inside Kit, but her laughter made it impossible not to grin with her. As she continued to giggle, he leaned over and kissed the side of her neck, making his way down to her breasts. By the time he reached her nipple, her laughter had changed to sounds of pleasure.

She tasted so good. As he drew a line with his mouth down to her stomach, her muscles flexed and twitched under his lips. She felt so alive, so warm and strong, and he wanted to connect with her, to be part of that—part of her. Reluctantly, he pulled away, smiling a little smugly at her sound of protest as his mouth left her skin. Quickly rolling on a condom, he kissed her mouth and eased inside her.

A groan escaped each of them as he sank into her heat. He went still for a moment, trying to catch his breath and control his swirling emotions. When he couldn't do either, he let himself slip into the moment, allowing everything to disappear except the feel of her as he moved. He couldn't stop exploring her, his lips and hands moving over her, sliding over sweat-slick skin and finding all the spots that made her shiver and gasp against his mouth.

It was amazing to him how much she wanted him. He found her mouth as his pleasure grew, and he tried to pour all his affection and gratitude and need for her into a kiss. With a groan, she broke the kiss, closing her eyes and arching her neck as she came a second time. Her body tightened around him, driving him over the edge, and he felt pleasure rush over him, unexpectedly intense and completely wonderful.

It took a long time to come down from that height. When he finally did, it was to discover another completely different—yet almost as addictive—feeling. He sank into the mindless, floating warmth, loving the press of her lax body against his, but his thoughts started to intrude too soon. With a reluctant huff, he pulled away. Kit resisted for a moment, her arms tightening to pull him back against her, and it was nearly impossible to not be lured back into the nest they'd made.

"Give me twenty seconds," he said, giving her a quick kiss. After tossing the condom and cleaning up in the bathroom, he hurried back to her, hoping she'd be just where he'd left her, warm and lax and happy.

"Eighteen...nineteen..." Her teasing counting broke off with a squeal as he jumped back on the bed and kissed her again.

"Twenty," he finished, the word muffled by the press of her lips. She laughed, and he felt it, both against his mouth and in his chest. In his *heart*.

Pulling back a little, he stared at her. When she started looking puzzled, he tried to put his thoughts into order so he could explain. Normally, with her, this was easy, but everything had been stirred up inside him.

"You... This..." He waved a hand, indicating her, the bed, his whole world now that she was in it. Pausing, he sorted his thoughts and feelings, settling on something simple that didn't even come close to the marvelous chaos in his brain right now. "I'm happy. Are you happy? With this? With me?"

She didn't even hesitate. "I've never been so happy."

When he kissed her, he could feel that she was smiling. He was, too.

CHAPTER 22

THE NEXT MORNING, KIT CLOMPED DOWN THE STAIRS TO THE lower level of the tower, a little grumpy that she'd had to leave Wes and their warm, rumpled bed. Justice rushed to the door ahead of her—not caring about her sulk—and waited impatiently, dancing from foot to foot, as she pulled on her coat and boots.

"I don't know how you slept through all of that last night," she said quietly as she tugged on her gloves. "However you did, I'm grateful for it." She smiled at the thought of the previous night, of how thoughtful and intense and perceptive Wes had been. It had been an impulsive decision, made when she was sleepy and being thoroughly kissed, but she didn't regret it at all. The only thing she regretted was having to leave so early to get to work.

She pulled open the door, expecting a wall of snow after the previous night's storm, but only six inches or so spread in a thick blanket over the area, with bigger drifts piled up against the tower walls...and her SUV.

With a low groan, she walked through the snow toward her vehicle and examined it in the pale dawn light. A four-foot white wall leaned against the north side of the SUV, making it look like she'd driven it sideways into a snowdrift.

"That is going to take a *lot* of shoveling to get out," she muttered, crouching down to look underneath, where snow had piled up until it reached the undercarriage. Justice trotted over to sniff at the frozen wave that had swallowed her SUV. "Why did you let me park here?"

The dog looked at her, cocking his head to the side, but then his attention snapped to the woods. By the way his tail started wagging, Kit knew he'd heard someone. She straightened, turning to face the same direction as Justice, her hand automatically reaching for her nonexistent gun. Mentally scolding herself for letting down her guard, she signaled the dog to move with her around to the other side of the SUV, putting it between them and whomever was in the trees.

Everything was quiet. Even the wind had died down to nothing, and the snow added a hushed feel to the early morning. Kit scanned the wooded area, trying to see movement or a color that didn't belong, but the low light turned the forest into a gloomy, impenetrable mass. Not for the first time, she wished she had Justice's keen senses—or that he had a voice and could tell her exactly what he'd smelled and heard.

There was a flicker of movement, and she whipped her head to the side, focusing on the spot where she'd seen it. Narrowing her eyes, she waited, but everything had gone still again. The silence was unnerving. With the snow and underbrush, anything—or anyone— moving through the trees should have made some kind of sound, but there was nothing. All was quiet.

The motion came again, just briefly, gone before Kit could identify what was out there. Thoughts of bears and moose and mountain lions and cop-hating people with guns ran through her head, and she forced herself to push her nervous speculation aside. Her imagination wasn't helpful at the moment.

The movement was closer this time—too close— and Kit shifted, taking a subtle defensive stance as a man in camouflage coveralls stepped out of the trees. Kit tensed even more, quickly scanning him. He wasn't carrying any weapons that she could see—no shotgun, thank goodness—but she was still wary. He was walking toward her, but he wasn't moving especially aggressively. When he waved—a jerky, slightly goofy gesture—she relaxed slightly, hoping that this was one of Wes's less-hostile neighbors.

Kit stepped out from behind the SUV, still keeping Justice next to her and a careful eye on the approaching man. He stopped ten feet away, arms relaxed at his sides.

"Hi," she greeted, and he gave her a nod. When he remained quiet, she figured any conversation was going to rely on her. "Are you Wes's neighbor?"

"Yup." His answer was more of a grunt, but he didn't sound unfriendly—just not that talkative. He looked to be in his fifties, with the sun-browned, leathery skin she was starting to associate with longtime residents of Colorado who never used sunblock. "Good to see Wes found a girl."

Swallowing a snort and a smart-ass retort, Kit limited herself to a nod and a bland smile. "I'm Kit Jernigan."

"Murphy." He didn't specify whether that was a first or last name. "Nice dog. You use him for hunting?"

"Tracking." She decided to keep her police-officer status to herself for the time being, hoping Murphy would share more with "Wes's girl" than he would with a cop. "You don't mind dogs, then?"

"Not unless they're biting me in the ass." He grinned, showing several gaps on the sides of his mouth where teeth should've been.

"He won't bite." Kit released Justice from his position next to her, and he headed straight for Murphy. "He might drown you in drool, but that's as aggressive as he gets."

After Murphy gave him a quick scratch, Justice trotted off to investigate some smells. Keeping half an eye on the dog and most of her attention on Murphy, she asked, "You hunt, then?" Since he wasn't carrying a gun, she wondered what he was doing in the woods so early.

"Trap," he said, and a light went off inside Kit's head.

She looked at Murphy with renewed interest. "You saw the person leaving the house, the one that burned down? That was you?" Although she tried to keep the question light, as if she was simply curious, she knew some intensity seeped through, judging by Murphy's wary glance.

"Yeah," he said a little reluctantly.

"How close were you?"

"Dunno." He raised one shoulder in a half shrug. "Twenty feet?"

"That was right before the fire?"

All he gave her was a slight nod, so she tried to widen her eyes as if she was impressed and a little scared. "Wow. You were that close to a possible murderer? I know you didn't know that at the time, but doesn't that freak you out a little, looking back on it?"

She could see him relax a little as he gave her a slightly condescending smile. "'Course not. She was just a tiny bit of a thing."

A woman. The murderer and arsonist was a woman. It was almost impossible not to start firing questions at him in true interrogation style. Kit turned slightly to focus on Justice as she tamped down the urge to drag the whole story out of him. "It was a woman?"

"Yup." Her restraint was rewarded when he continued, sounding more relaxed. "Young one, too. Pretty. Had dark hair like yours, but she wasn't..." Trailing off, he lifted his hand, indicating his face with an awkward gesture that would've made her laugh if she hadn't been so focused on the interview.

"She wasn't Asian?"

He looked relieved. "Right."

"Was she white, then?"

"Maybe?" His pauses were driving her batty, since she didn't know if he was going to elaborate, and the urge to ask a hundred questions pressed on Kit. "Could've been Mexican."

Kit mentally translated that to Latina, and her heart rate sped up. His description matched Elena so closely, but she had to be careful not to force the facts to fit her suspicions. "Isn't it unusual to see a stranger in town?"

He gave another of his semi-shrugs. "Not really. Mostly keep to myself. Wouldn't know half the people in town if I ran right into them. I stick to those woods south of town. Heading there now, in fact, to do some hunting. Don't run into many other people there— except for her, of course."

"I know someone who looks a lot like that." Kit pulled out her phone and quickly found the picture of Elena's driver's license she'd taken when researching. As she enlarged it so that just the photo filled the screen, she kept an eye on Murphy. She was so close to getting a possible identification, and she was afraid her witness would just wander off into the trees. Holding out her phone so the screen faced him, she said, "Is this the woman you saw?"

He squinted at it and nodded. "Sure looks like the same lady."

Kit's stomach swooped with excitement before she remembered that Elena—who'd just been identified as a possible killer—lived in a household of innocent people. "Did you see where she went after she left the burning house?"

"Nah." He was casual, and Kit was glad her poker face was holding. "Didn't want to scare her by following her."

"Probably a good plan." Justice ran past her, and Kit checked to make sure he wasn't running off into the woods. He was just playing in the snow, so she turned back to Murphy—who was staring at her wide-eyed. She blinked at his terrified expression, such a change from the relaxed, friendly one he'd just been wearing. "You okay, Murphy?"

"You're a cop?" He backed away from her, his eyes wide. "I wouldn't've said anything if I'd known... Forget it. Didn't see nothing. You've got no reason to bring me in."

She held up her hands, trying to convey that she wasn't going to hurt him—or drag him off to jail. "I'm not going to force you to do anything you don't want to do. I'm just trying to solve this crime. If this woman is a killer, then we need to make sure she doesn't hurt anyone else. I just want to keep you and everyone else in Monroe safe."

For a moment, he paused, and she wondered if she was getting through to him, but then his expression closed down hard. "You cops are all liars." He rushed backward, almost running, until he reached the edge of the woods. Within seconds, her only witness had disappeared into the trees. She'd only managed to take two steps after him.

My jacket. With a growl of frustration, she realized that, when she'd turned, she'd flashed him the MONROE POLICE DEPARTMENT printed in huge letters on the back of her coat. Shaking off her self-annoyance for stupidly scaring off her witness, she focused on the more critical issue—Sam and his family were sharing their home with a murder suspect.

And this time, she had more to go on than a hunch.

"Wes!" she called. After a few moments, one of the windows swung open, and he stuck his sleep-rumpled head out. Despite the urgency of the situation, the sight of him made her heart twist. "Can you give me a ride into town?"

"Give me four minutes." After he ducked back inside, the window closed behind him. She was too tense to even smile at Wes's extremely precise time estimation. Since she'd been taken by surprise by Murphy's arrival—and testimonial—she hadn't recorded their conversation. Kit mentally kicked herself for not using her phone to catch at least the last part of the impromptu interview. There was no way Murphy would give a formal statement. Even if they picked him up, she knew he'd keep his mouth closed. All she had was her word against Elena's.

She called Justice and hurried to the large shed where Wes kept his truck. Her mind spun as she tried to think of the best way to warn Jules and Grace. She decided to tell Theo first. Even if he was skeptical, there was no way he'd let Elena be around Jules and the kids if he knew there was even a chance she'd put them in danger.

They needed to trust Kit—their lives depended on it.

Wes came out of the tower, and Kit instantly felt some of the tension that had been twisting her stomach into a tight knot release. Things would work out. Now that she had more than a gut suspicion that Elena was guilty, Kit would be able to convince the other cops that Elena was an extremely viable suspect, and they'd arrest her before she could hurt anyone else. "Thanks for doing this," Kit said as Wes got closer to where she waited by the overhead door. "My SUV's snowed in, and your neighbor just confirmed my suspicions about a possible suspect in the arson-and-murder case. I need to report this."

"Murphy actually talked to you?" Wes asked, leaning in as if he was going to kiss her but then stopping and stepping back again as if reconsidering. Biting her lip to hold back the smile that wanted to break free at his adorably uncertain stutter-step, she closed the distance between them and reached up to kiss him. Even though she wanted to linger, she knew they needed to get to town, so she started to retreat. Wes stopped her, gently cupping the back of her neck, and pulled her into a final short-but-sweet kiss. Happiness made Kit feel floaty for a moment before she refocused on the Elena situation.

"Yes. He was very forthcoming when he thought I was your 'girl,' but he ran away when he saw the back of my coat." She turned to show him.

"That isn't surprising." Wes was quiet as he pressed his thumb to a scanner, and the overhead door started to lift before he spoke again. "My girl?"

Kit raised an eyebrow at him, trying not to smile at his pleased tone. She wasn't sure why, but pretty much anything Wes did this morning made her feel all warm and bright inside.

"Sure, but let's go with woman, rather than girl." She climbed into the passenger seat of his truck and slid over to the middle of the bench seat so Justice could get in.

"My woman." He was grinning as he got into the driver's seat. "I can live with that."

CHAPTER 23

As THEY MADE THEIR SLOW WAY DOWN WES'S ROAD, KIT tried to relax. *Nothing you can do until we get there*, she reminded herself. She wished she'd taken the few minutes to use Wes's radio to call in the information she'd just received, but then she caught herself. What could she have said over the radio? It was going to be hard enough to convince the other cops in person that Elena was their murder suspect. There was nothing she could've said over an unsecured channel that would've helped.

"With this snow, this drive will take longer than usual." His gaze fell to her right foot, and she realized she was pressing it hard to the floor, as if she had a gas pedal under it.

"I know." She consciously relaxed her muscles and resisted the urge to bounce her knee up and down in impatience. "Ignore me. I'm not a good passenger."

Although he kept his eyes on the narrow, snow-covered road, he smiled. "I don't believe that. You're good at everything."

She laughed. "Nope. Remember what I told you about me being the black death when it comes to computers?"

He shrugged, not looking like he cared about her technology-crashing curse, and gave her a sideways look that made her want to tell him to pull over so she could thoroughly kiss him again. *Elena's still free and doing who-knows-what*, she reminded herself, instantly sobering. She needed to get this taken care of, and then she could enjoy whatever it was that she and Wes had jumped into last night.

When they turned off onto the highway, it was evident that the plows had made at least one pass, and Wes was able to speed up a little. He shifted in his seat, drawing her attention. She rarely saw him look uncomfortable or anxious, and she wondered what was wrong.

"Would you…" He cleared his throat. "I'd like to go on another date with you, if you would be amenable."

Despite the worry coiling through her, Kit grinned. "I would be amenable."

His tension eased, and his smile returned. "Good. I'm hoping that we can avoid any fires or kidnappings this time."

"I think we should be able to manage that." She frowned. "Although we might need to leave town for that to happen."

Pulling out her cell phone, Kit saw that she finally had reception, so she tried calling Theo. When he didn't answer, she called Hugh.

"Greenie!" he boomed, making her pull the phone away from her ear so he didn't deafen her. "How was your wild night with our local fire spotter?"

"Ah…" Taken off guard by his accurate description—it had been a pretty wonderful wild night—she hesitated, shooting a sideways glance at Wes. By his pleased smirk, he'd heard Hugh's question. "Not really relevant. I'm headed to the station now. Are you at the viner?"

"Nope, I'm at Jules's. The mysterious Mateo Espina

will be here soon, and I have a couple more questions for him. Figured I'd catch him before he left town and started ignoring my calls."

"Is Theo with you?" As they rounded a curve, the rear of the truck slid out toward the shoulder. Without looking bothered, Wes corrected the skid and then slowed slightly. Even though Kit knew it would take even longer to get into town if they slid into a ditch, the creeping pace was driving her up a wall.

"Yeah, he's around here somewhere. Why?" He must've picked up on her tension, since his joking tone had changed to a serious one.

"I talked to one of Wes's neighbors. He saw someone coming out of the house right before the fire started."

"Which neighbor?" Hugh sounded intrigued, but wary, too.

"Murphy. Do you know him?"

"I know of him. What was he doing in the woods?"

She couldn't tell what that implied. "Checking his leg-hold traps. From what he said—"

"He told you he was in the woods, setting illegal traps?" Hugh interrupted, and Kit resisted the urge to thump her head against the dash.

"No. Wes warned me about the leg-hold traps. Murphy just mentioned the trapping part."

"There's no way Murphy talked to a cop."

Now Kit wanted to thump *Hugh* on the head. What did any of this matter when she'd found an actual witness who'd put Elena at the scene of the crime? "He didn't know until he saw the back of my coat. Then he ran."

"What'd he see?"

Finally. "He described a woman—small, young, dark hair, either white or Latina."

There was silence on the other end of the call, so Kit continued.

"I showed him a picture of Elena, and he immediately identified her as the woman he saw leaving the house right before the fire. She walked into the woods."

There was an extended pause before Hugh spoke again, long enough that Kit checked her phone to make sure she hadn't lost the call. She hadn't, but her battery was almost gone. Since she hadn't planned to spend the night with Wes, she hadn't brought her phone charger with her.

"Shit." Hugh believed her. She could tell by the panic filling that one word. "This whole time, she's—" He gave a grunt before his voice cut out abruptly. After a short, silent pause, there was a heavy thump.

"Hugh?" Kit checked the battery indicator again. It was deathly low, but the call was still connected. "Hugh?" Only silence answered her, but it didn't feel like the emptiness of a bad connection. Pressing the phone more tightly to her ear, she listened, trying to hear something, anything, on the other end of the call. There was a faint sound, hard to make out, and Kit plugged her other ear, blocking out the noise of Wes's truck engine. Faintly, she could hear someone breathing, and the wrongness of the sound made the back of her neck prickle with warning. Was that Hugh? If so, why had he stopped talking?

A double beep loudly indicated the call had ended, making her jerk the phone away from her ear. She stared at the "call ended" message for a moment, trying to determine what exactly had happened. "That's not good." Wes glanced at her, obviously picking up on the stress in her voice, but she focused on trying to call Hugh back. It went right to voice mail, and her pulse rate shot up as her fingers tightened around her phone. Why wasn't he answering? Quickly ending the call, she ignored the tension twisting in her stomach as she tapped Theo's number.

As it rang, she dug the fingers of her free hand into her thigh.

"Bosco," he answered, and all her pent-up breath escaped in a rush of relief.

"Theo, you need to check on Hugh." She spoke quickly, knowing she didn't have much more battery life left.

"Kit?"

"Yes, it's me. I was just talking to Hugh when he went silent. Can you check to make sure he's okay?"

"Yeah, sure." The background voices faded. "He's just upstairs. What's going on?"

"A witness just identified Elena as the person leaving the arson-and-murder scene."

"What witn—?"

After a triple beep sounded, her phone screen went black.

"No, no, no," she chanted, hunting around the cab of Wes's truck. "Please tell me that you have an iPhone-compatible charger in here somewhere."

By his expression, she knew before he spoke that his answer was no. "Sorry. My phone's still at the tower."

"It's okay." She said it more to reassure herself than Wes. "Theo was going to check on Hugh. Both of them are aware that Elena's a suspect. They'll protect the

kids and everyone else at the house until we get there."
Despite her words, dread ate at her stomach lining, and
she looked at Wes.

"Take us to Jules's house as fast as possible."

Without a word, he pressed on the accelerator, and the
truck shot forward. Kit only hoped that they wouldn't
arrive too late.

"Kit?" Theo said, glancing at his phone. He cursed,
muttering something about the lack of good cell phone
reception at the lookout tower.

Alex smiled slightly before ducking back. Theo's call
with Kit must've been interrupted. How convenient for
Alex. She slipped into Jules's room, making sure she
stayed just out of sight.

"Hugh?" Theo's voice was sharp with alarm as his
footsteps hurried down the hall toward where Alex had
left Hugh's unconscious body.

She raised Ty's baseball bat and waited for just the
right moment.

Two down, one to go.

Looking at the two trussed and unconscious cops,
Alex allowed herself just a second of satisfaction in
a job well done. She'd known that subduing the cops
would be the trickiest part of her plan. So far, though, it
had gone surprisingly smoothly.

Closing the closet door, she propped Dee's desk chair

under the knob. As she left the room, she pushed in the button lock on the door behind her, swinging the base-ball bat at her side. The door locked from the inside, so it wouldn't help hold Theo and Hugh if they managed to escape the closet, but it would keep any nosy children from accidentally discovering them.

She trotted down the stairs, giving Sam a smile as she passed him. "Good morning."

His usual silence and suspicious glare didn't bother her. It was a wonderful day, and she wasn't about to let a sullen teenager take away from it. Humming to herself, she propped the baseball bat against the wall by the front door and walked to the kitchen.

Jules, Grace, Sarah, and the kids were sitting around the table, laughing at something that Alex hadn't caught, as Otto leaned against the counter, sipping coffee and smiling a little as he watched his wife.

"Otto," Alex said sweetly, drawing everyone's atten-tion to her. She dropped her gaze, using her pretend shyness to hide her unusual giddiness. It was just that everything was going so well. Kit had been snowed in at Wes's tower, safely out of the way, and she'd been Alex's biggest obstacle until now. "Could you help me get something out of the hall closet?"

"Oh, I can help," Jules said, popping up out of her seat. "What do you need?"

"Actually, I need someone really tall, just for a second."

Jules sat back in her seat. "I have to admit that Otto does have a slight height advantage over me."

The other women laughed. "He's very handy that way," Sarah said, tipping her head back to smile up at him.

Setting his coffee mug on the counter, he took advantage of his wife's upturned face to give her a kiss and then followed Alex out into the hall. *It's like leading lambs to slaughter*, she thought happily. "Thanks, Otto. I tossed my hat onto the top shelf last night, and now I can't reach it. Would you mind…?"

He gave her a small nod, turning his back to her to look in the closet. Picking up the bat, Alex swung, connecting with the back of his head. For a second, he stayed upright, making her wonder if she'd not hit hard enough, but then he swayed and fell, crashing down like a felled tree. The loud thump as he connected with the floor worried her for a moment, but then a burst of laughter came from the kitchen. They were talking so noisily that they didn't even realize Alex was picking them off, one by one.

After zip-tying Otto's wrists behind his back, she rolled him into the closet, huffing a little with the effort of shifting his huge form. A small sound, barely a squeak, made Alex whirl around, pulling the pistol Bendsie had given her from her waistband.

Dee stood behind her, her mouth slightly open in shock. "What… What are you doing?"

"Getting revenge," Alex said, closing the closet door without taking her gaze or the gun off the little girl. "You can help."

Reaching out, she grabbed Dee and yanked the little girl against her. Dee let out a yelp as Alex pressed the muzzle of the gun against her head. "I didn't want to kill you," Alex said, moving toward the kitchen with Dee's back pressed against her. "I don't especially enjoy killing children. That's why I called Courtney and told her to come here and get you and your brothers. That didn't quite work out as planned."

Dee made a choking sound, as if she was having trouble breathing.

"This works, too." Keeping the gun against the girl's head, Alex walked into the kitchen.

CHAPTER 24

THE TRICK WITH DEE HAD WORKED PERFECTLY. IT WAS amazing how compliant adults became when a child was threatened.

Fifi the dog was locked in the basement, and Jules, Grace, and Sarah were all zip-tied—wrists and ankles— with duct tape covering their mouths, sitting in a line on the living room couch. The twins, also bound, and Dee were sitting against the opposite wall.

"Yell for Sam," Alex told Ty.

Clamping his lips together stubbornly, he glared at her. Apparently, the sweet little crush he'd had on her was over.

Unperturbed, she tucked her gun away and pulled Tio's special Swiss Army knife out of her pocket. Tapping the side so the blade extended, she hauled Dee to her feet and touched the tip of the knife to the girl's tear-streaked cheek. Jules shouted something, but the duct tape muffled the sound. Alex ignored her.

"Call for Sam."

Ty went white. "Sam." It came out soft and cracked. When Alex moved the knife closer, pressing the blade ever so lightly into his little sister's skin, he yelled loudly, "Sam!"

Smiling in triumph, Alex released Dee, returned the

refolded knife to her pocket, and retrieved her bat. "Sit," she ordered, and Dee slid down to huddle next to Ty. Standing to the side of the door, Alex waited, listening to the rhythm of his feet on the stairs, first one flight and then the next.

"Ty?" he called from the hallway.

"Run!" Ty yelled, making Alex smirk. Didn't he know his brother at all?

As she'd expected, Sam rushed into the living room, stopping abruptly when he saw everyone. Even as the other kids shouted warnings, Alex swung, clipping him in the back of the head.

Sam crumpled to the floor. *Last one down.* Alex smiled. The scene was set. Now all she needed to do was wait.

It didn't take long. Just a few minutes after she'd zip-tied Sam and rolled him to the side of the room out of the way, there was a knock on the front door.

"It's open," she called, grabbing Dee by the arm and pulling her close again. It had worked so well the last time. Instead of pointing the gun at the little girl's head this time, Alex kept the pistol low and hidden, but still prodding Dee's spine as a reminder to behave. Dee might be small, but she'd been surprisingly resourceful in the past. Elena had heard the helicopter-crashing story.

The room went silent. The only sound was the click of the front door closing. There was no click of footsteps. Thanks to his most recent employment, he'd learned to move soundlessly.

He stepped into the doorway, his gaze immediately landing on her. His eyes widened, and he stopped abruptly.

"Alex?"

She stared at him. Seeing him felt different than she'd expected. He looked different—older, harder...sadder. She felt an unexpected surge of love at the sight of him, but she quickly smothered it with anger. She had plenty of that stored up.

His initial shock was fading, replaced by raw joy. "Alex? You're alive?" He jerked forward a step, his arms coming up as if he was about to hug her.

She needed to put a stop to that. Lifting the gun, she pointed it at Dee's temple. His ecstatic expression cracked, horror replacing it as he finally took in the scene—the bound and terrified women and children all staring at him, wanting him to save them yet again.

That was over. Mateo Espina wasn't going to be saving anyone anymore.

"Hello, Big Brother."

———————

The drive to Jules's house felt like it took forever.

Justice must have picked up on Kit's unease, since he whined as he shifted in his seat, where he'd been contentedly watching the scenery for the entire ride. Absently, she stroked his ears, needing the contact as much as he did.

As they slowly made their way down Jules's claustro-phobic, snow-covered driveway, her tension increased with every curve in the road. There was no real reason to believe that anything was wrong, but her instincts were telling her in no uncertain terms that there was danger ahead. Darting a look toward Wes, she felt guilt bloom in her chest. In her hurry to get there, she'd dragged him into what could be a bad situation. It was too late for second thoughts, though. She just needed to do her best to keep him safe.

The snow-frosted house came into view, looking disarmingly like a Christmas postcard—in a slightly lopsided and weathered way. Three squad cars were parked in front, and Lexi, Viggy, and Xena barked from the back seats of their respective vehicles.

"I need you to go to the police station and get help," Kit said.

Wes hesitated but then tipped his chin down in a nod. "I will."

Despite the tension gripping her, she leaned closer and gave him a quick kiss, trying to soak in some of his steady calmness to soothe her jittery nerves. "Thank you."

He kissed her back and then cupped her face in his hands. His face was solemn and visibly worried as he looked at her intently. "Be careful." The words were simple, but his concern and fear for her safety were obvious. Kit appreciated that he was going for help as she'd asked. She knew it was bothering him not to back her up, to leave rather than protecting her, but he trusted her. He had confidence that she could do her job and that she'd keep herself safe.

"Always." Pulling away from him was hard, but she had to go. People—their friends—needed her help. Giving Wes a final look, she squeezed around Justice and got out of the truck. She didn't look back as he drove away. He trusted her to do her part, and she'd trust him to do his.

Sweeping her gaze over the front of the house, she

saw the window coverings were closed tightly over all
the downstairs windows. Climbing the front porch steps,
she listened carefully, but she couldn't hear anything.
Even the three K9s that had been barking had fallen
silent. With all three cops here, as well as at least some
of the house's residents, she felt there should've been
some noise, even if everyone was inside. She debated
knocking, but decided to just walk in. If nothing was
happening, she'd apologize to Jules later. The element
of surprise was more important right now than courtesy.

Carefully turning the knob, she pushed and met resistance. The dead bolt must've been engaged. Quietly
moving back down the stairs and around the side of the
house, she walked through the snow, checking all the
windows for some sign of what was happening inside.
She couldn't see anyone.

The closer she got to the back door, the eerier the
stillness seemed. The kids should be out playing. Grace
should be stuffing a handful of snow down the back of
Hugh's coat while Sarah and Otto laughed from a safe
distance. Jules should be watching her siblings with a
smile, leaning back against Theo for warmth. There was
something so wrong about the peacefulness of this early
winter morning.

Silently, Kit moved up the steps, noting that the glass
set in the wooden door was covered by a small, frilly
curtain. She tried the knob, and it turned in her hand. She
cracked the door open, moving slowly and as quietly as
possible. The hinges let out a small squeak, and she froze,
mentally cursing old houses and their noisy hardware.

When no one ripped the doorknob out of her hand,
she pushed it open another inch, far enough that she had

a good view of the empty kitchen. Kit slipped inside, gently closing the door behind her, and moved quickly through the deserted kitchen. She noted that there was half-eaten cereal getting soggy in abandoned bowls of milk on the table, as well as glasses of orange juice. Something—or someone—had interrupted their breakfast. Without taking her eyes off the hallway doorway, she slid a knife soundlessly out of the block, gripping it tightly in her hand. She crept past the basement door, freezing when she heard a whimper. It came again, and she identified it as a dog—Fifi, most likely. Mentally apologizing for leaving her locked up, Kit continued to the doorway.

In the hall, she could hear voices coming from the front of the house. Carefully creeping in their direction, she started to make out individual words and then sentences.

"You're dead."

Kit froze, recognizing the voice as Mr. Espina's, the surprise witness from the day before. He didn't say the words in a threatening way. Instead, his voice was full of grief and shock. Wishing she had her gun rather than a kitchen knife, Kit stopped next to the archway leading into the room where she could hear them talking. She needed to get a feel for what was going on before she simply blundered in, giving up any advantage of surprise.

"Disappointed?" That was Elena, but she sounded different. Instead of her usual hesitant, breathy tone, she was confident, almost brash.

There was a harsh inhale of breath. "No! How could you ask that? You were—are—my baby sister, Alex. Everything I've done has been because of you. I took down the Jovanovics and the Blanchetts so they couldn't hurt anyone else. I helped other women escape. My entire life since that day has revolved around getting revenge for your death."

Her laugh was humorless and awful. "Thanks, Big Brother. Abandon me when I needed you, but make sure all these other women don't have a bad day." Her voice went up an octave at the end, and silence fell in the room. "Too bad about what happened to them."

"You killed them." There was no question in his voice, just flat resignation.

"I did. Every single person you tried to save. Why should they be safe when I wasn't?"

"They were innocent, Alex."

"So was I!"

Kit jolted, hearing the sound of muffled protests. How many people were in there? How many would Elena manage to hurt before Kit could stop her? She wished she could see inside the room, but, from the clarity of Elena's voice, it sounded as if she was facing the entrance. If Kit tried to peek through the archway, there was a good chance she'd be spotted. It was difficult making a plan, though, when she didn't know what weapons—if any— were in play. From the shrill note in Elena's voice, she was very close to snapping. Kit needed to find out exactly what was happening in that room.

"You were *dead*!" Mr. Espina's voice rose to close to a shout. In the silence that followed, there was a child's sob, hastily choked back. Kit frowned, trying to identify the sound. Was that Dee? Her heart sank into her boots. She'd hoped that the kids would've headed off to school early, but it seemed that they were trapped in there, too. "I saw you get shot! You fell so far, there was no way you could've lived." His voice broke, making Elena's grating laugh sound even more inhuman.

"Too bad that wasn't me. The Jovanovics played you, *Brother*. You left me there. I prayed for you to save me, and you never came. You never came!" Her voice rose to a shout, but then she quickly got herself back under control, speaking in that coldly amused tone again. "So, I saved myself. It took years. You know what I did during that time? I made a plan. I executed it to perfection and killed every single person you tried to save. I wanted you to suffer as much as I did.

"Then Jules came along with the kids and changed things. You started sending them all here, where you could keep an eye on them and they could watch over each other, rather than just leaving them on their own to die. You thought this way would be better, didn't you? That you could actually save them this time?" She gave a short, bitter laugh.

"You were wrong. This time, I'm going to make you watch as I kill every one of these people who were somehow more worthy of saving than me. I want you to see them die so that you know you failed them, just like you failed me." Several people were quietly crying now, too many for Kit to tell who was whom. "You're already missing one from this group."

"Yolanda Hopper," Mr. Espina said quietly. "She asked for my help. As soon as she arrived in Monroe, you killed her and burned the house down to cover your tracks…didn't you?"

"Like I told her," Elena said carelessly. "I made a much better Elena Dahl than she ever would."

"Alex, stop. No more. Killing more innocent people won't help anything."

"Sure it will." The amused note was back in her voice, and it chilled Kit to the bone. The woman had just been casually talking about killing kids and the women who'd taken her in, who'd befriended and defended her, all to get revenge on her brother for not saving her, a brother who'd thought she was dead. "It'll hurt you. And that, Big Brother, is worth killing everyone in this room."

CHAPTER 25

"No!" Tio's cry spurred Kit into action. She launched through the archway into the room, peripherally taking in the scene, the bound and gagged women and terrified kids. In the center of the room, her back to the fireplace, was Elena, holding Dee in a headlock with a semiautomatic pistol pressed to her temple. Mr. Espina, his eyes wild with pain and grief, struggled against the duct tape holding him to a chair.

If Kit could've stopped, she would've at the sight of a white-faced Dee with a gun to her head, but her momentum pushed her forward. All she managed to do was drop the knife so that she didn't accidentally cut the little girl. Shock froze Elena in place just long enough for Kit to reach her. Pushing the hand holding the gun up, she took both Elena and Dee down in an inelegant tackle.

As they fell, Kit scrambled to grab the gun and shove Dee to the side, out of Elena's range. They hit the floor and slid as Dee wiggled free of the struggle. Everyone was shouting—some of the words muffled by duct tape—adding to the confusion. Now that Dee was clear, Kit narrowed her focus on Elena. If she could neutralize the threat, then the rest could be dealt with later. She squeezed Elena's wrist, hard, and the gun hit the floor, spinning in place just a few feet away from their fighting bodies. Both of them reached for it, but Kit's reach was slightly longer. Elena drove a fist into Kit's kidney, sending a flash of pain through her. Her body involuntarily stiffened, and her hand jerked. Instead of grabbing the gun, she only managed to shove it farther away.

With a roar of rage, Elena drove up her hips and flipped them so that Kit was on the bottom, cracking her head painfully against the floor. Cursing herself for underestimating Elena, Kit struggled to shake off the wave of pain and dizziness from the hit to her head. In her peripheral vision, she saw Dee scurry closer, and Elena swung a fist toward the little girl.

No! Kit mentally screamed, lifting her spinning head to crack her forehead against Elena's nose while reaching out and knocking the other woman's arm away before Elena's fist could connect. Dodging the hit, Dee grabbed the fallen kitchen knife and scrambled out of reach. Pain flared in Kit's skull, but it was worth it. With a roar, Elena unleashed a flurry of punches on Kit's face and midsection that she blocked as best she could, but the room was spinning and hazy from the double hit to her head.

Elena landed a lucky right hook to the left side of Kit's face, the pain and shock jarring her just long enough for Elena to roll toward the gun. Kit held on, going with her. She knew that if she allowed Elena to recapture the gun, everyone in this room would likely die. She used the momentum to keep them rolling, fighting to regain the upper position.

As they tumbled over, Kit's head cracked against the brick hearth, a bright flash of white filling her brain, wiping out her thoughts. As soon as the shock of pain faded, she scrambled to her feet and lunged for Elena, but it was too late. Elena's fingers closed around the grip of the gun. Turning, she aimed the pistol at Kit. Everyone in the room froze, and Kit realized that Sarah, Grace, the twins, and Dee were missing, and Jules and Sam were free of their bindings. *The knife*. Dee must've freed them while Kit was grappling with Elena. Despite her terror as she stared down the gun barrel, Kit felt a rush of relief that some of them had escaped.

"I sent for backup!" Kit tried to think, but the blinding pain in her skull and fear made it difficult. She swayed slightly before catching herself. "More officers should be arriving any second."

A flicker of uncertainty crossed Elena's face before she sneered. "I don't believe you. No one is coming."

"Wes dropped me off and then went to get the chief. Listen, you can hear the engines of the squad cars coming up the driveway." They both listened, and Kit was thankful that the wind had picked up again, covering her bluff.

"I don't hear anything." Despite her words, Elena shot a quick glance at the covered window before quickly taking in the room. Kit was pretty sure she'd just noticed that most of her hostages had escaped. Her lips tightened along with her grip on the gun as she refocused on Kit. "Guess I'll just have to kill the rest of you quickly, then."

She aimed the gun straight at Kit's heart.

Kit froze. She forced herself to not flinch away, to stare straight at Elena, to make the woman look right into her eyes as she killed her.

Elena's index finger whitened as she curled it around the trigger, and Kit braced herself for the shot.

"Alex!" Mr. Espina's voice cracked through the room, making Elena's head snap toward him. "Don't do this. It ripped me apart when I thought you'd been killed. We have a second chance to be a family. I want my sister back. Please, Alex. I love you."

Elena stared at him for so long that Kit started to hope that her brother had gotten through to her. Maybe this horrible day wouldn't end with another needless death.

"Your sister did die that day," Alex said.

Turning the gun toward her brother, she pulled the trigger.

Everyone went still, the room deadly silent. Elena stared at her bleeding brother, her expression as shocked as if her hands hadn't held the gun. "Mateo," she breathed, sounding small and scared as she stared at him, slumped in his chair, only the duct-tape bonds keeping him from falling to the floor.

Dragging her gaze from Mr. Espina's unconscious form, Kit lunged for Elena, hoping to take advantage of her distraction. Before Kit could reach her, though, Elena snapped out of her daze and raised the gun again, just inches from Kit's chest.

"Cut your losses," Kit said, trying to keep her voice calm and reasonable even though she wanted to scream. "Your brother is dead. More cops are coming. You aren't going to accomplish anything today. Save yourself. You've worked so hard on this. Why would you throw it all away now? You're out of time. Even if you manage to shoot a couple of us, you won't escape unless you leave right now. What good is your plan if you spend the rest of your life in prison?"

When Elena sent another hunted glance toward the

window, Kit knew she had her. All she had to do was make sure that no one died before Elena took off.

"Fine," Elena said, refocusing on Kit. "But you're coming with me." Moving behind her, Elena held the gun to Kit's upper spine and shoved her toward the archway. "If you do anything, I'm going to blow a hole in you. Even if you survive it, you'll never walk again. Remember that."

"W-wait!" Sam cried out as he stepped in front of them. Until that point, Kit had managed to contain her fear enough to function, but the sight of Sam putting himself in the line of fire sent utter terror running through her.

"Sam, no!" she cried, and he gave her a frightened but resolute look before refocusing on Elena.

"T-t-take m-m-me, inst-t-tead," he said, and Kit tensed, ready to do whatever she had to do to keep that from happening. Kit knew that whoever left as Elena's hostage was most likely not coming back. She was willing to take that risk with her own life, but not with Sam's. Not Sam.

Before Elena could respond, Kit blurted out, "Take me. You don't want to kill a kid."

"Don't tell me what to do," Elena growled, and Kit hid a wince at her blundering misstep. Despite her fear for Sam, she needed to be smart.

"If you take him, I'll chase you down." The gun barrel jammed harder into her back, but Kit ignored the pain and the way that her head injuries and adrenaline were making the room spin. She couldn't mess this up. Sam's life was at stake. "Think of how much you hate me. I ruined all your plans. How good will it feel to use me as your hostage and then kill me? It's got to be better than feeling guilty for shooting an innocent kid."

For a frozen moment, Kit thought she'd failed.

"Walk," Elena said, shoving the gun into Kit's spine again. The pain was almost a relief. She wasn't taking Sam as a hostage. He was safe. Kit's knees grew watery, threatening to dump her on the ground, but she forced herself to stay upright and walk toward the door.

As they passed, Sam gave her a tormented look. "K-K-Kit…"

She tried to smile at him, even as her mind worked. She needed to survive—for herself and for Wes and for Justice and for Sam. Whatever it took, she'd fight tooth and nail for her life.

With her hold on Kit's arm and the gun in her back, Elena pushed Kit down the hallway and through the kitchen at a jog. She didn't hesitate when they burst outside, steering them across the backyard and into the woods. Elena pressed her into a run, speeding up until all Kit could concentrate on was placing her feet so she didn't trip. Her relief at getting Elena and her gun away from everyone was mixed with terror. If Elena's plan was successful, Kit was going to die. Her only hope was to get away.

Thinking of an escape was almost impossible, though, with branches whipping her across the face and rocks wanting to trip her and send her sprawling onto the snowy ground. Her eyes were fixed on the game trail in front of them, hunting out roots and holes that threatened to trip her and possibly get her shot on the way down.

Even in their mad dash through the trees, she recognized the deer trail they were following. She and Justice had covered this ground before, and she knew they were headed toward the burned house. This was Murphy's territory.

Murphy's trapping territory.

Her gaze snapped back to the ground, this time with more intent. She looked for unnatural bunches of leaves or man-made markings, showing where he'd hidden one of his traps. It was a long shot, she knew, but it was better than no plan at all.

"Where are you going?" she gasped, wanting to keep Elena distracted. "Do you even have a plan?"

"Of course." It was a small comfort that Elena sounded just as winded as Kit was. "I always have a plan and a way out of town."

Way out of town. As her gaze continued searching the ground, she turned over Elena's words in her head. There was no public transportation in Monroe, so the only way out would be by car—or helicopter. Since there was no metal bird hovering over them, she assumed that Elena had a car waiting—or maybe a driver? An accomplice?

As they got closer to the burned house, Kit racked her brain. She'd done the canvass, for goodness' sake. Of anyone, she should know if there were any suspicious vehicles in the area, especially with so few people around. Mrs. Jones had been one of a sparse handful of people still in the area, and she would've immediately noticed a strange car parked in the neighborhood.

Mrs. Jones. She'd been missing her keys. "Planning on stealing the old Lincoln?" she puffed.

When Elena jerked in surprise, Kit knew she'd guessed right. It probably wouldn't save her life, but she was still happy to have one more piece of the puzzle—and to know exactly where Elena was heading.

A gleam of metal caught her eye, and she saw the unmistakable curve of a leg-hold trap buried in the leaves. She leaned sideways, using her weight to make Elena veer left.

"Knock it off," Elena growled, shoving the gun against her spine painfully. "It's just as easy to shoot you here."

Saving her breath, Kit gave Elena one more shove and then jumped, praying that it was far enough, that she would clear the spot. Elena made a surprised sound at the sudden movement, and her hand was jerked from Kit's arm. Just as she landed, Kit dropped, hearing the dull metal *clang* and a scream just before the crack of a close-range gunshot.

A sharp, agonizing pain shot through her thigh. Kit stumbled, almost falling. Blood pulsed from a hole in her leg, immediately darkening the fabric of her pants with hot liquid that chilled quickly. She stared at it, shocked, but then ripped her gaze away. She needed to run. Elena was still too close and had the gun. It would be easy for her to kill Kit right now. Adrenaline kicked in, and she stumbled forward, feeling a fresh gush of blood running down her leg as jagged pain stabbed her with every step.

Drops of red dotted the pristine snow, leaving a trail Kit knew a kindergartner could follow, but there was nothing she could do. If she stopped to bind it, then Elena would catch up with her, and then she wouldn't just have a hole in her leg—she'd have a matching one in her head. Gradually, the pain faded and the wound went numb, leaving only a strange wobbliness to the injured leg. She sped up, weaving through the trees, trying to put as many things as possible between her and the gun.

"Bitch!" Elena shrieked behind her, right before the gun fired twice more. "I'll track you down and kill you slowly for this! You can try to run, but I'll find you!"

Risking a glance back, she saw Elena prying open the vicious jaws of the trap that had locked around her ankle. Blood reddened the churned-up snow around the trap, and Kit felt a base pleasure in the fact that she wasn't the only one hurting. Turning back around, Kit fled, flying along the narrow path faster than she'd ever run before, ignoring her numb and shaky leg, even as it tried to buckle under her weight. She dodged around evergreens and plowed through brushy blockades, resisting the urge to look behind her, knowing that would just slow her down. She had to take full advantage of her head start, or she would be dead.

The ground sloped down, and Kit used it to run even faster. The snow and dead leaves under her boots were slick, and the rocky surface didn't give her any traction. Soon, she was going too quickly to stop, and her boot skidded on a loose rock. Her bad leg gave out, and her arms flailed out to the sides as she tumbled down, sliding and rolling and twisting as she bounced painfully off a tree trunk.

It took several seconds for her to realize that she wasn't moving. Her leg was starting to hurt again, but the throbbing helped her hold on to consciousness. From the stain soaking her pants, she was losing too much blood. Shaking her head to clear her brain, the urgent need to get as far from Elena as she could hit her again, and she tried to scramble to her feet. As soon as she shifted her right leg, pain tore through her, and she sucked back a scream that wanted to escape.

The second time, she managed to pull herself to her feet, but she only got a few feet before the world spun and her leg folded underneath her. Her brain threatened to panic. Elena was coming to kill her, and Kit couldn't even move her leg, much less stand. She slammed the mental door on the fear, desperately focusing on her breathing to keep the pain from overwhelming her common sense.

She needed to move. If that was impossible, then she needed to hide. If she couldn't run or walk, then she needed to crawl or even drag herself to a hiding spot. Looking around, she spotted a downed pine thirty feet away that would provide some concealment. Having a plan, even one as basic as that, helped to calm her shattered nerves, and she tentatively moved her leg again, gritting her teeth against the need to cry out. Just that small shift made black spots overtake her vision. Blinking rapidly, she managed to focus again, but she knew she couldn't hold on to consciousness for long.

There was no way she was standing or even crawling, so that left dragging herself across the ground. One arm at a time, she pulled herself toward the log, each movement sending jagged spikes of pain through her right thigh. Grabbing a sapling in her outstretched hand, she tugged her lower body across the patchy snow, using her left knee to propel her forward. Her injured leg hit a mostly buried rock, and agony shuddered through her, strong enough to cloud her brain and narrow her vision. Glancing back, she saw the bloodstained trail she was leaving in her wake, the red vivid against the white of the snow.

Stay conscious. Stay conscious.

Her mantra worked, and the woods around her came back into focus.

"Well, now, that's just pathetic." Elena's voice was close, too close. Kit turned onto her side, terror muting the tearing pain that movement sent through her, and saw Elena just a few feet away, limping. There were tears and bloodstains on the calf of her right leg, and Kit felt that vicious satisfaction again that Elena wouldn't escape completely unscathed. It made Kit's inevitable death a little less bitter. She knew the final shot was coming. Even if Kit could stand, there was nowhere left to run. She was trapped, just like a rabbit in one of Murphy's traps.

With a chilling smile, Elena raised the gun and took aim.

As Wes pulled his truck behind the chief's squad car, he felt his stomach twist in fear. The previously sleepy house had erupted into chaos. People and dogs were everywhere, their frantic motions projecting the emergency situation. He couldn't see Kit.

Quickly tying an improvised leash onto Justice's harness, Wes jumped out of the truck with the dog, running up to the closest person.

"Sam! Where's Kit?"

Sam turned toward him, and Fifi moved with the teen, pressing herself close to his legs. Sam looked terrified, with a green cast to his pasty-white skin. From his expression, Wes knew that the answer wasn't going to be good.

"Elena t-took h-h-her." His tone was thick with concern and self-recrimination. Turning away from Wes, he looked down at his dog. "F-Fifi, f-f-find K-Kit! C'mon, g-girl. You c-c-can d-do this. F-find Kit!"

"She's not trained yet, Sam," the chief said, his voice kind despite the tension underlying it. "Justice will find her, but you need to stay here."

Unable to bear another second of just standing there, Wes tightened his fingers around Justice's twine leash. "What door did they leave through?"

"The b-b-back," Sam said, and Wes ran through the side yard to the back porch, Justice, anxious and hyper, bounding along next to him. Sam started to follow, but the chief stopped him. Tuning out their argument, Wes focused on Justice.

Crouching down in front of the dog, he put a hand on either side of Justice's face. This was it. There was no more time to waste. Kit was out there with a homicidal Elena, and Wes needed to find her—now. Justice looked up at him, his body unusually still, as if even he understood the gravity of the situation. "Justice, find Kit."

Justice started circling, his nose to the snowy ground. After just a few seconds that felt like an eternity, he bayed and took off for the trees. Wes ran, Justice in front of him, pulling the leash tight. They crashed through the brush, ignoring the evergreen branches dumping their load of snow down his back and over Justice. The dog seemed to fly in front of him, and he cursed his own human legs for slowing them down. He ran faster, weaving through the trees, not knowing what Elena's plan was or how long she would keep Kit alive. Wes was grateful that he was used to running through the woods around his tower, that his lungs had become accustomed to the high altitude so that he could keep up with Justice as they sprinted after Kit.

Justice didn't hesitate, following the trail without slowing, but it still felt too slow. As they plunged through a grove of aspen, a gunshot rang out, clear and loud in the cold winter air. Wes froze at the sound, his heart plunging into his stomach, and the dog's momentum yanked him forward again. His legs felt numb as he ran, but he still pushed them harder, imagining Kit shot and bleeding and dying in the snow.

He almost tripped over the sprung leg-hold trap. The fresh blood smearing the trap and dotting the trail made fear rip through him. From the tracks, it was obvious that one of the women had gotten caught—but which one?

He ran after them again as fast as he could, only pausing for a brief moment to unhook the twine leash when it got caught in some brush. The trees thinned a little as they ran over the crest of a hill, enough so that he saw the two figures—one on the ground and one standing—at the bottom of the incline. He sped up, dodging trees and rocks, and Justice pulled him to an even faster pace. The dog started baying, and both women turned their heads.

Elena was the one standing, and her arms were outstretched, the dull black of a handgun in her hands. It felt as if Wes's heart stopped at the sight. Time slowed down, but that didn't help, since there was no way he could get close enough in time to stop what was going to happen.

Elena was going to shoot Kit, and there was nothing Wes could do but watch.

The sight of Wes and Justice made hope leap in Kit's chest for one illogical moment before she realized they were too far away. They couldn't help her. Kit felt around for a rock or a branch or some kind of weapon so that she could at least go out fighting, but there was nothing except leaves and snow and sandy dirt.

"My plan didn't go like I wanted," Elena said, adjusting her aim, "but at least I get to kill you. You were the most aggravating part of this place."

A *boom* echoed through the trees, and Kit's eyes snapped shut. She braced for the hit, wondering if it was going to hurt, sending a mental apology to everyone who'd be heartbroken at her death. She'd failed to stay alive, but at least she'd saved the others. Despite the comfort in that thought, she still felt a rush of fury and grief as she waited for the bullet that would end her life.

There was no impact. Opening her eyes, she realized that she was alive and unhurt and that Elena was the one on the ground, a hole through her middle and her eyes wide with shock.

Kit looked around, trying to understand what had just happened, how she'd been saved. Her gaze landed on a camouflaged figure standing in the trees a short distance away, smoke curling from the shotgun as he lowered it to his side. "Murphy?"

He gave her an odd half salute before he turned and walked away. Then Wes was there, and her attention was focused on him and Justice, one who was patting her down, looking for bullet wounds, and the other who was focused on licking her face.

She was alive. Despite everything, she'd survived. Wrapping an arm around Justice and the other around Wes, she felt a moment of sheer happiness.

At a low groan, she turned her head to see Elena's sprawled and bleeding body. Forcing herself to release Wes and Justice, she dragged herself to Elena's side. Grabbing the gun sitting in the snow by the other woman, Kit slid it toward Wes. "Clear that," she ordered roughly.

As she felt for a pulse, she used her other hand to cover the bleeding hole where the slug had entered. Elena's heart beat sluggishly, throbbing weakly against her fingers, and Kit turned her entire focus to stopping the bleeding. Elena may have been a monster, but Kit was still a cop—and she had to help. She couldn't let even Elena die if there was some way she could prevent it.

"Are medics following?" she asked Wes without turning toward him.

"I'm not sure. Justice and I just took off." His voice shook, and she wished she could spare a moment to reassure him, but she was too focused on stopping Elena from bleeding out and keeping herself from passing out. "We had to find you."

She opened her mouth to thank him for coming after her, for having her back, when she felt a sharp pain prick her stomach. Glancing down, she saw a knife blade pointing at her belly. It seemed surreal, so small and yet so deadly as it pressed against her skin. Shocked, her gaze flew to Elena's face to see her small, cold smile. In that moment, Kit could read everything in those dark eyes. Elena was going to punish Kit for interfering in her plan, for seeing through Elena's act when everyone else had believed her. Before she died, Elena was going to drag one last person with her.

Kit knew in that second that she was going to die in these snowy woods after all.

A loud boom rocked the world around her, making Kit flinch, and she saw the moment Elena's hand slipped off the knife, leaving it to fall harmlessly into the snow. When Kit moved her stunned gaze back to Elena's face, the smile was gone...and so was most of her head. Dark hair was caught in a spreading halo of blood.

Everything was quiet as Kit turned her head to look at Wes.

His arm was extended, Elena's gun smoking in his hands, a grim look on his face.

"Thank you," she said, the words echoing strangely inside her head. She could hardly believe everything that had happened. "You saved my life."

He stared at her, his gun hand falling to his side. Without looking away from Kit, he dropped the magazine and cleared the chamber, letting the bullet drop into the snow. Sliding the gun in his pocket, he crouched next to her and pulled her gently into his arms. Once she was pressed against his chest, his arms tightened until she could barely breathe.

She didn't mind, though. The pressure reminded her that she was alive.

Justice pressed against her other side. Wrapping an arm around the dog and the other around the man, she hugged them both tightly to her. "How am I not dead?" Her voice shook, but she forgave herself for that. After all, she'd just come closer to dying than she ever had—and considering the insanity of the last half hour, that was saying something.

Finally releasing her, Wes ran his gaze over her, quickly finding the bullet wound. "I thought I was going to have to watch you die." His hands trembled as he tore the fabric of her pants, exposing the bloody hole in her thigh. For some reason, that shakiness made her start to cry.

"I'll be okay," she said as much for her own reassurance as his. "I'm not dead. I'm not even injured that much. Well, except for my leg, but that's just a bullet hole."

His huff of breath was shaky at best. "Right. *Just* a bullet hole. Over here!" His last two words were a shout.

Everything was getting fuzzy around the edges, and her leg had pretty much stopped hurting again, even though Wes was pressing on it.

"Thanks for saving my life again," she said, unable to keep her words from slurring. Other voices around them caught her attention for a moment, and then they slipped away from her. Even Wes's face was getting a little blurry. "You seem to be making a habit of it."

This time, when unconsciousness tugged at her, she let it take her. Wes was here, and he'd keep her safe.

CHAPTER 26

"Why are we having a barbecue?" Kit asked, shifting her crutches so that Otto and Sarah could get into the kitchen. Otto gave her a nod, and Sarah offered a quick, one-armed hug as they passed, careful not to bump Kit's right leg.

"It's a yay-everyone-survived barbecue," Hugh explained, pulling plastic wrap off the platters of raw hamburgers and steaks. "Plus, nothing's blown up in the past, oh, ten days or so. And you're the injured one now, so everyone fusses over you, and they leave me alone. Plenty of reasons to celebrate."

"But why a barbecue? It's December."

He grinned at her as he headed for the snow-covered deck. "Because we're crazy that way."

Shaking her head, she pushed herself away from the counter and crutched over to the kitchen table where Wes was helping Tio with his drone. When she leaned over to kiss his temple, he turned and smiled up at her, that beaming, happy smile she didn't think she'd ever get used to.

Since the two were occupied with their drone construction, she moved into Hugh's living room, where everyone else had gathered.

She squeezed into the packed room. Dee, Ty, and

Sam were playing with the four shepherd puppies that Hugh and the others were bottle raising. In another few weeks, they'd be old enough to go to their new homes. Theo, Otto, and Hugh were each taking a puppy, and they were pushing her to adopt one as well. The pups were so cute that not much convincing was going to be necessary. Justice would love having a dog friend.

Fifi was lying next to Sam, being surprisingly tolerant of the puppies pouncing on her wagging tail and play-fighting with her paws.

Jules squeezed in next to her. "I feel like we're in a clown car. This house is going to explode if one more person or dog comes in here."

"Please don't mention explosions," Theo said, sounding like he was at least partly kidding. At the knock on the door, he moved to answer it.

Kit watched curiously, wondering who'd arrived. From her count, everyone in their group of friends was already there. Theo stepped back, allowing the person at the door to enter. To Kit's surprise, Mr. Espina, his left arm secured in a sling, stepped into the house. Everyone went quiet, except for some yips and squeaks from the puppies.

"Come in." Grace was the first one to break the silence. "It's good you came. Do you want a drink?"

He shook his head with the slightest shake, his grim expression not lightening at the invitation. Kit was struck by how hopeless he looked, and her heart squeezed for him. As much as Elena—Alex—had tried to blame him, none of what had happened had been his fault. "I just wanted to drop this off." He handed Jules a legal-sized envelope and then turned to leave.

"You sure you don't want to stay for a while?" Sarah asked.

Without turning around, he gave another one of those infinitesimal shakes of his head and left, quietly closing the door behind him. Everyone was silent for several moments, and Kit suspected they all felt the weight of Mr. Espina's grief.

Jules opened the envelope. As she examined the contents, her eyes grew wider and wider.

"What is it?" Theo moved closer, putting an arm around her as he scanned over the paper in Jules's tight grip. His eyebrows went up. "I don't know if this is a gift or a punishment."

"It's a gift!" Jules's laugh had an emotional catch to it, even as she teasingly elbowed Theo in the belly. "A wonderful gift." She held up the document so everyone could see it. "It's the title for our house. Mr. Espina gave us our home!"

A cheer went up, and Kit joined in, although she now understood Theo's comment. She'd seen the state of that house. It didn't seem to affect everyone's joy at the news, however. As ancient and dilapidated as the place was, it was home to Jules and her family, and Kit was enormously happy for them.

Once the excitement died down slightly, Hugh brought two bottles of beer from the kitchen. He handed the first to Kit and the other to Grace. They both thanked him—Kit verbally and Grace with a quick kiss.

"No drink for me?" Jules asked with feigned offense, still flushed with excitement and hugging the title to her chest.

"Nope." Hugh didn't look at all bothered by her

scolding. "I only have two hands. Kit gets all the free drinks she wants until she forgives us for ever doubting her, and Grace is my sweetie pie. Besides, you already got a house. Now you want a beer, too? Kind of greedy, don't you think?"

Theo, who must've slipped into the kitchen in the meantime, handed Jules and Sarah each a bottle.

Giving him a smile, Jules said, "Thank you, even if it is beer."

"What else would we drink at a barbecue?" Hugh asked, heading back out to the deck.

Kit asked, "Does anyone else think it's weird we're grilling out in December?"

"Hugh likes to host at least one winter barbecue a year. If we suggest waiting until it warms up, his feelings are hurt." Theo shrugged. "It's warm in here, at least." His gaze fell to Kit's leg. "You shouldn't be standing."

She waved off his concern. "I sit plenty. I can see why it's called desk duty, and I also see why everyone hates it. I can't wait to start taking calls again."

"Otto," Theo called, and the other man raised his head. "Kit needs to sit down."

The big guy immediately popped up off the sofa and came over, scowling. "Why are you standing on that leg? You just had surgery a week ago. It should be elevated."

They fussed at her until she was settled on the couch, her leg propped up on pillows stacked on the coffee table, with an amused Jules and Grace on either side of her. Grumbling, the guys finally left her alone. Deep down, she loved their concern. It was the same nagging she'd offer to one of her partners if they'd been hurt. It meant she was one of the team, and that finally filled the empty spot that had existed since her last department had turned on her.

"No wonder Hugh's grateful I took the attention off his injuries," Kit said, making the other two women laugh.

"They're even more over the top with you, though," Grace said, keeping her voice low so just the three of them could hear it. "They feel bad about not trusting your instincts with the whole Elena thing."

"I feel bad, too," Jules said, squeezing Kit's hand. "I can't believe I listened to her, that I defended her. I feel like such an idiot. I'm sorry, Kit."

Kit squeezed back. "You've already apologized about five thousand times, and the guys have apologized about twice that. It's fine. You're forgiven. I understand the need to go all mama bear when it comes to your siblings. Speaking of the kids, how are you all doing?"

"We're good." Jules took a deep breath that shook a little, but she looked relieved. "It's hard to believe we don't have to be scared anymore."

Sarah left the puppy fest and squeezed in on the end next to Grace. "How's the leg?"

"Better. It doesn't hurt that much anymore unless I do something stupid or Justice runs into me. It's more annoying than anything."

Grace grinned at her. "This is your chance, though, to have that big, bearded man of yours be your devoted slave. Have him fetch and carry for you."

With a snort, Kit said, "He already has everything set up at my house so it operates on voice control. It takes some getting used to. I keep opening and closing blinds by mistake, and I think I confuse Robo-Cat on a regular basis."

"He gave you the robo-cat?" Jules laughed. "It must be love."

Kit couldn't completely swallow her smitten grin. She was pretty sure it was love—on both sides. She couldn't imagine caring about someone more.

"H-hey, K-Kit," Sam said, looking up from where he sat cross-legged with a puppy in his lap and another trying to climb him like a mountain. "H-how long d-do you have to b-be on crutches?"

"Another month." She tried not to whine, but it was hard.

"C-c-can w-we train the dogs again after th-that?"

"Of course." She smiled at him. He seemed different now, lighter. "In the meantime, would you be willing to work with Justice, too? I'll pay you."

He scowled. "You're not paying me."

Surprised, she looked at him quizzically.

"We're training partners." Ducking his head, he ran his fingers over the back of one of the puppies in his lap. The back of his neck turned red. "We're friends, aren't we?"

"Of course we are." Kit had to blink rapidly to keep any tears from escaping. "Okay. I won't pay you, but I'll take care of Fifi while you're on vacation. How about that?"

"Deal." He gave her one of his rare, sweet smiles, and Kit had to force the happy tears back again.

"I'll give you weekly homework for both of the dogs. How's Fifi doing at your house?"

"G-good." He shot a look at Jules before turning back to the puppies.

"If 'good' means she only ate half of everything in the house, then yes, she's good," Jules muttered, although she didn't seem too annoyed. "She's so sweet that no one can really get upset with her."

Kit, Sarah, and Grace all grinned at her silently.

"What?"

"You're so keeping that dog," Sarah singsonged, and the rest of them laughed.

"Probably." Jules shrugged, not looking too upset about it. "And we're getting one of the puppies. I've resigned myself to living in a zoo."

"You'll love it," Sarah said.

"True." Jules smiled. "Everything seems so happy and easy now that we're not running anymore."

Sarah raised her bottle of beer. "I can drink to that. Here's to no longer hiding."

"Here's to no more explosions," Grace added, lifting her own drink.

"No more fires."

"Or snipers."

"Or helicopters dropping bombs."

"Or drug lords who want to kill us."

"Or murderers who live in our house."

Kit blinked, a little overwhelmed at hearing everything that had happened to this tiny town over the past few months. What had she been thinking to move here?

But then she looked at the people around her, knowing that she had real partners and friends and a sweet, drone-building Sasquatch of her very own. Monroe resembled a postapocalyptic deathscape, sure, but it had become *her* postapocalyptic deathscape.

She raised her glass. "Here's to mountain folk with good aim."

"Hear, hear!"

Taking a drink, Kit lowered her glass and looked around the room at her new partners and friends. The sound of Wes's laughter filtered in from the kitchen, and she smiled. It had been worth the frustration and loneliness and fear and even the painful hole in her leg to have found her place in this weird mountain town she'd grown to love.

Finally, against all the odds, she was home.

Curious what Fireman Steve has been up to?
Read on for a sneak peek of the Rocky
Mountain Cowboys, coming October 2018!

ROCKY
MOUNTAIN
COWBOY
Christmas

CHAPTER 1

STEVE HAD BEEN A BORNE FIREFIGHTER FOR LESS THAN FIVE minutes when the missing-person call came in.

"Grab some of the spare gear and let's go," the chief told him. "Search and Rescue will meet us there."

Steve was moving toward the equipment room before the chief even finished speaking. As he yanked on his borrowed bunker gear, a trickle of adrenaline warmed his blood. This was what he lived for. It'd been too long since he'd headed to a scene without a sense of dread weighing him down. The past couple of years had held too many tragedies and betrayals.

Borne would be different. He'd be able to go back to helping people, rather than cleaning up after it was too late.

Pushing away memories of his past two towns, Steve jammed his feet into a pair of boots and headed for the rescue. Swinging up into the passenger side of the cab, he turned to the chief, who was firing up the engine. The radio lit up as various people called in, giving their ETAs, and Steve grimaced slightly. He had a lot of names to learn. Starting over for the second time in less than two years wasn't much fun.

"Who's lost?" he asked. He'd deal with this call and then worry about the rest. Someone was missing, and that took priority.

"Camille Brandt, our local eccentric artist," the chief said, easing the rescue out of the station and into the swirling snow.

"Camille? She still lives in Borne?" Steve was surprised. He'd figured that the dreamy, shy girl he remembered would've escaped the small Colorado town as soon as possible to live in New York or California or some artists' paradise. As much as Steve loved his childhood home, Borne wasn't kind to those who marched to their own beat.

The chief gave him a quick sideways glance before refocusing on the road. Although the snow wasn't too treacherous yet, a strong north wind had picked up, tossing the inch of powder around and messing with visibility. "You knew her growing up?"

"Yeah." That didn't feel like the complete truth, though, so he added, "Sort of. She was three years younger than me, but I saw her around. Borne High School's pretty small."

The chief gave a laugh. "True."

"You didn't go there, did you?" As Steve asked the question, he looked out the window, noting what had changed and what had stayed the same since his last visit home. A few houses had been painted, and what used to be a taco shop now sold coffee. Other than that, it was still the Borne he'd always known.

"Nope." The chief turned onto a side street, careful not to bump a car parked at the curb. "Moved here fifteen years ago." A wry expression crossed his face. "Still a newcomer, according to most people."

Steve gave an amused grunt. That was Borne, all right. "Who reported Camille missing?"

"Mrs. Lin, Camille's neighbor," the chief said as he rolled up to the curb in front of Camille's grandma's house. *No*, Steve mentally corrected himself, *Camille's house*. The older woman had died a decade or so ago.

Reaching for his door handle, Steve said, "Hopefully, she's just at a friend's house, safe and warm."

The chief snorted as he opened his door. "Friend's house? I thought you said you knew Camille."

Before Steve could ask what he meant by that, the chief slammed the door shut. Climbing out of the cab, Steve ducked his chin into the collar of the borrowed bunker coat as the wind spat a handful of sharp snow pellets against his exposed neck. If Camille really was in need of rescue, they had to find her soon. It'd be dark in a couple of hours, and the weather would only get worse.

Jogging across the street, Steve caught up with the chief on Mrs. Lin's doorstep just seconds before she opened the door.

"Well, come in, come in," she fussed, stepping back so they could both enter. "You're letting the heat out."

Steve closed the door behind them, but Mrs. Lin didn't look any happier. Then again, he'd never seen her look happy about much of anything.

"Steve Springfield?" she asked, and he gave her a nod of greeting. "Does this mean you're finally back for good then? 'Bout time you stopped traipsing around the world and came home. Your poor parents will finally be able to relax and enjoy their retirement."

Steve set his molars to keep from telling Mrs. Lin that rather than "traipsing around the world," he'd only been a few hours' drive up into the mountains, that his "poor" parents were happily basking in the New Mexico sun, and that none of that was really her business anyway.

The chief must've guessed some of what Steve wanted to say, because he cleared his throat and flicked an amused glance at him. "Mrs. Lin, what time did you see Camille leave?"

"Like I already told the dispatcher, it was at ten forty-eight yesterday morning. I know that because I was on the elliptical downstairs, watching out the front window. I always go a full sixty minutes, from ten to eleven, and the display showed forty-eight minutes. Camille walked outside—without locking her door, even though I keep telling her she's going to be brutally murdered if she's not careful—and went into the woods across the street."

"You haven't seen her return?" the chief asked, scribbling in his small flip notebook.

"She hasn't gotten back yet." Mrs. Lin's tone was certain. "She's been gone for a day and a half. Her car hasn't moved. I even checked the snow for footprints by the garage and on the front walk. She's still out there, probably freezing to death, unless she's been kidnapped to be sold into sex slavery."

Steve blinked. "Doubt there's much of a risk of that around here."

"You've been gone for years," Mrs. Lin scolded. "Things have changed in Borne. It's not the sleepy little town you left."

"It's still pretty sleepy," the chief said as he wrote.

"There's been a huge jump in crime." Mrs. Lin folded her arms over her narrow chest and glared.

The chief didn't seem to feel her laser-like stare

burning holes in his downturned head. "Not really," he said.

"There *is* crime, Chief Rodriguez." Mrs. Lin's voice was frosty. "What about the felon who took Misty Lincoln's lawn furniture?"

"That was her ex-husband." The chief finally looked up from his notes. "And I believe he'd been awarded it in the divorce." Mrs. Lin huffed, but he spoke again before she could start rattling off any other local crimes. "Do you know where Camille was headed?"

Although she held her glare for a few moments, Mrs. Lin finally let it go. "Probably to find all sorts of trash for her…things." Mrs. Lin gestured vaguely in the direction of Camille's house.

Her…things? Steve opened his mouth to ask for clarification when the chief flipped his notebook closed. "Did you try calling her?"

"Of course. It goes to her voicemail—her *full* voicemail, so I couldn't even leave a message."

The chief moved to open the door. "Give the dispatcher a call if you spot her or if she calls you back."

Mrs. Lin gave them a tight nod as they left her house and walked toward Camille's. Steve kept an eye out for any footprints, but he had to concur with Mrs. Lin on that. The only things he spotted were some blurry indentations leading away from the house. He assumed they were from when Camille had left. Her elderly car was parked on the street, covered by a light blanket of fresh snow.

"I'm still not sure why you're so certain she's not with a friend," Steve said as he climbed the front steps and pounded on her door. There was just the silence of an empty house on the other side.

"Camille's not really the drop-in-on-friends sort," the chief said absently, peering into a window. "The few times I've seen her out in public have been at odd hours, times when she didn't think many other people would be out and about, I'm assuming. She's not exactly the town hermit—that's your brother Joe—but she's pretty close to earning the top spot."

Knocking one final time, Steve considered that. It didn't seem to fit the Camille he remembered. Sure, she was shy, but she'd been sweet, too, and pretty enough to stick in his head, even though she'd been three grades below him. When he thought of a hermit, he pictured someone cranky and sour. Camille Brandt had either changed a lot since high school, or the chief was exaggerating.

As they knocked on the side door that led into her workshop, Nate's pickup pulled up behind the rescue. His brother climbed out, and Steve waved him over. He noticed Nate's slight limp as he hurried to join them and felt a twinge of concern that he kept to himself, knowing his brother wouldn't appreciate the fussing. Nate had twisted his ankle while turning horses out into the pasture a few days earlier, and he'd refused to have it checked out. Ryan, another of Steve's brothers, climbed out of the passenger side of the truck and followed Nate. Even though Ryan wasn't officially a member of Search and Rescue or the fire department, Steve wasn't surprised to see him. Ryan always loved being where the action was.

"Camille's missing?" Nate asked as he reached them, zipping his coat a little higher. Steve couldn't blame him. The wind was vicious today.

"According to Mrs. Lin, she headed into the woods yesterday morning and hasn't gotten back yet," the chief summarized, waving toward the trees across the street. More vehicles arrived, and deputies, firefighters, and Search and Rescue members joined their growing huddle. As he hunched against the stinging assault of snow and wind, Steve eyed the trees, antsy to start searching.

The chief handed the scene over to a woman from Search and Rescue that Steve didn't recognize. She introduced herself as Sasha and quickly divided everyone into teams. Steve, the chief, Ryan, and Nate were together.

"Betsy will be here in about ten minutes with her tracking dog," Sasha said in a loud, clear voice that managed to carry over the wind. "I don't want to wait for them to arrive before we start searching, though... not with dusk approaching and the temperature dropping like it is."

Steve was glad for that. He was antsy enough with the delay as it was. Every search reminded him of when his two girls had been lost in the mountains, and the memory of those horrifying hours still hit him like a punch to the gut at times like these. The idea of someone—especially shy, sweet Camille—being caught in the frozen night, alone and afraid, made his stomach churn with worry. He needed to get out there and start searching for her. With the temperature dropping and the wind picking up, each minute could be critical.

The teams spread out and started making their way through the trees, calling for Camille. Their voices were quickly snatched away, dulled by the thick forest and the now-roaring wind. The trees creaked ominously, threatening to drop thick branches on their heads, and Steve moved a bit more quickly.

The sun was slipping toward the mountain peaks, and the light cast strange shadows. Steve's pulse kept leaping every time he caught a glimpse of a promising shape, and disappointment caught him after each false alarm. The searchers spread out, the space between the chief, Steve, and his brothers gradually increasing until the only sounds were the crunch of snow beneath his boots and his voice calling for Camille in the gathering dusk.

He held an image of her face in his mind from when they'd both been teenagers. She'd been so delicate-looking. It was hard to imagine her surviving a few hours in the snowy wilderness, much less a whole night. A fresh sense of urgency pushed him to move faster.

"Camille!" he called, raising his voice so it would carry over the wailing wind. He paused to listen, but there was no response—at least none that he could hear. Steve pressed on, tromping around trees and through snowy brush that threatened to trip him. Evergreen branches scraped against the heavy fabric of his borrowed bunker gear, showering him with their layer of snow. He drew a breath to yell for Camille again, but a distant yelp made him whip his head around as he realized the muted cry of pain had come from Nate. Steve turned and hurried through the trees to his brother's side. "You okay?"

"Fine." He didn't sound fine, and his face was drawn with pain. "Just took a bad step."

"Do you need to head back?" Steve asked, watching

closely as Nate lowered his foot to the ground. As soon as he put weight on it, he grimaced but waved Steve off.

The chief joined them. "Everything okay?"

"His ankle's bothering him," Steve said. "I'll help him back to the staging area."

"No, he's *fine* and going to continue searching," Nate gritted out, limping away.

"What's up?" Ryan called through the trees. "Something wrong?"

"We're good!" Steve called back, even as he exchanged a concerned look with the chief. He knew there was no point in fighting Nate on this. His brother was stubborn and took his search-and-rescue duties too seriously to give up without a fight—something that, in this case, would waste precious time.

So instead, they spread out again and continued to search. Although Steve knew that Nate was doing his best to push through, he'd slowed considerably, and Steve was torn between hurrying to find Camille as soon as possible and refusing to leave his obviously hurting brother behind. The tree branches clacked and groaned, snow whipping into Steve's face and shoving his shouts for Camille right back down his throat. The light was quickly fading, the thickening storm clouds and heavy evergreen branches around the searchers blocking most of the remaining sunlight.

Reaching to turn on his headlamp, Steve gave an annoyed grunt when his fingers only found his helmet. That was the problem with starting over at a new fire department, especially as a volunteer. Until he'd proven that he was there to stay, he was stuck wearing left-over equipment that definitely wasn't set up the way he liked it. He patted the pocket of his bunker coat and was relieved to feel the heavy cylinder of a flashlight. At least he wouldn't be stumbling blindly around the woods once the last of the light disappeared.

"Camille!" he yelled, his voice rough from repeatedly calling for her. His mind was busy running through all sorts of possibilities—what if she'd fallen off a ledge or had a seizure or encountered a bear or stepped in a ground squirrel's hole and broken her ankle? If something had happened, how many hours had she been stuck in the freezing temperature, possibly unconscious?

He moved more quickly, and Nate dropped even farther behind. Steve couldn't let that affect his speed, though. The priority was to find Camille. Nate was upright and moving. Despite his injured ankle, he was fine.

Camille might not be.

The trees thinned, and Steve shoved aside an evergreen branch as he stepped into a clearing. With the sun setting, it took him a moment to recognize where he was—the old scrapyard. The spot was familiar, a favorite place to search for treasure as kids, but it was also slightly menacing in the dim light. The scrapyard had grown as more and more people dumped junk cars and other metal trash, the piles mounded even higher with a solid layer of snow. It had been an exciting, almost magical place when he'd been a kid, but now he saw it through a parent's eyes, and there was danger everywhere. All of the worst-case scenarios he'd thought up while searching came back to him in a rush.

"Camille!" he bellowed, jogging through the snow, feeling his boot catch on uneven footing. So many parts and pieces were buried under sheets of white, just waiting to trip him up and send him flying. Considering the condition of the metal he could see, whatever he landed on would be sure to give him some mutant, vaccination-resistant strain of tetanus, too.

The wind roared, sending a piece of rusted sheeting flying end over end until it struck the remaining back half of an old Chevy van with a clatter. Glancing behind him, Steve saw Nate emerge from the trees, and a new urgency hit him. They needed to find Camille before Nate hurt himself even worse trying to stubbornly navigate the uneven terrain.

"Stay there!" he shouted, but Nate slogged through the snow, either not hearing or ignoring him. Knowing his brother and how he'd ignore his own pain if someone else was in trouble, Steve figured it was the latter. Biting back a growl of worried frustration, he moved even faster through the piles. "Camille!"

There! Had there been movement over by the ancient washing machine off to his left? He headed toward it but was forced to slow as he picked his way between an old piece of farm machinery and the remains of a bed frame. "Camille! It's Steve Springfield! Yell if you can hear me!"

A head suddenly popped up above the pile right next to him, seeming to appear from nowhere. "*Steve*-freaking-*Springfield*?"

Startled, Steve lurched sideways and barely avoided tripping over the junk surrounding him. He peered at the small figure, his eyebrows flying up as he took in her safety goggles and Elmer Fudd hat. "Camille?"

"Yes?" She drew the word out tentatively, and Steve

felt a rush of relief—and the slight annoyance that followed on the heels of worry. It was a familiar sensation, since his kids were too smart and adventurous for their own good.

"Are you hurt?" he asked, focusing on the parts of her that he could see. Between her heavy layers of clothes and the junk hiding her bottom half from view, it wasn't much. "Do you need help?"

"No?" Again, she said the word slowly with an upward incline at the end.

"Good. A lot of people have been worried about you."

"They have? Why?" She stared at him, her brown eyes wide behind the clear plastic of the safety goggles. Blond wisps of hair had escaped the hat and curled around her face. Eyeing her rosy cheeks and full pink lips that were parted slightly in confusion, Steve was transported back to high school, where he'd surreptitiously eyed her in the hall, feeling guilty for his interest in a freshman but unable to keep his eyes off her. Even then, there'd been something about the shy loner. They'd only talked a few times, but she'd had a way of looking at him that made him feel like he could move mountains. If she'd been closer to his age, he would've been tempted to ask her out.

"Mrs. Lin called and said you left yesterday morning and never returned," he explained. "Did you spend the night out here?"

Her eyes rounded, and her pink cheeks darkened even more. "What? No! I went home last night and came back out this morning. Why'd she call you?" she asked on a squeak.

"Not me specifically," Steve said. "She called

dispatch. I'm here because Fire and the county deputies respond to all search-and-rescue calls."

All the color left her cheeks, and Steve's smile slipped away. "Search and rescue?" Her voice was barely audible above the wind. "Looking for me? Everyone's here trying to search and rescue *me*? Are they all coming here? I'm not lost or hurt or anything. I don't need to be searched and rescued!" Looking more and more horrified, she ended on what could only be described as a wail.

"It's okay." Steve took a step closer, trying to soothe her. "Most searches are false alarms. We're used to that."

"*I'm* not used to it!" His reassurances didn't seem to be having much of an effect. "I'm not used to it in any way. Oh, geez Louise, everyone's been searching for me. They're all going to be running over here, aren't they?" The wind settled for a few seconds, and a dog's excited barking could clearly be heard. Camille winced at the sound. "Dogs? Dogs are leading people toward me? I'm not lost! I'm right here, where I usually am. There was just so much to pick up yesterday and today, since I need extra pieces for the Christmas orders, and it took me a little longer than I'd planned, but I didn't think there'd be search and rescuers and *dogs* and cops and Steve-freaking-Springfield..."

"Hey, now. Take a breath." Hiding his amused bafflement over how she kept adding *freaking* to his name, he kept his voice gentle but firm enough to cut through Camille's building panic. "Things will be fine. Everyone will be relieved to see that you're safe. The medics will check you over, and then we'll all go home."

"Medics? Plural? As in more than one? They'll check

me out in front of everyone, while people watch?" She seemed to alternately pale and flush, as if torn between horror and embarrassment. "No. No, no. That's not good. I'm fine. I don't need checking out. All my parts are where they should be, and I even wore my warmest hat, so my ears aren't even cold. I'm *fine*." She took a step back, her boot bumping against a sled piled with pieces of metal scrap. Steve wondered what she needed the parts for. There didn't seem to be any rhyme or reason to the items she'd collected.

Shaking off his distraction, he focused on the panicked woman in front of him. If he didn't do something, she was going to bolt, and then things would get messy—and even more embarrassing for her as the well-intentioned rescuers gave chase. Steve really didn't want that to happen. For whatever reason, he had an overwhelming urge to make things better for Camille. He just wasn't sure how.

"Springfield!" the chief called, circling a scrap pile some distance away. "Did you find her?"

"Oh, no." Camille's eyes grew wider and wider as the chief approached. "Here they come. All the people and medics and questions and *staring*…"

"Don't worry," Steve said, and Camille whipped her head around to look at him, wild-eyed. "I'll fix this."

He just needed to find the right… *There!*

"Oof!" Steve fake-yelled as he jammed his foot between the piece of farm machinery and the old bed frame he'd just skirted. He pinwheeled his arms dramatically for effect.

"What's wrong?" The chief jogged up to them, his face furrowed with concern. "Is Camille hurt?"

Steve straightened with exaggerated care. "Camille's fine. Mrs. Lin had it wrong. Camille went home last night." He gestured toward his foot. "I'm the one that's in need of a rescue. Give me a hand out?"

As he had hoped, the chief's attention instantly turned to his predicament. After examining the metal surrounding Steve's boot, he asked, "How'd you even manage to do this, Springfield?"

Pulling out his portable radio, the chief sighed heavily enough to be heard over the wind. "We found Camille in the scrapyard. She's fine, but the new guy got himself stuck."

Steve felt a twinge of annoyance at the amused condescension in the chief's tone, but then he glanced at Camille, who was looking just slightly less like she wanted the earth to swallow her. The mocking that was sure to follow this incident was worth it if his supposed clumsiness took some attention off her.

Ryan hurried toward them, took the scene in at a glance, and started laughing. "Oh, how the mighty firefighter has fallen."

Steve glowered at his brother. Of course Ryan took pleasure in his predicament. He'd always been the most competitive of all the Springfield brothers.

"Hey, Camille." Ryan turned his attention to the petrified woman, who gave him a dorky wave that made Steve smile. Her awkwardness was still incredibly endearing. "You okay?"

"Fine. I'm good. Nothing wrong here." She shifted back another step as if she was worried that Ryan would insist on checking her over, and Steve let out a grunt of pretend pain.

"A little help?" Steve asked Ryan, trying to pull his brother's attention away from Camille before she bolted.

"Nah," Ryan teased. "I'd rather help Camille. She's much prettier than you are."

Camille turned bright red and made a slight choking sound. Annoyed, Steve grabbed a handful of snow and tossed it at his brother.

"Hey!" Ryan brushed off his coat. "Careful there. You don't want to start a snow war. I'm not the one who's stuck."

The rest of the Search and Rescue members, firefighters, and cops trickled in, including Betsy and her tracking dog—a shaggy, excited mixed breed of unknown parentage.

"Camille, there you are. You need to get checked out." Nate started determinedly in her direction, but Steve reached out and snagged a handful of his brother's coat before he could pass. Knowing Nate's predilection for rescuing damsels in distress, he'd make a big fuss over her, and she very clearly did not want the attention.

"Hang on, Nate. I need you to pull back on this piece here."

"But..." Nate turned back toward Camille, who scooted farther away from them.

"Nope. She's fine. I'm the one who needs help right now." He wasn't a big fan of being the center of attention, either, but he was willing to make the sacrifice. After all, sometimes saving people didn't involve anything as dramatic as burning buildings. "Are you going to leave your favorite brother trapped?"

Although Nate gave him a suspicious look, he bent

and yanked at the metal frame. Ryan watched in amusement, clearly unwilling to help. Well, no surprise there.
At least he was distracted by the show.

Steve scanned the growing crowd of first responders
and spotted the Search and Rescue scene commander.
"Sasha," he called, hooking the toe of his boot a little
more firmly under the piece of metal it was wedged
against. "Camille's fine, and Nate, Ryan, and the chief
can help me with this. No reason for everyone else to
stand around getting cold."

Sasha studied the awkward-looking Camille and then
Steve for a long moment before giving him the slightest
wink. "Agreed. Okay, everyone! Head back to staging, and don't forget to check out with Boris. If you do
forget, we'll be searching the woods for *you*, and no one
wants to do that again!"

"Shouldn't someone do a medical check on Camille?"
Nate asked as everyone else started heading back toward
the trees. Steve wished his foot was free so he could kick
his brother with it.

"She declined medical attention," Steve said quickly,
and Camille looked confused for just a moment before
she started nodding.

"Yes. I declined that. I do decline it. It has been
declined."

Steve coughed to hide a laugh, settling for a smile
that instantly gentled the moment their eyes met. "Why
don't you walk back with Sasha? I bet she'd be willing
to let Mrs. Lin know that you're safely home."

Sasha grimaced. "Sure, stick me with Mrs. Lin duty. I'll
get you back for this, Steve Springfield. C'mon, Camille."

Meeting Steve's gaze, a flushed Camille mouthed

thank you before following Sasha back into the woods. Steve felt a warmth in his belly as he watched her walk away, towing her collection of found items on the sled behind her. Ryan gave him a long, calculating look before turning and hurrying after them, and Steve swallowed a groan. He'd made his interest in Camille—as innocent as it was—too obvious, and now his brother's competitive spirit had kicked in. When they were younger, Steve hadn't been able to look twice at a girl without Ryan trying to elbow in.

The trio was swallowed by the darkening woods, and Steve looked away. There wasn't anything he could do about that now.

When he glanced down, he saw Nate eyeing him with a knowing look. "Found a new way to be the hero, huh?" he asked in a low voice. Apparently, there was no fooling *this* brother.

A string of muttered curses brought Steve's attention back to the chief. "This isn't budging," he said. "I'm going to have to call someone to grab the tools from the rescue and haul them in here."

"Hold on," Steve said when the chief reached for his radio. "I felt it give. Nate, pull back just like that…" He contorted his face as he pulled out his foot, trying to make it look like a huge effort and not something that he could have easily done for the past ten minutes or so. "There! I'm free. Good work, team."

From the chief's suspicious scowl, he knew something was up, but he didn't challenge Steve's miraculous rescue. "Fine. Let's head back. It's only going to get colder."

Steve fell in behind the chief, careful not to move

so quickly that Nate couldn't keep up—and being even more careful not to let on that he was doing anything of the sort. Now that everyone else was gone, an eerie quiet spread over the snow-covered mounds. The wind whipped against his skin, and Steve tucked his chin in the collar of his coat, thinking about Camille and how glad he was that she hadn't been trapped in the icy dark all night. Even as the trees groaned and creaked around him, he smiled slightly, holding the picture of her in those goggles and that earflap hat in his mind.

He barely knew her, but for some strange reason, the thought of Camille Brandt, all grown up, was keeping him warm.

———————————

Why did this keep happening to her?

Camille flattened herself against the toilet paper display, resisting the urge to thump her head against the rolls. There was a reason she only came to the Borne Market early on Sunday mornings, and that was because she didn't want to be forced into awkward conversations with any of her neighbors. It helped that sixteen-year-old Kacey Betts worked the checkout on Sunday, and her focus stayed glued on her cell phone the entire time. Camille could slip in, buy what she needed, and slip right back out without having to make polite chitchat with anyone. Today, however, she and Kacey weren't alone.

Steve-freaking-Springfield was there.

The last time she'd seen him, he'd sweetly helped her escape her "rescue." She still hadn't forgiven Mrs. Lin for sending everyone and their brother on a search

for her. The whole situation had been mortifying, and
that was with Steve's help. If he hadn't been there,
it could've been so much worse. Camille's stomach
churned and her cheeks flushed at the thought of all that
attention—and the potential additional humiliation.

Now, though, she was in a whole new pickle.

Why, today of all days, did Steve have to need
groceries? Why did she have to have the urge for
peanut-butter blossoms? She glanced at the bag of
chocolate stars in her hands and sighed. If she'd just
eaten a spoonful of peanut butter and called it good, she
wouldn't be in this mess.

Come on, Camille, she scolded herself, *grow up
already*. Just because Steve was here didn't mean they
couldn't have a normal conversation. It wouldn't be
awkward unless she made it that way. Sure, she might
have had a huge crush on him as a teenager, and his
gallant actions at the scrapyard might have revived that
crush to its full, painful glory, but she was a mature
adult, capable of casual social interactions.

Camille winced a little at the mental lie. *Okay,
maybe not*. New plan: she was going to sneak past his
aisle and get to the checkout without him even noticing that she was in the store. Resolved, she peeked
around the corner of the display and saw that he was
focused on the products in front of him. Refusing
to let her gaze linger on his rugged profile or broad
shoulders, she forced herself to concentrate on her
goal—escape.

Now!

She shot forward, but her knee caught the edge of the
display, knocking down a column of toilet paper. Time

seemed to slow as the rolls tumbled down, hitting the floor in a series of dull thuds.

She scrambled to pick up the packages, her heart thumping fast in her chest, still hoping that she could still pull off her escape. The horrible awkwardness could still be avoided if she hurried. Maybe he hadn't heard her. The falling rolls hadn't been that loud. Not like cans of peanuts or unpopped popcorn or...a cylinder of ball bearings or—

"Camille?"

She stopped abruptly, keeping a death grip on the toilet paper. That wonderful voice was just a shade deeper than she remembered from high school, but the thrill that rushed up her spine at the sound of it was all too familiar. Turning her head, she met Steve's eyes before dropping her gaze to her armful of Charmin. She replaced the last of the fallen rolls, feeling her hairline prickle with sweat as her thoughts twisted into useless tangles.

Why, *why* was she always embarrassing herself in front of this man?

"Camille. How are you?" His voice was certain now, and as friendly and calm as it always seemed to be. The Springfield brothers had all been sought after in high school—even snarly Joe'd had a fan club—but Steve had always been Camille's favorite. No matter how popular he'd been or how handsome he'd gotten or how many girls had been crushing on him, he'd always stayed so steady and kind.

Now he was waiting for her to speak, though, and she needed to focus on the conversation. "Fine." *Good. Great.* She'd managed an answer, and it'd actually made sense.

"No issues after your time out in the cold?"

"No." He didn't respond right away, looking expectantly at her instead. She knew that meant she was supposed to add to her one-word answer, and she scrambled to think of something, anything she could say. "I was wearing clothes." *Ugh.* That didn't sound right at all. "I mean, there was no chance I'd get frostbitten since I had multiple layers on, plus my boots are waterproof. That's important... Keeping dry, I mean. Since, you know, wet is cold." Her voice trailed off at the end as she resisted the urge to wince. Why was it that she could put words together in her head, but they always came out all wrong?

"True." He sounded amused, and now she couldn't keep from grimacing. Of course he was amused. She was being ridiculous. "I'm glad you're okay."

"How about you?" *That's good*, she praised herself. *Turn the attention back on him. He'll talk, and you can just nod and stay quiet and everything will be okay.* "Is your foot all right?"

His smile widened, one corner tucked in wryly. "Yeah. It was always fine. I just thought you might want everyone's focus on someone else."

She knew it. His dramatic fuss had been so unlike the Steve Springfield she'd sort of known in high school. It had been so obvious to Camille that he'd been faking that she'd been surprised when Nate, Ryan, and the chief had fallen for it. "I did. Thank you." There. That was normal-ish. "I owe you one. I mean, it'd be hard to duplicate that situation with our roles reversed, but if you ever need to be saved, then I'm your man. Well, I'm your *wo*man. Not that I'm your woman in *that* way, of course." Closing her mouth so firmly her teeth clicked together, she swallowed a groan. Why did she never stop at normal-ish?

Steve was silent. When she managed to get up the nerve to peek at his face, he didn't look amused or offended or even baffled. Instead, he seemed…thoughtful. "Actually, I could use your help right now."

Taken off guard, she blinked. "My…help? Now? Here? At the grocery store?"

His mouth pulled down in a grimace as he waved a hand at the products lining the shelves. Dragging her gaze off him, Camille actually noticed what he'd been examining so intently.

"You need my help with…feminine hygiene products?" She wasn't sure why she'd used the technical term, but it was such an odd situation. Steve had reappeared out of the blue after sixteen years. He'd saved her from what could've been a horribly humiliating event in the woods, and he was now standing in front of the tampon display. She was just happy she was capable of talking at all.

"If you don't mind." He gave her a slight smile, not wide enough to create the charming creases in his cheeks she so vividly remembered. "This is an area I… Well, I don't really know what I'm doing."

"Okay." She cautiously moved closer, drawn by him as she'd always been, even as a gawky fourteen-year-old. "What kind of help do you need? Is this for your wife?" She remembered when she'd heard about his marriage, just two years after he'd left town after graduating from high school. Even though she and Steve had only exchanged a handful of words, Camille had still felt a painful twist in her chest at the news.

"No." He focused on the boxes as he tipped his head from side to side, the motion drawing Camille's attention to the way the rounded muscles of his shoulder angled to meet his neck. In his time away, Steve had not slacked off in the working-out department. "She died eight years ago."

"Oh." Jerking her attention off his body, she stared at the familiar line of boxes, not knowing the right response, as usual. "I'm so sorry."

He accepted her words with a tight nod.

Camille mentally scrambled to think of something to say. What could possibly follow "My wife's dead"? Camille hadn't known her, so she couldn't say something like "She was a wonderful woman," since she had no idea what his wife had been like. She didn't even know her name. Anything unrelated to his wife's death, on the other hand, felt so silly and blasé, as if she was blowing off what had happened to him as something small and casual and not the hugely devastating event it surely had been.

"So." He cleared his throat. "This is for my daughter."

"Right." Of course Steve was the wonderful kind of dad who went to the store to get tampons for his kid. Camille was not surprised at all—impressed and even more smitten, but not surprised. "What does she usually use?"

He rubbed his neck—it was like he was *trying* to get her to focus on his excess of muscles—and twisted his shoulders in an uncomfortable shrug. "She doesn't...not yet. I know it's coming, though. Zoe's almost twelve, and she's living in a houseful of guys, except for her little sister, Maya, and I want her to have"—he waved at the tampon display—"whatever she needs on hand when the time comes. It's been hard enough for her to grow up without her mom. The only thing I can do is to hopefully make things a little easier for her."

With a frustrated grunt, he turned to face Camille. "Unless this is just going to make it worse? Should I bring her here and let her pick out what she'll need instead?" Before she could answer, he groaned and scrubbed a hand over his face. "I've been a parent for fourteen years, and it didn't used to be this hard. Now that they're growing up, it feels like all the rules are changing, and I don't know what I'm doing anymore."

Camille's mind went blank. She was horrible at thinking of the right words in the moment—at three the next morning while lying sleepless in bed, sure, but in the moment, never. As the silence stretched, Steve's shoulders began to sag, and he looked so defeated that Camille couldn't stand it.

"My grandma raised me," she blurted out, horrified at the words that were leaving her mouth. Was she really going to tell Steve-freaking-Springfield this story, of all stories? What was she doing? Despite the impending humiliation, though, she kept talking while focusing on a box of panty liners. If she met Steve's warm hazel eyes, she knew she'd stumble over her words and it'd all come out sounding even worse. "I've always been shy, so I didn't have many friends." *Or any*.

"When I got my period, I was eleven. I panicked. My grandma was long past having to use any of this, so there wasn't anything in the house. Since I didn't know what to expect, I didn't know if tissues would be enough, so I used one of Grandma's dish towels, emptied my piggy bank, and came here."

She grimaced at the memory and at the fact that she was actually sharing this traumatizing story with anyone, much less Steve. Freaking. Springfield. "It wasn't an early Sunday morning like this, though. It was Saturday afternoon, packed with everyone doing their weekly grocery shopping, including the prettiest and meanest girl in sixth grade, Hayden Larchmont."

Her cheeks burned as red as they had two decades ago. "There I was, Grandma's embroidered dish towel stuffed in my underwear, feeling like everyone could take one look at me and just *know*, lurking in the candy aisle as I waited for Hayden's family to leave so I could grab what I needed and run. Finally, this lane was clear, and I hurried over—and I stood right here, in this very spot, staring at all this helplessly. I had no idea what to buy. Hayden and her mom came around the corner, and she stared at me standing in front of the tampon display and started to giggle, like she knew about the dish towel and *everything*, and I realized that soon everyone at school would know every humiliating detail, too. I was so flustered and embarrassed that I just grabbed a box at random and ran."

Now that the story was out, her word vomit spewed all over poor Steve, she had no choice but to leave before she melted into a puddle of liquid humiliation. She plucked two types of tampons and a box of pads from the shelf and piled them into Steve's arms. "Here. She can start with these. It might take some time for her to find out what works best for her, but one of these should get her through the first period."

Steeling herself, she turned and met Steve's wide eyes. His mouth was open slightly, but he didn't say anything.

"And for the record, I think you are a very good dad." Turning, she marched to the checkout counter, not looking back at him, even when he called out a thank-you. As Kacey rang up her chocolate stars, Camille stared at the debit card reader, trying very hard not to think about what she'd just done.

I told Steve Springfield the story of my first period.

There was no other option. Camille was going to have to move.

"How many times do I need to say this?" Steve frowned at his two girls. "No more blowing things up—especially not in the house."

"But Dad..." Maya gave him the sweet smile that worked a little too well when it came to getting out of trouble. "It was only a tiny explosion. Just a little *pop*."

"I didn't mean for it to blow up." Zoe frowned at the blackened parts in her hands as if she could read what had gone wrong from the bits that remained. "It wasn't an *intentional* explosion. I'm not sure what happened... Maybe a leak in the fuel line?"

"That shouldn't cause an explosion. A fire, maybe, but..." His eyes narrowed. "No. You aren't distracting me this time. Both of you know the rules. No working on combustible, explosive, or otherwise dangerous projects without an adult present. You"—he pointed at Maya—"are on stall-cleaning duty every day until Christmas." Ignoring her groan, he turned to Zoe. "You are cleaning out the shop. Once that's done, you're helping your sister with the barn chores." Although she grimaced, she accepted the punishment absently, and he knew her mind was still on the cause of the explosion. "No more working on this engine unless I'm directly supervising—or Joe, if I'm not available."

"What? No!" That had gotten her full attention. "Uncle Joe isn't around this close to Christmas. He's better at hiding from the customers than Micah is, and Micah's, like, *invisible* this time of year. I'll never get to work on my engine." Her big brown eyes, so painfully reminiscent of her mother's, widened as she pleaded with him.

"Fine." He knew he was too big a softy when it came to his children, but he couldn't help it. They were good kids—just a little too smart and creative for their own good sometimes. When they were little, it'd been easy to know the right thing to do, but parenting grew harder and harder the older his children got. Now, he often felt as if he were trying to put together one of Zoe's engines without a manual—and with a good chance that everything would blow up in his face. "No working on your engine unless it's in the shop and either one of your uncles is supervising or I'm there."

"Or Will or Micah?" Zoe added hopefully.

Steve snorted a laugh. "You know more about mechanics than either of your brothers, so no. Besides, they just encourage chaos." He turned his stern glance on Maya. "As does your sister, so she doesn't count as supervision, either."

Maya grinned. "This wasn't even close to making it into Zoe's top ten."

Closing his eyes, Steve groaned. "Go ride your ponies. At least they don't blow up."

"You should make a mechanical horse," Maya said

as the two girls headed for the door, stopping to pull on boots and coats. "No, a whole mechanical cavalry! That would be a-*maz*-ing."

"That'd take a lot of raw materials," Zoe said, although her thoughtful tone told Steve that she was considering the idea. He squeezed his eyes closed, making a mental note to tell his brothers to let him know if any large pieces of machinery suddenly disappeared.

"Before you create a robot army," Steve suggested dryly, "why don't you focus on designing a solar stock-tank heater for the back horse pasture."

Zoe's face lit up with excitement at the idea of a new project, and he looked at his two girls, marveling that they'd be teenagers soon. That reminded him of what he'd picked up at the store earlier that morning, and he frowned uncomfortably. There was no sense in putting it off. Camille had said she'd gotten her period when she was eleven, and Zoe would be twelve in a month. She could get it at any time, and Maya probably wouldn't be far behind.

"Girls." They must've caught a different note in his voice, because they immediately turned toward him. "I got something for you at the store."

They both lit up, and he tried to wave away their anticipation.

"It's nothing exciting." He felt his neck heat and mentally scolded himself as he rubbed it. This was basic biology, and the girls needed to know that it wasn't anything to be embarrassed about. He wanted them to ask questions and tell him what they needed. He hated the thought of them going through the unnecessary humiliation and discomfort that Camille had experienced.

"What'd you get us?" They'd moved closer. His long pause must've intrigued them; he had their full attention.

"You're getting older." He cleared his throat, reaching for the grocery bag. He'd tossed it on the kitchen table when he'd gotten home just in time to witness Zoe's explosion. "I wanted you to have these when the time came. I'll put them in the bathroom closet. There are instructions, and you can ask me questions if you have any." He remembered how he couldn't even pick out the right products without Camille's help. "If I don't know the answer, we'll…Google it or something."

Opening the bag, he held it out to show the girls what was inside. They both peered into the bag, and Zoe's eyes went wide. She jerked back, as if she could catch something from the contents, and her face flushed brick red.

Maya looked puzzled. "What are they?" she asked.

Without answering, Zoe turned and hurried toward the door. Steve took a deep breath, trying to think of the best way to answer. Before he could say anything, Zoe called, "C'mon, Maya."

"But what are they?" she asked, moving obediently toward her sister.

"Tampons," Zoe whispered, yanking open the door.

"Oh!" The confusion cleared from Maya's young face. "For when we get our periods!"

Steve didn't think it was possible for Zoe's face to get any redder, but somehow it happened. She seemed so embarrassed by just the sight of the bag's contents that Steve knew his vague plan for having a father-daughters open discussion about puberty was not going to happen anytime soon. Zoe couldn't run away fast enough.

"We'll talk about it later," she said to Maya under her breath, before basically shoving her sister through the door and following her outside.

Steve's gaze stayed on the door after it closed behind the girls, a creeping sense of failure enveloping him. How had he managed to fumble that so badly? It seemed to be happening a lot lately, especially with Zoe and Micah. Until recently, he'd always taken pride in being a competent dad, but now he seemed to be missing more pitches than he was hitting. He wondered if once she was an adult, Zoe would tell the story of when she was eleven and her dad completely humiliated her by buying her tampons. He silently cursed, wishing for the thousandth time that Karen had lived and was part of their children's lives. She would've known what to do. Unlike Steve, she wouldn't be failing their kids.

The door swung open, jerking him out of his mournful thoughts, and Zoe stuck her head back inside. Her cheeks were still red, and she didn't meet his gaze.

"Thanks for getting those, Dad. Love you."

She quickly disappeared again, shutting the door behind her. After a few shocked seconds, Steve smiled. Maybe Camille had been right. Maybe he was doing okay after all.

ABOUT THE AUTHOR

A graduate of the police academy, Katie Ruggle is a self-proclaimed forensics nerd. A fan of anything that makes her feel like a badass, she has trained in Krav Maga, boxing, and gymnastics, has lived in an off-grid, solar- and wind-powered house in the Rocky Mountains, rides horses, shoots guns, trains her three dogs, and travels to warm places to scuba dive.

ROCKY MOUNTAIN COWBOY CHRISTMAS

Beloved author Katie Ruggle's new series brings pulse-pounding romantic suspense to a cowboy's Colorado Christmas

When single dad Steve Springfield moved his family to a Colorado Christmas tree ranch, he meant it to be a safe haven. He quickly finds himself fascinated by local folk artist Camille Brandt—it's too bad trouble is on her trail.

It's not long before Camille is falling for the enigmatic cowboy and his rambunctious children—he always seems to be coming to her rescue. As attraction blooms and danger intensifies, this Christmas romance may just prove itself to be worth fighting for.

For more Katie Ruggle, visit:
sourcebooks.com

ROCKY MOUNTAIN K9 UNIT

These K9 officers and their trusty dogs will do anything to protect the women in their lives

By Katie Ruggle

Run to Ground

K9 officer Theo Bosco lost his mentor, his K9 partner, and almost lost his will to live. But when a ruthless killer targets a woman on the run, Theo and his new K9 companion will do whatever it takes to save the woman neither can live without.

On the Chase

Injured in the line of duty, K9 officer Hugh Murdoch's orders are simple: stay alive. But when a frightened woman bursts into his life, Hugh and his K9 companion have no choice but to risk everything to keep her safe.

Survive the Night

K9 officer Otto Gunnersen has always been a haven: for the lost, the sick, the injured. But when a hunted woman takes shelter in his arms, this gentle giant swears he'll do more than heal her battered spirit—he'll defend her with his life.

Through the Fire

When a killer strikes, new K9 officer Kit Jernigan knows she can't catch the culprit on her own. She needs a partner: local fire spotter Wesley March. But the more time they spend together, the hotter the fire smolders... and the more danger they're in.

For more Katie Ruggle, visit:

sourcebooks.com

SEARCH AND RESCUE

In the Rockies, lives depend on the
Search & Rescue brotherhood. But this far
off the map, secrets can be murder.

By Katie Ruggle

Hold Your Breath

Louise "Lou" Sparks is a hurricane—a
walking disaster. And with her, ice
diving captain Callum Cook has never
felt more alive...even if keeping her
safe may just kill him.

Fan the Flames

Firefighter and Motorcycle Club
member Ian Walsh rides the line
between the good guys and the bad.
But if a killer has his way, Ian will
take the fall for a murder he didn't
commit...and lose the woman he's
always loved.

Gone Too Deep

George Halloway is a mystery. Tall. Dark. Intense. But city girl Ellie Price will need him by her side if she wants to find her father…and live to tell the tale.

In Safe Hands

Deputy Sheriff Chris Jennings has always been a hero to agoraphobe Daisy Little, but one wrong move ended their future before it could begin. Now he'll do whatever it takes to keep her safe—even if that means turning against one of his own.

For more Katie Ruggle, visit:
sourcebooks.com

I AM JUSTICE

First in an action-packed, band of sisters romantic suspense series from award-winning debut author Diana Muñoz Stewart

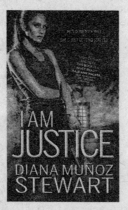

Justice Parish takes down bad guys. Rescued from a brutal childhood and adopted into the wealthy Parish family, Justice wants payback. She's targeted a sex-trafficking ring in the Middle East. She just needs a cover so she can get close enough to take them down...

Sandesh Ross left Special Forces to found a humanitarian group, but saving the world isn't cheap. Enter Parish Industries and limitless funding, with one catch—their hot, prickly "PR specialist," Justice.

"High-octane and sexy, this book is a must-read!"

—Julie Ann Walker, *New York Times* and *USA Today* bestselling author of the Black Knights Inc. series

For more Diana Muñoz Stewart, visit:
sourcebooks.com

ALSO BY KATIE RUGGLE